IT
HAPPENED
IN...
*m*anhattan

D1322774

July 2014

August 2014

September 2014

October 2014

IT HAPPENED IN...
*M*anhattan

EMILY McKAY

BARBARA DUNLOP

KATE LITTLE

MILLS & BOON

Published in Great Britain 2014
by Mills & Boon, an imprint of Harlequin (UK) Limited,
Eton House, 18-24 Paradise Road, Richmond, Surrey, TW9 1SR

IT HAPPENED IN MANHATTAN © 2014 Harlequin Books S.A.

Affair with the Rebel Heiress © 2010 Emily McKaskle
The Billionaire's Bidding © 2007 Barbara Dunlop
Tall, Dark & Cranky © 2002 Anne Canadeo

ISBN: 978-0-263-24593-6

011-0914

Harlequin (UK) Limited's policy is to use papers that are natural, renewable and recyclable products and made from wood grown in sustainable forests.The logging and manufacturing processes conform to the legalenvironmental regulations of the country of origin.

Printed and bound in Spain
by Blackprint CPI, Barcelona

AFFAIR WITH THE REBEL HEIRESS

EMILY McKAY

Emily McKay has been reading and loving romance novels since she was eleven years old. She lives in Texas with her geeky husband, her two kids and too many pets. Her debut novel, *Baby, Be Mine*, was a RITA® Award finalist for Best First Book and Best Short Contemporary. She was also a 2009 *RT Book Reviews* Career Achievement nominee for Series Romance. To learn more, visit her website, www.EmilyMcKay.com.

For my mother, Judy Beierle, who has taught me over and over to smile in the face of adversity, to meet challenges with bravery and hope, and to always, always find something to laugh about

One

Kitty Biedermann hated Texas.

That single thought had echoed through her mind from the time the flight attendant had said the words "unscheduled landing in Midland, Texas," until this moment, five hours later, when she found herself sitting in the bar adjacent the seedy motel in which she would be forced to spend the night.

The last time she'd been in Texas, she'd been dumped by her fiancé. Of course, he hadn't been just any old fiancé. He'd been the man she'd handpicked to save Biedermann Jewelry from financial ruin. So being dumped hadn't resulted in mere public humiliation or simple heartbreak. It meant the end of Biedermann Jewelry. So it was understandable that Kitty held a bit of grudge, not just against Derek Messina, but against the whole damn state.

Since being dumped by Derek, her situation had gone from bad to worse to desperate. She had needed Derek.

From the time she was a child, she'd been raised with one purpose—to land a husband with the smarts and business savvy to run Biedermann's. When Derek hadn't wanted her, she'd remained undaunted. But now, after six months of working her way through every single, eligible straight man she knew, she was beginning to feel…well, daunted.

With this latest trip to Palm Beach, she'd been scraping the bottom of the barrel. Geoffrey barely had two functioning synapses to rub together, but at least he could read, write and looked damn good in a suit. But even as meager as his qualifications had been, he hadn't wanted her.

Biedermann's meant everything to her. It was slipping through her fingers and there didn't seem to be anything she could do to catch it.

Now, with her elbows propped on the suspiciously sticky bar top and her chin propped in her palms, she stared at the murky green depths of her salt-rimmed margarita glass. She gave the glass a little shake, watching as the ice cubes within tumbled to the bottom of the glass. A lifetime of planning had fallen apart just as quickly. Was this rock bottom?

Her throat tightened against despair. Immediately she straightened, blinking in surprise. She was not given to fits of self-pity. Certainly not in public.

She shook her glass again, studying the contents. Exactly what was in this margarita? After a mere two drinks she should not be succumbing to such maudlin emotions.

Maybe this was what she got for giving the bartender a hard time. When she'd ordered a Pinot Grigio, he'd asked, "Is that like a wine cooler?" Apparently she shouldn't have doubted him when he said he'd make her a drink strong enough to knock her on her pampered, scrawny butt.

She was still contemplating the contents of her drink when she happened to glance toward the door and saw *him* striding in.

It was as if someone tossed a bucket of icy water on her. Every cell in her body snapped to life in pure visceral response. The stranger was tall and lean, somehow managing to look lanky but well-built all at the same time. He was dressed simply in well-worn jeans and a T-shirt that stretched taut across his shoulders, but hung loose over his abdomen. No beer belly on this guy. A cowboy hat sat cockeyed on his head, but he wore scuffed work boots instead of the cowboy boots she expected.

Her first thought—when she was capable of thought again—was, *Now* this *is a cowboy. This* was what women the world over romanticized. *This* was a man at his most basic. Most masculine.

Even from across the room, her body responded to him instantly, pumping endorphins down to the tips of her curling toes. Funny, because she'd always preferred her men sophisticated and suave. As well-groomed as they were well-educated.

She was, in fact, so distracted by this mystery cowboy who'd just sauntered in that she didn't see the other guy sidling up to her. The rough hand on her arm was her first clue someone had claimed the stool beside hers. Swiveling around, she realized that hand belonged to a guy who could not have been more different than the cowboy who'd snagged her attention. This man was short and, um…plump. He was bald except for a few wisps of hair grown long, combed over and plastered down with what she could only hope was some sort of styling product. His cheeks were rosy, his nose bulbous. He looked vaguely familiar, though she couldn't possibly have met him before.

"Well, hello there, little lady." He stroked a hand up her arm. "Whadda say we getcha some'tem cold to drink and we scoot on out to that there dance floor?"

"Pardon?" She—barely—suppressed a shiver of disgust at his touch. She tried to wiggle free from his grasp, but he had boxed her in between the bar and the woman on the stool beside her.

Why was he rubbing her arm like that? Did she know this man? After all, he *did* look familiar.

"You wanna take a turn around the room?"

"A turn at what?" she asked, genuinely not understanding him. She spoke four languages, for goodness' sake, but Texan was not one of them.

The man frowned. "Are you makin' fun a me?"

"No," she protested. Unfortunately, it was then that

she figured out where she knew him from. "Elmer Fudd!" she blurted out. "You look like Elmer Fudd!"

Normally, she would not have said anything, but she'd already gulped down two of those wicked margaritas. And all she'd eaten since lunch was a packet of airline peanuts. So her tongue was looser than normal.

Indignation settled over his pudgy features. He leaned toward her, scowling. "Whadja call me?"

"I...I didn't mean it as an insult."

"You *are* makin' fun a me." The man's face flushed red, only increasing his resemblance to the cartoon hunter.

"No! I...I...I..."

And there it was. She, who almost always knew exactly what to say and who could talk herself into and out of almost any situation, for better or for worse, was speechless. Horribly so.

She'd unintentionally insulted and offended a man who was probably armed right now. This was it. She was going to die. Alone. Miserable. In Texas. Murdered in a fit of rage. By a man who looked like Elmer Fudd.

Ford Langley could see trouble coming the second he stepped into The Dry Well, his favorite bar in Midland.

The Well was the kind of seedy dive that rednecks and oil rig workers had been coming to, through boom and bust, for sixty years or so. Since the Green Energy branch of FMJ, Ford's company, leased land for their wind turbines from a lot of the people in here, he figured they all knew who he was and how much he was worth. They just didn't care. Frankly, it was a relief places like this still existed in the world.

It was not, however, the kind of place women wore couture suits and designer shoes. Ford had three sisters with expensive taste. He knew a five-hundred-dollar pair of shoes when he saw them.

The woman sitting at the bar looked startlingly out of place. He'd never seen her there before. He came to The Well almost every time he visited Midland, and he definitely would have remembered this broad.

The word *broad* filtered through and stuck in his mind, because that's exactly what she looked like. The sexy broad who ambles into the PI's office in an old film noir movie. Lustrous flowing hair, long silk-clad legs, bright red lipstick, gut-wrenching sex appeal. With just enough wide-eyed innocence thrown in to make a man want to be the one to save her. Even though he knew instinctively that he would get kicked in the teeth for his trouble.

To make matters worse, she was talking to Dale Martin, who, Ford knew, had been going through a rough divorce. Dale had undoubtedly come in looking for what The Well provided best: booze, brawls and one-night stands. Given how completely out of his league the woman was, Ford could already guess which Dale was going to get.

When Ford heard Dale's distinctive drawl rising above the blare of the jukebox, Ford moved through the crowd, closing in on the brewing conflict, hoping he could cut trouble off at the pass.

He approached just in time to hear Dale accuse her of making fun of him. Hiding his cringe, Ford slung an arm around the woman's shoulders.

The stubborn woman tried to pull out of his grasp, but he held her firm. "I will—"

"Dale, buddy," he continued before she could ruin his efforts. "I see you met my date." He sent the woman a pointed look, hoping she'd take the hint and stop trying to squirm away. "Sugar, did you introduce yourself to my buddy, Dale?"

"It's Kitty," she snapped.

Dale was looking from him to her with a baffled expression. Which was fine, because Ford figured confused was better than furious.

"Right, sugar." Ford gave her shoulder an obvious squeeze. Winking at Dale, he added, "Kitty here's one of those feminist types."

She blinked, as if having trouble keeping up with the conversation. "Insisting that I be called by my given name and not some generic endearment does not make me—"

"She's a bit prickly, too." Based on her accent, he made a guess. "You know how Yankees are, Dale."

"I am not prickly," she protested.

But with Ford's last comment, a smile spread across Dale's face and at her protest, he burst out laughing, having forgotten or excused whatever she'd said to offend him. After all, she was a Yankee and obviously couldn't be expected to know better.

With Dale sufficiently distracted, Ford tugged the

delectable Kitty off her stool and nudged her toward The Well's crowded dance floor. "Come on. Why don't you show me what you can do in those fancy shoes of yours, sugar?"

At "sugar" he gave Dale another exaggerated wink. She, of course, squeaked an indignant protest, which only made Dale laugh harder.

When they were out of Dale's hearing range, she once again tried to pull away from him. "Thank you, I'm sure. But I could have handled him myself. So you can't seriously expect me to dance with you."

"'Course I do. Dale's watching."

Before she could voice any more protests, or worse, undermine all his hard work, he stepped onto the dance floor, spun her to face him and pulled her close. The second he felt her body pressed to his, he had to ask himself, had he really orchestrated all of that to avoid a fight or had he been angling for this all along?

She was taller than she'd looked sitting on the stool. With her heels on, her head came up past his chin, which was rare, since he dwarfed most women. As he'd suspected, her boxy suit hid a figure that was nicely rounded without being plump. She was delectably, voluptuously curved.

He felt the sharp bite of lust deep in his gut. Maybe he shouldn't have been surprised. He lived a fairly high-profile life back in San Francisco. As a result, he picked his lovers carefully for their discretion, sophistication and lack of expectations. He had enough responsibility without saddling himself with a spouse.

Unfortunately, it had been nearly six months since his previous girlfriend, Rochelle, had gone out for lunch one day with a friend who had kids and came home dreaming of designer diaper bags. He'd been happy to dodge that bullet and hadn't been in a hurry to find someone to replace her. Which probably explained his strong reaction to this woman. Kitty, she'd said her name was.

As he moved her into a shuffle of a Texas two-step, he felt her body relax against his. If his instincts were right, Kitty was smart, beautiful and used to taking care of herself. In short, she was exactly his sort of woman. She just may be the most interesting thing that had happened to him in a long time.

Kitty had never before found herself in this situation. Naturally she often danced with men she'd only just met. But she kept very careful tabs on the social scene in Manhattan. As a result, she usually knew the net worth, family history and sexual inclinations of every male in the room.

What some might consider mere gossip, she considered her professional obligation. She was in no position to date, marry or even notice a man who couldn't bring his own personal fortune to her family coffers. Unfortunately, ever since Suzy Snark had caught Kitty in her sights, the business of finding a rich husband had become increasingly difficult. Derek—damn him—had been the perfect choice. Until he'd gone and fallen in love.

But the truth was, she was tired of planning every move she made. This stranger with whom she was dancing, this cowboy, this man she'd never see again after tonight, made her pulse quicken.

From the moment she'd seen him sauntering through the door to the instant he'd pulled her body against his, she'd felt more alive than she had in months. Years, maybe. Somehow the scent of him, masculine and spicy, rose up from his chest and cut through the stench of stale smoke and cheap beer. His shoulders and arms were firm and muscular without being bulky. He had the physique of a man who worked for a living. Who lifted heavy things and shouldered massive burdens. The hand that cradled hers was slightly rough. This was a man who'd never had a manicure, never taken a Pilates class and probably didn't own a suit.

In short, he was a real man. Unlike the pampered men of her acquaintance. Most of whom, she was sorry to say, were likable, but were just a little bit…well, that is to say…well, they were sissies. And until this moment, she'd never realized that bothered her. She'd never known she wanted anything else.

Her face was only inches from his shirt and she had to fight against the sudden impulse to bury her nose in his chest. To rub her cheek against his sternum like a cat marking her territory.

It had been so long since she felt this kind of instant sexual attraction to someone. Geesh, had she ever felt this kind of attraction? She didn't think so.

Not that she planned on acting on it. A one-night stand was *so* not part of her five-year plan.

"I don't even know your name," she muttered aloud.

"Ford," he murmured.

He'd ducked his head before speaking so the word came out as warmth brushing past her ear. She suppressed a shiver.

"Like the car?" she asked.

He chuckled. "Yep. Like the car."

Geesh, indeed. Even his name was masculine. Why couldn't he have had a name that was just a bit more androgynous? Like Gene or Pat. Or BMW.

She didn't manage to stifle her chuckle.

"You're imagining me named after other car brands, aren't you?"

Her gaze shot to his. "How did you know?"

"It's pretty common. People usually think one of two things and you just seemed the type to wonder, 'What if he'd been named Chevy?'"

"Are you saying I'm predictable?" Even though the lighting was dim, she could see that his eyes were whiskey-brown. And just as intoxicating as the tequila in her drink.

"Not at all," he reassured her. "You could have been thinking Dodge."

"It was BMW, actually. I can't see you as something as clunky as a Dodge." Was she *flirting* with him? What was wrong with her?

"So you're a woman who appreciates precision engineering."

Actually, I'm a woman who enjoys precision in everything.

The words had been on the tip of her tongue. Thank God she swallowed them. Instead she asked, "What's the second?"

"Second what?"

"You said people usually think one of two things. If the first is other car names, then what's the second?"

His lips quirked in either amusement or chagrin. "They wonder if I was conceived in the back of a Ford."

"Ah." Perhaps that had been chagrin, then. And was that the faintest hint of pink creeping into his cheeks? As if he were just a tad embarrassed. "And were you?"

"That," he said firmly, "is a question I was never brave enough to ask my parents." They both chuckled then. A moment later he added, "But I have three sisters and their names are not Mattress, Kitchen Table and Sofa, so I think I'm safe."

She nearly asked what the names of his three sisters were, but she stopped herself. Somehow that seemed inappropriate. More personal, even, than the discussion of his conception. She didn't know Ford. Didn't want to know him longer than the length of this song. Personal details like the names of his sisters didn't matter. So instead, she gave in to her temptation to rest her cheek against the strong wall of his chest and to breathe in deeply.

After a moment he said, "I hope you don't judge Dale too harshly."

"Dale?"

"The guy hitting on you earlier."

"Ah. Him." She'd forgotten he even existed.

"He's been going through a rough divorce. His wife left him for a guy who's twenty-three years old."

"Ouch. That's got to be hard on the ego."

"Exactly. Which is why he's been a mite irritable lately. But what exactly did you say to him that made him so mad?"

She cringed, hesitating before answering him. "I said he looked like Elmer Fudd."

Ford seemed to be suppressing laughter. "I can't imagine why that offended him. Everybody loves Elmer Fudd."

"That's what I tried to tell him!"

They both chuckled. But then she looked up. For a moment, space seemed to telescope around them, blocking out everything else. The smoke, the crowd, even the blare of the music faded until all she could hear was the steady *thump-thump* of the bass echoing the thud of her heartbeat.

She felt her nerves prickle in anticipation. Desire, hot and heavy, unspooled through her body. Her very skin felt weighed down. Her thighs flushed with warmth.

Who knew that laughter could be such a turn-on?

Their feet stopped shuffling across the floor. That ridiculous grin seemed frozen on her face for an instant, but then it faded, melted away by the intensity of his gaze. There was a spot just over his ear where his otherwise straight hair curled. Before she could think, her fingers had moved to his temple to tease that wayward lock of hair.

He took her hand in his, stilling her fingers. He cleared his throat, and she expected him to say something, something funny maybe, something to lighten the tension between them, but he said nothing.

Who had ever imagined that she'd feel this needy lust for a stranger? Not just a stranger, but a cowboy. A Texan. When she'd sworn she'd never even set foot in this damn state again. She *so* hadn't seen this coming.

That's when it hit her. Here, tonight, was a night out of time. She would never be here again. She would never see him again.

In this strange place, with this man she didn't know, she had complete immunity. Freedom from her well-planned life. From her routines and her expectations of herself.

Tonight she could do whatever she wanted with no consequences. She could allow herself to do what she would normally *never* do. She could be stupid and reckless.

Without giving herself the chance to harbor second thoughts, she rose up on her toes and pressed her lips to his. His mouth moved over hers with a heated intensity. The sensual promise in his kiss made her shiver. She arched against him, letting her body answer the call of his. She slipped her hand into his and walked off the dance floor, tugging him along behind her.

As she wove her way through the crowd, the tempo of her blood picked up. After a lifetime of carefully planning, of controlling her actions and emotions, he could be her one rebellion. Tonight could be a vacation from her life.

And even if this was a mistake, he'd make sure she didn't regret it.

Two

Two months later

"You've got to stop moping around," Jonathon Bagdon said, then added, "And get your feet off my desk."

Ford, who'd been sitting with his work boots propped up on the edge of Jonathon's desk while he scraped the tip of his pocketknife under his nails, looked up for the first time since his business partner walked in the room. "What?"

Jonathon swatted at Ford's boots with the leather-clad portfolio he'd been carrying. "Keep your feet off my desk. Christ, it's like you're ten."

Ford's feet, which had been crossed at the ankles,

slid off Jonathon's desk. He lowered them to the floor and ignored the insult.

"The desk is worth twenty thousand dollars. Try not to scuff it."

Finally Ford looked up at his friend, taking in the scowl. He glanced over at Matt, the third partner in their odd little triumvirate, who sat on the sofa, with one leg propped on the opposite knee and a laptop poised on the knee. "Who shoved a stick up his ass this morning?" Ford asked Matt.

Matt continued typing frenetically while he said, "Ignore him. He's just trying to bait you. He doesn't give a damn about the desk."

Ford looked from one to the other, suddenly feeling slightly off-kilter. Together the three of them formed FMJ, Inc. He'd known these men since they were kids. They'd first gone into business together when they were twelve and Jonathon had talked them into pooling their money to run the snack shack at the community rec center for the summer. One financially lucrative endeavor had led to another until here they were, twenty years later, the CEO, CFO and CTO of FMJ, a company which they'd founded while still in college and which had made them all disgustingly rich.

Jonathon, though always impeccably dressed and by far the most organized of the three, might impress some as overly persnickety. But those were only the people who didn't know him, the people who were bound to underestimate him. It was a mistake few people made more than once.

In reality, it was unlike Jonathon to care whether or not his desk was scuffed, regardless of how much it was worth.

Still, to mollify Jonathon, Ford abandoned the chair he'd been sitting in and returned to his own desk. Since they worked so closely together, they didn't have individual offices. Instead, they'd converted the entire top floor of FMJ's Palo Alto headquarters to a shared office. On one end sat Jonathon's twenty-thousand-dollar art deco monstrosity. The other end was lined with three worktables, every inch of them covered by computers and gadgets in various stages of dissection. In the middle sat Ford's desk, a sleek modern job the building's interior designer had picked out for him.

With a shrug, he asked, "Is Matt right? You just trying to get a rise out of me?"

Jonathon flashed him a cocky grin. "Well, you're talking now, aren't you?"

"I wasn't before?"

"No. You've been picking at your nails for an hour now. You haven't heard a word I've said."

"Not true," Ford protested. "You've been babbling about how you think it's time we diversify again. You've rambled on and on about half a dozen companies that are about to be delisted by the NYSE, but that you think could be retooled to be profitable again. You and Matt voted while I was in China visiting the new plant and you've already started to put together the offer. Have I left anything out?"

"And…" Jonathon prodded.

"And what?" Ford asked. When Jonathon gave an exasperated sigh and plopped back in his chair, Ford shot a questioning look at Matt, who was still typing away. "And what?"

Matt, who'd always had the uncanny ability to hold a conversation while solving some engineering problem, gave a few more clicks before shutting his laptop. "He's waiting for you to voice an opinion. You're the CEO. You get final vote."

FMJ specialized in taking over flailing businesses and turning them around, much like the snack shack they'd whipped into prosperity all those years ago. Jonathon used his wizardry to streamline the company's finances. Matt, with his engineering background, inevitably developed innovations that helped turn the company around. Ford's own role in their magic act was a little more vague.

Ford had a way with people. Inevitably, when FMJ took over a company, there was resentment from the ownership and employees. People resisted, even feared, change. And that's where Ford came in. He talked to them. Smoothed the way. Convinced them that FMJ was a company they could trust.

He flashed a smile at Matt. "I can do my part no matter what the company is. Why do I need to vote?"

While he spoke, he absently opened his desk drawer and tossed the pocketknife in. As if of their own accord, his fingers drifted to the delicate gold earring he kept stored in the right-hand corner.

The earring was shaped like a bird, some kind of sea

bird, if he wasn't mistaken. Its wings were outstretched as if it were diving for a fish, its motion and yearning captured in perfect miniscule detail.

Ford's fingertip barely grazed the length of its wingspan before he jerked his hand out and slammed the drawer shut.

It was her earring. Kitty Biedermann's. The woman from the bar in Texas.

He'd discovered it in the front of his rented pickup when he'd gone to turn the truck in. Now he wished he'd left it there. It wasn't like he was going to actually return the earring to its owner.

Yes, when he'd first found the earring, he'd had Wendy, FMJ's executive assistant, look Kitty up, just to see how hard it would be to hunt her down. But then Kitty Biedermann turned out to be a jewelry store heiress.

What was he going to do, fly to New York to return the earring? He was guessing she didn't want to see him again any more than he wanted to see her. But now he was stuck with this stupid bird earring.

As much to distract himself as anything, he rocked back in his chair and said, "Okay, let's buy a company. What do they do again?"

"What do you mean, what do they do?" Jonathon grumbled. "This is the company you researched."

Ford nudged his foot against the edge of the desk and set his chair to bobbing. "What are you taking about? I didn't research a company."

"Sure you did." Jonathon held out the portfolio.

When Ford didn't take it, Jonathon settled for tossing in on Ford's desk. "The same day I sent out that first list of companies to consider, you e-mailed Wendy and told her to dig up anything she could find on Biedermann Jewelry. Since you seemed interested in them, Matt and I voted and…"

Listening to his partner talk, Ford let his chair rock forward and his feet drop to the floor. With a growing sense of dread, he flipped open the portfolio. And there was the proposal. To buy Biedermann Jewelry.

His stomach clenched like he'd been sucker punched.

Had Wendy misunderstood his casual, *Hey, see what you can find out about Kitty Biedermann?* But of course Wendy had. She was obsessively thorough and eager to please.

With forced nonchalance he asked, "Have you put a lot of work into this deal yet?"

"A couple hundred man hours," Jonathon hedged. "Biedermann's is circling the drain. We need to move fast."

Matt normally wasn't the most intuitive guy. But he must have heard something in Ford's voice, because he asked, "What's up, Ford? You having doubts?"

"It's a pretty risky deal," he said simply. Maybe he could gently redirect their attention.

But Jonathon shook his head. "It isn't really. Biedermann's has always been a strong company. They've been undervalued ever since Isaac Biedermann died last year. But I can turn them around." Jonathon's lips quirked in one of his rare grins. "Kind of looking forward to the challenge, actually."

Ford had seen that look in Jonathon's eyes before. Jonathon was ready to gobble up Biedermann's. Any minute now he'd be picking his teeth with the bones of Biedermann's carcass.

Unless Ford stopped him.

Which he could do. All he'd have to do is explain about Kitty. And the earring.

But what was he really supposed to say? *Don't buy the company because I slept with her?* He usually preferred relationships to last a little longer than one night, but he wasn't above the occasional fling when the chance presented itself. He'd never had a problem walking away the next day. He just wasn't a long-term kind of guy. He wouldn't even remember her name if it hadn't been for that lost earring.

"So what do you say?" Jonathon asked. "We all in?"

"Sure." And he sounded convincingly casual about it, too. He pushed his chair back and stood. "Hey, I'm going to the gym. That damn chair makes my back hurt."

"Don't be gone long. We've got work to do."

"When do you leave for New York?" he asked.

"Not me, we," Jonathon corrected. "As soon as I can get the board to agree to a meeting."

"Great." It looked like he was going to be able to return that earring after all.

Kitty sat at the head of the conference table, concentrating all of her considerable acting skill on looking relaxed. Today was the first of what would probably be many meetings to negotiate the deal with FMJ. She would never feel good about this, but what choice did she have? Everything she'd tried on her own had blown up in her face. Marty, Biedermann's CFO, had assured her this was her only option. Her last, best hope to salvage anything from Biedermann's.

Still, the thought of selling the company twisted her gut into achy knots. Beidermann's had been in her family since her great-great-grandfather had moved to New York from Germany and opened the first store in 1868. For her, Biedermann's wasn't just a company, it was her history, her heritage. Her family.

But it was also her responsibility. And if she couldn't save it herself, then she'd hand it over to someone who could, even if doing so made her stomach feel like it was about to flip itself inside out.

She should be more comfortable sitting at this table than most people were in their own bedrooms. And yet she found herself strumming her fingers against the gleaming wood as she fought nausea.

Beside her, Marty rested his hand over hers. He seemed to be aiming for reassuring, but his touch sent a shiver of disgust through her.

He stroked the backs of her fingers. "Everything will be all right."

She stiffened, jerking her hand out from under his. "I beg your pardon?"

"You seemed nervous."

"Nonsense." Still, she buried her hand in her lap.

She didn't handle sympathy well under normal circumstances. Now it made her feel like she was going to shatter. He looked pointedly at the spot on the table she'd been drumming on, to which she replied, "I'm impatient. They're seven minutes late and I have a reservation for lunch at Bruno's."

Marty's lips twitched. "You don't have to pretend with me."

Something like panic clutched her heart. So, he thought he saw right through her. Well, others had thought that before. "Don't be ridiculous, Marty. I've been pretending to be interested in your conversations for years. I'm certainly not going to stop now."

For an instant, a stricken expression crossed his face and regret bit through her nerves. Dang it. Why did she say things like that? Why was it that whenever she was backed into a corner, she came out fighting?

She was still contemplating apologizing when the door opened and Casey stuck her head through. "Mr. Ford Langley and Mr. Jonathon Bagdon are here."

Awash in confusion, she nearly leaped to her feet. "Ford Langley? Is here?"

Then she felt Marty's steady hand on hers again. "Mr. Langley's the CEO of FMJ. He's come in person for the negotiations."

She stared blankly at Marty, her mind running circles around one thought. Ford Langley.

He was here? He was the CEO of FMJ? Impossible. Ford Langley was an ignorant cowboy. She'd left him in Texas and would never see him again.

She must have misheard. Or misunderstood her assistant just now. Or misremembered the name of the stranger she'd slept with. Or perhaps through some cruel trick of fate, the CEO of FMJ and the stranger shared the same odd name.

Each of these possibilities thundered through her mind as she struggled to regain her composure. Mistaking her confusion, Marty must have spoken for her and told Casey to show in the people from FMJ.

She barely had time to school her panic into a semblance of calm before the door to the conference room swung open and there he was. Fate had pulled a much crueler trick on her than merely giving two men the same name. No, fate had tricked her into selling her beloved company to the same man to whom she'd already given her body.

What had he expected?

Okay, he hadn't thought she'd jump up, run across the room and throw her arms around him. But he sure as hell hadn't expected the complete lack of response. The coolly dismissive blank stare. As if she didn't recognize him at all. As if he were beneath her notice.

Her gaze barely flickered over him as she looked from him to Jonathon. Then she glanced away, looking bored. Someone from Biedermann's had stood and was making introductions. Ford shook hands at the right moment, filing away the name and face of Kitty's CFO.

She looked good. Lovely, in fact. As smoothly polished as the one-dimensional woman in the Nagel painting poster he'd had on his wall as a teenager. Beautiful. Pale. Flat.

Gone was the vibrant woman he'd danced with in The Well two months ago. By the time the introductions were done, one thing had become clear. She was going to pretend they'd never met before. She was going to sit through this meeting all the while ignoring the fact that they'd once slept together. That he'd touched her bare skin, caressed her thighs, felt her body tremble with release.

Which was exactly what he should do, too. Hell, wasn't that what he had *planned* on doing?

Just as Jonathon was pulling out his chair, Ford said, "Before we get started, I wonder if I could have a word alone with Ms. Biedermann."

Jonathon sent him a raised-eyebrowed, do-you-know-what-you're-doing? kind of look. Kitty's CFO hovered by her side, like an overly protective Chihuahua.

Ford gave the man his most reassuring smile while nodding slightly at Jonathon. He knew Jonathon would back him up and get the other guy out of there. Jonathon wouldn't question his actions, even if Ford was doubting them himself.

Something was up with Kitty and he intended to find out what it was.

Kitty watched Marty leave the conference room, fighting the urge to scream. An image flashed through her mind of herself wild-eyed and disheveled, pulling at her hair and shouting "Deserter! Traitor!" like some mad Confederate general about to charge into battle and to his death, all alone after his men have seen reason and fled the field.

Clearly, she'd been watching too many old movies.

Obviously her time would have been better spent practicing her mental telepathy. Then she could have ordered Marty to stay. As it was, she couldn't protest without Ford realizing how much the prospect of being alone with him terrified her.

The moment the door shut, leaving them alone in the room, he crossed to her side. "Hello, Kitty."

She stood, nodding. Praying some response would spring to her lips. Something smart. Clever. Something that would cut him to the bone without seeming defensive.

Sadly nothing came to mind. So she left it at the nod.

"You look…" Then he hesitated, apparently unsure which adjective best described her.

"I believe 'well' is usually how one finishes that sentence." Oh, God. Why couldn't she just keep her mouth shut?

"That's not what I was going to say."

"Well, you seem to be having trouble finishing the sentence," she supplied. "Since I'm sure I look just fine and since I'd much rather get this over with than stand around exchanging pleasantries, I thought I'd move things along."

He raised his eyebrows as if taken aback by her tone. "You aren't curious why I'm here?"

That teasing tone stirred memories best left buried

in the recesses of her mind. Unfortunately, those pesky memories rose up to swallow her whole, like a tsunami.

As if it were yesterday instead of two months or more, she remembered what it had felt like to be held in his arms. Cradled close to his body as they swayed gently back and forth on the dance floor. The way he'd smelled, musky yet clean against the sensory backdrop of stale smoke and spilled beer. The way her body had thrummed to life beneath his touch. The way she'd quivered. The way she'd come.

She thrust aside the memories, praying he wouldn't notice that her breath had quickened. Thankful he couldn't hear the pounding of her heart or see the hardening of her nipples.

Hiding her discomfort behind a display of boredom, she toyed with the papers on the table where she'd been sitting. She couldn't stand to look at him, so she pretended to read through them as she said, "I know why you're here. You came here to take control of Biedermann's." Thank God her voice didn't crack as she spoke. It felt as if her heart did, but that at least she could hide. For the first time since he walked into the room, she met his gaze. "You can't honestly expect me to welcome you. You're stealing the company I was born to raise."

His expression hardened. "I'm not stealing anything. FMJ is providing your failing company with some much-needed cash. We're here to keep you in business."

"Oh, really. How generous of you." She buried all her trepidation beneath a veneer of sarcasm. As she always did. It was so much easier that way. "Since that's the case, why don't you just write out a nice hefty check and leave it on the table on your way out. I'll call you in a decade or so to let you know if it helped."

"A big, fat check might help if all you needed was an infusion of cash. But the truth is, Biedermann's needs a firm hand at the helm and you can't have one without the other. You know that's not how this works."

His words might have been easier to swallow if he'd sounded apologetic instead of annoyed. No, wait…there wasn't really any way that anything he said could be easier to swallow.

"No. Of course that's not how it works. You'll go over the company with a fine-toothed comb. You'll tear it apart, throw out the parts you don't like and hand the rest back in pieces. In the end, everything my family's worked for for five generations will be gone. All so you can turn a quick profit."

"Tell me something. Is that really what's bothering you?"

Of course it wasn't what was really bothering her. What was really bothering her was that he was here at all. Her safe, what-the-hell-I'm-stuck-in-Texas fling hadn't stayed where it was supposed to. In Texas. What was the point of having a fling with a stranger if the man ended up not being a stranger at all?

But she couldn't say that aloud. Especially given the way he was looking at her. With his expression so intense, so sexual, so completely unprofessional, it sent a wave of pure shock through her system.

"W-what do you mean?"

"Come on, Kitty. This anger you're clinging to isn't about Biedermann's at all. This is about what happened in Texas."

She quickly buried her shock beneath a veneer of disdain. "Texas. I'm surprised you'd have the guts to bring that up."

"You are?"

"Of course." She strolled to the other side of the conference table. "I'd think you would be the last person to want to hash that over. But since you brought it up, maybe you can answer a question for me. Was anything you told me true or was it all pretense?"

"What's that supposed to mean?"

"You know. That whole charade you put on to pick me up back in Texas. That aw-shucks, I'm just a simple cowboy trying to make a living act."

"I never said I was a cowboy."

"No. But you had to know that's what I thought."

"How exactly was I supposed to know that?" His facade of easy charm slipped for a moment and he plowed a hand through his hair in frustration. He sucked in a breath and pointed out in a slightly calmer tone, "You weren't exactly forthcoming about who you were, either."

"I did nothing wrong." True, she hadn't exactly presented him with her pedigree when they'd first met, but surely it didn't take a genius to see she didn't fit in at that bar. If there had been an obvious clue he didn't, either, she'd missed it entirely. She refused to let him paint himself the victim. "I don't have anything to apologize for. I'm not the one who pretended to be some down on his luck cowboy."

"No, you're just the one who gave me a fake phone number instead of admitting you didn't want to see me again."

"If you knew I didn't want to see you again," she asked, "then why did you go to the trouble of hunting me down?"

"I didn't hunt you down. What happened in Texas has nothing to do with FMJ's offer."

"Then how exactly did the offer come about anyway?" she asked. "If you didn't go back to work and say, 'Wow, that Kitty Biedermann must be really dumb to have fallen for my tired old lines. I bet we could just swoop in and buy that company right from under her.'"

His gaze narrowed to a glare. "You know that's not how it happened."

"Really? How would I know that? What do I really know about you other than the fact that you're willing to misrepresent yourself to get a woman into bed with you?"

"I never lied to you. Not once. And despite the fact that you're acting like a brat, I won't start now."

"Maybe you didn't lie outright, but you certainly misled me. Of course, maybe that's the only way you can get a woman into bed."

Ford just smiled. "You don't believe that. The sex

was great." He closed in on her, getting right in her face as if daring her to disagree.

God, she wanted to. That would serve him right.

But when she opened her mouth, she found the denial trapped inside her. Between the intensity of his eyes and the memories suddenly flooding her, she just couldn't muster up the lie.

Instead she said the only thing that popped into her mind. "You can't convince me that FMJ is prepared to buy Biedermann's solely so you can get laid."

He grinned wolfishly. "Boy, you think highly of yourself."

"You were the one who brought up sex," she pointed out.

"You didn't let me finish. I was going to close with the suggestion that we both try to forget it happened."

"Oh, I won't have any trouble with that," she lied easily, barely even cringing as she waited for the bolt of lightning to strike her down.

"Excellent." He bit off the word. "Then you agree from here on out, it's all business?"

"Absolutely." Her smiled felt so tight across her face she was surprised she could still breathe. But she kept it in place as she crossed back to the door.

Jonathon and Marty were waiting in the office outside the conference room. If they'd picked up on the tension, neither commented. Thank goodness. She simply wouldn't have had the strength to come up with any more lies today. Between the lies she'd told Ford and the lies she was telling herself, she was completely out.

"Everything okay?" Jonathon asked, more to Ford than to her.

However, she didn't give the treacherous bastard a chance to answer. Instead, she dug deep and pulled out one more lie. "Mr. Langley was just assuring me Biedermann's is going to be in great hands with you." She held out her hand to gesture him back into the conference room. "Why don't you come in and we'll talk money."

Kitty's head was pounding by the time she finally made it back to her office alone. The simple truth was nothing could have prepared her for this.

She thought she'd been ready, but she hadn't, really. Not to sit in a conference room and listen politely while strangers discussed her beloved Biedermann's— while they calmly talked about compensation packages. While they talked about key positions in the company they'd need to replace.

Oh, they'd started by reassuring her that she would stay on as president of the subsidiary, but she knew she wouldn't have control. Not really. She'd be a figurehead, at best. A pretty adornment to make things look good. It'd be pathetic if it wasn't so sad. But the really pathetic thing was she would let herself be used that way.

She loved Biedermann's. She'd do whatever it took to save it. Even if she had to sell her soul to the devil. Or in this case, Ford Langley.

Three

If she thought her day couldn't get any worse, she was wrong. She ran into Ford in the elevator bay.

"Fantastic," she muttered as she punched the elevator button. "Thousands of people work in this building and I get to ride down with you."

"I waited for you."

"How kind." She didn't bother to meet his gaze or to inject any real graciousness in her voice. She certainly hoped he wasn't so dense that he couldn't hear her sarcasm.

"I wanted to apologize." He seemed to be speaking through gritted teeth.

Well, she certainly wasn't going to make this any easier for him. "For your behavior earlier?" she asked as the elevator doors began to open. She prayed there'd be someone else in the car with them, but her prayers went unanswered. Which was the norm of late. "Don't worry. I didn't expect better behavior from you. After all, I know what Californians are like."

It was a twist of something he'd said to her at that bar in Texas, when he'd teased her about being a Yankee. His gaze flickered to hers and for a second they seemed to both be remembering that night.

Damn it, why had she brought that up? She didn't want to remind him about that. She certainly didn't want him to think she remembered that night with anything approaching word for word accuracy.

"What I meant," he said, following her into the elevator, "was that the meeting seemed hard for you. I can't imagine it's easy to sell a company that's been in your family for generations."

She shot him a scathing look. "Please don't tax your mental capacity trying to imagine it."

The doors closed, sealing them inside. For a moment he thought she'd say nothing more, just ride with him in silence. Maybe this was it. Maybe she really was as cool a number as she'd seemed in the boardroom. Maybe selling her family company meant nothing more to her than—

Then abruptly she let loose a bitter laugh.

Okay, maybe not.

"You want to know the really funny thing?" she asked as she punched the 1 button. "This is exactly what I was raised to do."

"Run Biedermann's?" he asked.

"Oh, God, no. Don't get me wrong. My father adored me. Treated me like an absolute princess. But he never thought I was capable of running Biedermann's. I was supposed to transform myself into the perfect wife. I was supposed to catch myself a rich husband to run Biedermann's for me."

She slanted him a look as if to assess his reaction. Her tongue darted out to slip along her lower lip and his body tightened in response. He was not supposed to want her. This was about business. Not sex. Now, if only his body would get that memo.

Apparently she'd gotten it though, because she continued on as if the energy between them wasn't charged with the memory of soul-scalding sex.

She shook her head wryly. "His attitude was archaic, but there you have it."

"So you decided to prove him wrong," he surmised.

"No, I didn't even do that. I really tried to marry the perfect man to take over Biedermann's. I had him all picked out. Even got him to propose." When the elevator doors didn't shut fast enough for her liking she started punching the close button repeatedly. "He just decided to marry someone else instead. I won't bore you with the details of my love life. Not when they're available online in several different gossip columns."

The elevator started to drop and again she laughed.

"See, that's the funny part, right? Flash-forward a year. I've made a complete mess running Biedermann's, just like my father predicted. You swoop in to rescue the company. FMJ is going to take care of everything. But—" she hastily added, as if he were about to argue with her. "I'll still get to play at being president of the company. You'll be watching over my shoulder, so there's no chance I'll make things worse. I'll just get to sit there, looking good, while a big strong man fixes things for me. It's the job I was raised to do."

"Kitty—" he began, but the doors opened and she cut him off as they did.

"My father would be so proud."

She said it with the cavalier indifference of someone who was truly in pain. But damn, she was good at hiding it.

If he hadn't met her under other circumstances, if he'd never seen her with her guard down, he'd probably even be fooled. But as it was, he saw right through her.

If she'd been weeping and moping, maybe he could have ignored her despair. Or handed her off into the care of someone who knew her better. But these bitter self-recriminations...well, he remembered how he'd felt after his father died. The grief, the anger, the guilt, all rolled into one. He wouldn't wish that on anyone.

He fell into step beside her, and said, "Look, you're going through a hard time. You shouldn't be alone tonight. It's Friday night. Why not let me take you out for—"

"It's not necessary. I have plans."

"Plans?" he asked. "After a day like today?"

She waved a hand, still putting on a brave face. "It's

something I couldn't get out of. A commitment from weeks ago."

He quirked an eyebrow, waiting for her to supply more information.

Finally she added, "It's a fundraiser for The Children's Medical Foundation. At The Pierre. Very posh. You wouldn't be comfortable there," she finished dismissively.

She was either trying to insult him or she'd made up the engagement to put him off. He didn't believe for a minute that she planned on going to this charity event, even if she had bought the tickets months ago. She was just trying to get rid of him. But he couldn't stand the thought of her all alone, wallowing in her misery.

"Great." Why not pretend to buy her story? "I'll come with you."

She shot him a look icy enough to freeze his eyebrows off.

Okay, so he couldn't exactly imagine Kitty wallowing in anything. Here in New York she was as cool and collected as they came.

But he'd seen her outside her element. He'd seen her vulnerable. He knew that a passionate, emotional woman lurked beneath the surface of her icy cool perfection. If he peeled back the layers to reveal that woman, he'd probably find someone who could use a shoulder to cry on.

Kitty stopped in the lobby, ignoring the other people filtering out onto the street. "You don't need to do that."

"I don't have plans."

"Your partner—"

"Has a teleconference with some people in China."

"Who called a meeting for a Saturday morning?" she pressed.

"You know what they say." He flashed a smile. "If you don't come in on Saturday, don't bother coming in on Sunday, either."

"I'm fine," she insisted.

But she wasn't. He could see the strain in the lines around her eyes and in the tightness of her mouth. Of course, there was a chance his attempt to be kind was only making matters worse, but his gut told him to keep pushing. He was almost past her defenses, but charm alone wouldn't get her to open up. He needed to change tactics.

"Oh, I get it," he said. "You don't want to be with me."

"Exactly."

"You're probably afraid of how you feel about me." A lock of her hair had fallen free of its twist. He reached out and gave it a quick tug before tucking it behind her ear. He let his fingers linger there, at the sensitive place along the back of her ear.

She rolled her eyes. "That's not going to work."

"What?" he asked innocently.

"You're trying to bait me," she accused.

"Hey, I understand. You don't want to be alone with me. Can't say I blame you." He dropped his eyes to her lips. He let himself remember what it had been like to kiss her. To feel her breath hot on his skin. When he met her gaze again, he knew she remembered it, too.

"It's probably wise. We should spend as little time together as possible."

Her breath seemed to catch in her throat and her tongue darted out to lick her bottom lip. Then she seemed to shake off the effects. Her eyes narrowed in obvious annoyance. "Fine." She turned and started to walk away. "If you're so desperate for something to do tonight that you'll pull that cheap trick, you can come along. But don't blame me if tickets to this fundraiser are outrageously expensive at the last minute."

He smiled as he fell into step beside her. The spark was back in her eyes. The bite was back in her words. She'd be fine.

"I'll pick you up at your place," he offered.

"That's not necessary."

"I don't mind."

"Well, I do," she countered. "You don't honestly think I'm going to tell you where I live, do you?"

"You don't honestly believe I don't already know, do you?"

She turned and shot him an assessing stare. "You know where I live? What did you do, hire a private investigator?"

"I didn't have to. Jonathon has a whole team that researches that kind of thing when we're looking to acquire a company."

"I don't know whether to be creeped out or impressed." She reached the street and raised her hand to hail a cab, but this time of night the streets were packed. "Creeped out wins, I think."

"This is just company policy."

"What, all's fair in love and war?" she asked with an edge to her voice.

"This isn't love or war. This is business."

He held her gaze as firmly as he said it.

She jerked her gaze away from his, turning her attention to the passing cabs on the street. "This may be only business to you. But for me, it's both love and war. I love Biedermann's. And I've spent the last six months fighting for its survival. This may not be personal for you, but it's deeply personal for me."

A look of surprise crossed her face. Like she hadn't meant to admit that. Or maybe she just wasn't used to talking about her emotions.

After a minute he said, "Maybe that's part of the problem."

"Part of what problem?" He was about to respond, but she stopped him before he could. "And don't you dare tell me that 'the problem' is that I care too much. That I'm too emotionally involved to make rational decisions. Because I don't believe that my emotional state has anything to do with the flagging economy or the fact that malls across America are doing lower volume sales across the board." Her voice rose as she spoke, betraying her frustration. "If I could miraculously turn off my emotions and stop caring about Biedermann's, it wouldn't make a bit of difference. So if it's all the same to you, I'm going to go right on caring passionately about—"

Her voice cracked and she started blinking rapidly. Like she was trying to hold back tears.

He reached out a hand to her. "Kitty, I'm sorry—"

But a cab finally pulled up before he could finish the sentence. "Don't be sorry," she ordered as she opened the door. "Just find a way to fix it. Because if you can't, then we're both screwed."

She didn't look back as she climbed into the cab. He watched her go in silence.

She was one tough cookie.

Every other woman he knew was more in touch with her emotions. Or—he corrected himself— maybe just more willing to use her emotions to get what she wanted. Any one of his sisters would have been boo-hooing up a storm halfway through the meeting. But Kitty had just sat there in silence. Listening to every word that was said, but commenting little herself.

If it hadn't been for her outburst in the elevator, he might never have known how upset she truly was. She was unlike any woman he'd ever known. She wasn't willing to use tears to get what she wanted. He had to admire that.

But in other ways, Kitty was exactly like the other women he knew. She herself had admitted that she'd been on the lookout for a rich husband.

But somehow the poor bastard had slipped away. Or the lucky bastard, as the case may be. Frankly, he didn't know whether to feel sorry for the guy or not. Kitty was a hell of a woman.

Sure, he'd used steak knives that were less sharp than her tongue, but for him, that was part of her charm. He had enough women in his life that he had to walk on eggshells around. Thank God he didn't want to get married. Otherwise he might be tempted to drop to his knees and propose right now. He nearly chuckled imagining the scathing response that would earn him.

Ford had developed a certain cynicism about the institution at a very young age. He'd been about nine or ten when he first discovered that his father had a long-term girlfriend living one town over. Eventually, that girlfriend had developed into a second family, complete with two curly-haired little girls, quite close in age to his own sister.

At first the way his father balanced both families disgusted Ford. By the time he reached adulthood himself, it was no longer his father's behavior that troubled him. By then he'd realized both his mother and the other woman knew about each other. They'd been content to let the situation slide. As long as there was enough money to go around.

Since his father's death, Patrice and Suz had become friends in some sick little way. As for the girls, they now treated each other like the sisters they were. He seemed to be the only one who found the situation odd.

Now, standing on the curb watching the spot where Kitty's taxi had disappeared into the night, Ford nearly laughed himself. If she thought her revelation about her family would scare him off, she had another think coming. His family had more drama than a Greek tragedy.

Ford tucked his hands into his pockets and started walking toward the nearest subway station. It wasn't far back to the hotel and it was a nice night. He might as well enjoy the weather.

Only then did he feel the earring still in his pocket. It was just as well he hadn't returned it to her today. She might have been tempted to cram it down his throat.

Kitty's apartment, a walk-up in the eclectic Murray Hill neighborhood, surprised him. He'd have pegged her for an Upper East Side girl, or at the very least he imagined her in some glossy new high-rise. Instead, she lived in a prewar building that had seen better years.

When she let him into her fourth-floor apartment she wasn't dressed yet. She left him waiting in her living room for nearly an hour. Probably just to tick him off.

Her apartment was smaller than he'd expected, sparsely furnished with a few antiques. With the exception of a couple of framed black-and-white family pictures, the walls were bare. Either her taste was minimalist or she hadn't lived here long.

Ford spent the time hanging out on the sofa, first answering his e-mail on his iPhone, then reviewing some specs Matt had sent him, and then finally playing Tetris on his phone.

He might have left, but the truth was, the tension was palpable. Too much remained unsaid between them.

Under any other circumstances, he would have let it slide, being something of an expert on unresolved emotional issues. But with Kitty, it was different. He'd never before been in a position where he'd have to work with a woman he'd slept with. The last thing he wanted was some emotional complication mucking up the coming negotiations. If she was going to have a problem working with him, he wanted to clear the air now.

Finally her bedroom door opened to reveal Kitty encased in a shimmering deep purple gown with a low-cut, heart-shaped neckline. Her dark hair fell in sleek waves about her shoulders. He nearly laughed at the expression of surprise that flickered across her face when she spied him.

He stood. "You look lovely."

She fell into step beside him, not bothering to suppress an exasperated sigh. "You're still here."

"Much to your disappointment, I'm sure." He put a hand at her back to guide her to the door, only to discover a generous expanse of naked skin.

"Not at all," she murmured, suddenly all charm. "I had trouble with my zipper. You can't imagine how worried I was you might get tired of waiting and leave."

"Trouble with your zipper? For over an hour?"

"It's a long zipper."

He leaned away to look pointedly at the back of her dress. A delicate triad of beaded straps criss-crossed at her shoulders. Her skin was left bare all the way to just below her waist. The sparkling fabric molded to her bottom before falling in a straight line to the floor.

Just over the crest of her bottom he could see the faint outline of the zipper hidden in the seam. It couldn't have been more than four inches long.

"So I see."

Kitty was no scrawny fashion model. She had a body that managed to be both slender and voluptuous. Her bottom was lusciously rounded. Just looking at it made his blood throb with lust.

She elbowed him in a way that was both playful and seductive. "Stop looking at my zipper," she murmured huskily as she locked her door.

He shrugged as they started down the stairs. "If you don't want people looking at your *zipper*, you shouldn't display it quite so prominently."

"That's sexist," she chided.

"No, it would be sexist if we were at work and I ordered you to display your zipper. Or I hired you or fired you based on the size of your zipper. But this is a social situation, so I don't think either of those apply. Besides, a woman doesn't wear a dress like that unless she wants to be looked at."

He hailed a cab when they reached the street.

Kitty frowned, her bottom lip jutting forward in a pout. "Oh. We're going in a cab. How...prosaic."

"I try to avoid hiring a driver when I come to the city. They spend too much time looking for parking and driving around. It's a waste of gas and resources." He held open the cab door for her, admiring the swath of leg revealed as she slid into the car.

"Hmm. Like I said. How prosaic."

He climbed in beside her. "Being aware of the environment isn't prosaic." A hint of his annoyance slipped into his tone. "FMJ has made most of its money in green industries. Our image as a green company is a priority. Not just for the company, but for all of us."

She yawned delicately, but with obvious boredom. Annoyed by her attitude, he nearly called her on it, but before he could, it hit him. "You're doing this on purpose, aren't you?"

She looked taken aback. "I...I don't know what you mean. Doing what?"

"This." He gestured toward her body-skimming dress. "The sexpot dress. The self-indulgent pout. The childish behavior. It's all a way of keeping me off balance."

She blinked, and he couldn't tell if he'd insulted her or if she was merely surprised he'd seen through her. "You're just trying to distract me. To avoid that conversation we need to have."

"However did you get that idea?"

"Probably because you've been pushing me away ever since I walked into the conference room today. You've made it obvious that you don't want to relinquish control of Biedermann's. You may have fooled everyone else into thinking that's the only thing going on. But I can see right through you. I know the truth."

Oh, God. What did he mean? He knew *the truth?* What truth? That she was a total fraud? That she had no idea what she was doing?

He leaned closer, a seductive grin on his face. "I know what you're really afraid of."

"Afraid of?" she squeaked.

He brushed his thumb across her lower lip, once again sparking the desire that heated her blood every time he touched her.

She should not be attracted to him. He was so not what she needed right now. Or ever, for that matter. Geesh, he wasn't even wearing a tux. Okay, so he looked fabulous in an Armani jacket thrown over a gray cashmere sweater and black pants. And, yes, the understated elegance of his outfit made him look outrageously masculine. Never mind that he carried it off. Never mind that the day's worth of stubble on his jaw made her fingertips tingle with the urge to touch him. Never mind that she could tell already all the other men at the fundraiser would look overdressed and foppish by comparison. She couldn't possibly be attracted to a man who didn't even know when to wear a tie.

"Yes," he continued. "You're afraid of the attraction between us."

As his words registered, she was flooded with an odd sense of relief. He was still talking about sex. About what had happened between them in Texas.

Maybe it shouldn't have made her feel better, but somehow it did. Physical intimacy she could handle. Men had been pursuing her since she hit puberty. She knew how to handle that. She knew how to entice without promising anything. To lure and manipulate a man while staying just out of his reach.

What she didn't know was how to handle a man who was interested in her. Not her body. Not her net worth, but her.

Thank God, Ford was proving no different than any other man she'd ever met. She'd learned long ago the secret to keeping men at arm's length.

The mere suggestion of sex was enough to distract the average man. The possibility that you might one day have sex with him made most men so befuddled they never bothered to look beneath the surface.

To that end, she let herself sway toward him slightly, as if she couldn't resist his draw. Then she ran her tongue over the spot on her lip that he'd touched. It was a gesture sure to entice him, but she found it disconcertingly intimate. She could almost taste him on her tongue.

Suddenly memories flooded her of their one night together. How could she have forgotten what it had been like to kiss him? To feel his hands on her body? To give herself over so completely to his touch?

She felt her breath catch in her chest, found herself leaning toward him, not in a calculated way, but as if he were a magnet and the heart pounding away in her chest were made of iron, pulling her inexorably toward him.

He cleared his throat, breaking the spell he seemed to have cast over her. Nodding toward the cab door on her side, he said, "We're here."

When had that happened? Damn him. She was supposed to be distracting him. Not the other way around.

Feeling befuddled, she looked from him to the

crowded street outside her window, to the cab driver rattling off the fare. Her mind was embarrassingly sluggish, but finally she got moving.

Staying one step ahead of Ford was going to be harder than she'd thought. This was going to take some serious work.

Then just when it seemed like things couldn't get any worse, a camera flashed a few feet away. Great. Just what she needed.

Paparazzi.

Four

Ford stood near the bar, nursing a tumbler of weak Scotch, wishing he could have ordered himself a Sierra Nevada Pale Ale. He would have thought that at five hundred bucks a ticket, they could have stocked the bar with some decent beer. But of course, the best beer in the world wouldn't have distracted him from what was really bothering him. His date.

From the moment the first camera had flashed outside the hotel and she'd practically leaped from his side, she'd been avoiding him. At first, he'd assumed she just didn't want their picture taken together. That she was averting the potential scandal. But things hadn't improved since they'd made it into the event.

She'd immediately sent him off to get her a glass of

white wine and she'd been dodging him ever since. Not that he wasn't having a grand ol' time, between the event organizer who'd hit him up for a ten-thousand-dollar donation and the drunk society maven twice his age who'd been hitting on him. He hadn't had this much fun since his root canal.

Then he spotted Kitty across the room. On the dance floor. With another man. A guy who couldn't have been more than five-six and had very clingy hands.

Ford wasn't used to women blowing him off. After all, he'd only come out tonight because he'd wanted to make sure she was okay. After the near waterworks in the elevator, he'd been worried about her emotional state. Judging from the way she was laughing at Mr. Grabby's joke, she was doing just fine. But enough was enough.

He handed his drink to a passing waiter and wove his way through the crowd to the dance floor. He cut in, sweeping Kitty into his arms before she could protest. But he could tell she wanted to. As her hand settled into his, a scowl twisted her perfect features.

"I'm starting to think you're avoiding me."

"Whatever gave you that impression? After all, it's not like you wheedled your way into coming with me uninvited or anything."

He grinned at her, some of his annoyance fading at the bite of her sharp tongue. In Texas she'd been relaxed and open. Who would have guessed he'd find her bristly defenses just as appealing. "I'm a grown man. I don't wheedle."

"Hmm…" She paused as if considering her words. No doubt searching for the best way to skewer him. "How about coerce? Or maybe bully? Are those descriptions more to your liking? Are those masculine enough for you?"

He stared down at her, studying her expression. As they danced, his body brushed hers. He couldn't help remembering what it had felt like to dance with her in that bar in Texas. There, her body had melted into his; here, she held herself more stiffly. This was less a dance, more a battlefield.

"I don't like to think," he said seriously, "that I've bullied you into anything."

She arched an eyebrow. "Then perhaps you shouldn't be trying to buy my company out from under me."

"That's business."

"I thought you said it was *all* business?" she countered smoothly.

"That's not what I meant and you know it." She felt good in his arms again. Solid, yet soft. Curved in all the right places. Tempting and a little bit dangerous.

Suddenly he couldn't remember why he was supposed to leave her alone. Something about the business deal, right? It was a bad idea to mix business with pleasure. He knew that.

But Biedermann's was in serious trouble and FMJ looked like the only people stepping forward to help out. Besides, if everything went as planned, this would leave her even richer than she was now. Kitty was a businesswoman first and foremost.

But she was also a woman. A very desirable, powerful woman. He'd be an idiot to ignore the tension simmering between them. Not just because the sex would be fantastic, but because the more they tried to ignore it, the more likely it was to get in the way of business. He couldn't let his former relationship with Kitty muck up this business deal. He wouldn't let his buddies down like that.

Ford smiled. "What's going on with Biedermann's is all business. This thing between us isn't business at all."

"There is no thing between us."

Her voice was so emotionless, he almost believed she meant it. But his body had been inside hers. He'd watched her face as she climaxed. Women didn't forget that kind of thing. Sure, he could let her go on pretending they had no past, but that would just make things worse down the road if this blew up in both their faces.

"There was something between us back in Texas. I'm betting there still is."

She hesitated, her feet missing the rhythm for a moment. But then she picked up the beat again and fell into step. "You're wrong."

"And you're avoiding the obvious," he said. "You're acting like we didn't have hot, steamy sex in the back of my truck."

Her gaze narrowed into a glare. "And you're acting like a sixteen-year-old girl who put out on prom night and now wants to hear the quarterback still respects her."

He nearly chuckled at the image, but that seemed to only irritate her more.

She leaned closer to whisper vehemently, "You want to know the truth? Yes, the sex was hot and steamy. But it was just sex. Sex with a nameless, faceless stranger. It was never meant to be anything more than that. If you'd wanted a long-term relationship you should have put an ad up on one of those Internet dating sites."

"Trust me. I'm not a relationship kind of guy. I'm just not willing to be whipped. Least of all by you. Why would I? So far, you've been insulting, arrogant and generally a pain in the ass."

Surprise flickered across her face and he might have felt a twinge of guilt if every word he said wasn't true. Possibly even an understatement.

"Don't get me wrong," he continued. "It's kind of cute. In a spoiled brat kind of way."

"Cute? Spoiled brat?" She sputtered as if searching for a response. "How da—"

"How dare I? I dare because whether you like it or not, we have to work together. Whether *I* like it or not, for that matter. I thought talking about what happened in Texas might make things easier for you." Though the music continued to play, they'd slowed to the point they were no longer dancing. "Apparently I was mistaken. You don't want to talk about it? Fine. Just make sure you don't bring any of this baggage into the boardroom when we start negotiations."

She pulled her hand from his. Her gazed narrowed to a venomous glare. "Thank you for clearing that up for me. Here I was worried FMJ's offer might have been motivated by some chivalrous impulse on your part."

"Sorry, sugar." He softened his words with a grin. "I don't have a chivalrous bone in my body."

"I'm glad you've disabused me of that notion. Now I can go about being my normal…what was that phrase you used? Oh yes, pain in the ass…without feeling bad about it. That makes things much easier."

Shooting him one last haughty look, she spun on her heel and left the dance floor.

"I 'disabused her of the notion'?" he muttered to the empty spot where she'd been. "Who the hell talks like that?"

He stood there for a minute until he realized the couples around him were staring with interest. He flashed his best charming rogue smile and shrugged. "Women."

Several men tried to hide their smiles. A couple laughed outright. The women either rolled their eyes or just looked away. But he could see in their eyes that they were more amused than they wanted to be.

If the audience was keeping score, it looked like he'd won another round. It didn't feel that way, though. If only he'd believed her when she said she wasn't interested in sleeping with him. Hell, he'd even be satisfied with believing himself.

Kitty's heart pounded in her chest as she maneuvered through the maze of bodies on the dance floor. Nausea clung to her, sticky and thick. She wasn't sure how much longer she could maintain any semblance of calm around Ford. Her nerves were frayed to the point of exhaustion.

Selling Biedermann's was something she'd never

thought she'd consider. Just meeting with FMJ to discuss it had been abhorrent. But she'd done it. She'd dug deep to find strength she'd never known she had and she'd done the right thing for the company. And this was how fate had punished her.

Why, oh, why, did it have to be him? Why did he have to be the *F* of FMJ? Six billion people in the world and the one she never wanted to see again just happened to be the one who held her future in his hands. It was cruelty piled on top of humiliation. It was completely…nauseating.

She flattened her hand against the restroom door and shoved her way inside. The room was thankfully empty. A fact that she only had a second to appreciate before another wave of nausea washed over her. She bolted for the closest stall just as bile mixed with the rich appetizers she'd been so hungry for when she'd first arrived.

Talk about humiliation.

As if throwing up—in public—wasn't bad enough. As Kitty knelt on the bathroom floor with one hand propped on the toilet paper dispenser and the other wedged against the wall, she heard footsteps outside the stall.

"Oh, my, are you all right?" asked a wavering voice from behind her.

The voice sounded kind—benevolently maternal. Kitty wasn't taken in. Too many "kind" women were starving for gossip.

"I'm fine," Kitty managed. She raised her left leg, felt around in the air a bit for the door, then kicked it shut.

"Is there something I can get you, dear?"

Hmm…a cool washcloth? A glass of water? Retrograde amnesia? Any of the above would do.

Kitty shoved the hair out of her face and straightened, wiping at the corners of her mouth with the back of her hand.

"Perhaps I could notify your date that you're not feeling well?"

Nosy and persistent, then. Kitty stood, smoothing down her dress. In her haste, she stepped on her hem and pulled it out. But that couldn't be helped. Praying she looked better than she felt, she left the sanctuary of the stall. Kitty turned to see an elderly woman hovering by the sinks. Though she had to be nearing ninety, the woman was well-dressed and obviously took pains with her appearance.

Kitty remembered something her grandmother had often told her. There's no situation that can't be improved with a fresh coat of lipstick.

Sayings like that had made Kitty roll her eyes as a teenager. Inexplicably, Kitty chuckled. "I think I'll just freshen my makeup."

The older woman smiled. "Always a good idea, if you ask me."

Kitty faced the mirror. Her hair had lost its smooth sheen and now looked tousled beyond repair. Her face was ashen, her lips dry. Even her eyes seemed to have developed dark circles. She could only suppose they'd darkened to match her exhaustion.

And here she'd thought she looked pretty good just a few hours ago when she'd left the condo.

She sighed. By the sink there was a selection of hand lotions and perfumes, along with a bottle of mouthwash and a stack of tiny cups. She filled one of the cups with water to rinse out her mouth.

Spitting as delicately as she could, Kitty said, "This is quite embarrassing. I don't think I've ever thrown up in public before."

"Think nothing of it, dear. Every woman goes through it."

Kitty raised her eyebrows. "Every woman—" she started to ask in confusion.

"Well, not every woman. But when I was pregnant with Jake, my second, I couldn't keep anything down, either."

"Oh, I'm not… That is, I've just been under a lot of stress."

The woman gave her a pointed look. "Is that what they're calling it these days?"

"I'm not—" But Kitty's protest died in her mouth. "Pregnant."

Her vision tunneled, fading to black at the edges but staying piercingly bright in the center, where she could see her reflection in the mirror. Pale. Frightened. Terrified.

What if she was?

She couldn't be. But even as she thought it, reality came crashing back.

She was losing Biedermann's. Ford was back in her life. Running her company. So why wouldn't she be pregnant?

* * *

Ford stood in the grand ballroom of The Pierre, scanning the room one last time as the nasty truth sank in. Kitty had left him standing on the dance floor, dashed off for the bathroom and then—somehow—sneaked past him on her way out.

As unpleasant as the idea was, there was no other explanation. Kitty was nowhere to be found. Hell, he'd waited long enough for her to put in an appearance.

Maybe he had it coming. After all, this wasn't an actual date. He'd pushed his way in. Bullied her into agreeing, to use her word.

Still, he wasn't going to let her get away with this.

Forty-five minutes later, he was standing at her door, a lavish bouquet of orchids in his hands.

Her hair was loose about her shoulders, no longer sleek, but tousled as if she'd been running her fingers through it. Her face had been scrubbed clean of makeup, leaving her cheeks rosy. Her mouth was still impossibly pink, though.

She'd changed out of her dress and had a long silk robe cinched tight around her waist. The result was that she looked like one of those forties movie starlets. Somehow, even devoid of makeup and expensive clothing, she still exuded class. As if she'd been simmered in wealth since childhood and now it fairly seeped from her pores.

She eyed him suspiciously, her gaze dropping to the orchids and then back to his face. "What are those for?"

Since she didn't seem inclined to invite him in, he

elbowed past her into the apartment. "They were my excuse to get in the building. One of your neighbors was leaving. I told him I was here to apologize for a date gone bad so he'd let me in."

"And he believed you?"

"What can I say? I was persuasive."

After a moment of indecision, she closed and bolted the door. "Don't worry. It won't happen again. I'll hunt him down and kill the jerk."

"Don't do that. If you're mad at me, take it out on me." While she considered his words, he surveyed her apartment. A dingy kitchen led off from the living room and he headed there with the flowers. "Do you have a vase?"

"I thought the flowers were just a ruse."

"That's no reason not to enjoy them. Do you have any idea how hard it is to find flowers at midnight on a Friday night?"

He grabbed a vase out of one of the cabinets. It was an ornate job with elaborate curlicues. As he filled it with water, he waited for her response. She always seemed to have some snappy comeback.

It was her silence that alerted him something was wrong. He dropped the flowers into the vase and turned, thinking maybe she'd retreated to her bedroom or even left the apartment. Instead he found her sitting on the living room's sole sofa with her elbows propped on her knees and her face buried in her hands.

His nerve endings prickled with alarm.

He sent up a silent prayer. *Please don't let her be*

crying. Between his three sisters, Patrice and Suz, he'd faced down his share of weepy women.

The one thing his vast experience with crying women *had* taught him was that running like hell would only make things worse.

"Hey," he began awkwardly. "What's—"

Then Kitty stood, her eyes red, but dry.

No tears. Thank God.

She crossed to stand before him, her posture stiff with anger. "What's the matter?"

She got right in his face, stopping mere inches from him. "I'll tell you what's the matter."

She shoved a hand against his shoulder. Surprise bumped him back a step. "You are the matter."

She bopped him on the shoulder again. This time he was ready, but she was stomping forward, so he backed up a step anyway. "You come here and push your way into my company. Into my life. Into my apartment. You push and you push and you push."

With each *push* she shoved against his chest and with each shove he stepped back, trying to give her the room she needed. But she followed him step for step.

"Maybe it's time someone pushed back."

By now he was—literally—up against a wall. With his back pressed to the living room wall, he had nowhere else to go. She stopped mere centimeters away from him, her hands pressed to his chest, her eyes blazing with anger.

"I'm—" he began.

But she didn't let him finish. "Don't you dare say

you're sorry. Sorry won't cut it. *Sorry* doesn't even *begin* to cut it."

"I—"

"Well?" she prodded.

He gripped her shoulders, resisting the urge to shake her. "Stop. Interrupting. Me."

Her chin bumped up and she glared at him through stormy eyes. "Well?" she demanded again.

"I—" What?

Suddenly, he couldn't remember what it was he'd been about to say. All he could think was that this was what he'd wanted for the past two months. He wanted to see her again. To sleep with her. To strip her clothes off her, lay her bare before him in a proper bed and spend hours worshipping her body.

"'I—I—I—'" she copied, mocking his stammer. "Is that the best you can do?"

Man, she was annoying sometimes.

"No," he said. "This is."

Cupping her jaw in his hands, he shut her up the best way he knew how. He kissed her.

Five

What exactly did she have to do to insult this man? She'd sneered at him. She'd acted like a tease. She'd ditched him in the middle of their date. She'd insulted him and made fun of him. And now he was kissing her?

What was wrong with him?

Worse still, what was wrong with her?

A hot and heavy make out session with Ford was the last thing she needed right now. She wanted peace and quiet to process the events of the night. She wanted to kick Ford out of her apartment. She wanted him out of her life. She wanted to go on kissing him forever.

After months of living on memories, he was actually kissing her. Months of pretending she'd forgotten him, of believing she'd never see him again, of shoving him out of her mind during the day, but then dreaming of him when she slept. After months of waking in the middle of the night, panting, heart racing, body moist and heavy with need. After months of that, he was here. In her apartment. Kissing her.

His tongue nudged into her mouth, tracing the sensitive skin behind her lip. She shuddered, opening herself fully to him. He tasted of smoky Scotch and heat, of neediness and lust. So familiar, even though she'd only been with him once. Her body sparked to life beneath his touch.

Suddenly it didn't matter that he'd sneaked back into her life uninvited. It didn't matter that he'd deceived her. That he pushed too hard. That she couldn't intimidate or control him. All that mattered was that he just keep kissing her.

Her body remembered his touch as if it were yesterday. No matter what lies she'd told him earlier, *she* remembered. She remembered every second of their time together. As if for those few hours they'd been together she'd been more alive than at any other time in her life. As if she'd been more herself than she was in real life. The way he'd kissed her then. The cool night air on her skin when he'd kissed her in the parking lot of that god-awful bar. The heat of his hands against her flesh. The cold metal of his truck door pressed against her back.

His fingers had fumbled as he pulled her shirt over her head. She'd lost an earring. Yet when he'd touched her breasts, he hadn't been clumsy. His touch was deft. Gentle. His fingertips rough as they'd pinched her nipples, sending fissures of pleasure through her body.

He'd shoved her skirt up to her waist and his jeans had been rough against the insides of her thighs. He'd shoved her panties aside, touched her *there*. A slow, rhythmic rasping of his thumb that had driven her quietly wild. By the time he'd plunged into her, she was already on the brink of climax. The feel of him pumping inside of her combined with the chafing of his fingers had sent her over the edge.

Now, kissing him in her living room, with memories flooding her, his touch was so achingly familiar. Her body trembled with need. Moisture seeped between her legs as desire pulsed through her. She was ready for him already.

His arm snaked around her back, holding her body to his as he walked her backward, one step, then two, still kissing her. His mouth nibbled hers as if he would devour her one tiny bite at a time. And she felt power-less to stop him.

The backs of her knees bumped against the arm of the sofa just as his hand cupped her breast through the bodice of her robe. The silk provided little protection against his roaming hands, not that she wanted any. She felt her nipple tighten, hardening to his touch. Heard a groan stir in his chest.

He pulled his mouth from hers. "This isn't how I wanted this to happen."

But he poured kisses along her neck as he said it.

Proof that he was as powerless against her as she was against him.

Her hands clutched the lapels of his jacket. Pulling back, she tried to glare at him. Which was hard to do through the fog of her desire.

"How *you* wanted it to happen? What about what I want?"

He grinned wickedly, his hand flicking open the folds of her robe. Brushing the outside of her panties, he said, "I think I know what you want."

Her panties were damp with her need for him. She knew it. Maybe it should embarrass her, this desperate lust for him, the way he only had to kiss her and she went wet for him, but it didn't. Not when she knew he felt the same way. She may be wet, but he was hard. Panting. Pulsing against her hand when she ran it down the front his pants.

"You do, don't you?" Her voice came out husky. "Know what I want, I mean."

"I do."

His gaze was disconcertingly serious as he muttered the words. For an unsettling second, she considered the possibility that maybe this was about more than just sex for him. For both of them. But she shoved the concern aside.

Sex was all they had. All she wanted.

Because she couldn't think about anything else. Anything beyond this minute. This very second. She couldn't think about the mistake she might be making. Or the mistake she'd already made.

She couldn't think about the pair of pregnancy tests she'd hastily thrown out when the doorbell rang. Couldn't think about the twin pink lines on those pregnancy tests. She couldn't think about the baby already growing in her belly.

Logic told him to slow down, but she didn't let him. One minute he was merely kissing her, the next she was tumbling over the arm of the sofa, pulling him on top of her. He barely caught himself in time to keep from squashing her. He braced one hand on the back of the sofa and the other right beside her head.

For all her height, she felt tiny beneath him. He didn't want the weight of his body to pummel her. "That was close," he muttered.

"Not nearly close enough," she purred, bucking against him. Her hips rocked against his. Not in a light and playful way, but frantically, as if she were seconds from losing all control. One of her legs crept up the outside of his thigh, hooking around to anchor her hips to his.

Then she bucked against him one last time, rolling him off the sofa altogether, following him down onto the floor. Thank God for plush carpet, though even that hadn't been able to keep the breath from being knocked out of him.

Or maybe it was just her that took his breath away. Kitty. Demanding. Arrogant. Unapologetic. And sexy as hell.

She walked her hands down his chest, slowly pushing

herself into a seated position astride his hips. Her robe gaped open, barely covering her breasts as it caught on her nipples. The sash was still tied at the waist, but the robe revealed enough for him to see she was naked except for her underwear. A little scrap of fabric that felt silky and damp beneath his touch. Just kissing him had made her wet. His erection leaped at the very idea, straining against the front placket of his pants.

Head thrown back, she shifted her hips forward, grinding herself against him. She groaned low in her throat, a sound both erotic and unbearably tempting. How could he resist her? Why would he even try?

He slipped his thumb under the hem of her panties and found the nub of her desire. He stroked her there and the moan turned into a chorus of yeses. The steady chant echoed through his blood, pounding against the last of his restraint.

When she reached for his zipper, it didn't even occur to him to stop her. With a few quick movements, she'd freed him. He lifted his hips as she pulled at his pants, not even bothering to take them all the way off.

She nudged the fabric of her underwear out of the way, then lowered herself onto him. With one smooth movement, he was inside of her. Hot, tight, and unbearably sweet. He squeezed his eyes tightly closed, trying to reign in his pure lust. Sucking a breath in through his teeth, he narrowed his focus. Pleasure rocked through his body, but he stayed just ahead of it. He didn't want to come too quickly. He wanted her right there with him.

He moved his thumb in slow, steady circles, matching the rhythm of her rocking hips. With his eyes still closed, he focused on the sound of her breath, the quick gasps and low moans. The yeses had dissolved to a series of meaningless guttural sounds.

He felt her muscles clenching around him. Then he made the mistake of opening his eyes. He looked up to see her poised above him, her back arched, her breasts thrusting forward as her hands clutched her heels. With her neck arched her hair fell down her back in wild disarray. He'd never seen anything more primitive, more primal, more gut-wrenchingly erotic.

And then she focused her groans into a single word that sent him spiraling beyond control.

"Ford!"

Sleeping with Ford just about topped the list of stupid things she could have done. Ford had said she'd had a hard day and he didn't know the half of it.

And as if sleeping with him wasn't bad enough, she'd *slept* with him. When he'd picked her up and carried her to her bedroom, she'd actually tugged him down onto the bed with her, draped her body over his and promptly fallen asleep. She'd snuggled with him, for cripes sake.

When she'd peeled herself off him in the morning to sneak away for a shower, she prayed he'd at least have the common courtesy to disappear. But no. Not Ford. He made coffee.

How the hell was she supposed to defend herself against a man who'd made her coffee?

"Oh," she said joylessly. "You're still here."

"We have to talk."

"So you keep saying." She crossed the narrow kitchen to the coffeepot and poured herself a cup. "Maybe you think we're ready for couples' therapy."

He cut to the chase. "We didn't use a condom last night."

Ah. So that was why he'd stuck around.

Hoping to antagonize him into storming out, she said, "I suppose you blame me for that."

"I didn't say that. I just wanted to let you know you don't have to worry about your health. I get tested annually for anything that—"

"I know," she interrupted him. "When I got back from Texas I had myself tested. Yes, we were pretty safe, but as we both know condoms aren't one hundred percent effective at anything."

She broke off sharply. *Please don't do something stupid. Like cry. Or tell him the truth.*

"So," she continued. "I knew that wasn't a concern."

Just keep sipping your coffee. He'll leave soon and you can do all the stupid things you want.

He pinned her with a heavy stare. "Do I need to worry you'll get pregnant?"

It took all her willpower not to spew coffee all over the kitchen. Instead she equivocated. "Do I look worried?"

"That's hardly the point. You never look worried."

Well, at least she still had someone fooled. With a

self-effacing shrug, she said, "When you're raised the way I was, you learn to keep your emotions to yourself."

"Well, you learned well, then." There was a hint of something dark in his voice. Bitterness maybe, but she didn't want to consider what he might mean by that. She couldn't let herself think too much about his emotions just now.

She ignored his comment. "You don't have to worry about last night."

"You're certain?"

"Let's just say that if I got pregnant from last night, it would be a medical miracle."

Thank God he didn't press her for a more precise answer. Still, she didn't breathe deeply until he'd left and she'd thrown the dead bolt behind him.

Maybe doing something stupid like this was inevitable.

She stood in her kitchen for a long time, sipping her coffee, making excuses for her behavior. What she wanted most was to simply crawl back into bed with her sketch pad and MP3 player. To spend the whole day pretending the rest of the world didn't exist. Of course, she didn't have that luxury.

Come Monday, Ford would start pressuring her to cement the deal with FMJ. Whatever else happened, she couldn't afford to sleep with him again. There was too much at stake, for Biedermann's and for her. After all, she was going to be...

Kitty broke off her train of thought to stare down at her nearly empty coffee mug. Could pregnant women even drink coffee? Shaking her head, she dumped the last splash of coffee in the sink and washed out the mug. She'd have Casey look that up on Monday.

She paused in the act of drying the mug. Yeah, that'd be subtle. No one would ever guess she was pregnant, between puking every few minutes and having her assistant research the effects of caffeine on pregnancy.

At some point, she'd have to tell Ford about the pregnancy, but she wasn't ready for that just yet. She needed more time to process it. To figure how she felt about the tiny life growing inside of her and what it meant for her life.

She had no idea how Ford might respond to the news he was about to be a father. But she knew that whatever his reaction was going to be, she'd need to have her own emotional defenses in place before she dealt with him.

How long could she justify not telling him? A couple of days maybe. But she had to tell him and she had to do it soon.

The very thought made bile rise in her throat. She dashed for the bathroom, only to have her nausea fade, leaving her feeling queasy. The minty zing of her toothpaste helped. When she put away the toothpaste, she saw the two pregnancy tests she'd taken the previous evening.

She'd stopped to pick them up at a drugstore on the way home from the fundraiser. Her heart had pounded the whole time, sure she'd see someone she recognized. Or that at the very least someone would comment on the absurdity of a woman in formal wear buying pregnancy tests late at night. She hadn't cared. She'd needed to know.

She had still been reeling from the shock when Ford had shown up on her doorstep. He'd caught her at her most vulnerable. Again.

But it wouldn't happen a third time. From now on, she'd be prepared to deal with him. But first, she had to deal with other issues. She pressed a hand to her belly.

Logically, she should still be freaking out about being pregnant. But for some strange reason, she wasn't. Maybe some weird pregnancy hormone had been working its magic on her subconscious for the past two months. Whatever the reason, she felt strangely at peace.

Why did being pregnant have to be such a bad thing? All her life she'd dreamed of being part of a bigger family. She'd longed for sisters and brothers. How many times had she made her grandmother read *Little Women* to her? Dozens.

The only thing she'd wanted more than siblings was a real mother. Her grandmother had done her best. She'd loved her and cared for her, sure. But she hadn't done the things other mothers had done—or rather the things Kitty had imagined other mothers did. She'd never climbed onto the jungle gym at the park. She'd never built forts out of old sheets draped over the furniture. She'd never crawled into Kitty's bed to cuddle her and chase away the monsters.

Those were things Kitty's childhood had lacked. But they were experiences she could give to her child.

She could lavish this child with love. She could become the kind of mother she'd always wanted for herself. She could create the family she'd craved for so long.

What about Ford? What kind of father would he be? She bet he'd be the kind of dad who coached Little League and charmed all the teachers into rounding up his kids' grades. He'd spend too much on birthday presents, and...

Whoa. Where had all that come from? Wondering what kind of father Ford would make was the last thing she should be worrying about. It was a completely absurd exercise. Like wondering whether or not the tooth fairy was ticklish. Ford was Mr. Not-Willing-to-Be-Whipped.

There was no way he'd be interested in coaching Little League. This morning, he'd given her the perfect opportunity to tell him about the baby, but she'd balked. She hadn't exactly lied, but she hadn't told him the truth, either. And she suspected it had less to do with her mental defenses than it did with the possibility that she already knew how he'd react.

Ford wasn't looking for long term. Not with her. Not with a child. When he found out the truth, he would cut and run.

At least, dear God, she hoped he would. She could only pray he wouldn't do something noble like offer to *marry* her.

She'd been a burden all her life. For once in her life, she wanted to pull her own weight.

Yes, being pregnant now was inconvenient, what with everything that was going on at Biedermann's.

But it didn't have to be a bad thing. Not at all. The more she thought about it, the more convinced she became. She could be a good mother. She could do this. This was one dream that would not be snatched away from her.

True, she'd probably never be able to run Biedermann's the way she'd dreamed of. But being a failure as a CEO didn't mean she'd also be a failure as a mother. After all, her father had been a fantastic CEO, but a less than stellar parent. That was proof enough, if she needed it, that the two jobs didn't require the same skills. It came down to this: she'd have to be a good parent, because she was likely to be the only parent her child ever knew.

Whenever he and Jonathon traveled together, they got a hotel suite. The combined living space always made it easier to have teleconferences with Matt and to work late in the evenings. It was an arrangement that had worked well. And Jonathon certainly didn't care that Ford was returning to the hotel, having obviously been out all night. And had he slept with any other woman, Ford would have kept his mouth shut.

But Kitty was not any other woman. This morning she'd seemed fine. But the truth was, he had no idea what she was really feeling. He couldn't dismiss the possibility that he'd screwed things up. And if he had blown this deal because he couldn't stop thinking with a certain male part, then Jonathon deserved to know the truth.

"I made a mistake," he admitted as soon as he walked into the hotel suite.

Jonathan didn't even bother looking up from his laptop. A fruit plate and a bowl of oatmeal sat untouched beside his computer. "That's never a good announcement at 7:00 a.m. on a Saturday morning. But you're a big boy. I'm sure you can handle it."

"I slept with Kitty."

Jonathon's head snapped up. "Kitty Biedermann?"

"It was stupid, I know," he admitted.

A pot of coffee and a couple of cups sat untouched on the room service tray, so he poured himself a cup. He looked up to see Jonathon with a bemused half smile on his face.

"We just got here. That's fast, even for you." When Ford didn't answer, Jonathon's smile morphed into a contemplative squint. "That's not it, is it? You knew her already."

"I did. We met in Texas about two months ago." He took a sip of the coffee, relishing the heat as it burned its way down his throat. A stiff drink was what he really wanted for a conversation like this. Scalding hot coffee wasn't a bad second, though.

Jonathon studied him for a long moment, absently popping a grape in his mouth as he did. "You were the one who wanted to buy out Biedermann's."

Ford shook his head. "Biedermann's was on your list."

Jonathan stabbed a bite of cantaloupe. "Technically, that was the NYSE's list. I just referenced it when I was looking for another company to buy. There were seven or eight other companies on that list. You were the one who did all that research on Biedermann's."

Jonathon paused, chewing slowly as he watched Ford. "Unless you weren't researching the company at all. You were researching her, weren't you?"

"Look. I made a mistake. It wouldn't be the first." Ford took another drink of his coffee, wishing again it was something stronger. "I asked Wendy to find out what she could about Kitty Biedermann. She was overly enthusiastic. I didn't even know Biedermann's was on the list until you'd done most of the work."

"You should have said something then."

"I didn't think it would be a big deal. Neither of us was looking for a long-term relationship. I knew what happened in Texas was just a one-night stand and it would never happen again."

Jonathon quirked an eyebrow. "Which explains perfectly why you just slept with her a second time."

"It's not a big deal."

"So you keep saying. Are we going to have a problem with the acquisition?"

Ford thought back to Kitty's attitude. Last night she'd been passionate and demanding. This morning she'd been coolly reserved. "I don't think so," he said honestly. "She's devoted to Biedermann's. She'll do the right thing for the company. As for me, she's not emotionally involved. She's just not the boil-a-bunny type."

"How well do you know her?" Jonathon asked.

"Well enough to know that…" Then he noticed that Jonathon leaned over his laptop as he spoke, typing rapidly. Ford just rolled his eyes. "You're looking her up on Google, aren't you?" In answer,

Jonathon just shrugged. "After all the information about her that Wendy dug up, you think you're going to find something on the Internet that we didn't already know?"

Jonathon shrugged. "It never hurts."

Annoyed, Ford continued speaking. "I know her well enough to know she's not going to back out of a business deal for personal reasons."

Jonathon tapped his fingers across the mouse pad while he waited for the slow hotel wireless connection to load the results page. "I hope you're right. Kitty owns nearly sixty percent of the company. If we don't have her on board, the deal will never go through, regardless of whether or not we can convince anyone else."

"I know that." His tone was a little sharper than he'd intended.

Jonathon raised his hands in a gesture of defense. "Just reminding you." He clicked on a page, then sat back, waiting for it to load. "If she backs out now, we've wasted a decent chunk of change. And I don't like wasting time, either."

"She's not going to back out. Selling Biedermann's to us is going to make her a lot of money. That's all the incentive she needs. She's been rich all her life and we're going to make her richer. There's nothing else we need to know."

But by then Jonathon had leaned forward to read whatever Pandora's box Google had pulled up. He let out a low whistle.

"What?" Ford demanded.

"You might want to read what Suzy Snark has to say before you say anything else that'll get you in trouble."

Tension seized Ford's stomach. "Who?"

"Suzy Snark. She's a gossip blogger here in New York. Talks about Kitty every once in a while." He looked up at Ford. "You didn't really read that report from Wendy, did you? Suzy Snark was mentioned multiple times."

The tension that had started in his gut seeped through the rest of his body, leaving him frozen on the spot. He should just cross the room and take the damn laptop from Jonathan, but no matter what orders his brain issued, his feet weren't following them.

Finally he said, "Stop being so damn cryptic and just tell me what the damn thing says."

"Trust me, you're going to want to read this yourself."

He took the laptop from Jonathan and sat back down on the sofa, only vaguely aware of Jonathan walking away to give him privacy. As he read, his tension coalesced into cold, hard anger.

A few minutes later, Jonathan returned, holding out a shot of Scotch from the hotel's courtesy bar. Ford carefully set the laptop on the coffee table before accepting the drink. He took several long drinks, then realized his knuckles were turning white from gripping the glass too tightly.

Finally he stood and headed for the door with grim determination, almost too angry to speak.

"Where are you going?" Jonathan asked.

"To find Kitty."

Six

By the time Monday morning rolled around, Kitty felt marginally more prepared to face Ford. After he left her apartment Saturday morning, she'd decided she simply couldn't face him again so soon. So she'd abandoned the familiarity of her apartment for a hotel not far from Biedermann's offices. She'd spent the weekend with her phone turned off, huddled under the blanket watching an *I Love Lucy* marathon and ordering room service. She'd bawled when Little Ricky was born and then found herself unable to stop crying. Poor Lucy always tried to do the right thing, but always made a mess of things. Sometimes her own life felt like an episode of *I Love Lucy,* but without the laugh track or the comforting presence of Ethel Mertz.

Maybe this mess would seem more bearable if her own pratfalls could be cushioned by the unconditional love of her own Ricky Ricardo. Maybe if Ford…

No, she stopped herself. She couldn't think like that. He wasn't hers. He never had been and he certainly wouldn't be now that she was keeping this secret from him.

Maybe, she justified to herself, one lie of omission deserved another. In Texas, he hadn't told her that he was a business tycoon whose company was worth billions. So Saturday morning, she didn't tell him the whole truth, either.

But of course, she hadn't outright lied. After all, he truly didn't need to worry that she'd gotten pregnant then. By the time they'd had sex, she was already two months pregnant.

All of her rationalizations almost made her feel better. Until Monday morning rolled around and she found Marty pacing in her office. With his tie loosened and his hair tousled, he looked as bedraggled as she felt.

She dropped her handbag on the chair by the door and shrugged out of her coat before tossing it carelessly on top. "Honestly, Marty, have you even been home? You look as if you slept here."

Marty knew her as well as anyone did. Keeping the truth from him would be quite the challenge. Today was a day to channel her inner bitch if there ever was one.

He ignored her comment. "Where have you been all weekend? I've been trying to reach you since Saturday. We all have."

Kitty's stomach tightened. This didn't sound good. "I went away for the weekend." Another lie. Sort of.

What could she possibly have done wrong now? She hadn't even been here. Running his fingers through his hair again, Marty asked, "Have you been online this morning?"

She faked a yawn to cover any panic that might have crossed her face. "You know I can't stand staring at a computer screen before coffee. Speaking of which, could you be a dear and get—"

"No, Kitty. Not this morning." He rounded her desk and popped open her laptop. "Come have a look."

By the time she reached it, the Suzy Snark blog was loading onto the screen. At the top of the page was a picture of her and Ford climbing out of the cab in front of The Pierre Hotel. Whatever nasty comment Kitty had been about to make was swallowed by her dread.

She stared blankly at the screen, her eyes unable to focus on the jumble of words on the screen. After a second, she realized Marty was looking at her expectantly.

"Well," he said.

She dropped petulantly into her office chair. "Why should I care what some gossipmonger has to say?"

"You should care because it affects your business."

"I sincerely doubt it."

"Are you even going to read it?"

You bet your booty she was. But not now, with Marty looming over her, watching the painful process. "Maybe later. After coffee."

Marty twisted the laptop to face him and began reading aloud. "Christmas has come early for those of us who love juicy gossip—"

"Honestly, Marty," she interrupted. "Is this really necessary?"

"Yes." His tone was unexpectedly firm. "You need to read this before anyone from FMJ shows up."

She mimicked his tone. "Fine. Then be a dear and get me that mocha latte and I'll be done reading it by the time you get back."

As soon as he was gone, she leaned forward and began the laborious process of reading.

Christmas has come early for those of us who love juicy gossip. Readers of this column are probably wondering why Kitty Biedermann's love life has been so dull lately. Ever since her breakup with Derek Messina, she's been nursing her broken heart in private. But no longer!

This time she's set her sights on entrepreneur Ford Langley of FMJ. The two were seen together at the posh Children's Medical Foundation fundraiser just last night. It's not surprising the enterprising Kitty would try to land such a hunky catch. The shocker is that they may be entering into professional negotiations as well as personal ones. There are rumors that Biedermann's is about to get gobbled up by FMJ.

And that's not even the biggest news. An inside source says Kitty may be expecting more than just a hefty bonus from FMJ. The only question is, once Langley finds out about Kitty's little bundle of joy, will he still be interested in saving Biedermann's Jewelry? Or will the heiress have to raise her baby and run her company all on her own?

Kitty felt bile rise in her throat as she sat back in her chair. Oh, dear lord.

Before she even began to ponder the issue, Marty reappeared. The mocha latte he set down in front of her did nothing to settle her stomach. His stony expression did little to quell her fears.

"I got a decaf. Just in case she's right." He must have read her answer in her expression, because he propped his hip on the edge of her desk and muttered a curse. "How did she find out?"

"I don't know," she admitted.

"Guess."

But she couldn't guess. She'd known herself for less than seventy-two hours. How had Suzy-stinkin'-Snark found out about it?

"I bought a pregnancy test," she said aloud. "Someone must have seen me do it."

Marty sighed. "And if it was someone who reads the blog and recognized you, they would have contacted Suzy right away."

Marty's obvious annoyance rankled. "Why are you acting all put out over this? This is my private life she's exploiting."

"And it affects our business. Why were you out with Ford anyway? Did you think making a conquest of him would make this buyout any easier on you? Do you really think FMJ is going to want to do business with you when you act like this?"

She could only stammer in response. For years she'd put up with Marty's passive-aggressive kowtowing, and now—the one time she could have really used him in her corner—he was turning on her?

Kitty was saved from having to formulate a defense when Ford appeared at the door.

"Oh, goody," she muttered. "Because I wasn't feeling beleaguered enough."

Ford swept into the room with all the subtly of a tsunami, and he brought flotsam and jetsam in his wake. Jonathon and Casey followed him.

"I assume you've both seen it."

Kitty opened her mouth to answer, but before she could, he turned to her assistant. "We're going to have to make a preemptive strike. We'll schedule a press conference. But not for this afternoon. We want to appear proactive, but we don't want to lend credence to the blog by appearing to be reacting to it. So announce the press conference, but schedule it for a few days out. Wednesday maybe. Jonathon, why don't you and Marty get started on that? Casey, you can—"

Fear propelled her to her feet. "A press conference?" She tried to scoff convincingly. "Over a piddling gossip blog? Isn't that overreacting?"

Ford turned the weight of his gaze on her. He crossed his arms over his chest. "Not at all. FMJ's acquisition of Biedermann's hasn't been officially announced yet. It doesn't look good that the news was leaked."

Right. The acquisition. The news of her pregnancy had overshadowed everything else. She'd forgotten that the blog even mentioned the buyout.

"But," she protested. "It was leaked to a *gossip* blog. One that no one is likely to read. And it's even less likely that anyone who does would care about business."

"This blog may have a wider readership than you think. We all read it within a few hours. We have to assume others have, too. If we work fast, we can minimize the damage."

"Why should we respond at all? We certainly don't want people thinking that whatever this woman posts online is true."

Marty's gaze had been ping-ponging back and forth between them. Ford narrowed his gaze at the other man, giving him a why-are-you-still-here look. Before Marty could respond to the unspoken question. Jonathon ushered both Casey and Marty out with such practiced ease, she couldn't help wondering if he and Ford had orchestrated the move.

"Wow," she murmured. "I'm impressed. Normally it's impossible to get Marty out of my office when he's got a bone to pick." She gestured between Ford and the door through which Jonathon had just vanished. "Did you guys plan out that two-pronged approach? Not that I mind. If we have to talk about that blog, I'd much rather do it without an audience."

"Damn right we have to talk about that blog. Was she right? Are you pregnant?"

* * *

"Does it matter?" Kitty countered smoothly.

Her lack of denial was all the confirmation he needed. Ford gritted his teeth against the questions he wanted to throw at her. As prickly as she was, it wouldn't take much to push her into a full-fledged argument.

"I'd prefer a quiet wedding, but I'll leave that up to you. We should—"

She spun to face him. "We're not getting married."

"Of course, we're getting married." A hard note crept into his voice. "I'm not going to desert my family."

For a long moment, she seemed to be considering him. Then she patted her belly with exaggerated care. "Well, lucky for you, this baby and I aren't your family."

Kitty stood there, one hand propped on her hip, chin up, all defiant bravado.

"You're saying it's not mine?"

"I'm not *saying* it isn't yours. It *isn't* yours."

"But you are pregnant?"

Her chin inched up a notch. "What I am is none of your business. Not your burden. Not your problem."

"You couldn't be more than a couple of months pregnant," he pointed out.

"What's your point?"

"The timing is perfect for me to be the father."

She quirked an eyebrow, her expression full of arrogance. "What, you think I came back from Texas so satisfied that I couldn't even imagine being with another man?"

"I suppose I would like to think that. But the truth is, you're not the type to sleep around."

"Oh, really?" she asked, her voice brimming with challenge. "And you're such an expert on me? How long have you known me, Ford, really? A week? It's less than that, isn't it? The truth is, you have no idea what I'm capable of."

If she was lying, she did a damn good job of it. There wasn't so much as a sputter of doubt in her eyes to give her away.

He waited for the surge of relief. Pregnant or not, she was letting him off the hook. All he had to do was take her at her word and walk away.

He studied her standing there, taking in the defiant bump of her chin, the blazing independence in her eyes. She was dressed in slim-legged pants and a fuzzy sweater that made her look touchable. But that was the only hint of softness about her, otherwise she was all hard angles and bristly defenses.

Kitty was pregnant. There was a baby growing inside her belly. A tiny life. Maybe his. Maybe not.

But his gut said it was his. Every possessive, primitive cell in his body screamed that her child must be his.

Of course, that didn't mean it *was*.

"You're right," he said finally. "I don't know you well, but I'm a good judge of character. I know you well enough to know you're capable of lying to get what you want. The only thing I don't know is what it is you want."

She squared her shoulders and met his gaze. "What I want is to save Biedermann's. If FMJ can do that, then we'll have a deal. If not, I'll find someone else who can."

* * *

"Are you sure you don't want Marty here?" Ford asked as he sat down at the conference table. "He is your CFO."

"I'm sure." They were working late, trying to get all the details of the acquisition hammered out before the press conference later in the week. Thanks to Suzy Snark, they needed to work much faster than they might have otherwise. Instead of sitting herself, she stood near the windows, staring out at the cityscape below. Marty made her so damn nervous. She'd asked Ford to set up this meeting between him, her and Jonathon precisely because she couldn't ask the kinds of questions she needed to with Marty in the room.

Of course, Jonathon made her nervous, too, with his steady gaze and his brilliant head for numbers. He was exactly the kind of person who made her feel twitchy with fear. But Jonathon couldn't be avoided. She no longer trusted herself to be alone with Ford.

Which was why she waited until Jonathon had settled into a chair at the conference table before speaking.

"If I'm going to hand my family's company over to your tender care—" Kitty stressed the words *tender care,* letting them hear her doubts that their management of Biedermann's was likely to be either tender or careful "—then I need assurances that you actually have a plan in place."

Jonathon cleared his throat. "If you've read the proposal we sent, you'll see your compensation package is—"

Ford interrupted him. "I don't believe it's her compensation package she's worried about."

She looked over her shoulder, surprised by his comment. He sat at the table, leaning back in his chair, one ankle propped up on the opposite knee. The posture was relaxed, but there was an intensity to his gaze that made her breath catch in her chest.

"Yes." She forced fresh air into her lungs. "Exactly."

Now, Ford sat forward, steepling his hands on the table before him. "Unless I'm mistaken, Kitty is the rare CEO who is less worried about what she's going to get out of this settlement than how the company is going to be treated." He pinned her with a stare that she felt all the way to her bones. "Am I right?"

In that instant, the intensity of his gaze laid her bare. All the artifice, all her defenses, the image she'd worked her whole life to build and maintain seemed to vanish like a whiff of smoke, leaving her with the disconcerting feeling that he could see straight through to her very soul.

"You are," she said simply.

"I don't understand." Jonathon frowned, looking down at his laptop as if he expected it to sprout flowers. "Why did you ask to meet with us alone if you weren't worried about your end of the deal?"

"I thought you'd be more honest in private." Which was also true and was as good an excuse as any. "I don't care how much money I walk away with. I don't care what kind of golden parachutes you offer to the board members. I care about whether or not the stores themselves survive. When this is all over with, is there going to be a Biedermann's in nearly every mall in America? Are there going to be any of them left?"

The question hung in the air between them. Since they seemed to be waiting for her to say something else, she continued.

"If FMJ gobbles us up, that may solve the immediate problem of our declining stock prices, but that's only part of the problem." She turned to Jonathon. "Our stock price wouldn't be going down if we had strong retail performance. I want to know how you plan to improve that."

She expected Jonathon to answer. After all, he was FMJ's financial genius. However, it was Ford who spoke.

"You're right. For too long, you've been relying on people shopping at your stores because they're already at the mall. However—"

Ford broke off as his cell phone buzzed to life. Reaching into his pocket, he grimaced as he pulled out the phone. "Sorry."

He turned off the volume on the phone, but left it sitting on the conference table by his elbow. "It's not enough…"

Even though he continued talking, her attention wandered for a second. She'd seen the name displayed on the phone when it rang. *Patrice.* What were the names of his sisters? Chelsea, Beatrice and…something else. Certainly not Patrice, though.

Not that it mattered in the least. He probably had the numbers of dozens of women stored in his phone. Hundreds maybe. It wasn't her business.

She forced her attention back to his words.

"We don't want shoppers to stop in at Biedermann's because they're at the mall. We want to attract them to the mall because there's a Biedermann's there. We need Biedermann's to provide them with services and products that they can't get anywhere else."

"We have strong brand recognition," she protested. "We offer more styles of engagement rings than any other store."

"But engagement rings are a one-time purchase. You need something that will bring customers back again and again."

The phone by his elbow began to vibrate silently. Again she glanced down. This time the name display read Suz.

"You can answer it if you need to," she said.

He frowned as the phone stopped vibrating and the call rolled over to voice mail. "I don't."

"Are you sure? Second call in just a few minutes."

Jonathon was scowling, clearly annoyed. He quirked an eyebrow in silent condemnation when the phone started vibrating again a few seconds later. Rosa this time.

Was that the third sister's name? She couldn't remember.

"Just answer it," Jonathon snapped.

Frowning, Ford stood as he grabbed the phone. "Hey, miha. What's up?" With a slight nod, he excused himself from the room.

For a long time, Kitty and Jonathon sat in silence, the tension taut between them. She suspected he didn't like her any more than she liked him. With his frosty demeanor and calculating gaze, every time she glanced at him she half expected to see little dollar signs where his pupils were.

However, after a few minutes of drumming her nails against the armchair, her patience wore out. Or perhaps her curiosity got the better of her.

"Does he always get so many personal calls at work?"

Jonathon scowled, but she couldn't tell if he was annoyed by the interruption or by her questions. "It's after hours. But his family can be quite demanding."

"Those were all family members?" Maybe she'd misremembered the names. Or perhaps misread them?

Jonathon's scowl deepened. Ah, so he hadn't meant to reveal that.

"I know he has three sisters, but—"

"If you're curious about his family, you should really talk to Ford about it."

And let him know she was scoping out his potential as a father? Not likely.

She met Jonathon's gaze and smiled slowly. "The problem, Mr. Bagdon, is that whenever Ford and I are alone, we end up doing one of two things. Neither of them is conducive to talking about his family."

Mr. Cold-As-Ice Jonathon didn't stammer or blush. Instead, he held her gaze, his lips twisting in an expression that she might have imagined was amusement in a man less dour.

"Interesting," he murmured.

"What?"

"You expected me to be either embarrassed or distracted by your honesty."

"But you're neither?" she asked. What was it with these guys from FMJ that none of them reacted the way normal men did?

"Certainly not enough to be tricked into telling you the information you're fishing for."

Well, if her motives were going to be so transparent, then she might as well be honest. "Very well, then. Let's be frank. I am curious about Ford, but I don't want to ask him about his family."

"Because…" Jonathon prodded.

She smiled. "If there's one thing you and I can both agree upon, it's that the relationship between Ford and I is complicated enough as it is. Yes, I could talk to him about it, but I wasn't merely being provocative with my earlier comment. Every time Ford and I are alone we're either fighting or having sex. I don't see any reason to add emotional confidences into an already volatile mix merely to satisfy my curiosity."

Jonathon studied her for a moment, his expression as nonplussed as it always was. Finally he nodded. "Very well. What do you want to know?"

What didn't she want to know might have been a better question. Ford seemed such a dichotomy. She thought of the easygoing charmer she'd met back in that bar in Texas. He'd seemed such a simple man. Not stupid by any means, but uncomplicated. It was that quality that had drawn her to him in the first place. With his laid-back charisma and magnetic smile, he'd coaxed his way past her defenses as easily as he'd mollified Dale.

That alone should have made her suspicious. A man that could assess and defuse a tense situation like that was no mere cowboy. Far more telling was the way he'd charmed her. She never let down her defenses. Never let anyone close. She should have known that any man who could tempt her into a quickie in the parking lot was a man to be reckoned with.

What was that saying? Fool me once, shame on you; fool me twice, shame on me.

Well, she was suitably shamed.

Regardless of all that, Ford—this chameleon of a man, whom she barely knew and couldn't possibly hope to understand—was the father of her child. She had no way of anticipating how he would react if he were to learn the truth.

She clearly took too long to formulate her question, because Jonathon leaned forward. "If you've got a question, you should ask now. He might not be on the phone with his family much longer."

Suddenly, she was struck by an awful thought. Her skin went clammy as panic washed over her. Dear God, what if the reason Jonathon didn't want to talk about Ford was because he was married? Choking down her dread, she asked, "By family, you don't mean wife, do you?"

Jonathon laughed, a rusty uncomfortable snort of

derision. "Ford? Married? Hell, no. He's that last man on earth who would cheat on a wife."

She clenched her jaw against her innate dislike of being laughed at. "Well, I hardly know him. How am I supposed to know that?"

Jonathon's smile faded. "Ford's father kept a mistress for the last fifteen years of his life. He had a whole other family he had set up in a house one town over. While he was alive, he kept all those balls in the air himself. But when he passed away, he'd named Ford executor of his will. All of sudden Ford had to find a way to make peace between these two families."

"My goodness. What did Ford do?" She asked the question almost without realizing she'd done it.

"Ford did what he always does." Jonathon's expression had turned from icy to grim. "He smoothed things over."

Okay, so she wasn't exactly an expert on women, seeing as how most of her friends were men. She could only imagine how she would feel if she found out that the man she'd loved had had another family secreted away somewhere. She'd be pissed. No amount of "smoothing things over" would make that all right. And yet, if anyone could do it, she believed Ford could.

"They must just hate each other," she murmured.

"Surprisingly, they don't." Jonathon shrugged as if to say he didn't get it, either. "They resented each other for a long time, but now they're friends, strange as that sounds. Ford's younger sister—his full sister, that is—

Chelsea is about the same age as Beatrice. Ford managed to convince both Suzanne and Patrice that the girls all needed each other. Of course, it helped matters that his dad had died practically broke. So Ford was pretty much supporting everyone."

"How old was he?"

"Twenty-three or so."

She'd read somewhere that he'd made his first million by the time he was twenty-two. If he was supporting five women not long after that, he must have been highly motivated indeed to keep making money. From what he'd told her, his sisters were only now in college.

She glanced toward the door to her office through which Ford had disappeared. "This kind of thing, with the constant phone calls. This happens often?"

"Only when there's some crisis they want him to solve. They tend to…um, disagree a lot. When they do, they all call Ford to sort it out for them."

"So he solves all their problems, but he never lets them get too close, does he?"

Jonathon sent her a piercing look. "Why do you say that?"

"Because it's what I would do."

Seven

From where she sat, she could see Ford through the open door of her office. He stood with his back toward them. Tension radiated from him. She could see it through the lines of his shoulders, in the way he shifted them as he spoke, as if he were trying to stretch out the knotted muscles. But she could hear the tone of his voice, as well. Not the words, the tone. Quiet and soothing.

She wondered, did his family know he was lying to them? If not with his words, then with his intent.

She was watching Ford so closely that Jonathon surprised her when he said, "You say that because you think you're so much alike."

There was the faintest hint of condemnation in his

voice. It made her chuckle. "Oh, God, no. Not at all."
Finally she looked back at Jonathon. "He's so
charming, isn't he?"

"I don't know what you mean."

"I saw it in Texas. The way he can manipulate
people. Talking them into things. Get them to do things
they normally wouldn't."

"You're saying he charmed you into bed with him."

She slanted a look at Jonathon, tilting her head to
the side as she studied him. "Do you always do that?
Willfully misunderstand what people are saying?"

"I've found most people say things they don't really
mean. And mean things they're not willing to say
aloud. I've found it's best to make sure everyone is on
the same page."

She nodded. "Very well, then, maybe he did charm
me into bed with him. But I certainly wasn't unwilling, if that's what you were asking. No, what I meant
was that he has the ability to charm everyone. But I
don't think he lets many people close."

No, like her, he kept everyone at arm's length. His
charm was as much a weapon as her sarcastic quips. She
couldn't say exactly why she knew that to be true, simply
that she understood it on a gut level. The same way she
knew that if fate hadn't thrown them together again, she
never would have seen Ford after that one night in Texas.

Somehow the thought made her sad. Ford wasn't
hers to keep, but she was glad she'd had this chance to
see him again. To get to know the man he really was.
Even if that man wasn't someone she could let too close.

Jonathon didn't respond, but studied her with that same steady gaze she found so disconcerting.

"Have I satisfied your curiosity?"

Kitty flashed him a cavalier smile. "You've certainly answered all of my questions."

More to the point, he'd told her everything she really needed to know about Ford. If he found out he really was the father of her child, he'd do everything in his power to take care of her. But he'd never really let her or the baby in. He'd never love her or the baby the way she wanted to be loved. She'd just be another burden to him.

And wasn't that just the last thing she needed? Another man to coddle her. Yippee.

Ford couldn't tell how much progress he and Jonathon had made on convincing Kitty to accept their offer, but he sensed something had changed while he'd been on the phone with his sister. He'd come back to the table to find Kitty looking pale and withdrawn. To make matters worse, not much later, Jonathon had gotten a call, as well, and had to leave the meeting.

Now half a day had passed and they were no closer to signing papers. Kitty had vanished after lunch, leaving him to go over the quarterly financial statements with Marty, whose eager nervousness reminded him of a puppy with ADD.

To make matters worse, he'd wandered over to Kitty's office. He hadn't planned on coming there. That's just where he'd ended up. As if he no longer had any control over where his feet took him.

A quick glance in her office told him it was empty. She better not have left early. He'd already turned to leave when he heard a noise from the other side of the office. The door to her bathroom was open.

"Kitty, are you there?" he asked, crossing her office.

He was a few steps from the bathroom when the door slammed closed. "Go away," said her muffled voice.

He should have taken at her word, but he made the mistake of hesitating just long enough to hear the recognizable sounds of someone throwing up. He cringed.

"You okay?"

"Go a—" More retching.

That sounded bad. Not that hurling ever sounded good. He should definitely leave. He'd almost made it to the door when a voice in his head stopped him in his tracks. *She's obviously sick, and you're running for the door. What kind of jerk are you?*

But she'd told him to go.

Of course she did. No one likes puking. You think she's going to ask for your help? No way. But you can't just leave her there.

He walked back to the bathroom, praying the door would be locked. That would be the perfect excuse to just turn and walk away. He tried the knob. And the damn thing wiggled.

He opened the door to see her wiping her mouth with the back of her hand. Thick strands of dark hair had fallen down from its twist to hang in her face. Her gaze blazed with anger.

"I said go away." But her hands trembled as she lowered herself to sit on the ground beside the toilet.

He'd done the right thing.

Shutting the door behind him in case anyone came in, he said, "You don't have to be so proud."

"Great. A lecture. Thanks." She pressed her cheek to the tile wall. "Next time you're throwing up, I'll fly out to California to razz you."

"Yeah, I'll give you a call," he shot back. He pulled a paper towel from the dispenser and ran it under the faucet before handing it to her. "Here."

"Thanks." She wiped carefully at the corners of her mouth, then folded that edge to the center and pressed the damp cloth to her forehead. A sigh of relief escaped her lips.

The sound stirred something deep within his belly. Some primitive urge to care for and protect. To possess.

Okay, she should not look sexy right now. That was just wrong.

He looked around for something else to do and saw a mug sitting on the ledge under the mirror. After rinsing it carefully, he filled it. He squatted by her side and held it out.

After a second, her eyes flickered open. She stared at him for a moment. If she saw the heat in his gaze, she didn't comment, but the tension seemed to stretch between them as she sipped the water. He half expected her to come back with one of her customary jabs. Instead she said merely, "Thanks."

"You're welcome. Can I get you anything else?"

"One of my lollipops. Top drawer of my desk. Right-hand side."

Glad to have something to do, he headed straight for her desk. The first thing he saw when he pulled out the top drawer was an artist's sketchbook. A large pencil drawing dominated the page. In the bottom left-hand corner was a scared little girl in a pinafore dress, with black curls and huge eyes, like a cross between Shirley Temple and Betty Boop with just enough Kitty Beidermann thrown in to make the character unmistakable. She clutched her hands in front of her in exaggerated terror. Behind her loomed an enormous monster, all pointy teeth and glistening drool. Its arms arched over her head, wicked claws gleaming. The monster's body was formed by the letters *F, M* and *J.* The overall effect was both humorous and compelling.

So, she fancied herself an artist, did she?

He grinned as he picked up the sketchbook and flipped the page. However, the other pictures weren't cartoons but rather sketches of jewelry. It was the same tongue-in-cheek, gothic sensibility, but applied to intricate drawings of necklaces and earrings.

"Find one of the yellow ones, if you can," she called out from the bathroom.

He looked back in the drawer and saw a pile of lollipops. After digging through for a yellow one, he headed back to the bathroom, flipping through the sketchbook as he went.

When he reached the bathroom, he tucked the book

under his arm to pull the wrapper off the lollipop. He held it out to her. "These help?"

She plopped it in her mouth and rolled her eyes at him, either in relief or at his obvious doubt. After several strong sucks that caved in her cheeks and worked her throat in a way that was alarmingly erotic, she nodded.

"They're specially formulated." She spoke between sucks. "High in Vitamin C. Sour flavor. Helps with the morning sickness."

This was morning sickness? Undeniable proof of the baby growing in her belly. The baby that was maybe his, maybe not his. But she was definitely making herself known. He felt as if a hand reached into his chest and gave his heart a squeeze.

Kitty swayed a bit, apparently still feeling wobbly, and he automatically reached out a hand to steady her. Her touch on his arm felt weak and trembling. That hand squeezing his heart tightened to a fist.

Before she could protest, he wrapped one arm around her shoulder and gripped her arm with the other, guiding her out of the bathroom to the sofa in her office.

They'd just left the bathroom when her door opened and Marty strolled in. He stopped dead in his tracks, looking from Kitty and back to Ford, then to the open bathroom door through which they'd obviously just walked. Together.

Marty's gaze narrowed and his cheek muscles twitched into a frown. "I'm glad with all the work we have to do that you two are finding ways to amuse yourselves."

Ford waited for Kitty to explain her morning sickness. Instead she pressed her body against his side and slithered her arm around his waist. With exaggerated slowness, she pulled the lollipop from her mouth and smiled. Then she slanted him a look meant to turn men rock-hard.

"Me, too," she murmured with the faintest wink.

Marty gave a disgusted squawk and fled the room, apparently imagining that they were about to go at it again right in front of him.

As soon as the door shut behind him, Kitty sprawled on the sofa, stretching her legs out in front of her indelicately and popping the lollipop back in her mouth with absolutely no artifice.

"Oh, thank God he's gone. Like my nausea wasn't bad enough without having to listen to him."

"You could have explained."

"Trust me. The last thing I need is Marty feeling sorry for me." She shuddered with mock disgust, closing her eyes again to concentrate on her lollipop.

Her hand rested on her belly, her fingers absently toying with the swatch of knit that covered the exact spot where he imagined her baby growing. The way she'd stretched across the sofa, her belly appeared perfectly flat with only the gentlest slope to her stomach. No one would guess she was even a day pregnant. She must not be very far along. More than a month, since she'd already taken the test, but not much more. Maybe two.

The recesses of his brain started doing a little involuntary math, but he shoved the thought aside. She'd said it wasn't his. She was letting him off the hook. That was enough. He didn't want to be a dad and he sure as hell didn't want to inflict himself as a father on any poor kid. It wasn't just him she was letting off the hook. It was all of them. Until she was far enough along to get proof one way or another, he had to take her word for it anyway.

To distract himself from those disconcerting thoughts, he pulled the sketchbook out from under his arm and started flipping through it again.

"What is this?" he asked.

She opened a single eye to gaze at him. When her gaze fell on the sketchbook, she tensed for a second. Then she closed her eye and forced a breath that almost sounded relaxed. "Just doodles."

"They don't look like doodles. They look like jewelry designs."

He held up the page to reveal a sketch of a necklace and earrings. The set was full of intricate curlicues and elaborate swirls in a style that managed to reference Victorian styles while still looking modern.

"It's just something I drew up. It's not even very original."

"What do you mean?" He turned the page to look at the next design.

"I modeled it after some of my grandmother's old jewelry. The ones I had to sell. Most of the drawings in there came from pieces of my grandmother's. A swirl here, a flower there. Just bits I combined together from one piece or another."

He looked up from the drawings. Her free hand still rested on her stomach, but her fingers had started tugging at the knit. Normally Kitty's innate confidence bordered on arrogance. If he didn't know better he'd think she was fidgeting.

He flipped to the next page, staring at the image for a moment before turning the page ninety degrees to get a better angle. "Is this a case for an iPhone?"

She pulled in her legs, straightening. "You know not everyone likes their gadgets to look like gadgets."

It was the same scrolling design as one of the earlier pictures, but this time the perfect size and shape to enclose a cell phone. The page held three drawings, one of the back; the second depicted elegant, tiny, clawed feet, which wrapped around the front of the phone; the third showed the delicate hinges along the side. He could imagine it in gleaming sterling. The overall effect was a brilliant merging of gothic Victorian and geeky tech. Between the clawed feet and the ghoulish tiny gargoyle face on the back, the piece almost had…a sense of humor.

Like the drawing of FMJ gobbling up Kitty.

"Did you think of this?" he asked.

"It's similar to my great-grandfather's cigarette case."

"Wait a second." He flipped back a few pages to the drawing of the earrings and pendant. He squinted at the scrawled writing he'd dismissed initially. In tiny letters he saw the words *Bluetooth?* and *ear buds?* "This isn't jewelry, is it? These are gadgets. This isn't a necklace, it's a case for an MP3 player."

She reached to pull the sketchbook from his hands. "You don't need to poke fun at me."

"I'm not." He held the book just out of her reach. "I think it's brilliant."

Her gaze narrowed in suspicion as she stepped closer to him, still reaching for the notebook. "It's completely unrealistic."

"Says who?" he asked.

"Everyone I've ever showed it to."

"Which is?"

"My father. The board of directors. No one's gonna buy geeky jewelry."

He scoffed, dismissing her concern. "Let me guess. Your father was one of those guys who thought iPhones would never sell, either."

She set her jaw at a stubborn angle. "Besides which, Biedermann's *sells* jewelry, we don't make it." Once again she reached for the notebook. "We don't have the means or the experience to even do a mock-up of that kind of thing, let alone manufacture it."

"Biedermann's doesn't." He thumbed through the pages until he returned to the first image that had caught his attention. He flipped the book around to display the picture of FMJ. "But FMJ does." He grinned. "Sometimes it's good being the evil monster."

She blinked in surprise, then chuckled for a second. But then she studied his face, finally pulling the sketchbook from his grasp. "It's too risky."

"No, it isn't. Matt has a whole electrical engineering department that would love to take a whack at this. Let me just fax him a couple of the pages."

"No."

"But—"

She turned on him suddenly. "Biedermann's is practically hemorrhaging money right now. The absolute last thing we need to do is venture into something like this. If we took a risk like this and it failed, we'd never recover."

"Then the trick is not to fail."

"That's so easy for you to say. Everything you touch turns to gold, right? Buy a company, sell a company. It's all the same. You make millions in your sleep. Besides, if you're wrong, and Biedermann's dies off completely, you can still sell off chunks of us to recoup some of your losses. FMJ could probably use the tax write-off anyway. It may not matter to you whether or not Biedermann's flounders or flourishes, but it matters to me."

As gently as he could, he said, "You know, Kitty, for someone who claims to be desperate to save Biedermann's, you're sure not willing to take many risks to do it."

"I am willing to take risks. I'm just not willing to risk everything."

A second later, she'd snatched her purse out of the desk and was gone. And, damn it, she'd taken her sketchbook with her. He was going to have to find a way to get it back, because he was going to send those drawings to Matt. This could be the key to everything. The niche market Biedermann's was looking for. Not just upscale jewelry, but high fashion accessories for the gadgets nearly every American owned.

Biedermann Jewelry. It's not just for engagements anymore.

He nearly chuckled at his own little joke. This could really work. Between Matt's electronic genius and Kitty's artistic brilliance, they could hit a market that no one else had tapped. Biedermann's would be back on top. And best of all, Kitty would be responsible for that.

He could do this for her. He could fix her professional life.

God knew there wasn't much he could do for her personal life.

Eight

From the blog of New York gossip columnist Suzy Snark:

Fiddling while Rome burned. Polishing the brass on the Titanic. Both phrases imply great negligence in the face of disaster. New Yorkers may want to add a new idiom to that list: Getting a massage while your company is being bought out.

I know, we usually eschew the nitty gritty business details for outright gossip, but this tidbit was too salacious to keep to myself. Besides, the business geniuses at FMJ have scheduled a press conference for this afternoon to announce their acquisition of Biedermann Jewelry. I thought you might want something to consider while they're trying to convince their stockholders it's a good thing they're squandering their own resources to bail out Ford Langley's girlfriend.

Readers will be shocked to learn that while Biedermann Jewelry stock prices continue to plummet, heiress Kitty Biedermann continues to receive daily spa treatments. Sources say she spends upward of two thousand dollars a week on mani-pedis and facials. In a time when her personal finances must be taking a hit, that's got to hurt.

Is the heiress addicted to pampering? Is she simply careless? Or is there something else going on here? Perhaps she sold all her Biedermann stock back when it was still worth something. Too bad she didn't see fit to tip the rest of us off, as well.

"Is any of this new blog true at all?" Ford asked.

She glanced at the image on his iPhone. Her stomach clenched at the sight of the scarlet swirl at the top of the screen. Another Suzy Snark blog. Just what she needed.

"Ah," she quipped, trying to sound completely blasé. "Suzy Snark. What fun."

"Have you read it?"

"I don't read trash."

He held out the iPhone. "You need to read this."

Panic clutched her stomach. Her gaze darted from the phone to his face. She wanted nothing to do with any of that rubbish.

"Why don't you try to sum it up for me?" she suggested in her best spoiled-brat voice.

"It accuses you of negligence." Ford continued to hold out the phone as if he expected that to be all the encouragement she needed.

Though her heart seemed to stutter in her chest, she didn't reach for the phone. What exactly had Suzy Snark discovered?

Ford continued, his tone full of exasperation. "She says you've been spending your days at the spa. Getting massages and pedicures when you should be working."

"Is that all?" Her heart started thudding again, a rapid tattoo she was sure Ford would be able to hear.

"What do you mean 'is that all?' Is there more?" he demanded. "Is there something you're not telling me?"

Instead of answering, she tried to sidestep the question. "It's just a stupid gossip blog. You and Jonathon place entirely too much importance on what this woman writes. What does it even matter?"

He shoved his phone back in his pocket. "It matters. It may just be a gossip blog, but who knows how many people read it. This woman maligns you every chance she gets. Has it occurred to you that Suzy Snark may be the reason Biedermann's stock is in free fall?"

She sucked in a breath. "No. It hasn't."

"I did some preliminary research. Every time she posts about you, the stock price dips. Starting with today's press conference, we're going to defend you against this woman's lies. Now why don't you—"

But he must have seen the truth in her expression,

because Ford broke off. He studied her in silence for a moment before slowly shaking his head. "She's not lying, is she?"

"I wouldn't know. I didn't read the blog."

Ford ignored her comment. "Is she right? Have you really been spending hours of every workday at the spa?"

"I'm not going to defend myself to you."

"You're going to have to defend yourself to someone. The fact that you haven't denied any of this makes me think it must be true."

"What is it you want me to admit to? Going to the spa sometimes? Fine, I do that. Every woman I know gets regular manicures and pedicures. Most men I know, too. It's not a crime."

"No. But if you're doing it during office hours, every day, then it looks bad. It looks like you're not doing your job. It looks like you don't care about the company. And if you don't care about it, then why should anyone else?"

"Is that what you think? That I don't care about Biedermann's? I would do *anything* for Biedermann's."

"So you keep saying. But, frankly, I'm not seeing it."

"Are you kidding me? Since I took over as CEO, I've poured everything I have into this business. I've spent every waking moment trying to educate myself on how to be the best CEO I can. I've listened to every damn business book published in the last decade, from *Barbarians at the Gate* to *The 4-Hour Workweek,* none of which have been remotely helpful, by the way. I've worked eighty-hour weeks. I've abandoned my social life completely.

"None of that made any difference. The stock price just kept going down. So I decided to buy whatever stock I could in hopes of keeping the price up. I liquidated all of my assets. Sold everything I had. Furniture, art, jewelry. Things that had been in the family for generations. I quietly auctioned it off piece by piece. A year ago, I moved out of the townhouse where I grew up, where Biedermanns had lived for over a hundred years. I sold it and moved into a *walk-up*."

To her embarrassment, her voice, which had been rising in pitch steadily, broke on the word *walk-up*. She knew where she lived was the least of her worries, but somehow it signified all the things wrong in her life.

Knowing she was being ridiculous didn't make it sting any less when he said, "Come on, you make it sound like life without a doorman just isn't worth living. Surely it's not that bad."

"Have you ever lived without a doorman?" she asked.

"I live in a craftsman remodel down by campus in Palo Alto," he deadpanned. "I've never had a doorman in my life."

"Well, I now live on the fourth floor in a building without an elevator. I grew up with staff, for cripes sake. Our housekeeper worked for my family for forty-five years. After I let Maggie go, she couldn't even afford to pay the tuition for her granddaughter's college."

Maggie had been like family. No, more than that. To a girl who'd never known her mother, Maggie *had been* family. And Kitty had had to fire her. Sweet Maggie had tried to comfort her, made her hot tea and murmured

optimist platitudes like, *I've always wanted to travel.*
Maggie had been too proud to accept a handout once
she was no longer employed, so Kitty had done the
only thing she could do. She'd tracked down Maggie's
granddaughter and hired her at Biedermann's.

"Then why did you sell the house?" Ford was
asking her. "And if you had to sell it, why not move
someplace nicer?"

At his question, she bumped her chin up defiantly.

"Because," she shot back. "When the stock price
started to drop, I couldn't just stand by and do nothing.
So I bought as much as I could. And then when it kept
dropping, I couldn't even pay the taxes on the townhouse. Selling the house was the only option."

"You should never have invested your personal
assets in—"

"I know that, okay?" she snapped. "I was trying to
help Biedermann's and I made a stupid mistake. I'm
really good at making stupid mistakes, thank you very
much."

It was just one of many, many stupid mistakes.
Sometimes she felt buried under the weight of them.

"I'm just trying to—" he began.

But she cut him off with a belligerent glare. "I don't
need your help."

He talked over her protests. "If Biedermann's really
does go under, you'll have lost everything."

What could she say to that? All she could do was
shake her head and blink back the tears. "If Biedermann's
really does go under, then I've lost everything anyway."

But that wasn't entirely true anymore, was it? She'd have the baby. She'd have the family she'd always wanted. It was a small consolation that was turning into everything.

"So tell me this," he said. "If you're so desperate to keep Biedermann's afloat, why this elaborate act? Why don't you want anyone to know what you're doing? Why spend your days at the spa getting massages and facials? You've got to know how bad that looks."

She met his gaze. "I can't—" she began before breaking off. Then she swept a hand across her forehead, pushing her hair out of her face. "I can't explain that."

"Well, try. Make me understand what's going on here. Give me something, anything, that makes this make sense."

"This is just what I do."

Whenever the influx of written material got too much to handle, she took Casey, went to the spa and had her assistant read aloud to her. The paperwork was so overwhelming. Business documents were the worst. She just couldn't wrap her head around the pages and pages of words. Listening to them read aloud helped. But what kind of CEO had her assistant read everything aloud? Christ, it was like she was a preschooler at story time. How could she explain that to Ford?

Instead she said, "It's like a…a coping mechanism or something."

"You mean the massages are a way of relieving stress?"

She all but threw up her hands in frustration. "No. I mean, I was raised never to reveal my weaknesses. You always have to keep up appearances."

"I don't understand."

"No. Of course you wouldn't. My mother died when I was young. My father was completely loving and indulgent, but Biedermann's always came first, so he wasn't around a lot. I was raised by my grandmother, who was already well into her sixties when I was born. It…"

She struggled for words. Finally she finished with, "It made for an unusual upbringing. I grew up in the 1990s, but really, it's like I was raised in the 1950s. To my grandmother, appearances were everything. I know she loved me, but in the world she lived in, you never let anyone see your weaknesses. You never aired your dirty laundry."

And a child with a disability—a child who was imperfect—was the ultimate dirty laundry. She'd been such an embarrassment to her whole family. Such a disappointment. How could she stand disappointing anyone else?

"So, going to the spa is your way of whistling in the graveyard? Of pretending everything is okay when it obviously isn't? You're not fooling anyone."

"I fooled you, didn't I?"

"You didn't fool me so much as make me doubt your sanity." His words were like a slap. He must have regretted them, because he sighed and scrubbed a hand down his face. "Look, you've got to defend yourself against Suzy Snark's allegations. Whoever she is, you've got to let people know she's wrong about you."

"And tell them what? That I was completely unprepared to take over as CEO? That I have no discernible leadership skills? That I have nothing to offer the company at all? How would admitting any of that help matters?"

"At least people would know you cared," he said finally.

Then she sighed, suddenly exhausted by the conversation. "My pride is all I have left."

For someone who'd lived her life in the public eye, Kitty seemed surprisingly nervous during the press conference. He doubted that anyone in the press noticed.

They stood side by side, along with Jonathon and Marty, a united front against the questions of the press. After he'd made the initial speech about FMJ's decision to acquire Biedermann Jewelry, Jonathon had stepped forward to outline the basis of FMJ's financial plan for Biedermann's.

As Jonathon spoke, Ford stopped listening. It was all stuff they'd discussed before. Instead he focused his attention on Kitty. She stood beside him, dressed in a gray pin-striped dress that wrapped around her waist. It managed to mimic the feel of a business suit, but its curve-hugging lines looked outrageously feminine. Her hair fell in dark, glossy waves, shadowing one side of her face. Bright red lipstick highlighted the bow of her lips. She looked like she'd stepped out of a Maxim photo shoot. A teenage boy's idea of how a woman should look in the workplace. A sexpot in a business suit.

Probably every man in the audience was mentally undressing her.

Hell, he wasn't a teenager and even his body had leaped in response to the sight of her. He'd had to battle some primitive urge to drape his jacket around her shoulders and bundle her back to her office, where he could strip her dress from her body and worship her like an acolyte.

At least until he'd noticed how nervous she was. Outwardly, she seemed fine. More than fine, actually. The press no doubt saw the confident, beautiful—if a little overblown—woman that she intended for them to see. That he'd seen at first glance.

It was only at second glance that the illusion began to slip. Her smile, though open and alluring, was a little stiff. It was too unwavering. There was no play about her lips.

This wasn't just nerves. This was perfectly contained, well-schooled nerves. This was someone who spent a great deal of time and energy learning to hide her panic.

The idea that Kitty—so composed, so polished and poised—might be fighting panic knocked him off balance. So off balance, in fact, that he let the press conference go on much longer than it should have.

Before he knew it, there was a blond reporter who looked about twenty-two saying, "Ms. Biedermann, when your father died unexpectedly last year, you were obviously woefully unprepared to take over as CEO of

Biedermann Jewelry. Can you explain why you insisted on serving in a position you have neither the skill nor the training to hold? And furthermore, how do you answer allegations that it's your gross incompetence that has led to Biedermann's current predicament?"

Ford kept waiting for Kitty to interrupt the reporter. Sure, Kitty was obviously nervous. But he'd seen the subtle signs of nervousness from her on other occasions in which she'd gone on to cheerfully lambaste him.

From what he'd seen, Kitty never backed down from a fight and never took crap from anyone. So he was blindsided when the reporter made it past the phrase "woefully unprepared" without getting the verbal equivalent of a body slam. Why wasn't Kitty defending herself?

By the time he heard the phrase "gross incompetence" he was done waiting for Kitty to don her own boxing gloves. He stepped up to the microphone. "If there are any signs of gross incompetence, I haven't seen them. FMJ would not have invested this kind of money in a company whose leadership we questioned."

"Then is FMJ merely investing in Biedermann's?" a different reporter asked. "Or can we expect you to do your signature restructuring and complete overhaul?"

"We'll be announcing some very exciting things for the stores soon." He flashed his best charming smile. "I promise you this, within a year everyone in this room will be shopping at Biedermann's."

"And about rumors that this acquisition is fueled by a romantic relationship between you and Ms.

Biedermann?" This question was again from the annoying blond.

Ford shot Kitty a glance to see if she was finally going to light into the woman, only to see Kitty still had that deer-in-the-headlights look.

So he ducked his head and gave the reporters his most boyishly mischievous smile. "Well, you found me out. This is all just a ruse to ask Kitty Biedermann out on a date. I figured a techie geek from California like me wouldn't have a shot with a blue blood like Kitty Biedermann. Hell, I couldn't even get her to return my phone calls before." A chuckle rumbled through the audience of reporters. "But seriously, my relationship with Ms. Biedermann is purely professional. On my first night in town she took pity on me and allowed me to accompany her to the Children's Medical Foundation fundraiser. We attended as business colleagues."

"So you're not the father of her baby?"

"Ms. Biedermann's personal life is a private matter. Let's keep this about business."

And with that, Jonathon took the cue to wrap up the press conference. A few minutes later, Ford guided Kitty out the room and whisked her up to her office. By the time he had her alone, his shock had given way to anger.

"What the hell was that?" he asked even as he slammed the door shut behind them.

She spun around, her eyes wide. "What?"

"The way you behaved out there with the press. That's what."

"I don't know what you mean," she stammered.

She pressed a palm to her stomach as if to still the fluttering in her belly. He grabbed her by the wrist and held her hand out between them. "Look at you. You're shaking."

She jerked her hand away and thrust it behind her back. "So what if I am? Those things make me nervous."

"Yeah. I noticed. But that's no excuse for letting that reporter walk all over you."

Kitty glared at him. "What was I supposed to do?"

"You were supposed to defend yourself."

"How could I defend myself? She was badgering me with questions. There was nothing I could do."

"Kitty, I've watched you go toe-to-toe with a drunken rancher twice your size. Hell, every time we meet you try to rip me a new one. You know how to hold your own in a fight. That ninety-pound reporter shouldn't have had a chance."

She turned away, obviously searching for an explanation that would placate him. Finally she said simply, "That reporter was telling the truth."

"About us?" he asked. "We agreed what happened between us is nobody's business but our own. If you had a problem lying in a press conference, you should have told me that before—"

"Not about us," she interrupted. "About me." Again she turned away from him, but this time he sensed it was because she couldn't bring herself to meet his gaze. "All those things she said about me were true."

"Kitty—"

"About me being 'woefully unprepared.'" There was a disparaging sneer in her voice. "About my gross incompetence. It's all true."

He stared at the stiff lines of her back, barely comprehending her words. She looked like someone waiting to be hit.

For a moment he could only stare at her while he sorted through his confusion. "What do you mean? You're not incompetent."

"You only think that because I do such a good job hiding it. But I don't know what I'm doing. I wasn't prepared to run Biedermann's. The board never should have named me CEO."

"Kitty, being a CEO is a difficult job. People are rarely prepared for it. In your situation it was worse because your father's death was so unexpected and you were grieving for him. I'm sure it feels overwhelming. But that doesn't make you incompetent."

She glanced over her shoulder, sending him a watery smile. Where those *tears* in her eyes?

"You're not listening to me. No amount of preparation would have been enough. I'm just not smart enough."

And then he made his biggest mistake. He laughed.

She flinched. Exactly as if she'd been slapped. She was facing the windows again, so he didn't see her expression, but he would bet those tears were spilling down her cheeks by now.

He wanted to cross the room to her, take her in his arms and offer her comfort, but he knew that stubborn pride enough to know she wouldn't want him to see her crying. He wouldn't add insult to injury by making her face him.

"Kitty, I'm sorry, but the idea that you're not smart is ridiculous."

"Ford—"

"I've listened to you verbally skewer just about everyone you talk to. You can work a crowd like no one I've ever seen. Anyone who can hold their own in a room full of wealthy socialites could not possibly be stupid. If you weren't smart, believe me, I'd have noticed by now."

She shot him an exasperated look. "Why are you arguing with me about this? When my father and grandmother were still alive, they protected me the best they could. When my father died unexpectedly, I should have had the sense to step aside. But I was selfish. I love this company more than anything. I thought that would be enough. But I only made a mess of things."

She seemed so dejected, so unlike her normal self, he reached out a hand to her, but she deftly slipped out of his reach.

"You mentioned at the press conference that you'd be doing some restructuring. If you really intend to do everything in your power to ensure Biedermann's is financially viable, then you'll fire me."

Nine

"What the hell is up with Kitty?"

Ford cornered Casey looking for some answers. Casey glanced up from the pot of coffee she was making just as Ford shut the door to the break room.

Casey slanted him a look from under her shaggy bangs. "Do you mean, like, today? Or ever?"

The previous times he'd spoken to Casey, she'd impressed him as being little more than a surly reprobate. He'd wondered how such a girl had gotten a job at Biedermann's, let alone kept it. Nevertheless, the best way to get the dirt on someone was through his or her assistant. Besides, she seemed to be the only person Kitty might confide in.

So Ford flashed Casey a sympathetic smile. "Kitty must be pretty tough to work for, huh?"

The girl's characteristic frown darkened to a full-fledged glower as she shoved the coffeepot onto the heating element and flicked the on/off toggle. "If you're just looking to talk trash about Kitty, you'll have to find someone else. I'm not into that kind of negative bonding. This job's too important to me."

He held up his hands in a gesture of innocence. "I was just trying to be sympathetic."

"You were just trying to dig for information," Casey said shrewdly as she pulled a clean coffee mug from the cabinet.

"Maybe I was," he admitted, more than a little surprised by Casey's show of loyalty. Since the negative bonding Casey had accused him of obviously wasn't going to work, he decided to take a different tack. "Kitty's not always the most forthcoming person. I'm trying to figure her out. That doesn't make me the enemy."

Casey shot him a suspicious look, but said nothing as she poured cream and then sugar into the mug. She sent an equally dark look at the coffeemaker, which was gurgling slowly. Poor girl was obviously torn between her need for caffeine and her desire to storm out in a huff.

"I'm trying to help her. But I can't do that unless I understand what's going on. Something's—"

"You're trying to get her fired."

"I'm not." Hell, that was the last thing he wanted. Keeping Kitty employed and well taken care of would at least minimize his guilt. "I'm trying to save her job. But she's not giving me anything to work with. She's—"

"She's too proud," Casey said quietly, without meeting his gaze.

"Exactly." Encouraged by the lack of belligerence in Casey's tone, he pressed on. "Do you have any idea why she would think I should fire her?"

"She said that?" Casey's voice held a note of panic.

Wasn't that interesting. "You're really worried about her losing her job."

"Hey, I know what people around here think. That she's such a b—" Casey broke off and seemed to be considering the hazards of cussing in front of the man who was ultimately her boss. "Such a witch—" she corrected "—to work for that I'm the best she can get. But it's not like that."

Ford said nothing. He'd wondered himself how exactly a surly, semicompetent girl like Casey had landed a prime job like the assistant to the CEO of a major company.

"She's the best boss I ever had," Casey continued. "And if I lost this job, I'm guessing I'd lose the scholarship, too."

"The scholarship?"

"Yeah. The scholarship that pays tuition for community college for all Biedermann employees. 'Cause there's no way I could pay for college on my own. I'd have to drop out of HCCC."

"Oh. That scholarship."

He'd read just about everything on Biedermann company policy, and he'd never heard of an employee scholarship. Which made him think Kitty was paying for this girl's college out of her own pocket. Kitty, who'd had to sell her home and had auctioned off family heirlooms, was paying the tuition of this ill-mannered, unskilled girl.

Was Kitty...*softhearted?* It was easier to imagine the Dalai Lama sponsoring an Ultimate Fighting match.

But what other explanation was there?

He shoved a hand through his hair. Damn it, why did she have to be so full of contradictions? Why did she have to be fragile one moment, all bristly defenses the next? Why couldn't she just be the manipulative witch that everyone thought she was? That would make his life so much easier.

If he ever wanted to be free of Kitty and all the complicated emotions she stirred up, he was going to have to find a way to save Biedermann's. And save Kitty's job.

And apparently Casey's job, too.

"Look," he said to Casey. "I'm trying to do the right thing here. Not just for the company, but for Kitty, too. If you help me out, if you help me understand what's going on here, I'll make sure you don't lose your job. Or your scholarship."

Even if he had to start paying the girl's tuition himself. And wouldn't that be just great. 'Cause all he needed in his life was one more woman dependent on him.

Casey pursed her lips and studied him. "What do you want to know?"

"Kitty told me her father never expected her to run Biedermann's. Do you know why?"

Casey shook her head. "No. I never met the old man, 'cause I was hired after he died. But office gossip is he always wanted her to marry someone who'd take over as CEO. You ask me, it's why that skeezie Marty is so mean to her."

"You think Marty expected to be made CEO?"

She shook her head, pouring coffee into her mug now that the maker had finally stopped dripping. "Haven't you noticed that icky way he looks at her? Like she's his golden lottery ticket or something. I think he wanted to marry her himself." Casey jabbed her coffee with a spoon and gave it a brisk stir. "That guy creeps me out."

Ford felt a sucker punch of jealousy. He struggled to bury it. Kitty's love life wasn't his business. Or so he kept telling himself. Still, he found himself asking, "Did she and Marty ever go out?"

That was not him giving in to his curiosity. If Marty was smarting from a broken heart, that might be motivation enough for him to make things unpleasant for Kitty. He might even be leaking information about Kitty to Suzy Snark.

"Naw." Casey waved her hand, dismissing the possibility. "Kitty wouldn't stoop that low." But then Casey tilted her head to the side, considering. "But Marty isn't, you know, smart about women. And you know what Kitty's like. Marty might have thought she was hitting on him."

Ford had to stifle a groan. Yes, he did know what Kitty was like. She used her beauty and sensuality like a defensive shield. Whenever someone got too close, she'd turn into Kitty the vamp. Had she accidentally hit Marty with that overblown charm of hers? Had she crushed his expectations, and somehow turned a man who should have been her friend into an enemy?

"Ah, Kitty," he murmured half under his breath. "Maybe you really are stupid."

Beside him, Casey stiffened. "Hey, that's just mean."

"No, wait," he jumped in to correct her. "I didn't mean—"

"She's not stupid, she's dyslexic, and if you don't know the difference then you're the idiot."

"She's dyslexic?" Ford barely heard Casey's words as shock spiraled through him.

Dyslexic? Kitty was *dyslexic?*

"She hides it well, right? I guess when you have a disability like that, you're used to dealing—" Casey broke off and did a visible double take. "Wait a sec. You didn't know?"

Guilt flashed across Casey's face, but then she turned and scurried from the room, cupping the mug in both hands, shoulders hunched defensively.

What did he even know about dyslexia? He'd gone to high school with some kids with dyslexia, one of whom had gone on to become a rather famous jazz musician. Ford hadn't kept in touch with Steve, but they'd been friends in school and he remembered how much trouble Steve had had learning.

Suddenly Ford remembered things Kitty had said or done that hadn't made sense before now. In all the meetings they'd been to together, whenever someone handed out information, she'd never even look at it. Proposals, contracts, synopses, whatever. She'd just slip it into her leather folio without so much as a glance. Her behavior gave the impression of careless disregard for the work of others. But that wasn't it at all.

And what was that she'd said once? Something about listening to books about business. Not reading them. Listening to them.

If she had trouble reading, her job would be nearly impossible. Add to that the possibility that she may have inadvertently offended her CFO.

He thought about his own relationship with Jonathon. At FMJ, he, Jonathon and Matt functioned more as a triumvirate than their titles would imply. Still, he'd be unable to do his job as CEO without Jonathon. Their relationship and their success stemmed from their absolute trust.

No wonder Kitty was floundering as the head of Biedermann's.

Ford broke into a quick jog to chase after Casey, who was now halfway down the hall. "Hey, hold up."

Casey rounded on him, her expression hardened into protective defiance. "You can't say anything to her about this."

"Of course I'm going to talk to her about it."

"You can't," Casey pleaded in a whisper. "If she finds out I told you, she'll fire me! She's totally crazy about hiding it. I'm not even supposed to know."

"Then she didn't tell you herself?"

"No way." Casey sent a furtive glance down either end of the hall as if she expected corporate spies to be lurking around every corner.

"So you figured it out on your own."

"Yes." Casey started walking again, apparently satisfied that no one was listening in on their conversation. "Like, my interview for the job was a dead giveaway. She didn't care if I could type or use a computer or anything. She just had me read aloud. And that's pretty much my whole job. Every time she goes to get her nails done or to get a massage, she has me come along to read to her."

Which explained why Kitty spent so much time at the spa. What had she called it? A coping mechanism.

He remembered what she'd said about how appearances were everything. No wonder she didn't want anyone knowing she had a learning disability. Unfortunately all the things she'd done to protect herself ending up making things worse.

Casey sent him a pleading look. "You're not going to tell her all of this, are you?"

"I have to."

He felt like he finally understood her. He only hoped it wasn't too late to help her.

Just when Kitty thought her day couldn't get any worse, Ford showed up at her apartment. Again.

She stood with her hand on the edge of the door,

glaring at Ford through the foot-and-a-half gap between the door and the jamb. "Let me guess, some idiot
in the building let you in again."

"It was a different guy this time. But he'd watched
the press conference and I convinced him we really
were in love and just didn't want anyone to know it."

"What is it with you sneaking into my building?"

"It's nothing personal. I just didn't think you'd let
me up."

"I wouldn't have. Probably because I didn't want to
see you. Funny how that works, isn't it?"

She couldn't really blame her fellow tenants for
being unable to keep Ford out of her building when she
couldn't keep him out of her mind. He was a charming
bastard, that was for sure. She'd always thought of
herself as an expert at manipulating men. So why was
it none of her tricks worked with him? Worse still, why
was his persistence so appealing?

That was the real problem. Not that he wouldn't
leave her alone, but that she didn't want him to. She
moved to shut the door in his face, wishing she could
block out her feelings as easily.

But he blocked her with his foot in the door. "Why
didn't you tell me you were dyslexic?"

Her stomach clenched at his words as a wash of
chilly panic flooded her. How had he found out? It was
a secret she'd kept her whole life. The one she'd done
everything to protect. She'd been prepared to resign
from Biedermann's rather than talk about it. And he'd
found out anyway.

Damn him. Why couldn't he just stay neatly in her past the way one-night stands were supposed to? She shoved aside all her emotions, burying them deep in her belly, pretending they didn't rise up in the acid of her sarcasm.

"Why didn't I tell you I was dyslexic?" she repeated. "The question is, why would I? It's completely irrelevant and frankly no one's business."

He reached out a hand as if he were going to pull her into his arms, but she deftly avoided his grasp. She'd been staying one step ahead of intimacy her entire adult life. Why should he be any different?

He clenched his jaw, staring her down with his hands propped on his hips. His very body presented a formidable line of offense. "You should have said something."

"I hardly even notice it," she lied, moving to the far end of the room before turning and circling back. "You have a birthmark on your shoulder. We've never talked about that, either."

"I wasn't about to resign over my birthmark."

"Well, maybe you should," she said glibly. "It's hardly your best feature."

"Stop it."

She stilled, taken aback by the edge in his voice as much as his words. Glancing around, she realized she'd made a complete circuit of the living room and now stood before him once again. She was back where she'd started.

Sometimes her whole life felt like that. As if she was

going in circles, always moving, always pretending she was making progress, but never getting anywhere.

Tears burned her eyes as she felt her throat close off. God, she would not do this. She would *not* cry in front of him.

It was bad enough when she'd done it at the office. When she'd had the excuse of the stress of the press conference to fall back on. She wouldn't do it again.

She tried to move past him, to just keep moving. As she always did. Because moving in circles was better than standing still, even if she wasn't getting anywhere.

But he snagged her arm as she walked by. He turned her to face him. "You don't have to pretend this doesn't matter to you. You don't always have to be so tough."

She laughed; it sounded bitter and unpleasant even to her ears. "You can't possibly understand what my life has been like. Do you have any idea how many people would love to see me fail?"

He studied her for a minute, clearly considering her words. "Have you ever considered that there might be just as many people who'd like to see you succeed?"

She blinked, surprised by his words. But he was wrong. Stubborn, but wrong. "You don't know what you're talking about."

"I know enough," he continued, "to know that people with dyslexia aren't stupid. And that there are plenty of dyslexic people who are very successful."

"There may be. But I'm not one of them." He looked like he wanted to say something, but she glared at him defiantly. "Don't."

"What?"

"Don't try to sugarcoat this. You never would have before you knew about my disability."

"I wasn't about to—"

"Yes, you were. I could see it in your eyes. You were about to tell me that it's not my fault that Biedermann's is in this situation. Or worse still, that things aren't as bad as they seem. Because I know better. *You* know better. If Biedermann's wasn't circling the drain, FMJ wouldn't be here, offering to buy us out. If things weren't desperate, you wouldn't be here at all. And trust me, the last thing I want is for you to treat me differently now that you know I have a disability."

"Okay," he said slowly. "I won't lie to you. Things are bad." He stroked a soothing hand down her arm. It was a gesture that was benignly gentle. Paternal, almost. "But that doesn't necessarily mean you're responsible. Businesses fail for a variety of reasons. You're not—"

"Yes, I am. I'm the company's CEO. That means I'm responsible. Biedermann's has thrived for five generations. Until I took over. And for the past four quarters we've released negative earnings and our stock is plummeting. If FMJ were in the same situation, you wouldn't flinch from taking responsibility yourself."

"Maybe you're right." He stroked her arm again in that maddening way. The touch was generically tender. As if he was gentling a horse or comforting a child. As if knowing she was dyslexic made her less desirable. "If you don't think you can serve as CEO, then we'll find something else for you to do. Your sketches were amazing. You could launch your own line of jewelry."

His words stirred up a long-buried yearning. Her own line of jewelry. It was what she'd always wanted. Her barely acknowledged greatest dream. His words might have even placated her, if she didn't know just how impossible that dream was. He was leading her on just to appease her vanity. Worse still was the way he stroked her arm.

His touch was so completely innocent, so totally sexless, it sparked her anger. She was more than her dyslexia. She wasn't a child. She wasn't a spooked animal. She didn't need to be comforted or soothed or reassured.

"Stop that." She jerked away from his touch.

"What?"

"That thing you're doing where you stroke my arm. With that calming, gentle touch." She propped her hands on her hips and glared at him.

"What is it you want from me, exactly? You want me to admit how hard this is on me?"

"That would be a start." There was a note of surprise in his voice. As if he hadn't expected her to cave so easily.

"Of course, it's hard. Biedermann's is ingrained in my family. My father and grandparents always took so much pride in the company. This is what people in my family have been doing for five generations. Ever since I was a child, running Biedermann's was all I ever wanted to do."

"Surely it wasn't what you always wanted."

"Of course it was," she snapped; for an instant her irritation edged out her softer emotions. "My father brought me to work with him from the time I was a toddler. You know, I never missed having a mother." She turned away, embarrassed by the confession. Afraid that it made her sound heartless. Or worse, that it was a lie. That she truly *had* missed having a mother. That if her mother had lived, Kitty might have been a completely different person. More lovable. Her natural defensiveness kicked in and when she spoke her tone was bitter with resentment. "My father loved me enough for two parents. I had the best of everything. I went to the best schools. And when those weren't good enough, I had the best tutors. He coddled me all my life. Maybe that's why it was so shocking when I found out the truth."

To her surprise and embarrassment, her voice broke on the word *truth*. She brought her hand to her cheek and felt the moisture there. She brushed fervently.

Before she could hide them, he was suddenly at her side. With a gentle touch of her shoulders, he turned her to face him. She swallowed past the lump in her throat, resisting the urge to turn away from him.

"What truth?" he asked gently.

"That I'd never be able to run Biedermann's. That I'd never be more than just a pretty accessory." Through the sheen of her tears, she saw the flicker of disbelief. "He'd taken me out of school and hired private tutors. He carefully regulated everyone I came into contact with. He was only trying to protect me, but it meant I had no idea what I was capable of. Or rather incapable of. I was in college before I knew how odd my upbringing was. Before I realized I was reading at a third grade level and I'd never graduate. In *college*." She let out a bitter bark of a laugh. "I hate to think how much money he had to donate to get me in in the first place."

Tears streamed down her face. She looked up at him, fully expecting to see the panic most men displayed when faced with tears.

But there was no panic. No terror. And he wasn't running away. Instead, he leaned down and brushed a gentle kiss across her lips before he pulled her close and wrapped his arms around her.

She sank against him, relishing his strength, even as it annoyed her. She didn't want to want him. She wanted nothing more than to be left alone with her misery. But apparently he wasn't going to let her do that. And she wasn't strong enough to make him go away. Not when she had such a short amount of time with him anyway.

When he leaned down to take her mouth in a kiss, she met him, move for move. She pressed her body against his, needing the feel of his muscles moving beneath her palms.

His hands moved over her body, peeling away layers of clothing as easily as he'd stripped away her emotional defenses. He swept her up into his arms and carried her to the bedroom as effortlessly as he'd swept back into her life. His every touch heightened her desire.

She needed him. She needed this. Here, in the bed, they were equals. A perfect match.

With him, she could be herself as she could with no one else. But as much as she wanted this moment to last forever, she knew it couldn't. Her heart filled with bittersweet longing, even as he made her body soar. Even as pleasure shuddered through her nerve endings, she knew it was the last time they'd ever be together.

She had to tell him the truth about the baby and once she did, everything between them would change forever.

Ten

"This wasn't what was supposed to happen," she murmured.

Boy, she'd said a mouthful there.

"Ain't that the truth?" he muttered.

She pulled back just enough to look up at him. Through a sheen of dried tears she gazed into those liquid brown eyes of his and felt some cold icy part of herself melt.

Finally he asked, "What was supposed to happen?"

"You were supposed to leave." She ducked her head back to his chest.

"I was?" He tipped her chin up and studied her expression. "Is it so bad that I stayed?"

She let out a sigh that was part tearful shudder, part

exasperation. Her lips curled in a wry smile as she answered. "Yes, it is."

"I don't get it." His smile held both humor and something darker. "I know why I *shouldn't* stay, I just don't get why you don't want me to."

"Think highly of yourself, don't you?" She stretched as she said it, arching against the wall of his chest, relishing the feel of his strength. "But I can't argue with that at all," she continued. "In bed we're great together. It's out of bed that we're a disaster."

As easily as she'd slipped into his arms, she pulled herself free. The tears were gone, but her eyes felt dry and scratchy, as if she'd bawled for hours.

"You think we're a disaster together only because this thing with Biedermann's is between us," he pointed out.

"Not only because of that," she murmured, grabbing her clothes, but didn't explain.

"Not only. But mostly."

She bumped up her chin. "Even with only Biedermann's between us, that would be enough. The company is my whole life."

"True," he admitted. "But we're not on opposing sides here. You keep treating me like the enemy, but I'm not. FMJ is here to help. We're here to fix things for you."

"That's just it. You don't see anything wrong with that, do you?"

"With what?"

"The fact that you want to fix things for me." The fact that she had to explain it at all was only more proof of the problem. "That you want to help."

"No, I don't. It's what we do at FMJ. It's what *I* do."

"Exactly. If I let you, you'd swoop in and take over everything for me. FMJ would manage Biedermann's and I'd never have to make another decision in my life. Just sit back and live off my stock dividends and never worry about anything ever again."

"Most women wouldn't be complaining about that," he pointed out wryly.

She thought of what Jonathon had told her about his mother and sisters. Maybe they were content to live like that, but she never would be. "I think you're wrong about that."

"Look, you said yourself you were raised to find a rich husband, marry him and let him run Biedermann's for you. How is what I'm proposing any different?"

"For starters, you're not actually proposing, are you? It's different when people are married. You're suggesting a business arrangement. Out of pity, no less."

"Fine," he said, an unexpected bite of irritation in his voice. "You want to get married? We'll get married."

For a second, she just stared at him in shock. What did he expect her to do? Leap with joy? Instead, she let out a bark of laughter. "You want to marry me so I'll feel better about accepting money from you? That's ridiculous."

"Why? Because you're too proud to accept help?"

"No. Because people should get married because they love each other, not out of some misguided sense of…" She searched around for the right word, before finally pinning him with a stare. "Why exactly did you propose again? Was it pity?"

"It was *not* pity." He returned her gaze steadily. "Did you love Derek?"

"I…" That had been different. With Derek, it had been all business. Not this crazy mixture of business, lust and emotion. "That was different."

"How?"

"I could trust him." At least, she'd thought she could trust him. More to the point, she could trust herself with him. She knew how she felt about him. She admired Derek's business sense and his ambition, but she never could have loved him. When he dumped her, he'd wounded her pride, but her heart hadn't felt the slightest hiccup.

Quite simply, she'd never loved Derek, but she did love Ford. With him, it would be totally different. She'd be so vulnerable. She'd be at the mercy of her own emotions. And he would treat her just like he treated everyone else. He'd be charming, thoughtful and solicitous. Without ever actually caring about her at all.

Of course, she couldn't say any of that aloud. So instead she said, "And I understood his motives."

"I just thought—" Ford broke off, struggling to put into words what he could barely understand himself. "Look, you're pregnant. The single-parent thing is really hard. I watched Patrice struggle to do it for years. And Mom, after my dad died. It's a tough gig." He must have read the absolute horror on her face, because he let his words trail off before finishing lamely, "I don't know. I thought, maybe I could help out with that."

"Wow," she began with exaggerated disbelief. "You thought that *maybe* you could 'help out' raising your own—" And then she stopped dead as she realized what she'd just said. "You should just leave."

"What was that you were going to say? Raising my own *what?*" He grabbed her arm as she reached for the doorknob. "My own what? My own *child?* That's what you were going to say, wasn't it?" He searched her face, but she'd quickly schooled her expression to reveal nothing. "Wasn't it?" he demanded.

She yanked her arm from his grasp. "I misspoke."

"No, you didn't. You know that baby is mine. Tell me the truth."

Kitty met his gaze, chin up, eyes blazing. "I have no idea who the father of this baby is. Yes, I slept with you, so it could be yours. But I sleep with a lot of men. It could be anyone's."

He just shook his head. "You little liar."

"You don't believe me?" she asked coolly.

"Not for a minute. Saturday morning, when I was worried because we didn't use a condom, you told me you'd been tested when you got back from Texas. But we had used a condom in Texas. There was no reason for you to think you might have picked something up from me. Unless you were just being incredibly careful. Which you wouldn't be unless what happened in Texas was rare. Like, once in a lifetime rare."

An odd mixture of frustration and relief washed over Ford. *Why the hell hadn't he thought of this earlier?*

It was so obvious now that he'd thought it through. No one else could be the father of her child, because there was no one else. For Kitty, there was only him.

And he didn't even want to think about how much better that made him feel. How that strange pressure in his chest started to ease up. All he knew was this: he was the father of Kitty's child. Now she had to marry him. There was no reason not to.

"We're getting married," he announced. "That's final."

"That," she sneered, "is the stupidest thing I've ever heard. Getting married because I'm pregnant may actually be more stupid than getting married because you feel sorry for me."

"I'm not going to fight with you about this."

"Good, because I'm not going to fight with you about it, either. You can't make me marry you. You want to support the baby. Fine. Send a check. If you even want to be a part of the baby's life, I'm okay with that. We'll negotiate custody or something. But I'm guessing you won't even want that."

Fury inched through him, slow and insidious. Because she was right. He couldn't make her marry him. And, damn it, he wished he could.

"You can't keep me from my child," he warned her.

"I won't even try. I'm betting I won't have to."

"What's that supposed to mean?"

"Ford," she said, shaking her head. "You go through life keeping everyone at arm's length. You don't let anyone close to you. And you're so charming most people don't even notice."

"But you did," he muttered.

"Well, I consider myself something of an expert at holding people at an emotional distance." She flashed him a smile. If he didn't know her so well, he might not have seen the sadness in her gaze. "So I recognized the signs. You have a mother, a step-mom, or whatever she is, and three sisters. Sure, you support them financially. You fix problems for them, but that's the extent of your relationship with them. You don't let them choose. If they're too much of an emotional burden for you, then I'm guessing a baby is way more than you're ready for."

He wanted to argue with her, but the best he could come up with was a grumbled "This isn't over yet."

What could he really say? He *didn't* let anyone close to him. Not even his family. What kind of husband would he make? What kind of father?

Kitty and the baby would be better off without him. The best thing he could do for them was show himself out.

She'd always considered her active social life a part of her job. She didn't have much formal training and had not even graduated college. She wasn't the kind of woman who could inspire the confidence of the board or the stockholders. But there was one area of business in which she excelled. Schmoozing.

For that reason, dinner parties and gala balls

weren't mere social engagements. They were work. Tonight's gallery opening was no different, with one exception. Normally, when she worked a room, it was with the intent of making contacts and keeping her ear to the ground for useful information. But today she wasn't looking for information. She was looking for a spouse.

She may have scoffed at Ford's proposal of marriage, but she had to agree he had a point. Being a single mom would be tough.

But she certainly couldn't marry Ford. She was far too emotionally involved with him. Oh, who was she kidding? She was in love with him. He made her feel things no other man had ever made her feel. But for now, she was hoping that was a temporary condition.

Surely all she needed was some time away from him. Time for her feelings to fade and her heart to heal. And that would never happen if she married him.

And if he asked her again, she might not have the strength to say no.

Her only hope was to go back to her original plan. Find a husband who could help her run Biedermann's. Once she was safely engaged, Ford would leave her alone and she could start the long, arduous process of getting over him. What she needed now was a husband who would care about her baby, but never press her for a truly intimate relationship. Luckily she knew Simon Durant would be the perfect man for the job.

She moved through the crowd, her gaze shifting as she looked for a head of artfully tousled black hair.

Finally, she saw him at the back of the room, his arm draped over the shoulder of a whippet-lean man a good decade younger than he was.

Simon's face brightened when he saw her. "Kitty, darling! With all that nonsense in the news, I didn't think you'd make it."

Simon greeted her with double air kisses to her cheeks. Cosmo, the pretentious young artist whose show this was and whose shoulder Simon had recently been draped over, merely nodded before turning his attention elsewhere. But then, Cosmo had never liked her.

Kitty squeezed Simon's hand in greeting. She nodded in Cosmo's direction as she asked, "Do you think he'll notice if I steal you away for a few minutes?"

"He's talking to an art critic, so I doubt it."

Simon linked his arm with hers and guided her toward the open bar.

"So you've been following the stories in the news?" she asked.

"Mostly no, but the gossip has been hard to avoid. I don't suppose the delicious Mr. Langley is…"

He let his voice trail off suggestively.

"Gay?" she supplied. "Unfortunately, no." But wouldn't this all be much easier if he were? She certainly never would have found herself in her current situation. "I have a problem, Simon, and I think you might be able to help me with it."

They'd reached the bar. Kitty ordered a bottled water and Simon ordered a mango mojito. "You know I'll do anything for you."

She waited until they'd received their drinks and were out of the range of nosy ears before leaning close and saying, "Okay. Then marry me."

Simon choked on his drink, spewing a froth of orange liquid a good three feet. "Marry you? Honey, you're not exactly my type. And I didn't think I was that subtle or you were that dumb."

She smiled. "I'm not. And, for the record, neither are you."

"In that case, why would we get married?"

She sipped her water. "Simon, you're a brilliant businessman, but your family doesn't appreciate you." The Durants owned a chain of hotels. It was a business that had been around almost as long as Biedermann's. However, the Durant family tree was massive, sprawling and loaded with acorns of brilliant businessmen. Unlike her own family tree, which had been winnowed down to her one scrawny branch.

"You're not reaching your full potential at Durant International. You're too far down in the line of succession. Right now you're stuck as—what is it?— junior VP of public relations?"

Simon cringed.

"We both know you're capable of so much more." Kitty leaned forward, her zeal showing just a little as she sensed his interest being piqued. "Marry me, take over as CEO of Biedermann's and we'll kill numerous birds with one stone. You'll get a job you can be proud of and you'll come into your inheritance."

He quirked an eyebrow. "My inheritance, eh?"

"Rumor has it your very conservative grandmother is withholding your inheritance until you marry and settle down."

Simon's eyebrows both shot up. "The rumor mill has been active indeed."

"Is it true, then?"

"Let's just say Grandmother Durant has never approved of my lifestyle, but I have plenty of other sources of income. And I don't care about the money."

"Ah, but you do care about her. And I suspect it bothers you that you've never lived up to her standards. She'd be very pleased if we married. You could even provide her with a great-grandchild."

Emotion flickered across Simon's face, barely visible in the dim lighting of that gallery. Something dark and a little sad. She knew in that instant that her instincts about Simon had been right.

While he was decidedly gay, he regretted some of the things his lifestyle had cost him: his family's respect and the chance for a family of his own. She might just be able to tempt him onto an easier path. They'd never have a real marriage, but they were friends at least. Which was more than some couples could say.

Simon frowned as if he were seriously considering her offer. Hope surged through her. Maybe this would actually work. If it did, it would all be so simple. Such a fine solution to all of her problems.

"And what would you get out of this marriage?" he asked.

"I'd get a talented CEO. With you at the helm, Biedermann's stock would start to climb again. I'd keep the company out of the hands of FMJ. It's so perfect, I almost wonder why I didn't think of it before."

Simon studied her. "I was wondering that myself. After all, you haven't gone to lengths to hide the fact that you've been looking for a husband to bail you out."

She nearly laughed. "Don't tell me I've offended you by not propositioning you before now?"

"Not at all. I'm just curious why you're suddenly so desperate." Simon gave her a piercing look. "You know I'd never be the kind of husband you deserve."

She nodded. "Of course I know that. But we're friends. I think it would be very easy for us to settle into a marriage of sorts."

He cocked his head to the side and asked, "If you're serious, why come here? Why not just call? Why ask now? It's not often a man gets tracked down in the middle of his lover's art show and propositioned."

She had to laugh at that. "It seemed like the kind of thing to discuss in person. And I'm in a bit of a hurry."

"You make a very tempting package, my dear, but—"

"But you're not tempted?" she asked with a sigh.

"It's more that I think you'll regret it later. In my experience, when someone propositions you late at night, on impulse, it's because they're running away from someone else."

"I'm not running away from Ford." But the panicked note in her voice alarmed her.

Simon leveled his gaze at her. "Really? Why don't you tell me what happened?"

"Nothing happened," she insisted, determined to leave it at that. However, she kept talking, seemingly unable to stop the flow of words. "That man is impossible. He's insulting and rude. And he…" She struggled to regain the composure she felt slipping. "And he asked me to marry him."

Before she knew it, she'd told Simon the entire story. From the unplanned pregnancy to her incompetence as a CEO to Ford's offer of marriage.

When she finished, she looked at Simon, fully expecting a flood of sympathy. Instead he gazed at her in that penetrating way of his.

"What?" she asked.

"I'm just trying to figure out why you need me to be your husband and your CEO, if Ford has already offered to do the job."

"I can't accept his proposal. He only offered because he feels sorry for me."

"Sorry for you?" Simon asked.

She fumed. "I think he sees it as a point of honor."

Simon laughed at her. "Sure there's pity sex. But there's no such thing as a pity marriage. No man is that honorable."

Humiliation burned her cheeks as she asked, "Then why would he offer to marry me?"

Simon shrugged. "You'll have to ask him. Maybe he offered for the reason most men ask a woman to marry them. Maybe he loves you."

Shock coursed through her body. Love? Ford might love her? For one awful moment, her heart leaped into her throat, then sanity returned. "That's impossible."

"Are you sure?" Before she could answer, he pressed on. "Do you love him?"

"I don't—" But she could only shake her head. Not in denial, but in confusion. Was what she felt really love? Not a temporary blip of imaginary love, but real love. The kind strong enough to sustain an actual marriage? "I don't know."

"Then you better figure it out." Simon pulled her close and leaned down to brush a kiss across her cheek. But before his lips made contact with her skin, someone yanked him away from her and punched him soundly in the face.

"You didn't have to punch him."

Kitty sat beside Ford in the back of a taxi, but she'd crammed herself as far against the door as she could. Her arms were crossed over her chest as she gazed belligerently forward, her legs crossed away from him so that as she tapped her foot in irritation it scraped against the door. The cab driver kept glaring at her in the mirror, but she ignored him. Occasionally, the driver sent him a pleading look for backup, but Ford ignored him, too. Hell, he had bigger problems. Much, much bigger.

"What were you thinking?" she demanded.

What was he supposed to say to that? He hadn't been thinking. When he'd walked into that gallery and seen another man leaning down to kiss Kitty, he'd simply lost it. Never mind that the man doing the kissing was gay. Ford hadn't known that until after he'd punched him, when a pint-size, flamboyant man had shrieked and run across the room to kneel beside the fallen man. A lot of drama had ensued. Ford figured he was lucky the police hadn't been called, because an arrest was the last thing he needed to add to his humiliation.

To make matters worse, he'd obviously been set up. He'd gone to that art gallery in the first place because half an hour earlier he'd gotten a picture e-mailed to him of Kitty snuggling up to that guy. He'd been furious. It hadn't mattered that the e-mail had been from someone claiming to be Suzy Snark. He'd deal with that issue later. For now, he had more pressing issues.

Kitty shifted in her seat so she was almost facing him. "Do you have anything to say for yourself?" she asked in slow, baffled tones. "Any explanation for why you'd do that?"

There was a note of expectancy in her voice. Was there some answer she wanted him to give? Did she understand his actions? Because he sure as hell didn't.

He glanced at her only briefly before looking back out his window. He didn't know what to say. Because the truth was, he *did* have to hit him. When he'd seen Simon kissing Kitty, the need to hit him had been so strong it had almost been a compulsion.

In that moment, all the heightened emotions of that past week—all the anxiety, all the desire, all the frustration—all that emotion had crystallized into pure, blinding fury.

"Do you have anything to say for yourself? Anything at all?"

"I don't want to talk about it."

She threw up her hands in a *what the hell?* gesture. She snorted, turning toward him. "Of all the stupid—"

"I know. Shut up." He turned to face her, too. "You think I don't know what I did was stupid? I know. I'm thirty-two years old—damn it—I know better than to punch a guy just because he's kissing my woman. I. Know. Better."

Her eyes widened slightly at his words. She looked as if she wanted to turn and run, but in the tight confines of the taxi, there was nowhere to go. And since she wasn't saying anything, he kept talking.

"I'm not a complete moron, despite all evidence to the contrary. I don't fight. That's just not who I am. Back when we were kids, Jonathan got into plenty of fights. Matt, too. But not me. I was always the one talking the other guy into backing down. I've always been too smart to fight." He scrubbed a hand through his hair. "I guess you just bring out the idiot in me."

Her gaze narrowed slightly. "That's all you have to say for yourself?"

"What else do you want me to say?"

"Nothing. Nothing at all." Then she leaned forward and tapped on the glass separating them from the cab driver. "Pull over here," she ordered.

"Come on, Kitty, you can't get out here. It's late and you're a twenty-minute cab ride from your apartment."

"I'm not getting out. You are."

Eleven

Kitty watched Ford climb from the cab with a sinking stomach. If she didn't know it was too early for her to feel the baby moving, she'd have sworn the little bugger was giving her a swift kick in the gut. And not in a good way.

She'd given Ford the perfect opportunity to tell her he loved her. And all he'd come up with was "You just bring out the idiot in me."

That was the best he could do? Not "I love you." Not even "I couldn't stand the sight of another man touching you." Geesh, she would have settled for "I was jealous." But oh, no. That's not what she got. She got "You just bring out the idiot in me."

Well. What could she have said to that? "Gosh, I'm so glad I could help"?

Simon had been wrong.

Ford didn't love her.

But she did love him.

Something she hadn't known for sure until she'd been sitting there beside him in the cab, heart thudding away in her chest, waiting to hear his answer. Praying for a declaration from him.

And the instant he'd made that stupid idiot comment she'd known that she'd been kidding herself until now. She wasn't immune to Ford. He had the power to crush her very soul.

How could she even see him again? How could she risk falling even more in love with him?

No, she needed some distance. Not to mention some time. She had never backed down from a fight in her life, but she knew Ford. He wouldn't leave her alone. He'd never give her heart time to build up calluses. Which meant she had to go into hiding.

A few minutes later when the cab pulled to stop in front of her building, she leaned in the window as she paid. "Can you wait? I'll be down in just a few minutes."

It didn't take her long to pack a bag and return to the waiting cab. It was risky, leaving just now, when the deal with FMJ was still up in the air, but she just couldn't stay. She'd always thought losing Biedermann's was the hardest thing she'd ever have to go through. Turned out she was wrong. Losing Ford was so much harder.

By morning, Ford was ready for some answers. And, frankly, he figured he had them coming. Unfortunately, Kitty was nowhere to be found. She wasn't at work, she wasn't at home. She wasn't even at any of the spas he could think of calling.

In the end, he decided to check with the one person he least wanted to see. Simon Durant.

He tracked Simon down at the other man's apartment on the Upper West Side.

When Simon opened his front door sporting an already bruising black eye, Ford didn't waste any time. He figured the man was seconds away from throwing him out already.

He tried to contain his anger, but it crept into his voice as he asked, "What the hell did you say to Kitty?"

Simon's eyebrows shot up as he gestured for Ford to follow him into the living room. "Why do you assume I said anything to her?"

"Because she's gone."

"Gone?" Simon dropped onto the sofa, stretching out his legs along the seat.

"Yes, gone. As in, she's not answering her phone, she's not at home, and no one can tell me where she is."

"Ahh. I see." Simon nodded sagely, but didn't offer anything else. Then he looked meaningfully at the chair across from him.

Ford sat begrudgingly. This wasn't a social visit, but Simon clearly enjoyed toying with him. "So what did you say to her?"

"Hmm, let me think." Simon tapped his forefinger on his upper lip as if deep in thought. "First she asked me if I would marry her."

Ford had to repress the urge to leap across the coffee table and wrap his hands around the other man's throat. But hitting Simon last night obviously hadn't helped anything, so Ford sat, drumming his fingers on his knees, and prayed that Simon would reach the end of the story before he reached the end of his patience.

"And what did you say?" Ford gave Simon a verbal nudge.

"Well, no. Obviously." Simon sent him a look that seemed to ask, *Are you always this dumb?*

"Obviously."

"And then she told me that you had asked her to marry you. It's all very *Midsummer Night's Dream,* don't you think?"

Ford ignored him and asked, "Then what happened?"

"Then she cried a little." Simon's flippant tone vanished under the weight of this accusation. "And you know, Kitty never cries."

Ford could only swallow and nod.

"Do you know she's under the impression you asked her to marry you because you pity her?"

"That's absurd," Ford said automatically.

"I'm glad you think so." Simon flashed him a wane smile. "That's what I said. I told her I thought you were in love with her."

Ford felt like his stomach dropped out of his body as his mind went wheeling.

"Well?" Simon asked after a minute.

"Well, what?"

"Are you? In love with Kitty, I mean."

"No" was his automatic response, but even as he said the word he felt a pang deep in his heart.

Kitty was probably the most amazing woman he'd ever known. Smart, sexy as hell, and so damn pretty it almost hurt to look at her. None of which was even half as impressive as her pure strength of will. Her independence. In her lifetime, she'd managed to overcome challenges he couldn't even imagine. And she was so damn determined to do it all on her own.

It was kind of ironic. For the first time in his life, he wanted to help someone. He wanted to shoulder all the burdens or to stand by her side when she shouldered them herself. He wanted to be there for her no matter what. Not just for her, but for the baby, too. He wanted to try his hand at being the kind of father he'd never had.

If only she'd let him. Of course he was in love with her. Who wouldn't be? "Yes," he said finally.

This time, the smile Simon sent him was beaming. "Well, then." He straightened. "We have some work to do, don't we?"

If Kitty had any illusions that Ford would come rushing after her to sweep her off her feet, they faded quickly. As one week passed into the next, she faced the possibility that he wasn't coming for her. True, she'd made herself difficult to find, but not impossible. After all, the hotel was just a few blocks down from Biedermann's headquarters.

At first, she mostly just sulked. It wasn't so much that

she expected him to find her, but rather that she hoped
he would. In her mind she replayed scenes from all the
classic romantic movies she'd watched growing up. The
ones where the man chases down the heroine on New
Year's Eve or at the Empire State Building to declare his
eternal love. She wanted their story to have that kind of
ending, even though she knew it was impossible.

When she wasn't entertaining romantic fantasies
about Ford, she ate and slept, the two activities her
doctor most approved of. She was surprised how tired
being pregnant made her feel, but thankful that lots of
rest and near constant eating kept the nausea at bay.

As far as work was concerned, she turned over the
negotiations with FMJ to Marty. Following Ford's
advice, she came clean to Marty about her dyslexia. He
was shocked, but far more sympathetic than she'd
imagined he'd be. He called daily with updates about
the acquisition, but she found it hard to care.

Still, she knew the negotiations had not yet been finalized. So when Casey came by for a visit and mentioned that Ford had scheduled another press conference,
she was immediately suspicious. If Ford was ready to
talk to the press, it could mean only one thing. If he
wasn't going to announce that the deal was finalized, did
that mean FMJ was pulling out?

Whether she was ready to face him or not, it was
time for her to come out of hiding.

Staring out at the sea of reporters, Ford had to
swallow down his nerves. He'd done dozens of these

things in the past, hell, maybe hundreds, and they'd never bothered him at all.

But he knew if he had any chance of winning Kitty back, it would be right now. And she was out there somewhere, just waiting to see what he had up his sleeve.

He'd known—of course—that the one sure way to guarantee she came to the press conference was to tell Casey to keep her away.

He didn't have long to worry about it, because before he knew it, Matt was giving him the nod that it was time to begin.

"Acquiring Biedermann Jewelry was quite the departure for FMJ. Up until now, we've been known for pioneering green technologies. However, we were confident that with the right leadership and creativity Biedermann's could once again become a leader in the industry.

"Though our agreement with Biedermann's hasn't been finalized, we're so enthusiastic about the new direction we're taking things we wanted to give everyone a sneak peek at what we're doing.

"Casey there is passing out swag bags, and if you'll look inside, you'll see what I'm talking about. We're launching a line of stylish accessories for personal mobile devices."

A murmur went through the crowd as people began digging through the bags. Each of the twenty bags contained the Victorian-inspired iPhone case and the gothic Bluetooth earpiece. The earpiece had taken the most work, but luckily Matt had figured out a way to retrofit an earpiece FMJ was already manufacturing.

"These are all just beta versions," Ford continued over the whispers. He smiled broadly. "So go easy on them. The final versions will be in stores within a few months, along with the rest of the line. All of which, by the way, are designed personally by Kitty Biedermann herself."

Kitty could not have been more surprised than anyone else in the audience. She sat in the back row, feeling a little like Jackie O. hidden under sunglasses and a hat. So far, no one had recognized her.

When she'd opened the bag Casey had handed her with a wink, she'd actually gasped aloud. Thankfully her gasp was one of many exclamatory noises, so she didn't think anyone had noticed.

She dumped the two boxes on her lap and then carefully opened the first, unwrapping the tissue paper that surrounded the iPhone case. Her hand trembled as she held it. It was something she'd never dreamed she'd see. Her design come to life, strange and a little absurd though it was, with its Victorian curlicues and its gothic clawed feet.

After a lifetime of dreaming of it, she was finally holding one of her creations in her hands. Even better, the people on either side of her were murmuring excitedly. Her father had been wrong. There was a market for her work.

And Ford had given it to her.

By the time she returned her attention to the press conference, Ford was answering questions.

"Will Ms. Biedermann continue to design the line?" one reporter asked.

"I certainly hope so. As you can see, her designs are very original."

"Does this mean she won't be serving as CEO of Biedermann's?"

"Ms. Biedermann is extremely smart and talented. Like many other people who are dyslexic, she's shown tremendous resilience in overcoming her disability. Needless to say, FMJ will be happy to have her in whatever capacity she chooses to fill."

Kitty's head snapped up as panic poured through her body. He'd just casually dropped her dyslexia into the conference like it was nothing. What was he *doing?*

Ford had paused as shock rippled through the crowd, but now he continued. "Her learning disability has made her job as CEO extremely difficult, as you can imagine."

"So then she won't be continuing on in her current position? FMJ is going to replace her?" one of the reporters asked.

Ford's gaze sought out Kitty where she sat in the back of the room. He'd seen her trying to blend in when she'd first arrived. Not that Kitty could disappear in a crowd. Her intrinsic style and grace made her stand out.

When he'd made the announcement about her dyslexia, she'd near leaped to her feet. She yanked off her sunglasses and was glaring at him through the crowd. Was she anxious to hear his answer or sending him a telepathic message to explode? He couldn't tell. For now, all he could do was answer the reporter's question as honestly as he could.

"On the contrary. FMJ is going to do everything in its power to support her in whatever she decides. Biedermann's is still her company. However, the position she holds within the company will ultimately be her decision."

After that, he answered a few more questions and then wrapped up his part. He neatly handed the podium over to Matt to talk about the specs just as they'd planned. He wanted to slip out quietly. The last thing he wanted now was to get waylaid by some nosy reporter. No, there was only one person he wanted to talk to right now. And only one question he wanted answers to. Now that he'd revealed her biggest secret to the world, would she still want to talk to him?

She caught up with him right outside the conference room, falling into step beside him as if it hadn't been nearly two weeks since he'd seen her. As if there weren't repeated marriage proposals hanging in the air between them.

Finally the tension got to him and he broke the silence. "They seemed enthusiastic about the new line."

She slanted him a look, but the sunglasses were back on and he couldn't read her expression. "It was a big risk announcing it this early."

"It was. But Biedermann's stock price has been

climbing steadily since I scheduled the press conference. It had been fluctuating based on the Suzy Snark blogs. No matter what happens, Biedermann's is no longer in danger of being delisted."

After today, she would be fine even without him, if that's what she chose.

She stopped him, placing a hand on his arm. "Why did you do it? If our stock prices are climbing then theoretically I don't have to accept your buyout offer now. You made it easier for me to walk away from you."

"That's one way to look at it." He grinned wolfishly. "But all of Matt's Bluetooth stuff is proprietary technology. If you want Biedermann's to actually sell those gadgets of yours, now you have to sign the papers."

"So it was a trap?"

They'd reached the hotel lobby by now, and she stopped cold. He turned to face her. He'd been wondering when they would get to this part of the discussion. The part where she ripped him a new one for spilling the beans about her dyslexia.

But instead of the blazing anger he expected to read in her expression, he saw only shattering vulnerability.

"You can't honestly expect me to trust you after this. After you—" Her voice broke. Without meeting his gaze she pushed past him to walk briskly through the hotel lobby.

He caught up with her in a few steps. Grabbing her arm, he turned her to face him. "I brought up your dyslexia in the press conference to prove you can trust me."

"That makes perfect sense. Betray someone's trust to prove that they can trust you." She tugged on her arm, glaring at him. "Except I hadn't even trusted you enough to tell you about my dyslexia. You wheedled that information out of my assistant."

She used the word *wheedled* with relish. Obviously she remembered he'd objected to it the last time.

"No, you're right," he told her. "You didn't tell me. But then you didn't tell Casey, either. I can almost excuse you not trusting me. But Casey? That kid would do anything for you." He shook his head in exasperation. "Have you ever wondered what all this deception has cost you?"

She stared at him blankly, as if she didn't understand his words, but at least she was listening.

He tipped her chin up so she was looking full at him. For a second he studied her face, taking in the lines of strain around her mouth, the clear green intensity of her eyes. Her perfectly kissable bow of a mouth, painted a tempting scarlet.

His heart seized in his chest. He may have royally screwed this up. If she didn't forgive him, this may be the last time he was this close to her. But he couldn't think about that now.

"Kitty, your family made you believe your dyslexia was something to hide. Something to be ashamed of. But it's not. It's—"

"Don't try to tell me it's no big deal. That it doesn't make me different than anyone else." She twisted her chin away. "Because it is a big deal. It makes everything harder."

"Which is exactly why you need to be able to ask for help. You need to surround yourself with people you trust." His frustration crept into his voice. "No one does everything on their own. The rest of us mere mortals need help all the time. Why shouldn't you?"

But she just shook her head. "You don't get it, do you? This was my secret. It wasn't yours to tell."

"Exactly. And you were never going to tell it. You would have let people go on thinking the worst of you forever rather than have even one moment of vulnerability. So I made the decision for you. I did it because it was the right thing for you.

"For once in my life, I did the right thing, not just the easy thing." He laughed wryly. "I could have just left things as they were. I probably could have even talked my way back into your bed." He waited for her to protest, but she didn't. They both knew he was right on that account. "Instead, I did that one thing that I knew would piss you off, because I knew it would make your life better."

"So you did it because you wanted to piss me off?"

"No. I did it because I love you."

Kitty's heart, which had been racing with fury and fear, seemed to stop in her chest. She squeezed her eyes shut for a second as emotion flooded her.

He *loved* her?

When she opened her eyes he was still there. Watching her expectantly. "Look, neither of us is any good at this. We're both slow to trust. Neither of us let other people close. And it would undoubtedly be easier on both of us if we walked away right now. But I don't want to do that, and I'm betting you don't want to do that, either."

She opened her mouth to speak, but her throat closed off and all she could do was shake her head mutely.

"So I say we decide right now. We stick with this and make it work."

She wanted to believe him, but her heart didn't know how to trust what her mind heard.

"Biedermann's—" she began.

His hand tightened around her arm. "This doesn't have anything to do with Biedermann's. This is about you and me. And the baby we're going to have." He paused, his gaze dropping from her eyes to her belly. "I love you, Kitty. And I want to be a father to our baby. The only question is, do you trust me enough to let me?"

Her heart stuttered in her chest. Did she trust him? The question had barely flitted through her mind before she knew the answer. Of course she did.

An unexpected bubble of laughter rose up in her throat. Ford cocked an eyebrow at her giggle, his expression still expectant. But before he could ask why she was laughing, she threw her arms around his neck.

"Of course I trust you. Which is so silly because just a few minutes ago I didn't think I did."

She felt his arms wrap around her and tighten, felt his face nuzzle into her hair. Only when she felt the shudder of his deep breath did she realize how nervous he must have been.

She pulled back to meet his gaze. "You know I love you, too, right?"

His lips quirked into a half smile. "I thought my chances were pretty good."

"What would you have done if I'd have said no?"

"I'm not the kind of guy who takes no for an answer."

"Meaning?" she asked.

"Meaning, I would have pursued you until you said yes."

Just a few weeks ago, that answer would have infuriated her. Now she knew it was just exactly what she needed. *He* was just exactly what she needed.

She forced a mock frown. "You know, that was pretty gutsy. Asking a jewelry heiress to marry you when you didn't even have a ring to offer."

To her surprise he smiled broadly. "Hey, this I have covered." He reached into his pocket, pulled out something small. When he opened his palm, he revealed a single earring shaped like a bird.

"My earring," she gasped. She picked up the earring and let it dangle between her fingers. "I thought it was lost forever. I can't believe you kept it all this time."

He cupped her cheek in his palm. "Maybe I was just waiting for the right time to give it back to you."

As he pulled her into his arms one more time, she thought back to the first night they'd met. Maybe part of her knew even then that he was the perfect man for her. Or maybe she was just very, very lucky.

Either way, she was smart enough to hold on tight to this wonderful man and never let him go.

Epilogue

From the blog of New York gossip columnist Suzy Snark:

> Faithful readers of this column have no doubt been disappointed with the lack of drama in Kitty Biedermann's life. Ever since her springtime wedding to hunky business magnate Ford Langley, her life has been dreadfully dull. But that is all about to change. Late last night, with all the theatrics one would expect from Kitty's daughter, Ilsa Marie Biedermann-Langley made her first appearance.
>
> The tiny diva will be living at her family's full-time home in Palo Alto, California, but you

can expect frequent visits to the city. After all, Kitty's new line of accessories are the must-have items of the season, once again putting Biedermann Jewelry at the top of the fashion food chain.

"Ilsa made the Suzy Snark column," Ford said, looking up from his laptop.

Kitty's head snapped up. "She did?" Her gaze narrowed. "That Suzy Snark better watch it. If she—"

"Don't worry, it's all good stuff." Still, he chuckled at his wife's fierce reaction. It was their first morning back from the hospital. He and Kitty were sitting quietly at the table, him with his laptop, her with her sketchpad. Baby Ilsa slept quietly in the bassinet they'd rolled into the kitchen. For the moment, all was peaceful and quiet. Not that it would be for long. He could already tell that Ilsa had her mother's sassy temper. Which was just the way he liked it.

* * * * *

THE BILLIONAIRE'S BIDDING

BARBARA DUNLOP

Barbara Dunlop writes romantic stories while curled up in a log cabin in Canada's far north, where bears outnumber people and it snows six months of the year. Fortunately she has a brawny husband and two teenage children to haul firewood and clear the driveway while she sips cocoa and muses about her upcoming chapters. Barbara loves to hear from readers. You can contact her through her website, www.barbaradunlop.com.

For my beloved grandmother,
Lucy May Mallory

One

Emma McKinley should have been nervous as she stepped off the elevator onto the Garrison Hotels' corporate floor. But her emotions had been wrung dry days ago.

It all started with her father's sudden death. Then she discovered McKinley Inns' massive debts. And then she learned of the bizarre financial offer made to her sister in order to save the family corporation.

The only thing left inside her now was a grim determination. And it was focused on Alex Garrison, the CEO of Garrison Hotels.

She clamped her bag against her Donna Karan blazer and marched her matching pumps straight down the marble-pillared hallway. She'd never been in the Garrison offices before, never had a reason to talk to her family's rivals. But it didn't take a genius to figure out the double doors at the far end would lead to Alex Garrison's inner sanctum.

She ignored the stares from admin staff whose desks were tucked into discreet alcoves along the way. Nobody seemed inclined to stop her. Just as well, she wasn't in a mood to be stopped. She might not have an appointment with Mr. Garrison, but she had a moral right to confront him in person.

How dare he take advantage of her little sister, Katie, mere weeks after the funeral, with his veiled threats and outrageous propositions?

Emma drew a breath into her tightening lungs.

Maybe she did have some emotion left in her after all.

"Excuse me, ma'am," came a female voice on her left as the hallway widened into a posh reception area.

Emma didn't answer. She didn't glance across the desk at the woman, and she didn't break stride. Ten feet from his door. Eight feet.

"Ma'am." The voice was louder this time, more strident as a neatly suited, thirty-something woman jumped up from her chair.

Five feet.

"You can't go—"

Emma clamped her hand around the elongated, ornate gold door handle.

"—*in there.*"

Emma swung the door wide open.

Four men in dark suits, sitting at a round, mahogany meeting table, turned sharply to stare at her. Two were gray-haired, with bushy eyebrows and accusatory squints that told her she'd made a terrible blunder. The third was a younger, blond man. His sparkling blue eyes and restrained grin told her he welcomed the interruption.

The fourth man shot to his feet, pushing a leather chair backward with the motion. Dark-haired, dark-eyed and broad-shouldered, his stance told her he was more than ready to take on her and anybody else who breached his privacy.

"I'm so sorry, Mr. Garrison," came the secretary's breathless voice from behind Emma. "I tried—"

"Not your fault, Simone." The man's slate-gray gaze never left Emma. "Can I help you with something?"

Emma's grip tightened on her shoulder bag. Everyone else in the room faded to mist as her anger returned in force. She focused on Alex Garrison. "Did you think there was the *slightest* chance I'd let you get away with it?"

Simone gasped.

"As you can see." Alex's jaw clenched over the steel-threaded words. "We're in the middle of a meeting."

"I don't care if you're—"

"If you'd like to make an appointment."

"I would not."

"Then I'll have to ask you to leave."

"Do you know who I am?"

"No."

"Liar."

"I'll call security," said Simone.

Alex raised his eyebrows, gazing blandly back at Emma. She realized with a jolt that he really didn't know who she was. How was that possible? Katie was the public face of McKinley Inns, sure. But...

"Do we *need* security?" he asked.

"I'm Emma McKinley."

His nostrils flared and he jerked back ever so slightly.

Then, after a silent pause, he lifted a gold pen from the tabletop and tucked it into the breast pocket of his finely tailored jacket. His burgundy silk tie gleamed under the discreet lighting as he straightened to full height. "If you'll excuse us, gentlemen. I believe I can spare five minutes for Ms. McKinley."

The men started to rise.

Alex held up a broad hand. "Please. Ms. McKinley and I will use the boardroom."

He gestured to a wide oak door and indicated she should precede him.

She crossed the room and turned yet another ornate gold handle. The doorway opened into an impressively large boardroom, dominated by an oblong table of polished, inlayed wood. The twenty chairs surrounding it were covered in burgundy leather, and a bank of windows running down one side let in the August sun that was hanging over uptown Manhattan.

She heard the door click shut, and she pivoted to face him.

"I trust you can make this quick," he said, taking a single step toward her, planting his oxfords wide apart.

He was even larger and more impressive up close, with broad shoulders and a deep, muscular chest. Stark sunrays highlighted the uncompromising planes of his face. His chin was square, the set of his lips grim, and his eyes were the color of gunmetal gray after a glistening rain.

She got the feeling few people crossed him and lived to tell the tale. If she didn't know he'd been born with a silver spoon in his mouth, she'd swear he grew up on the streets of Brooklyn.

Not that any of it mattered. He wasn't getting his hands on her baby sister or their company.

"You are *not* marrying Katie," she stated bluntly.

He gave a careless shrug. "I believe that's up to Katie."

"My father isn't even cold in his grave."

"Doesn't change your financial situation."

"I can fix our financial situation." Maybe. Hopefully. They could always mortgage the Martha's Vineyard property.

Alex cocked his head to one side. "I can have your loan called within twenty-four hours. Can you fix your finances that fast?"

Emma didn't answer. He knew darn well she couldn't fix

them that fast. It would take weeks, maybe months to work through the maze of mortgages, letters of credit and personal guarantees signed by her father.

Her chest tingled and tightened. Why, oh, why did her father have to die so young? She missed him desperately. And she'd counted on having his guidance for decades to come.

"Ms. McKinley?"

"Why do you even *want* McKinley Inns?"

Garrison Hotels had dozens of properties, bigger, more opulent facilities. McKinley occupied a small, high-end niche, where Garrison could compete with any luxury hotel chain in the world.

"You're joking, right?"

She shook her head.

"Like anyone, I want to expand. And you're an opportunity."

"And you don't care who gets trampled in the process?"

The man's reputation was well and truly deserved. Though his press coverage had become more flattering over the past months, Emma wasn't fooled. He was a coldhearted takeover artist who profited from other people's misfortune.

He took another step forward and crossed his arms over his chest. "I don't think Katie made the situation clear. I'm the one doing *you* a favor."

Emma's spine snapped straight. She tipped her chin to look him in the eyes. "By marrying my sister and taking over our company?"

"By saving your company from bankruptcy. You're insolvent, Ms. McKinley. If I don't take you out, somebody else will. That's the way capitalism works."

"Don't patronize me."

A cold grin flexed one side of his mouth. "Way I see it, this is a win-win."

"The way *I* see it, this is a lose-lose."

"That's because you're idealistic and impractical."

"At least I have a soul."

He shifted his stance. "Last time I checked, a soul wasn't a requirement for a business license in the state of New York."

"She will *not* marry you."

"Did she explain the deal?"

Yes, Katie had explained the deal. Alex wanted their company. But he'd spent thousands of dollars over the last two years improving his image, and he was afraid of negative publicity from preying on two newly bereaved sisters.

Oh, he still wanted to prey on them. He just didn't want anybody to know about it. Hence the cover of marriage and all the joyous goodwill that would go with it.

"She told me," said Emma tightly.

"Then you know you'll keep half the company." His impassive expression turned to a scowl. "And I'm crazy for offering you that much."

"You actually expect to buy a bride."

"At that price. Yeah."

Emma honestly didn't know what to say.

"Are we done?" he asked.

Were they done? What did she do now? Make a hollow threat? Storm out the door? Swear he'd never get his hands on her precious inns when they both knew that's exactly what he would do?

He seemed to sense her hesitation. "Nobody gets hurt," he said. "The publicity will help us both. The press will go nuts over the merging of two great hotel families. We'll feed the story to female reporters, who'll get all misty-eyed at—"

She raked her bangs back from her forehead. "Are you *listening* to yourself?"

He blinked. "What do you mean?"

"You don't find that plan just a little cold-blooded?"

"Like I said, nobody gets hurt."

"What about Katie? What about David?"

"Who's David?"

"Her boyfriend. The sweet, gentle caring young man she's been dating for six months. He'll be heartbroken and humiliated."

Alex paused. For a second she thought she saw an actual emotion pass through his eyes. But then it was gone, replaced by hard gloss slate once again. "David will get over it. He can marry her later, when she's worth a lot more money."

Emma opened her mouth, but no sound came out.

"What about you?" Alex asked into the silence.

"I'm pretty upset," she answered, in the understatement of the century.

He rolled his eyes. "Your emotional state is irrelevant. Do you have a steady boyfriend?"

"No." And what did that have to do with anything?

"Problem solved."

"Huh?"

"You marry me."

Emma reached out to grip the back of a leather chair, afraid she might lose it right there. "What?"

Alex stood there, looking for all the world like a rational person, while tossing out the most outrageous proposal she'd heard in her life. Marry him? *Marry* him?

"It doesn't really matter which sister," he continued without a thread of emotion in his voice. "I only picked Katie because she's—"

"The pretty one," Emma finished, straightening away from the chair and squaring her shoulders. For some reason it killed her to have him of all people say it out loud. Not that everybody didn't think it. It was just that Alex cut to the heart of the issue with such dispassionate accuracy, that it hurt more than usual.

"That's not—"

"I am not marrying you, and Katie is not marrying you."

Alex's voice took on a soft warning note. "Option three is calling your loan. Then you get nothing."

Emma tightened her arm on her shoulder bag. "Option three is me working out the finances first thing tomorrow morning."

His mouth crooked in another half smile. "In that case, I'll leave my offer open for twenty-four hours."

She turned and stalked toward a side door. Her exit was all bluff and bravado, and they both knew it. For that alone, she'd never forgive him.

"No need, Mr. Garrison," she said tightly.

"Under the circumstances," he rumbled behind her, as she reached for the handle and twisted.

"You might want to call me Alex…Emma."

She didn't turn back, but her name on his lips sent a shiver up her spine.

Two hours later, the office door closed behind the Rockwell brothers, and Ryan Hayes turned his stare on Alex. "I assume you nailed down the details with her?"

Alex closed the top manila folder, carefully straightening the pile on the polished tabletop in front of him. "Not quite."

Ryan narrowed his gaze. "What do you mean not quite?"

Alex sighed and leaned back in his chair, rubbing a fingertip across his temple. Gunter's plan was looking more ridiculous by the minute. "I mean, the details aren't nailed down yet."

"But you are getting married."

"I'm trying," Alex snapped.

Ryan shook an admonishing finger. "You are not touching McKinley Inns without a bona fide McKinley bride on your arm. Jeez, Alex, they'll crucify us in the press."

Alex gritted his teeth. He'd turned this thing over in his mind a thousand different ways. If it was up to him, he'd call the loan right now and take over the damn company. This was business, not a day care for dilettantes.

But Ryan and Gunter were both major shareholders in

Garrison Hotels. And they were both convinced that Alex's reputation as a hard-ass was hurting business. They even thought some recent, decisive takeover bids had harmed employee morale and impacted on convention business.

As a result, they were forcing him to behave like a boy scout in public. He wasn't allowed to argue, wasn't even allowed to scowl. Soon they'd have him kissing babies and helping little old ladies across the street.

"Why don't *you* marry her?" he asked Ryan.

"Because I'm not the one with the image problem," Ryan countered. "Besides, I'm not the CEO, and I'm not the public face of Garrison Hotels. Profits were up fifteen percent for the quarter."

Alex glanced at his watch. "That could've been anything." He wasn't ready to accept that the kinder, gentler Alex was responsible for such an enormous turnaround.

"So what are the details?" asked Ryan.

Alex looked up. "Huh?"

"What's left to sort out with Katie."

"Nothing. It's not Katie. It's Emma now. And she's still making up her mind." Alex couldn't believe he'd proposed to two different women in the space of forty-eight hours.

Ryan cocked his head. "I thought you proposed to the pretty one."

"The pretty one said no. So I proposed to Emma instead. *She* doesn't have a boyfriend."

"I guess not," Ryan scoffed.

Alex's spine stiffened. Sure, Emma wasn't a knockout like Katie, but there was no need to get insulting. "What's that supposed to mean?"

"It means she's tough and scary."

Alex stood up. "Wimp."

Emma wasn't tough and scary. She was frustrated and panicking. Which worked in his favor, actually.

Ryan stood with him. "One sister or the other. You make this work or bail on the project."

Bail on the project? Alex didn't think so. McKinley had prime beachfront property on Kayven Island. Prime beachfront property whose value was *about* to go through the roof when the cruise ship facility was finally announced.

He might have to sweeten the deal or find another vulnerability to exploit. But he wasn't walking away from this one.

"What are we going to *do?*" Katie's face was pale as she leaned across the table at the Chateau Moulin restaurant off the lobby of the McKinley Inn Fifth Avenue. The flickering hurricane lamp emphasized her worry, reflecting in a window that was blackened by the park beyond.

"I don't know," Emma answered honestly with a shake of her head. "I'll have to call the bank in the morning."

"And tell them *what?*" Katie's voice rose to high C, matching the note of a grand piano tinkling in the corner.

"We'll restructure the mortgages, maybe use the Martha's Vineyard property as extra collateral."

"You know that won't work."

Emma didn't answer, because Katie was right. Equity in the Martha's Vineyards property wouldn't make a dent in the amount their father owed.

Things had been tough for McKinley the past few years. Bookings were down, costs up. Their father was always reluctant to let staff go. And they were locked into major renovations on three ski resort properties, while snow conditions had remained poor two winters in a row.

They were over a barrel, and Alex Garrison knew it. The man might be amoral, but he wasn't stupid.

"I'm going to have to marry him," said Katie, raising her palms in a gesture of defeat.

"And what about David?"

"I'll explain it to him somehow."

Emma took a drink from her martini glass, mimicking her sister's voice. "I'm so sorry, sweetheart. But I'm going to have to marry another man for his money."

"I won't say it like that."

"There's no way to say it and make it sound good."

"Well, are *you* going to marry him?"

Emma didn't answer as the waitress set salads in front of them.

"At least I don't have a boyfriend," she hissed, after the waitress left.

Katie straightened, looking tragically hopeful. "Is that a yes?"

"No, it's not a yes." Then Emma paused, desperately trying to gather her thoughts. "We can't..." She clenched her jaw. "It's not right... It *galls* me to even think about giving in to that man."

"At least we'd keep half the company."

Fair point. Emma took another sip of her drink. If Alex got the bank to call in the loan instead, they'd be lucky to keep one hotel.

If only they had more time. If only they knew someone who could underwrite them quickly and extensively. If only their father's heart hadn't given out.

The three of them were a team. They'd weathered storms before, and she was sure they could have found a way out of this maze.

"Emma?" Katie prompted.

Emma picked up her fork and stabbed into the shrimp salad. "We'll need to talk to Legal."

Katie's blue eyes dimmed in the lamplight. "To declare bankruptcy."

Emma drew a bracing breath. No. They weren't declaring bankruptcy. Not when they had a slightly more palatable choice.

They were going to throw their lot in with Alex Garrison. If they didn't, they'd be out on the street, and he'd be undermining their father's life's work by this time tomorrow.

At least with Alex there was a chance. If they had a few good years, maybe they could buy him out.

And it wasn't like Emma had a boyfriend waiting anywhere in the wings. Nor was she likely to have one in the foreseeable future. Plain-looking, plainspoken hotel executives who traveled half the year weren't exactly hot prospects on dating dot com.

Truth was, a marriage on paper wouldn't be that big of an inconvenience for her. A justice of the peace, a couple of publicity snapshots, and they'd barely have to see each other again.

She looked Katie straight in the eyes, not giving herself time to rethink the decision. "We have to talk to Legal so we can make sure Alex can't do something crazy with our inns."

Katie's eyes went wide. "You're going to do it?"

Emma dropped her fork and drained her glass. "I'm going to do it."

Two

Mrs. Nash had been calling Alex *Alex* his entire life. But since he'd moved out of his penthouse and back into the family's Long Island mansion six months ago—another of Ryan's brilliant plans to improve his image—she'd taken to calling him Mr. Garrison. Every time she did it, Alex glanced around for his father.

The old man might have been dead for three years, but he still had the power to make Alex jump. It was bad enough that Alex had taken over his father's study, he didn't need to take on his name as well.

"Call me Alex," he grumbled, glancing up from the financial section.

Mrs. Nash squared her shoulders in the doorway. "*Mr. Garrison.*" Her faint British accent grew more pronounced when she was annoyed. "A Ms. McKinley has arrived to see you."

Alex flipped his newspaper down at the fold, his senses coming on alert. "Which one?"

Mrs. Nash's formidable brow went up. "Ms. Emma McKinley, *sir.*"

"Okay, now you're just trying annoy me."

"Sir?" There was an undeniable twinkle behind her blue-gray eyes.

"It's Alex. *Alex.* You changed my diapers and smacked my butt."

She sniffed. "And I dare say, it didn't help much, did it now?"

Alex set the newspaper on his spotless, mahogany desktop and stood from the tufted leather wing chair. "Can we at least dispense with the sir?"

"Yes, Mr. Garrison."

He drew closer to her as he headed for the door. "You're fired."

Her expression remained impassive. "I think not."

"Because you know where the bodies are buried?"

"Because *you've* never memorized the combination to the wine cellar."

He paused. "Excellent point."

"Very good then…sir."

"Insubordinate," he muttered as he passed her.

"Will Ms. McKinley be staying to lunch?"

Good question. Was Emma going to say yes and make both their lives easier? Or was she going to stay up there on her high horse and cause him no end of trouble? Alex gave it a fifty-fifty chance.

He drew a bracing breath. "I have no idea."

Mrs. Nash nodded and carried on into the study, where she'd straighten the newspaper and erase any lingering trace of his presence. It was eerie, living in a house that forgot about you every time you left the room. Sometimes he'd leave subtle traces, a book out of place on a bookshelf, a sculpture slightly to the left on the mantel. But he hadn't tripped her up yet.

He headed down the hallway under the watchful eyes of his ancestors. The portraits were newly dusted and plum-line straight. His father was last, looking dour and judgmental, probably wishing he could grill Alex on the bottom line. Alex imagined that's what his father hated most about being dead—standing by silently while Alex ran amok with the family business.

He rounded the corner to see his latest business problem standing in the sky-lit rotunda foyer, clutching a patterned handbag against an ivory, tailored coatdress. Her shoulder-length, chestnut hair was tucked behind her ears and pulled sleek by a pair of sunglasses perched atop her head. Her lashes were dark against coffee-toned eyes, her lips were shaded a lustrous pink, and diamond studs twinkled against her earlobes. She was immaculately made-up and clearly nervous.

That could be a good sign, or it could be a bad sign.

"Emma." Alex held out his hand, deciding to pretend they hadn't parted on sarcastic terms.

"Alex," she nodded with a brief, brusque shake.

"Would you care to come in?" he asked, gesturing toward the hallway.

She peered suspiciously down the wide corridor.

"To my study," he elaborated. "We might be more comfortable there."

After a second's hesitation, Emma nodded. "All right. Thanks."

"Not a problem." He waited until she was beside him, then fell into step.

"How was traffic?" he asked, instantly regretting the impulse to make small talk. He wasn't nervous. He was cool as a cucumber when it came to business deals. And this one was no different than any other.

If she said no, she said no. He'd either change her mind or come up with plan B. Ryan was making way too much of this wedding thing, anyway. Alex's future didn't depend on Ms. McKinley's whims.

His study was back to being immaculate, as he knew it would be. The newspaper had been folded and placed in the front center of the desk. Alex knew he should sit behind it, putting himself in a position of power. But instead he touched one of the wing chairs clustered around the stone fireplace, gesturing for Emma to sit down.

She nodded her thanks, sinking into the chair and crossing one shapely leg over the other. She smoothed her ivory skirt and tucked the frivolous handbag in beside her.

Then she folded both her hands over her slender knees and looked up.

He quickly cleared his head of the picture her legs made and sat down across from her.

"Traffic was fine," she said.

He nodded, telling himself to get straight down to business. "And you've made up your mind?"

She drew back ever so slightly. Then she nodded. "Yes. I have."

He cocked his head. "And?"

She twisted a sapphire-and-emerald band around her right ring finger. "I'll marry you."

She sounded like she was agreeing to the gallows.

Well, it wasn't going to be any picnic for him either. He was about to saddle himself with a reluctant wife, curtailing his social life, curtailing his sex life and, given her current expression and body language, conjugal relations weren't going to be any part of this union.

Which meant he was celibate. For the duration. Wasn't that just wonderful.

"Thank you," he forced out.

She gave a sharp nod and made to rise.

"Wait."

She arched a brow.

"You don't think we have more to discuss?"

"What's to discuss?" she asked. But she did sit back in the chair and recross her legs.

"For starters, who do you *absolutely* have to tell?"

"That I'm marrying you?"

He shook his head. "That it's a fake."

"Oh."

"Yeah. That part. My business partners know."

"My sister knows."

"Anyone else?"

"My lawyer." It was her turn to sit forward. "You can expect a call from him on the prenup."

Alex coughed out a laugh. "You want a prenup?"

"Of course."

"You check my net worth in *Forbes* last year?" A prenup protected him a whole lot more than it protected her.

The expression in her brown eyes was more than a little judgmental. "Of course not. I couldn't care less about your net worth."

He found that somewhat hard to believe. But, whatever. The important thing was to get this farce moving along. "First thing we have to do is get engaged."

"I thought we just did that."

He opened his mouth, but she kept talking.

"You said 'marry me or I'll bankrupt you.' And I decided to take the lesser of two evils." Her pretty lips pursed. "And, you know, I really don't think it gets any more romantic than that."

Sarcasm? She was getting millions of dollars, while he was accepting an inferior business deal for the sake of his reputation, and she was handing out sass?

"You're not very grateful, are you?" he asked.

"Your blackmail victims are usually grateful?"

He shook his head in disbelief. So much for Emma being panicked and intimidated. "You were expecting champagne and flowers?"

"I was hoping for a bank loan and a good actuary."

"Well, you got me instead."

She nodded slowly, peering down her delicate nose at him. "That I did."

This bickering wasn't getting them anywhere. Alex stood, shaking off his restless energy. "If we're going to make this work, there are a few things we'll have to do up front."

"Like learn to tolerate each other?"

"Like convince the press we're in love."

Emma's lips slowly curved into a grin. First time he'd actually seen her smile. It gave her eyes a golden glow and put a dimple in her right cheek. And when the tip of her tongue touched her front teeth, he felt a jolt of desire right down to his toes.

At this rate, he was going to have to rethink which sister was the pretty one.

"What?" he asked, tamping down the unwarranted reaction.

"I've now figured out the difference between us."

Alex squinted. Had he missed something?

"I'm firmly grounded in reality, while you dare to dream the impossible."

He wouldn't have put it quite that way, but true enough.

"I think we can probably learn to tolerate each other," she continued. "I don't see how we could convince anyone we're in love."

Alex took a pace forward, catching the scent of her perfume, tamping down yet another jolt of desire. This was crazy. He couldn't be attracted to Emma. He wouldn't *let* himself be attracted to Emma.

"You know your biggest problem?" he asked.

She stood up, but he still had eight inches on her. "No, but I bet you're going to tell me."

"It's your defeatist attitude."

"Actually, my biggest problem is you."

"Sweetheart, I am your salvation."

"Humble, aren't we?"

"When you work hard and pay attention, you don't need to be humble." He inched closer, dropping his voice. "There are only six people in the world who know I'm not in love with you. I'm about to convince the rest."

"The *entire* world?" She arched a sassy brow.

"You need to think big, Emma."

"You need to think realistically, Alex."

"They're not mutually exclusive."

"Statistically? I believe they are."

"Then you need to be the exception." Alex grinned to himself. He could give back as much sass as he got. "And, Emma, *my darling,* I am exceptional."

She eloquently rolled her eyes. "Can I get something in the prenup prohibiting your ego?"

"Only if your lawyer's a whole lot better than mine."

She took a half pace back. "So that's your big plan? We gaze adoringly at each other in public, while our lawyers duke it out in the back room?"

He gestured for her to sit back down. "That pretty much covers it. Now, back to our engagement."

She sat down and her chest rose and fell beneath the tailored dress. "I assume we're talking about a very ostentatious ring?"

"Absolutely." He eased down into his own chair. He'd been giving this some thought. In the event, of course, that one of them said yes. "Thing is, we don't want them talking about *if* we're engaged. We want them talking about *how* we got engaged."

Emma paused. "I'm not going to like this, am I?"

"You a Yankees fan?"

She shook her head, and he could see the exact second she got his point.

Her brown eyes went round, and her complexion paled a shade. "No. Oh, no. Not the *JumboTron.*"

"It'd make a splash."

"I'd have to kill you."

"Bad plan. You wouldn't be in my will yet."

"You may not have noticed, but Katie does the McKinley publicity. She's the extrovert."

"If you'll recall, I *did* try to marry Katie."

Emma's expression tightened for a split second, and he realized his words might have sounded like an insult.

"She's taken," Emma declared. "Deal with it."

"I didn't mean—"

"Sure you did. No JumboTron. Got it?"

Alex hadn't meant he preferred Katie. He didn't care one way or the other. But another denial would be overkill. And it would probably just tick Emma off.

"How about if I surprise you?" he asked instead. "Add a bit of realism to the situation."

"This is silly," said Emma, straightening in her chair and getting all prim and proper on him. "We should be talking about the business merger. Who cares how we get engaged?"

Had she missed his point entirely? This whole thing was all about his reputation and his image.

"I care," he stated flatly. Sass was one thing, but she needed to understand his interests. "You're getting one sweetheart of a monetary deal, and I'm getting some good PR. The *how* matters. The *ruse* matters."

She opened her mouth to rebut, but he was done debating.

"Make no mistake about it, Emma. You and I are going to convince the world we've fallen in love or die trying."

"I don't know how I'm going to do it," Emma said to Katie as they walked off court number twelve at Club Connecticut. Distracted by Alex's plan, she'd lost decisively to her sister, game, set and match.

She wasn't an actress. And she wasn't a public person. While some hotel socialites hit the club scene and made the front pages of the tabloid press, Emma jealously guarded her privacy.

"Is he being a real jerk?" asked Katie, sympathy in her voice as she gestured to an empty umbrella table with four white deck chairs.

"No jerkier than we expected," said Emma honestly. "Problem is, he's got this whole fantasy, fool-the-press thing planned. And I'm definitely not up for playing the simpering Wall Street bride."

Katie frowned for a minute as she took her seat. "Well, I suppose he has to get something out of it."

"He's getting our hotels."

"Only half."

Emma raised her eyebrows at her sister. Did Katie honestly think Alex was being reasonable? "We promised him a wife, not a trophy bride for the front page."

Katie shrugged. "So he wants to show you off a little. Why not go with the flow?"

Emma peeled off her sweatband and shook out her hair. "Because the flow will be trite and embarrassing. And, if you'll recall, the flow is also one very big lie."

Katie smirked. "No harm in looking good while you're lying."

Emma pulled a bottle of water out of the acrylic ice bucket in the center of the table. "Quit laughing at me."

"I'm sorry. It's just—"

"That it's me and not you?"

Katie's tone changed. "Of course not. I'm grateful. You know I'm grateful."

Emma sighed. "I have to find a way to convince him to keep this low-key. A justice of the peace. A small announcement in the classified section."

Katie reached for a bottle of water, cracking the cap. "Or I could lend you some clothes and you could hit the party circuit on his arm."

"You're not helping."

"Wouldn't hurt you to get out and about. You know you work too hard."

"Not hard enough to save the company."

"Hey, you're saving the company now."

Emma sat back in her chair. She wasn't saving the company through her guile and business acumen, that was for sure. "It feels like prostitution."

"Without the sex?"

"Without the sex."

"Then it's not prostitution, is it? Lighten up, Emma. We'll go to Saks."

"Oh, yeah. Saks will solve the problem." Because as long as Emma had the right wardrobe, she could easily prance through uptown Manhattan casting mooning looks in Alex's direction.

She shuddered.

"Oh my," Katie muttered, her attention shifting to a spot over Emma's shoulder.

"Oh my, what?"

"He's here."

"Who's here?" Emma twisted her neck, trying to get a look.

"Alex," said Katie.

Emma froze. *"What?"*

"Alex is here."

She turned to face Katie. "He's not a member."

"Maybe not."

"It's a private club."

"Like the desk clerk's going to tell Alex Garrison he can't have a day pass."

Emma's chest tightened to a tingle. "What's he doing?"

"Coming this way."

"No."

Katie nodded. "Yes." Then she smiled broadly. "Hello, Alex."

Emma felt a warm palm come to rest on her bare, sweaty shoulder. Her muscles hummed beneath the touch, jumping to some bizarre rhythm. Like she'd never been touched by a man before.

She resisted the urge to shrug him off.

"Hi, sweetheart," Alex's voice rumbled in her ear.

Then his lips branded her temple, and the breath whooshed right out of her body. In fact, it was a light, insubstantial touch, but it jump-started her pulse and sent her nerve endings into a frenzy.

She had to tell herself in no uncertain terms to *calm the heck down.*

Giving her shoulder a final squeeze, he eased his big body into the vacant chair next to her and casually helped himself to a bottle of water. "So, how was the game?"

He was wearing a white polo shirt with a single blue stripe over one shoulder. The open collar showed off his strong neck and tanned skin, while the knit weave delineated his broad shoulders and well-defined pecs.

When Emma didn't answer, he raised a dark brow in her direction.

"Fine," she ground out. Now that she was starting to recover, her anger was bubbling up. A kiss at Club Connecticut was almost as bad as the JumboTron. And Alex knew it. The stares from the surrounding table were penetrating.

He nodded easily. "Good."

"I took her in straight sets," said Katie, her tone far too friendly for Emma's liking.

Emma leaned closer to Alex. "I thought we were going to *talk* about this?" she hissed.

He draped an arm casually over the back of her chair. "I'm through talking," he said.

"Well, I'm not."

"Really? That's unfortunate." He glanced around. "Because I think it's too late."

"Cheat," Emma muttered, knowing he'd won through brute force. At least a dozen people had seen that *oh so calculated* kiss.

Alex laughed. Then he raised his voice and looked at Katie. "Congratulations on the win."

Katie grinned in return. "Emma seemed to be having trouble concentrating this morning."

"Really?" Alex gave her shoulder another annoying squeeze, and her body responded with another annoying crackle. She didn't like it. She refused to like it. It had to be revulsion, because it couldn't be anything else.

"Have anything to do with last night?" he asked her loud and clear.

Two tables away, Marion Thurston's stenciled eyebrows shot to her dyed hairline. It seemed to take the woman a moment to gather her wits, but then she reached for a cell phone and hit a speed dial button. It didn't take a rocket scientist to figure out who she'd called. It was a very poorly kept secret that Marion Thurston fed stories to society columnist Leanne Height.

Emma leaned close to Alex again. "I am definitely going to kill you."

"You're still not in the will."

"I no longer care."

Alex laughed again. "Are you busy tomorrow night?" He looked at Katie. "You, too. I booked a table for the Teddybear Trust casino event."

"I don't gamble," said Emma.

"Well, it's time you learned," he said easily.

"I'm in," said Katie. "Is there room for David?"

"Ahhh. The elusive David."

"I don't want to learn," Emma grumbled.

"Blackjack," said Alex. "I'll bankroll you."

"You're not going to—"

His voice turned steely. "I'll bankroll you."

"Fine. You want to put a tattoo on my forehead while you're at it?"

He lifted her hand for a fleeting kiss, his gentle voice at odds with the steely look in his eyes. "No. Just a diamond on your finger."

"We've got trouble on the wedding front," said Ryan, plunking down in a guest chair in Alex's office.

Alex looked up from the McKinley Inns prospectus. "What kind of trouble?"

"The kind that starts with one archrival DreamLodge and ends with Kayven Island."

An adrenaline shot hit Alex's system. "Old man Murdoch knows about Kayven?"

"He has to," said Ryan, sitting forward in the leather chair. "There's no other explanation."

Dread crept through Alex's system. "For what?"

"He's putting together a bid for McKinley."

"Son of a bitch." Alex rocked to his feet, the possibilities winging through his mind. "The whole chain?"

Ryan stood with him. "Just the Kayven property."

Alex closed his eyes for a split second, wrapping his hand around the back of his neck and squeezing hard. "And the women would keep the rest?" It was a dream come true for Emma.

"Yeah," said Ryan.

"How long've we got?"

"He's presenting the offer start of business Monday."

"Who's your source?"

"Adam down in accounting mentioned that his brother-in-law over at Williamson Smythe was looking at the same geologicals as we were."

"He put it together from *that?*"

Ryan shook his head. "Adam doesn't know a thing. I pieced it together myself from six different sources. We're still the only player with the big picture."

Alex's mind clicked through potential scenarios. All of them ended with a DreamLodge win and a Garrison loss. "I can't let him make that offer."

Ryan nodded.

Alex had to shut Murdoch down. So how did he shut Murdoch down before Monday morning? Marry Emma was the obvious answer. "I wonder how she feels about Vegas...."

"You can't marry Emma in the next forty-eight hours."

Alex snorted. "The jet's at JFK—I could marry her in less than five."

"You don't think a quickie Vegas wedding would look *slightly* opportunistic?"

Alex's voice rose. "I'd rather look opportunistic than screw the whole deal."

"And what happens when Murdoch talks to her?"

"By the time Murdoch talks to her, she'll be Mrs. Alex Garrison."

Ryan shook his head. "Not good enough. We don't want Murdoch talking to her at all."

"We can't stop him from talking to her." It was a free country, and DreamLodge owned as many communication devices as anybody else.

Ryan eased back down in his chair, resting one ankle on the opposite knee. "We can if he thinks there's no point in talking to her."

"There are hundreds of millions at stake."

"Yeah," Ryan agreed quietly. "And we're going to make him think it's all ours."

Alex recognized the cunning gleam in Ryan's eyes. A renewed calm came over him, and he took his seat behind the desk, picking up a gold pen to twirl between his fingertips. "How?"

"We need four things," said Ryan.

Alex was all ears. There was a reason he'd taken Ryan on as a partner. The man was a strategic genius.

"McKinley's financial statements," said Ryan. "Some serious intel on DreamLodge, a quick and dirty marketing mock-up, and a diamond ring on Emma McKinley's finger."

Alex could take care of the ring and the marketing plan. He supposed he could come up with some kind of rational explanation for wanting Emma's financial statements over the weekend. But he didn't have a single contact at DreamLodge. "What kind of intel?"

Ryan hesitated for a single beat. "Can you call Nathaniel?"

Alex blinked at the sound of his cousin's name. "That's a pretty big gun."

"There are hundreds of millions at stake."

Right. Nathaniel it was.

Three

Emma slipped a thick, white McKinley-crested robe over her damp body, slipping on her glasses and flicking back a wisp of hair that had escaped from her clip. The hot tub motor whirred softly in the background as she padded across the penthouse from her bedroom to the living area.

She'd long since gotten past the strangeness of living in a hotel. Now she just enjoyed the view, the expert cleaning service and the convenience of hot meals at any hour of the day or night. McKinley's head offices were on the third floor of the Fifth Avenue Inn. So on blustery winter days, she was only an elevator ride from work.

She pushed the on button on the television remote and curled up in one corner of the wine-colored sectional sofa, tossing a brocade pillow out of the way. It was eleven-fifteen, Friday night. She'd skipped dinner, and she was thinking a cheese tray and a glass of Cabernet would go well with *Business Week Wrap-up* on ANN.

She called an order in to the concierge, then settled back to watch Marvin Coventry interview the CEO of Mediterranean Energy. The company was under scrutiny following a merger with a British company and an alleged payout to a UN envoy's nephew.

A knock sounded a few minutes into the interview, and Emma watched over her shoulder as she headed for the door to let in Korissa.

"Did they remember to add extra grapes?" she asked, while the CEO squirmed under the reporter's questions. Good. His shareholders deserved an explanation.

"I have no idea," came a male voice.

Emma twisted her head to come face to face with Alex Garrison. Her eyes went wide, and she jerked the lapels of her robe together. "I thought you were Korissa."

"I'm Alex." His gaze took in her robe, her haphazard hair and her clunky glasses.

"What are you *doing* here?" She hadn't expected to see him again until tomorrow night at the Teddybear Trust fundraiser, and she definitely wasn't ready to go another round with him. She tugged at her lapels, especially not dressed like this.

He glanced down at the briefcase in his left hand. "I thought you'd like to see my financial records."

"At eleven-thirty at *night?*"

"You said you wanted a prenup."

Sure she wanted a prenup. But not *now*. Right now she wanted to sleep, and to regroup before facing him again. "I'm not—"

"No time like the present." He glanced pointedly at the room behind her, then shifted almost imperceptibly forward.

Emma stepped sideways to block his path as the nearly soundless whirr of a room service cart announced Korissa's arrival.

The woman halted her brisk steps and glanced questioningly at Alex. "Shall I bring another glass?"

"That would be nice," said Alex. And before Emma could protest, he slipped through the door beside her.

Emma wasn't about to make a scene in front of Korissa, but the man was *not* staying. She moved out of the way of the cart.

"Nice," Alex murmured, glancing around at the Persian carpet, the marble fireplace and the Tiffany chandelier.

"Thank you," Emma said stiffly, while Korissa transferred the cheese tray, wine and fresh flowers to the dining table.

Then Korissa left the penthouse and closed the door behind her.

Emma yanked the sash of her robe tight. "This is not a convenient time."

He set the briefcase down on the dining table and held up his palms in surrender. "I apologize. But I just got out of a meeting."

His gaze seemed to snag on her outfit once again.

"I take it you had a free evening?"

"No, I did *not* have a free evening. I had a conference call, three supply contracts to approve and an accounting meeting that lasted past ten."

"But you're free now." He opened up the case.

She stared pointedly down at her robe. "Do I look free?"

He fought a grin. "You look…"

"Forget it."

"I was going to say cute."

"You were going to say awful."

His brow furrowed for a split second. "Why do you always—"

"What do you want, Alex?"

He shook his head, then he lifted an envelope from his briefcase. "I want to swap financial statements."

"Call me in the morning." She wanted to sleep. Nothing more, nothing less.

"I'm booked up all day."

"Well, I'm booked up all night."

He stilled. His glance shot to her bedroom door. "You have company?"

It took a moment for his meaning to set in. Of all the nerve. "*No,* I do not *have company.*"

"I thought maybe you were having a final fling."

"I'm not a final fling kind of girl."

He checked her out one more time. "Really?"

"And if I was, would I dress like this?"

"I told you, you look cute."

She groaned in frustration.

He abandoned his briefcase and moved toward her. "Seriously, Emma. I don't know where all this insecurity comes from."

She had no idea how to respond to that. Zero.

His voice went soft. "You're a beautiful woman."

"Stop it," she rasped. He was obviously practicing his lines, spinning his lies, trying to put her off balance for his own reasons.

He came to a halt directly in front of her, the intensity of his perusal causing waves of reaction through her body. "Don't sell yourself short, Emma."

She tried to breathe normally, tried to squelch the unmistakable creep of desire working its way along her limbs. "You have…surprising taste."

His mouth curved into a slow grin.

It was a smooth mouth, a shapely mouth, a very sexy mouth, set under a luminous laserlike gaze that surrounded a woman and made her feel like the only person on the planet. Emma felt herself being dragged under his spell.

"You think I prefer silk and satin?" he asked softly.

"I think you'd prefer black lace and heels." As soon as she spoke, she regretted the impulse.

His nostrils flared ever so slightly. *"Really?"* And his eyes telegraphed his thoughts.

"Not on *me.*"

He glanced at her cleavage. "Why not?"

This was getting crazy. "Alex."

He nodded to her bedroom door. "You got something back there I might like?"

God help her, she did. A little teddy and matching panties that Katie had bought her on her birthday.

Not that Alex would ever see them.

A trace of laughter rumbled deep in his chest. "Still waters run deep?"

"I have nothing," she lied.

He reached up and smoothed a stray lock of her hair. "Sure you do. Go ahead, Emma. Let me in on your deep, dark secret."

She blinked into the polished obsidian of his eyes, steeling herself against his pull, promising herself she wouldn't let him take control of their relationship. She needed to stay strong. She needed to stay focused. She had something he wanted, and the transfer was going to be on *her* terms.

But then his palm paused on her temple, distracting her thoughts. His fingertips brushed her hair, and every reluctant nerve in her body zeroed in on his point of contact, zinging hormonal messages that flushed her skin and softened her lips, and pushed her body in toward him.

His hand slipped down to her neck, cupping her hairline, pulling her slowly, inexorably toward him. His head tipped to one side, and she followed his lead, accommodating his advance, waiting, wondering, coming up on her toes in anticipation.

Then he stopped. She felt his hesitation as if it were her own. *Yes,* her primal brain screamed. *No,* her rational mind answered.

His breath puffed against her skin. "My own deep, dark secret is…" He paused. "That I…" Another pause. "Want…" Then he sighed. "Your financial statements."

The words were a dose of cold water.

And she was glad.

Truly.

Kissing Alex would have been a supremely stupid move. Not that she wouldn't be forced to kiss him at some point during this escapade. But it didn't have to be in her apartment, while they were alone, while she was half-naked.

What was she *thinking?*

She pulled determinedly away. "Okay. But then you do have to go."

He gave her a sharp nod of agreement, blinking away a funny glow that simmered deep in his quick-silver eyes.

She wasn't going to explore that glow. She wasn't even going to think about that glow. This was business.

All *business,* she told herself as she crossed to her computer. She clicked a link to the financial server and brought up the last quarter rollups, hitting the print button.

Alex watched in silence as the printer whirred to life and rapidly spit out twenty pages.

She scooped them from the tray and briskly handed them over.

"Thank you," he said, as he reached for the doorknob.

"You're welcome," she replied, calculating the seconds until he'd be gone.

But then he paused, and his flinty eyes narrowed. His lips parted. "Emma—"

"Good night," she prompted with finality.

He sucked a breath between his teeth, but he didn't persist. Instead, he gave a brief nod of resignation. "Good night."

And then he was gone. She twisted the door lock behind him, her fingers clamping hard on the metal bolt. Okay *that*— whatever it was—could *not* happen again.

She'd made a deal with Alex. It was no different than her staffing the front desk in Hawaii or taking a stint as a cocktail waitress in Whistler. Her father had always been proud of Emma's ability to roll up her sleeves and pitch in.

In this case, maybe she was rolling up her lips. But it was the same thing. She'd kiss Alex eventually, but it would be a business kiss. It would be for show, and it sure wouldn't happen while they were alone and she was half naked and lusting after his body.

She shivered, stepping back from the door, telling herself she was doing exactly what her father would have done. She was making the best of a bad situation.

When her mother died, and he was left with two bereft little girls, he'd picked himself up and dusted himself off. He'd learned to braid their hair, wallpaper their rooms and bake chocolate chip oatmeal monster cookies. When their Montreal hotel burned to the ground, he'd made the best of that, too. With fearless, un-flagging optimism, he'd buried his remorse, swept up the ashes and rallied the troops.

Well, Emma could be fearless. And she could bury whatever knee-jerk hormones were messing with her reaction to Alex. She'd make her father proud or die trying.

Emma was on guard Saturday night.

When they pulled into Tavern on the Green, she waited until Alex stepped out of the limo before she moved across the back seat. Mindful of the reporters waiting on the other side of the red rope line, she smoothed her champagne cocktail dress, and readied herself for a graceful exit.

Next to the open door, Alex turned to face her. He gallantly offered his hand, and she bit back a protest. She didn't want to touch him at all, definitely not first thing. But there was no way to refuse the invitation.

Surrounded by the tiny white tree lights and the glowing lanterns of the portcullis, she took a breath and reached out. As soon as their fingertips made contact, a warm glow whooshed up her arm. She smiled bravely as cameras flashed in all direc-tions.

Her gaze caught on Alex's soft, gray eyes. But she quickly blinked her attention away as he played out his role for the cameras. She tried to appear adoring without actually looking at his face—bad enough he was holding her hand. Bad enough she was imagining some cosmic connection between them as they strode the gauntlet of reporters firing questions.

Then Alex wrapped an arm around her waist and brought her to a halt for the photographers. They were pressed together, from knee to shoulder, and she could feel every single breath he took.

"Act like you adore me," he muttered under his breath.

"I'm trying," she returned, holding a smile, cursing her traitorous body that was cataloguing every nuance of Alex.

"Try harder." He gave the photographers a final wave, then propelled her toward the entrance.

Emma resisted the pressure of his hand on the small of her back. "Katie and David were right behind us."

"They can catch up."

"But—"

"Until you become a better actress, we're not standing around for the paparazzi."

"I'm smiling, already."

"That's a grimace."

"That's because I'm in pain."

His arm immediately slacked off. "I'm hurting you?"

"Mental anguish." And that wasn't a lie.

"Give me a break." He resumed the pressure on the small of her back as a balding man in a finely cut suit stepped forward to greet them.

"Mr. Garrison," said the man with obvious enthusiasm. "So very good of you to join us."

"Good evening, Maxim," said Alex, reaching out to shake hands. "May I present my um, girlfriend, Emma McKinley."

His voice softened ever so slightly over her name. Emma's heart tripped for a split second, while Maxim did a double take.

"Maxim is the chairman of Teddybear Trust," Alex explained.

The burly man smiled broadly as he reached for Emma's hand. "And you're the president of McKinley Inns. We haven't met. But I've heard a good deal about you, Ms. McKinley."

"Please, call me Emma." Her smile was genuine now. "I have the utmost respect for the Teddybear Trust."

The foundation had built a new children's wing at St. Xavier's last year, and they'd funded countless pediatric cancer research projects.

"This way," said Maxim, gesturing through the cut glass doorway to the Tavern on the Green foyer. "Drinks are in the Terrace Room. And might I suggest the Pavilion as a starting point for casino games?"

"Blackjack?" asked Alex, tossing Maxim a wry grin.

Maxim grinned back. "Last year was unfortunate for you." Then he winked at Emma. "But I know you'll bring him good luck tonight."

"I'll try my best," she promised Maxim, thinking that karmic forces might not be so quick to reward them for lying to the entire city.

Then Alex recaptured her hand and nodded to the doorman as he placed a quick kiss on her knuckles. Emma struggled to keep her head clear as they crossed into the richly decorated entry. The lobby was festooned with fine crystal and stained glass, while magnificent chandeliers refracted light as they started their way through the winding hallways.

She caught their reflection in a beveled mirror, shivering at the image of Alex, straight and tall, his strong hand resting on the small of her back, only a hair below the plunging V of her sparkling dress.

"Would you care for a drink?" His deep voice rumbled through her.

"A Chablis," she replied, then cleared her throat against the sultry sound. They were playacting here. He was pretending to be her date for the benefit of the reporters and the other patrons. And she was pretending to like him for exactly the same end.

She dragged her gaze away from the mirror and vowed to ignore every facet of his sex appeal. She needed to get a grip here.

He pointed to a doorway. "Through there, then."

They entered the Crystal Pavilion, catching the obviously curious glances of other guests.

Did they recognize Alex? Did they recognize her? She craned her neck, looking behind her for her sister's reassuring face. "We've lost Katie and David."

"We don't need a chaperone."

"But—"

"Tonight's about you and me." He smiled, nodded and waved a greeting to someone across the room.

They stopped next to the bar, and Alex rested a forearm on the polished top, giving the waiter their order before turning his attention to Emma. "You should try to relax and enjoy yourself."

Emma couldn't imagine relaxing under these circumstances. She couldn't imagine relaxing around Alex at all.

"In a few minutes you get to start spending my money," he said.

"I've never gambled in my life." She didn't mean it to sound snippy, but it came out that way.

"Somehow that doesn't surprise me." He snagged a handful of nuts from a crystal bowl on the bar and tossed them in his mouth.

"What's that supposed to mean?"

"It means you're way too conservative."

The waiter set the drinks down on Teddybear Trust coasters.

"I am not," Emma insisted.

Alex stuffed a bill in the tip snifter and nodded his thanks to the man. "Are too," he chuckled low to Emma as they walked away.

She huffed out a breath.

"You can prove me wrong, you know." He handed her the glass of Chablis, gently steering her back to the hallway. "Just belly on up to the blackjack table and make sure everyone knows I'm bankrolling you."

She took a sip of the crisp wine and let the alcohol ease into her system. "Is that what the modern urban male does for the woman he loves?"

"Since it's no longer practical to slay you a mastodon. Yeah. That's what we do."

She hid an unexpected grin behind another sip of the wine. "What if I want the mastodon instead?"

"Are you going high maintenance on me?"

"Apparently."

He pointed to another entryway. "Through here to the tables."

"Truthfully, I don't know how to play blackjack."

He shrugged. "It's easy."

Beyond the glass wall, lighted gardens spread out before them, lanterns swaying in the breeze as the well-dressed guests mingled from the restaurant to the patio and back again. The dealers, dressed in black jackets and bow ties, chatted with the guests as they doled out the cards.

Alex steered her toward a green felt table with high chairs and small white squares printed on the fabric.

"Hop up," he whispered against her ear, and she tried not to react to his nearness.

But then his arm casually brushed her bare back, raising goose bumps and sending pulses of energy to very inappropriate spots on her body.

"There you are." Katie's voice interrupted the moment. "This is fabulous!"

"Fabulous," Emma echoed, grateful for the buffer.

Katie hopped up next to Emma. There were already two men

at the opposite end, of the table facing the dealer. That left one empty seat in the middle.

David stood behind Katie's chair, and Emma gave him a smile.

"Buy me some chips," Katie told him.

In her peripheral vision, Emma saw Alex place some bills on the table in front of the dealer.

"I thought we were going to the roulette wheel," David said to Katie.

Katie patted the tabletop. "I want to play blackjack."

The dealer slid four stacks of purple chips in front of Emma. She half turned to Alex. "What do I do now?" she whispered.

She could almost feel his smile. She inhaled his scent, and the fabric of his suit gently touched her bare back.

"Make a bet," he whispered back. "Put it in the white square."

The man at the far end bet two green chips, and the other bet a black one.

"What are the colors?" she asked Alex.

"Don't worry about it."

The dealer placed stacks of black chips in front of Katie.

Emma pushed two purple ones into the square in front of her, and the dealer gave them each a face-up card.

She glanced at everyone's cards, wondering if the man had made a mistake. She leaned back to talk to Alex. "They can see—"

"It's okay. You're only playing the dealer."

"Well, the dealer can see what I've got," she hissed. How was that fair?

"Trust me."

Emma tipped her head to look into his eyes. Trust him? Was he kidding? He'd made it clear last night—somewhere between gross revenue and capital depreciation—that he was looking out for his own interests. In fact, he'd strongly advised her to do the same.

Of course, in this case, it was his money. Who cared if she lost?

"Emma?"

"Hmmm?"

He nodded at the table. "Look at your hand."

She glanced down. A queen and an ace.

"You won," he said as the dealer pushed a couple of chips into her square.

"Hit me," said Katie next to her.

Even though it was just luck, a warm glow of pride grew in Emma's chest. She'd won. Her very first time gambling, and she'd won. Whatever happened from here on in, at least she had that.

"Bust," sighed Katie, while David shook his head.

The dealer cleared the cards.

"Bet more this time," said Alex.

Emma stacked another chip in her square.

"It's going to be a long night at this rate," Alex breathed.

"Why don't you do it then?"

He leaned in closer, his hand sliding up to her bare shoulder. "Because we want the world to see *me* spending a lot of money on *you*, remember?"

She turned so that her nose almost contacted his cheek. His spicy scent surrounded her, and his broad palm moved ever so slightly against her shoulder. It would be so easy to sink into this fantasy.

She reached for her wine. "How about if you bet my money instead?"

He chuckled. "Doesn't work that way. Now bet."

"You're such a chauvinist."

"Yeah, I am. Get used to it." He straightened, ending the conversation.

Fine. He wanted to bankroll her? Emma moved an entire stack of chips into the white square. *Take that, Alex Garrison.*

"That a girl," he said.

"Holy crap, Emma," said Katie.

Emma turned to her sister.

"That's ten thousand dollars."

"What?" Emma nearly swallowed her tongue.

The first card landed in front of her.

"Those are five-hundred-dollar chips," Katie pointed out.

Emma's stomach contracted. She quickly reached for the stack of chips, but Alex stopped her by putting his hand over hers.

"Too late," he warned.

She turned to stare at him, her eyes wide in horror. She couldn't bet ten thousand dollars on a hand of cards. That was nuts.

"Play the game," he calmly advised.

"Why didn't you *tell* me?"

"Tell you what?"

"Alex."

"Play the game."

"No way." She started to rise, but her hand was trapped by his.

"You won," he said.

"What?"

He nodded to her cards. "You won again. You really should gamble more often."

Emma slowly looked down at her hand, a ten and an ace. She gave in to her wobbly knees and sat back down on the stool.

"Bust," said Katie.

David shifted behind her.

"How much did you lose?" Emma asked her sister. David didn't look too happy about this.

"Five hundred dollars."

Emma cringed. "Ouch."

Katie tossed two more chips in her square.

"I think we should move to roulette," David suggested.

"This is fun," said Katie. "We're having fun. Aren't we, Emma?"

"I'm having fun," said Alex, a definite edge of laughter to his voice.

David's nostrils flared as he drew in a deep breath.

The dealer passed out the cards.

"You know you just let fifteen thousand dollars ride?" asked Katie.

Emma's gaze flew to her chips. Good God. Why hadn't Alex stopped her?

After a long, tense minute, she won with a three-card nineteen. She immediately swiveled her chair sideways. "I can't take this anymore."

Alex trapped the chair with one knee to keep it from recoiling. "You're winning."

Their legs touched, and the warmth of his body seeped into her thigh. "I'm having a heart attack," she told him. And it was definitely on more than one front.

She started to climb off the high stool, and he quickly offered a hand to steady her. "You don't walk away from a hot streak."

"Watch me."

She shifted. Whoops. She hadn't counted on being all but trapped in his arms. A half step forward and she'd be pressed up against him. If she tipped her head, they could kiss. Or she could bury her face in his neck and flick out her tongue to see if he tasted as good as he smelled.

Of course she didn't. But the desire was strong. So was the image.

He watched her with those smoky eyes for a long moment. "Okay." He finally said. "Ever played craps?"

"No."

"Good." Then he gestured toward the hallway, putting an end to the intimate moment. "Craps tables are in the Chestnut Room."

She turned to Katie. "Are you coming?"

"Not for craps," said David.

Katie peered at her boyfriend's expression. "We'll catch up," she told them.

Emma nodded. Then she began walking with Alex. "Can we at least switch to ten-dollar chips?"

"No."

"I can't bet five hundred dollars at a time."

Alex might be comfortable with a high-rolling, high-stakes lifestyle. But she sure wasn't.

"You're already up several thousand," he said.

That was true. She felt a little better. She could lose all this, and he'd still be even.

"If you don't start losing soon," Alex continued. "The Teddybear Trust will be bankrupt."

Emma stopped, and her mouth formed a spontaneous O. She'd forgotten all about the Teddybear Trust. "I'm doing this all wrong, aren't I?"

Alex chuckled, his hand going to her back to get her going again. "I'll say."

She gave a sigh of frustration.

Then, unexpectedly, his lips brushed her temple. "You're delightful, you know that?"

Her chest contracted around the compliment.

But then Edwina and Fredrick Waddington materialized next to Alex, and she realized the compliment was part of the ruse. Everything about tonight was part of the ruse. Alex wasn't an easygoing, philanthropic businessman. He was only playing his part.

She forced out a smile as he performed the introductions. No more fantasy. No more intimacy. No more physical reactions. From this minute on, she was remembering it was a game.

Four

No matter how hard Emma tried, she couldn't seem to lose. A crowd had gathered around one of the craps tables, and every time she attempted to pass the dice, they'd erupt in a torrent of protest, shoving them back into her hands.

She took a deep breath.

Standing behind her, Alex rubbed her shoulders. "With a bet like that, you're either going to save the charity or buy us a new hotel."

She shook the dice up between her hands. "We don't need a new hotel. This is getting embarrassing. Don't you see Maxim glaring at me?"

"He's not glaring at you."

Emma glanced surreptitiously at her host and watched him run a finger under the collar of his shirt. It was bad enough that she was winning. But the entire crowd was winning along with her.

"How do I lose?" she whispered to Alex.

"Roll a seven."

"Okay." She blew on the dice.

Alex chuckled at her theatrics, and she dug her elbow into his ribs.

"A little support, please," she breathed.

"Come on, seven," he rumbled in return. "You do know you'll lose two hundred grand."

"It's not my money."

"Yeah. It's mine." Despite his protest, he sounded completely unconcerned.

It wasn't his money anyway. It was the Teddybear Trust's money. And she was going to put it back where it belonged or die trying.

She tossed the dice. They scattered along the green felt table, bouncing amongst bets that probably totaled a surgical wing, hitting the far wall of the table, then rolling to a stop. A six and a one.

Delight zipped through her.

She'd done it.

"Quit grinning," Alex warned as the crowd groaned.

Right. The other betters were disappointed. She quickly hid her smile against Alex's chest.

His strong arms went around her, and he made a show of stroking her back.

Okay. So much for not reacting to his latent sensuality. Every fiber of her body was revving up in reaction to his heat.

"Don't worry," he said, loud enough for everyone else to hear. "It's only money. And it's for a good cause."

The groans and grumbles around them gradually turned to good-natured jokes. One man pointed out the tax benefits of their loss, while another suggested they'd all be on Teddybear Trust's Christmas card list this year.

Alex didn't seem to be in a hurry to let her go. No wonder.

He had a big audience here—a big audience that would soon start asking questions about their relationship.

Hugging was the smart thing to do. So for just a second, Emma stopped fighting. She relaxed into his strength and let the tension roll out of her body. Gambling was way too stressful, even when she was trying to lose.

Alex's palm smoothed her hair, while his lips touched the top of her head in a tender kiss. It felt way too good, and sirens went off in all corners of her brain.

She ignored them as long as she could. But finally she pulled back. Still, he kept one arm firmly around her waist. Although it went against her mental promise, she didn't try to disentangle herself.

Some of the players moved away from the table, and the stick man called for a new shooter.

Katie and David appeared from the crowd.

"How'd you do?" asked Katie.

"She lost all my money," said Alex with a playful squeeze.

"Well, it has gone to a good cause," Emma pointed out.

"You lost my entire thirty-thousand-dollar stake," said Alex.

She'd forgotten it was that much.

But one glance at his expression told her he didn't care. Certainly he didn't care. He wanted the whole world to know she was here on his dime.

That was the game. His *game,* she reminded herself, trying to ease out of his hold. "Take the tax deduction and quit complaining."

He resisted her pressure.

She tugged harder.

Alex just grinned at her.

"Ladies and gentlemen," Maxim's voice came over the sound system. "You're invited to take a break from the casino games and join us in the garden for a surprise, grand prize draw."

"The gardens are lovely," said Emma, pulling firmly out of Alex's grip and moving to safety beside her sister. "Let's go watch the draw."

"Thanks to the generosity of an anonymous donor," Maxim continued. "Our grand prize this year is a Mercedes-Benz convertible."

The crowd gave an appreciative *ahh*.

"Check the top right corner of your admission ticket for your lucky draw number."

Emma linked arms with Katie and they followed the flow of people moving toward the lighted greenery. She was trying to focus on the gardens, on Katie, on *anything* but Alex. Or, more to the point, on anything but her reaction to Alex.

"Is David okay?" she asked Katie, concentrating on how the oak trees sparkled with thousands of white lights and lines of lanterns glowed against colorful flower tubs and hanging baskets. The garden was absolutely breathtaking at night.

Katie shrugged her shoulders. "Why do you ask?"

Emma studied her sister's expression. "He seems quiet." David was normally joking and jovial. Kind of like how Alex was tonight.

Nope, wait. Not Alex. *Not* Alex.

"Maybe he thought I'd win," said Katie.

"How much did you lose?"

"A couple of thousand." Katie tossed her blond hair. "I really don't know what his problem is." Then she whistled low, pointing to the car. "Oh, baby. I can sure see myself cruising around the park in that."

"Not bad," Emma agreed, checking out the sleek lines of the silver convertible. The chrome shone, and the paint fairly glowed under the brilliance of the garden lights.

"Ladies and gentlemen," came Maxim's voice as he stepped up onto the dais next to the spectacular car. "I have to say, Teddybear Trust donors are the most generous people in the country!"

A cheer went up from the crowd.

He bobbed his head in acknowledgement of the gesture.

Then, as the applause died down, he reached into a crystal bowl, stirring the slips of paper around with great drama. "And…the winner of this gorgeous, brand-new Mercedes-Benz convertible is…number seven-thirty-two!"

Alex ruffled Emma's hair from behind. "That's mine," he murmured in her ear. Then he leaned up and winked. "I'll be right back."

Emma stared at his retreating back. "He won?" she asked out loud.

Katie stared at her for a moment, her blue eyes going wide. "He won!" she cried.

"I see we have a winner," called Maxim as he spotted Alex moving through the crowd. Alex stepped up smartly onto the stage and handed Maxim his ticket.

"Mr. Alex Garrison," Maxim announced after a cursory glance. "Tonight's winner, and one of Teddybear Trust's most valued sponsors."

Alex made a show of sizing up the car. Then he stepped up to the microphone at the small podium. "Lady luck is definitely with me tonight," he announced with a broad grin. "And I'm hoping she'll stick around for a few more minutes."

He turned to Maxim. "Many, many thanks to Maxim and all of the dedicated volunteers at Teddybear Trust." He paused, gazing at the car for another moment. "Although I'd dearly love to take this baby out for a spin on the expressway, I'm afraid that won't be possible."

The crowd went silent.

"Because I'm donating it back to Teddybear," said Alex. "For their September auction."

Applause burst out as Maxim stepped forward and clasped Alex's hand with both of his.

Emma couldn't help the surge of pride that rose in her chest. Act or not, Alex had just donated serious money to a good charity.

He turned back to the microphone. "If you'll be patient with me for another minute. There's one more thing I want to say." He cleared his throat. "I was only half joking about lady luck. Truth is, I attribute tonight's luck to one very special lady." He stepped back for a beat.

"Emma," he continued, nodding in her direction.

It was a little overboard as courtship went. But, okay. She could go along. He'd earned this one. She smiled warmly up at him, trying to look love-struck.

He grinned back, his obsidian eyes sparkling under the tree lights. "Emma, will you do me the honor… Will you marry me?"

Emma froze. Her stomach plummeted to the patio.

A collective gasp went up from the crowd, followed quickly by a smattering of applause that grew and grew, while heads turned her way.

This was as bad as the JumboTron. No, it was worse than the JumboTron. At least at a baseball game, she'd have some anonymity. Half the people here tonight knew her, or had known her father.

Katie nudged her, and she realized Alex was staring at her expectantly.

While she tried to form a coherent thought, he reached into his pocket and pulled out a small velvet box. He'd planned this, the rat.

He was the anonymous car donor. The entire evening of chivalry and philanthropy had been designed to back her into a corner.

"Emma, say something," Katie hissed.

"I can't," she whimpered under her breath.

"We made a deal with him," Katie reminded her.

Yes, they'd made a deal. But not for this. Not for such a ridiculous showy, sentimental display. Her reputation was at stake. And, besides, she'd specifically vetoed this very thing.

Katie gave her a slight shove toward the dais. "Get up there."

She wasn't going up there. She couldn't do it. Her feet had become concrete.

"Emma?" Alex singsonged in an overblown, adoring voice. The faker.

"Bankruptcy," whispered Katie in a warning tone.

Bankruptcy.

Emma forced one foot forward. Then she moved the other. Then she pasted a sickly-sweet smile on her face and made her way toward him.

The crowd's applause escalated, and people congratulated her all along the short route. She let her vision go soft, and the multitude of faces blur in front of her.

Up on the stage, Alex gallantly took her hand. "Will you marry me?" he repeated, popping open the velvet box.

She barely glanced at the ring. She just wanted to get this over with and get out of there. She hastily nodded her head. "Yes. Yes, I'll marry you." *And then I'm going to kill you.*

His grin said he was reading her mind again. It also said he'd won this round. He took the marquise solitaire out of the box and slipped it onto her finger.

Then, as the crowd roared its approval, he leaned down.

He wasn't...

He wouldn't...

He *would!*

She tried to step back, but his arms slid around her.

Under his breath, he commanded, "Kiss me." And she realized she had no choice.

Several hundred people were watching, and this was the crux of a multimillion dollar deal. She tipped her head and saw him smile.

She promised herself she'd make it quick. She'd pucker up, get it done and get the heck away from this sham. But then his lips touched hers, igniting twenty-four hours' worth of pent-up passion.

His mouth was warm and firm, and way too mobile for a perfunctory photo op. Fine smoky scotch had flavored his lips, the residual alcohol tingling her sensitive skin.

She told herself to end it, but his arms pulled her tight, and fireworks went off inside her head, counterpoint to the flashes of cameras in her peripheral vision. A primal hormone kicked in, and her eyes fluttered closed. Her body went limp, and she opened to him, giving him access, returning his parry, her body alight in raw desire.

Ever so slowly, his arms loosened. Then he drew back, finishing with a brief, tender peck on her ravaged lips. Then the cheers of the crowd penetrated her consciousness, as every photographer in the place finished a montage of their kiss.

A cold wash of reality hit Emma. Keeping a professional distance was going to be a lot more difficult than she'd imagined.

Alex couldn't believe how easy that had been. Maxim had been more than eager to participate in the Mercedes scam. Sure, it meant Teddybear got a sizable donation, but Alex had a feeling the man was more excited about the flamboyant engagement. Whatever.

Alex shrugged as his limo pulled away from the portcullis in front of the McKinley Fifth Avenue. He'd seen Emma to the penthouse elevator and now picked up the phone to dial Ryan's number. He guessed a lot of people had a romantic streak.

"Yo," said Ryan in a sleepy voice.

"The ring's on her finger," said Alex as the limo turned into traffic.

"It went well?"

"She said yes." That was the salient point. The kiss had seemed salient there for a few minutes, too. Surprisingly salient.

But the kiss was fleeting, even if it was unexpectedly arousing. That diamond ring was money in the bank. "Boy Scout Garrison is now *Romantic Fool* Boy Scout Garrison." Gunter would be thrilled with the publicity, but Alex sure wasn't wild about the inherent celibacy.

"Better you than me, buddy," Ryan chuckled, knowing full well the engagement had clipped Alex's dating wings.

A soft murmur sounded in the background, cuing Alex's radar.

"You alone?" he asked.

"You kidding?"

Alex swore.

Ryan chuckled again. "Grit your teeth and think of the profit."

"I am thinking about the profit." But Alex was also thinking about Emma's kiss. For someone who prided herself on her solemn strength, her lips sure packed a punch. And she'd looked fantastic in that sparkling dress that showed off miles of creamy smooth skin.

He'd run his fingertips over it as often as he'd dared. Which turned out to be a mistake, since it was hard to think about the money when all he wanted was more of her body and more of her lips. And that wasn't about to happen in any meaningful way. Not now, not ever.

The woman with Ryan giggled, and Alex heaved a frustrated sigh.

"Buck up," Ryan advised.

"Right." Alex stabbed the end button and tossed the phone on the bench seat beside him. It was going to be a *very* long marriage.

Emma had had a very long Monday morning.

The following morning, she wiped away the sweat that had gathered near her hairline, tuning out the chatter of two women in a whirlpool tub near the spa's fern garden.

She should have known better than to get mixed up with Alex. When a deal was too good to be true, it meant it was *too good to be true.* Yeah, the man was bailing them out financially, but the personal price was much too high.

She hated the spotlight. And if this morning's flurry of activity was anything to go by, the spotlight was exactly where she'd be stuck for the next few months. Out of desperation, she'd left her office, skulked down the back staircase and dragged a lounger behind the curve of the marble wall here in the hotel spa in a bid for peace and privacy.

"Emma?" came Katie's voice from around a spreading palm.

"Back here," Emma reluctantly confirmed.

Katie appeared in high heels, a straight white skirt and a matching blazer. "What are you doing?"

Emma paused for a significant second. "What do you *think* I'm doing?"

"I don't know."

"Well, I'm hiding."

"From *what?*"

"Not from what, from who."

Katie stripped off her blazer. "Then who?"

"Philippe."

"Why? And aren't you going to ruin your laptop?"

"Because he's a caterer. And because he's an insane stalker. And yes, probably."

The two women in a nearby whirlpool laughed, and Katie took a couple of steps closer, lowering her voice. "You're being stalked by an insane caterer? Is there such thing as an insane caterer?"

"I think they're all insane," said Emma. "I'm being stalked by at least a dozen. Philippe is just the most persistent of the crowd."

"Can't security take care of them?"

Emma pressed the save button on her laptop and turned her complete attention to Katie. "Oh, sure. Then all the reporters can have a field day on McKinley security staff roughing up skinny men in berets."

Katie glanced behind her. "We have reporters, too?"

Emma sighed and pushed back her damp hair. "Yes. We have reporters. In the lobby, out front, on the mezzanine floor."

"Nobody bothered me."

"That's because Alex Garrison didn't make a spectacle of you last night."

Katie took a seat on the far end of the lounger, curling one leg beneath her as her face lit up with the memory. "You have to admit, if that had been real, it would have been incredibly romantic."

Emma didn't have to admit any such thing. It was grandiose and tacky. She'd never, not in a million years, marry a man who thought proposing in public was romantic.

She snapped the laptop closed. "It wasn't real."

Katie sighed. "I know that."

"So quit getting all starry-eyed on me. Alex was *acting*." A small difference, maybe. But a rather important one.

Katie toyed with a lock of her hair. "He's a good actor."

"He probably had his marketing staff coach him."

Katie laughed at that.

"Mademoiselle McKinley?" came a nasal male voice.

A sudden shift in Emma's blood pressure left her feeling light-headed. She stared at Katie. "You were *followed?*"

"I'm not exactly double-o-seven," Katie protested.

"Aarrgghh."

"Mademoiselle McKinley?" Philippe Gagnon repeated. Then he appeared around the corner of the marble wall. "Ah, *there* you are.'

Katie nearly choked on a laugh as the brisk, wiry sixty-something man stepped in front of them and clasped his palms together over his chest.

"There is so much we must do," he began.

He sure had that right. And on the top of Emma's list was a clandestine trip to the Bahamas. She'd find a small secluded beachfront hut with no phone, no radio, and *no* caterers.

Katie, on the other hand, seemed completely unperturbed by Philippe's interruption. She stood and held out her hand to him. "I'm Katie McKinley, sister of the bride."

"*Enchanté,* mademoiselle." He gallantly raised her hand to his lips and kissed her knuckles. "I am Philippe Gagnon. Sous chef, trained at the Sorbonne and apprenticed under John-Pierre Laconte. I have cooked for princes and presidents."

Katie turned to Emma, her grin growing wide. "Did you hear that, Emma? He's cooked for princes and presidents."

"Shoot me now," Emma muttered as a trickle of sweat made its way between her breasts.

Philippe shook an admonishing finger. "No, no. None of that from the bride. I am here now, and I will take care of everything."

Emma sat up straight. "Oh, no you—"

"*Emma.*" Katie shot her eyes a look of warning.

But Emma wasn't getting dragged into this circus. "I am not—"

"This is a most stressful time for you, mademoiselle." Philippe fluttered a hand toward the exit. "Those bohemian food hacks in the lobby. I will have them gone. Poof."

Then he held up his palms. "No, no. No need to thank me. After that, I will talk to the reporters. Give them a tidbit or two, non? Satisfy them for a short while."

Emma stared into the man's pale blue eyes, seeing an unexpected shrewdness in their depths. It took her less than a minute to revise her opinion of him. "You can get all those people out of my lobby?"

"But, of course," he said. "You must stay calm. I must keep you calm."

If by keeping her calm, Philippe meant protecting her privacy? He was hired.

* * *

Mrs. Nash punctuated her presence on the pool deck by clacking a pitcher of orange juice down on the table next to Alex's lounger.

He glanced up from the executive summary of the McKinley strategic plan.

He didn't know what he'd done to annoy Mrs. Nash, but it was obvious by the set of her lips that something was up. He tried to gauge her expression, but the sun was bright, and his eyes were grainy from lack of sleep.

He decided to go for the direct approach. "Something wrong?"

"What could be wrong?" Then her lips returned to the prune position. "Though I see you're getting married."

"I am," he confirmed, wondering if that was really the problem. Surely she wasn't offended because he hadn't told her personally. Sunday was her day off.

She peered at him over the half glasses that were secured around her neck by a sparkling gold chain.

He was clearly supposed to be catching onto something here. But he really didn't have time for games. Another ten minutes of cramming for the showdown with old man Murdoch from DreamLodge, and he was diving into the pool to wake himself up. He would barely get in thirty lengths and a shower if he wanted to be at the DreamLodge offices before eight.

And he definitely wanted to be there before the start of business. He wasn't taking any chances that Murdoch would get to Emma before Alex got to him.

Mrs. Nash finally relented. "To a woman I've never met?"

Alex gave his head a brief shake. "You met her last week."

Mrs. Nash drew in an expressive breath. "No. She was at the estate last week. We were never introduced."

Okay. That was an oversight. Alex could see that now, and he would definitely introduce them as soon as possible. "I'll—"

"And I see she's recently come into some property…"

And what, exactly, did Mrs. Nash mean by that? And what was that funny tilt to her chin?

Her tone dropped to interrogation timbre and the pace of her words slowed. "*Hotel* property."

"Yes." Alex measured his response. He was way too tired to justify his personal life.

At his admission, her voice turned snappy again. "You ought to be ashamed of yourself, young man."

Young man? "What happened to *Mr.* Garrison?"

"Sweeping that innocent girl off her feet."

Alex sat forward. "Wait a minute—"

"Did you send her the usual hothouse bouquet? Take her to Tradori's? Book your suite at the Manhattan?"

"Whoa." How did Mrs. Nash know about his suite at the Manhattan? "I've been completely up front with Emma."

"Ha. The poor woman didn't have a ghost of a chance. Her father only recently passing."

Now that just plain wasn't fair. Alex rose to his feet. "She had every chance."

Mrs. Nash shook her head. "Alex, I love you dearly. You are like a son to me."

"I didn't do anything wrong."

"I know your weaknesses."

"I know my weaknesses, too." And they certainly didn't include lying to women in order to steal their property.

They might involve misleading a competitor to cinch a business deal, or lying to the world at large in order to merge two hotel chains. But those were completely separate issues. And defensible ones.

Not that he had to explain himself.

Of course he didn't have to explain himself.

Unfortunately, something in her expression triggered a psychological remnant of his childhood. And he couldn't seem to bring himself to disappoint her.

He made a split-second decision to bring her into the circle. "Emma knows why I'm marrying her."

Mrs. Nash's expression changed. "She knows it's for her hotels?"

He nodded. "I offered her a financial bailout, and she took it. Now, if you'll excuse me, I have a meeting."

He stripped off his shirt, stepped out of his sandals to head across the deck.

Mrs. Nash followed on his heels. "A marriage of convenience, Mr. Garrison?"

"Yes, Mrs. Nash. A marriage of convenience." It wasn't like he was breaking the law.

"Well, we both know where that leads."

"To profitability and an increase in our capital asset base?"

"To misery and a cold, lonely death."

A stillness took over Alex's body. He hooked his toes over the edge and gazed into the still, clear water. "I am not my father."

"You are more like him than you care to admit."

"I'm nothing like him."

She clicked her teeth, and he could feel her shaking her head.

"I know what I'm doing, Mrs. Nash."

"Due respect, Mr. Garrison. You haven't a bloody clue."

Yeah. That was respectful all right. Alex tamped down the urge to engage in the debate. He was out of patience, and he was out of time. He drew a strangled breath, tensed his calf muscles and dove into the pool.

Five

It was three minutes past eight by the time Alex found a parking spot and strode up the wide staircase into the DreamLodge headquarters lobby. The airy, open room was impressive—quiet, understated and classy. But then Clive Murdoch hadn't built his empire on stupidity and poor taste. He was Alex's number one competitor for good reason. The man wasn't to be taken lightly.

Briefcase in hand, power suit freshly pressed, and his hair trimmed right to his collar, Alex scanned the floor directory next to a bank of elevators. The executive suite was on number thirty-eight.

He pressed a button and one of the doors immediately slid open.

The ride up was direct and smooth. And on the top floor, he emerged and introduced himself to the receptionist, hoping name recognition would get him in to see Clive Murdoch without an appointment.

"I'll see if he's free, Mr. Garrison." The young woman smiled behind a discreet headset and punched a number on her phone.

"Alex?" The sound of another woman's voice sent a ripple of warning up his spine.

He quickly blinked the surprise from his expression and turned to face Emma. Then he took a few steps forward to put some distance between them and the receptionist. "Emma," he crooned. "Right on time, I see."

"What are you—"

"I was worried you'd be late, sweetheart." He gave her a kiss on the forehead, while his mind scrambled for a contingency plan.

"What are you doing here?" she asked.

"What are *you* doing here?" he returned. "And why aren't you wearing your ring?" A good offense? It might work. He sure hadn't come up with any better ideas in the past fifteen seconds.

"I have an appointment," she said.

"So I heard," he bluffed.

"Heard from who?"

He quickly grabbed an answer for that one. "The hotel business is a tight-knit community."

She frowned. "It is not."

"Yes, it is." He frowned back at her, pretending he had a right to be annoyed. "I can't believe you'd book a meeting with Murdoch without me."

And, quite frankly, he couldn't believe she'd agree to meet Murdoch on his own turf for a negotiation. Didn't she understand the home court advantage?

"It's still my company," she said.

"And I'm a player in it. Where's your ring?"

She curled her left hand and tucked it behind her. "We haven't signed a thing."

They'd talk about the ring later. He had a lot to say about the damn ring. "You said yes in front of five hundred people."

Her complexion darkened a shade. "And we are *definitely* talking about that one later."

He should hate it when she used that tone of voice. But he didn't. It energized him instead of annoying him. It made him look forward to later.

"Fine," he said, keeping his tone deliberately flat. "But for now we have a meeting."

"*I* have a meeting."

He gave her a cold smile. "Sweetheart, your last solo business meeting was yesterday."

"Why, you—"

He cut her off with a quick kiss on her taut, tender lips. Then he drew back and dared her with his eyes, all the while raising his voice so the receptionist would hear. "Don't worry about it. We can pick up the ring after lunch."

"I'm going to kill you," she muttered under her breath.

"Later," he whispered. "After you give me hell for proposing to you." Then he took her hand and turned to the friendly receptionist. "Is Mr. Murdoch ready to see us?"

Emma couldn't believe Alex had crashed her business meeting. How had he found her? How had he even known to look for her? And didn't he have his own business to run on a Monday morning?

She felt like a fool traipsing into Clive Murdoch's office half a step behind him. She looked like a fool, too, if Clive's expression was anything to go by. He'd called last week to say he'd been working on a deal with her father. He wondered if she'd be taking over from here on in.

She'd said, "absolutely." She'd said she was at the helm, making decisions, running the company. And here Alex had cut her off at the knees.

"Clive," Alex greeted brusquely, sticking out his hand.

"Alex." Clive nodded, offering a guarded handshake.

He looked to Emma. "Ms. McKinley?"

"Soon to be Mrs. Garrison," said Alex, a definite edge of aggression in his tone.

Emma shot him a glare. What did he think he was doing?

"Good news travels fast," said Clive.

Alex pulled out a chair at the round meeting table, gesturing for Emma to sit in it.

She thought about rebuffing his offer, but his expression wasn't one to mess with. So she took the chair. She'd set him straight on business protocol later.

"Yet," said Alex, still standing, that same thread of steel in his tone. "You made an appointment with my fiancée anyway."

"Alex," Emma interrupted.

"I made the appointment last week," said Clive. His shoulders were tense, his voice hard-edged.

"Things have changed since last week," said Alex.

"Mr. Murdoch," said Emma, trying to calm things down.

"Call me Clive," said Clive.

"Don't," said Alex.

Emma stared at him in total shock. "Will you *stop* this?" Then she looked at Clive. "We're here to listen."

Alex's hands closed over the back of one of the chairs. "We're here to make a point."

She glared at Alex. "You don't even know—"

"McKinley assets are not for sale. Not now. Not ever. None of them."

For sale? Clive hadn't said anything about a sale.

"You haven't even heard my offer," Clive stated, the word *sale* obviously no surprise to him.

Emma stilled. How had Alex known they were talking about a sale? She hadn't even known they were talking about a sale.

"We don't need to hear your offer," said Alex. Then he

reached out a hand to Emma. "In fact, we don't need to be here at all."

Emma glanced back and forth between the two men as they stared each other down. What had she missed? What did Clive want to buy? Why wouldn't Alex consider it?

"Can somebody please—"

"I'm your contact," Alex informed Clive, tossing a business card on the table. "You think you have any more business with McKinley, you call *me.*"

Clive didn't touch the card. "You walk out that door, the offer's closed."

Alex shrugged, and it occurred to Emma he might be negotiating. Was this how it was normally done? Did he expect Clive to follow them to the lobby and up the ante?

Clive smirked. "The offer was *way* above market."

"It was chump change, and we both know it."

Wow. Emma could never have been that gutsy. She did wish she knew what they were talking about, but it seemed to make the most sense to play along.

She took Alex's hand, and they left the office.

"What now?" she asked as they waited for the elevator.

Alex glanced down at her. "Now, there's someone I want you to meet."

She glanced over her shoulder. "So, will he follow us?"

Alex looked behind them. "I doubt it."

"But…"

"But what?"

The elevator door slid open.

"I thought he'd follow us out and up the offer."

Alex gestured for her to precede him. "He didn't make an offer."

"But he was going to."

Alex trapped the elevator door to keep it from closing. "Yes, he was going to."

The truth dawned on Emma. "We really walked away without even hearing what it was?" What kind of a way was that to conduct business?

"Of course we walked away. Get on."

"But maybe it was—"

Alex leaned in, lowering his voice. "Stop talking and get in the elevator."

Emma hesitated. Then her glance slid over to the receptionist. Right. This argument was unseemly. But what on earth was Alex thinking?

She lifted her chin and marched inside, gritting her teeth until the door closed. "Maybe it was good," she shouted. "Maybe it was *fantastic.*"

Alex gave a dry chuckle. "Which do you think is more likely, Emma? That Clive Murdoch got rich by benevolently paying more than market price for hotels, or that Clive Murdoch is a shrewd old man looking to take advantage of your inexperience."

She glared at Alex. "Guess we'll have to tell him to get in line for that one, won't we?"

A muscle near his temple ticked for a moment. "I'm not old. And I'm not taking advantage of you, Emma. I'm saving you from bankruptcy."

"Benevolently, I'm sure," she returned with syrupy sweetness. "And with no thought whatsoever for your own welfare."

"You knew the score from minute one."

The elevator pinged and the door glided open.

"How do I know you're not taking advantage of my inexperience?" she pressed. "And, by the way, that was insulting. I've been in the hotel business my entire life. I've done everything from tend bar to renovate a ski resort."

"That's your credential? Tending bar?"

"Most recently, I was the vice president of North American operations. I'm not some naive newbie."

"Yeah?" he challenged as they started across the lobby. "Then why did you agree to meet Murdoch in his office?"

Emma didn't get the point of the question. "Because it was Mr. Murdoch I was meeting with."

Alex pushed open the double glass doors. The temperature went up twenty degrees while car horns and tire screeches replaced the echoing quiet of the lobby. "You should have had him come to you."

"What difference would that make?"

They dodged other pedestrians as they made their way down the stairs.

"Tactical advantage." Alex's lips quirked in a grin. "Newbie mistake. Good thing I was there to rescue you."

"*You* didn't even let him make the offer."

"The offer sucked, Emma. I brought a car. Just across the street."

"You don't know that."

"No—I'm pretty sure I brought a car. That blue Lexus over there, under the red sign."

"You don't know the offer sucked."

Alex stopped at the bottom of the stairs and turned to face her. "I knew about your meeting. I knew he wanted to buy. I knew how to shut him down. Don't you think there's maybe a slim possibility that I know the market value of a hotel?"

"Not half high on yourself, are you?" As soon as the sarcastic words were out, Emma regretted them.

Alex had made a fair point.

She'd been out to prove herself on this deal with Murdoch. She'd even gone so far as to secretly hope that whatever he had in mind would save McKinley Inns, so that she wouldn't have to give half of the company to Alex, and she could avoid going through with this farce of a wedding.

But Murdoch hadn't wanted to make a business deal beneficial to McKinley. He'd simply wanted to make a purchase. He'd been looking for a bargain.

Not that she'd ever admit any of it to Alex. He had enough of an advantage over her already.

"Like I said before," Alex interrupted her thoughts. "There's somebody I want you to meet."

"Your lawyer?" Now that the engagement was out of the way, the prenup was next on the list.

"No. Not my lawyer. My housekeeper."

For a man with a reputation as a cold-blooded hard case, Alex sure had a soft spot for his housekeeper. Oh, he tried to hide it. But it was there in the inflection of his voice as they came down his long driveway in Oyster Bay.

"She can be irritable at times, and she's as judgmental as anyone I've ever met. But she's been with the family since before I was born, so I try to humor her."

"Because she scares the life out of you," Emma guessed.

Alex hesitated just a shade too long. "Don't be ridiculous."

They drove beneath spreading oaks and past fine-trimmed lawns. The last time Emma had come to the Garrison estate, she'd been focused on the upcoming conversation with Alex. This time she paid more attention to the landscaping, doing a double take as they passed a magnificent rose garden.

"What did you tell her about me?" Emma asked as she craned her neck to watch the stunning blooms. *Wow.* The Vanderbilts' gardener had nothing on the Garrisons'.

"That I was marrying you for your hotels," he said.

"You did not."

"Actually, I told her I was helping you out of a financial jam. She guessed the part about the hotels."

That surprised Emma. "Well, at least I don't have to lie to her."

"You don't have to lie to anyone else either."

Okay, now that was about the most ridiculous thing Emma had ever heard. "Yeah, I have to lie."

"We tell them we're getting married," he explained. "We tell them we couldn't be happier—which, when you consider the money, has got to be true. And we tell them we're co-managing McKinley Inns. All perfectly valid."

"And what do we do when they ask about our feelings? You planning to pull a Prince Charles?"

He glanced her way, raising an eyebrow. "A Prince Charles?"

"When Prince Charles was asked if he loved Diana, he said 'whatever love is.'"

Alex chuckled.

"Hey, you pull a Prince Charles on me, and I'll pull a Mrs. Nash on you."

"What's a Mrs. Nash?"

"I don't know, but she does something that intimidates you, and I'm going to find out what it is."

"You're crazy."

"Like a fox." Emma glanced back out the windshield to see the three-story white building rising up in front of them. "I swear your house is bigger than some of my hotels."

"That's why I bought an apartment in Manhattan."

"You kept getting lost?"

Alex laughed.

The building grew closer and seemed to get taller. White stone pillars gleamed in the morning sun. Dozens of dormered windows delineated the three, no, *four* stories, while a fountain dominated the circular drive's center garden.

"You spin me around three times in there, I swear you'll never have to see me again."

"Good tip," said Alex as he brought the car to a smooth halt in front of the polished staircase.

She pulled a face, but he just laughed at her.

They exited the car and started climbing the wide steps.

"We have to talk about this," said Emma, trying not to feel outdone by Alex's status and old money.

"About my house?"

"About everything. How this marriage thing is going to work. How much time we'll have to spend together. How we'll coordinate our schedules."

Alex reached for the handle on the massive front door. "We can coordinate schedules over breakfast."

She supposed they could schedule a regular morning call. "What time do you get up?"

"Around six."

Emma nodded. "I usually eat about seven. We could talk on the phone over coffee."

"The phone?"

"You'd rather e-mail?"

"I'd rather eat at the same table. Dining room, breakfast nook, kitchen, pool deck, I don't care—"

"What are you talking about?"

He reached for the ornate knob on the huge double doors. "Breakfast. Pay attention, Emma. We're talking about breakfast."

"Where?"

"Here, of course."

Emma stopped dead. "Here?"

"Can you think of a better place?"

"My penthouse."

He smirked as he pushed open the door. "You want to share your bedroom with me?"

"We don't have to live together."

"Sure we do. We'll be married."

In name only. And even if they did spend time in the same residence, it couldn't be here.

Emma walked tentatively into the cavernous rotunda foyer,

gazing upward. It definitely couldn't be here. "Regular people don't live like this," she said. "It's practically a palace."

"That's because great-great-great Grandpa Hamilton was British royalty. The second son of an earl."

Emma gazed at the row of portraits sweeping off down the main hallway. "Why does that not surprise me?"

"The Earl of Kessex," said Alex. "It's a small holding just south of Scotland. However, his older brother inherited the property and the title. So Hamilton became an admiral in the British navy. I guess he always wanted the trappings because he bought the original eight hundred acres and built this place."

Emma made her way slowly down the hallway, peering at the old portraits of nobility.

"This guy," said Alex, pointing to a distinguished man in a dress navy uniform, gold tassels on his shoulders, medals adorning his chest, with a saber clutched in his left hand. He looked proud, serious, intense. In fact, take away the hat, the moustache and about twenty-five years, and he looked surprisingly like Alex.

Emma stepped back and glanced from one to the other.

"Yeah, yeah," said Alex. "I know."

"It explains a lot," said Emma. "It's genetics that make you so intent on expanding the family empire."

"Oh, I *like* her," came a woman's voice. She had a British accent, and her staunch declaration was quickly followed by the tapping of her heels on the hardwood floor.

Embarrassed, Emma pulled away from Alex.

The woman was taller than Emma, maybe five feet ten in her sensible shoes. Her hair was dyed sandy blond and cut fashionably short so that it feathered around her narrow face. She had on a straight skirt, a high collar and minimal makeup, and a pair of reading glasses dangled from a gold chain around her neck.

"You don't deserve her," the woman said to Alex.

"Mrs. Nash. May I present Emma McKinley, my fiancée."

It was the fist time Alex had used the title, and it made Emma's stomach clamp with guilt.

"You're quite certain you want to do this?" Mrs. Nash asked Emma, carefully searching her expression.

"Quite certain," said Emma. And she was. There were a million reasons against marrying Alex. But the one reason in favor of marrying him was pretty compelling.

"Well, let's get a look at you, then." Mrs. Nash glanced her up and down with a critical eye.

"Mrs. Nash," Alex protested.

"Amelia's," she pronounced.

Emma looked to Alex.

"Emma can pick her own wedding dress," said Alex.

Her wedding dress? So far Emma had blocked that tiny detail from her mind—along with the church, the flowers, the cake and the groom. Most especially the groom. And the kiss from the groom. And the shiver of arousal she got even now when she thought about their engagement kiss on Saturday night.

"If you're going to do this," said Mrs. Nash. "And let me go on record here and now as being dead set *against* your doing this. For the sake of the family, you're going to do it right."

"We can do it right without Amelia's dress," said Alex.

"You definitely don't want Cassandra's." Mrs. Nash spoke to Emma. "Or Rosalind's."

"I was thinking of something from Ferragamo or Vera Wang," said Alex.

"New?" asked Mrs. Nash with obvious horror.

"What's wrong with Cassandra and Rosalind's dresses?" asked Emma, partly to appease Mrs. Nash, but also partly to put Alex in his place. If he thought he was picking out her wedding dress, he had another think coming.

"Rosalind died young, dear."

"Oh, I'm so—"

"It was in nineteen-forty-two," Alex put in.

"Oh." Okay. So maybe condolences weren't necessary.

"And Cassandra." Mrs. Nash clicked her tongue. "She was a most unhappy child." She cast a knowing look at Alex. "And you two have quite enough problems without the dubious karma of that dress."

"It's a very generous offer," Emma said to Mrs. Nash. "But I'm sure I can find something on Fifth—"

"Do you want the world to believe you're marrying for love?"

Emma hesitated, thinking of poor Princess Diana. "We do."

Mrs. Nash divided her disdain between both of them. "I must say, if I'm to be a coconspirator in this folly, then you will have to take my advice."

Emma almost said *yes, ma'am.*

"A Garrison," Mrs. Nash continued, "would never buy a wedding dress off the rack. Now, let's take a look at the ring, shall we?"

Alex slanted an accusatory glare at Emma, and she guiltily inched her hands behind her back.

"I, uh, left it at home."

"Indeed." But then, instead of leveling a criticism, Mrs. Nash gave a decisive nod. "Just as well. We'll be needing the Tudor diamond for this."

Emma didn't know what the Tudor diamond was, but it sounded old and sentimental, and most certainly valuable. She shook her head. "I don't want any of Alex's heirlooms."

"But of course you do."

"No, really—"

Alex slipped an arm around her shoulder. "Mrs. Nash is right, Emma."

She shook her head more vigorously, fighting the reaction to his touch. Why did this stupid sensation have to rise up every time he put his hands on her? It was beyond frustrating, and it made no sense whatsoever.

Sure, he was a fit, sexy man who smelled like cedar musk. And he was rich and smart, with a brilliant if convoluted set of ethics that she couldn't help but admire.

And he sometimes seemed to have her best interests at heart. And every once in a while he showed a soft spot or a wicked streak of humor. She liked that. She didn't want to, but there was no point in denying he could make her laugh.

"You need to save those for your real bride," she insisted.

"That would be you," said Mrs. Nash. "*You* are his real bride."

"No, I'm…" She turned to Alex for support.

He shrugged his shoulders, and she felt completely adrift. The heirloom ring, on top of everything else, suddenly seemed ridiculously overwhelming.

"We need to get organized," Emma told him. Maybe if they made a list—the prenup, the ceremony, where they'd live, how long they had to stay together. Maybe then she'd feel like things were under control.

"Exactly," Mrs. Nash agreed. "And we'll begin with the Tudor diamond. It's being stored in the safe in the Wiltshire bedroom. I trust you remember the combination, Alex?"

"I remember the combination, Mrs. Nash."

"Well, we're not keeping the liquor in there, so you won't have had a use for it lately."

"I should have fired you years ago," said Alex, but there was clear affection in his tone.

Their banter made Emma feel even more like an interloper. "I'm sure the ring isn't intended—"

"You might take a look through the rest of the collection while you're up there," Mrs. Nash added. Then she winked at Alex. "Nothing says commitment quite like flawless emeralds."

Alex nodded to Mrs. Nash and patted Emma's shoulder. "Shall we?"

No, they shouldn't. She had to slow this thing down. They *had* to get organized. "We need to talk," she said with renewed vigor.

"We can talk in the Wiltshire bedroom."

Six

"**Y**ou'll definitely have to write these into the prenup." Perched on the edge of the four-poster bed, Emma had given up trying to reason with Alex. Instead, she slid a serpentine pattern ruby-and-diamond choker over her forearm. She'd have to be blind not to appreciate the brilliance of the jewels against her pale skin. A more mercenary person might be plotting ways to keep the necklace.

McKinley Inns had certainly allowed Emma and Katie to grow up with a lot of advantages in life, but it was still a relatively small company, and there'd been lean times with their family business. It was hard to imagine a threat to the Garrison wealth. Alex had produced an emerald necklace that looked to be a hundred years old. And she could only guess at the fortune tucked away in the leather and velvet boxes of the multi-shelved safe.

Alex extracted yet another case from a high shelf. "Would that be in favor of you or me?"

"I'm an option?" she joked. "Because a girl could get attached to some of these things."

So far, they'd discovered a sapphire pendant, several diamond bracelets, a man's ruby ring, even a tiara dripping with so many teardrop diamonds that Emma was sure it should be in a museum.

Still, the serpentine choker outshone them all.

"Afraid I can only lend them to you." He smiled at her as he crossed the room, his eyes going a shade of smoke she was beginning to like. "But we'll say yes to some of the party invitations, so you can show them off."

"Only if we bring along a bodyguard." She'd be scared to death wearing the necklace in public.

"You don't need a bodyguard." He waggled his eyebrows. "You've got me."

She couldn't help but grin at that one. "Okay. But only if you bring along great-great-great Grandpa Hamilton's saber."

"You don't think it might attract attention?"

"I thought attracting attention to us was your mission in life."

He snapped open the newly discovered case. "Touché."

"I, on the other hand." She gave in to temptation and looped the heavy choker around her neck. "Am trying to be classy and circumspect about our engagement."

Alex set the case down on the edge of the bed, motioning for her to turn around. "Let me."

Emma stood and faced away from him so that he could work with the clasp.

He brushed her hair out of the way and took the two ends from her fingertips.

"Thanks," she whispered, allowing herself a few seconds to enjoy the brush of his hands and the fan of his breath.

He smoothed the necklace and touched her shoulders, half turning her so she was facing a big oval mirror above a mahogany vanity table. "Take a look."

Emma's hand went to her throat where the necklace sparkled with the brilliance of two dozen flawless gems. She took a few steps closer, watching the diamonds reflect the light and the heavy gold glisten with her movements.

"Stunning," she breathed out loud.

"Stunning," Alex agreed, his voice a low rumble.

She glanced up and met his eyes in the mirror.

The smoky gray had turned to dark slate. His gaze dropped to the necklace, and in slow motion he brushed away a few stray strands of her hair.

Then he leaned down.

She knew she should stop him. She *had* to stop him. But her body was already anticipating the taste of his lips, his smooth warm lips against the delicate curve of her neck. Desire sizzled within her, and she held still, waiting, wanting.

His lips touched her skin, nudging the necklace out of the way, drawing her in with a gentle kiss. Her hands grasped the vanity top, steadying herself as her need for him took the strength out of her knees.

He broke contact, but then kissed her again. This time the tip of his tongue drew a circle above her collarbone. He blew on the moist spot, and her entire body contracted in response. Then he moved to the other side of her neck with a full, enveloping, overwhelming kiss.

Higher, then higher still. He kissed her jawline, her cheek, then his hands tunneled into her hair, bringing her head around as he zeroed in on her mouth.

When his lips met hers, passion and longing welled up from every corner of her being. She released the vanity, grasping his arm instead, clinging to the strength of his bicep and turning fully into his embrace.

While one hand guided her chin, his free arm snaked around her waist, pulling her firmly into the cradle of his thighs. His muscles were hot and hard as steel, transmitting the unmistakable signals of male desire.

His mouth opened wide, and she answered greedily. His tongue plundered her inviting depths, sending pulsating messages of need through her veins. She subconsciously arched her spine, moving closer, pressing her pelvis, her breasts, her thighs tight against his body.

The world outside disappeared, and her only thought was Alex. His incredible scent, his unbridled power, and the salty, tangy, heady taste of his skin fueled her hunger and hijacked any semblance of reason.

"Emma." Her name vibrated on his lips.

His hand slid to her bottom, grinding her high and tight against him, leaving her no illusions about the state of his arousal. The knowledge shot through her, ricocheting out from the apex of her thighs, streaking electricity to her toes and fingertips.

She cupped his face, smoothing her palms over his rough, masculine skin. She dug her fingers into his hair, kissing him harder, kissing him deeper. There was a primal magic to this passion, something she'd never, ever felt before.

In some dim recess of her mind, she knew they'd have to stop. But not now, not yet.

His breathing grew ragged. With both hands, he lifted her from the floor, slipping her skirt up her thighs, wrapping her legs around his waist so that the fabric of his suit abraded the thin silk of her panties. His thumbs slipped beneath the delicate elastic, and her muscles clenched around the touch.

Alex swore under his breath.

Emma couldn't disagree.

"We have to stop," he groaned.

She nodded, not sure she was capable of forming words.

His thumbs circled higher, forcing a moan from her lips.

"Don't do that," he growled.

"Then stop—" She moaned again.

His hands retreated. He drew his head back to gaze into her eyes. "I want you," he confessed bluntly, then waited for her reaction.

She took a breath. Then another. Then another, desperately gathering her bearings. "That can't be good."

"On the contrary," he said as he slowly lowered her to the floor. "I have a feeling it could be very, very good."

She moved away, out of range, shaking her head. "Don't you say that."

"Not saying it won't change a thing."

Maybe not, but it was all she had. She couldn't take this. She'd never felt so wickedly free, as if some unbridled hedonist had taken over her body. She would have said anything, promised anything, *done* anything.

"We can't ever do it again," she murmured.

"That's one solution," he agreed. But then his voice dipped low, and he leaned slightly forward. "Or else we do, do it again. But we never, ever stop."

The room temperature seemed to spike as they stared at each other. For a moment, Emma actually hesitated over the choice.

Abrupt noises came from the other side of the bedroom door.

"*Mr.* Garrison," Mrs. Nash cried from the hallway.

Her rapid footsteps were followed by more measured ones and a litany of rapid-fire French.

"Philippe," said Emma as Alex reflexively sprang toward the door.

It burst open, and Mrs. Nash marched inside.

"Will you *please* be so kind as to inform this odious man that the Garrison wedding feast dates back to William the Conqueror, and that we are *not* serving Garrison guests microscopic portions of bottom-feeding crustaceans smothered in outlandish butter sauces while I'm alive and breathing." She took a breath.

"A slab of beef and a dollop of dough?" Philippe demanded, coming abreast of Mrs. Nash. "You have the nerve to call that food?"

"I call that the Queen's supper," Mrs. Nash snapped in return. "You Brits don't know how to do anything but *boil*."

"I'll boil you, you—-"

"*Excuse* me?" Alex interrupted, glancing back and forth between the two.

Philippe seemed to recover his composure. "Forgive me, Mr. Garrison. Mademoiselle." He clicked his heels together and fixed his attention on Alex. "I am Philippe Gagnon. Sous Chef, trained at the Sorbonne and apprenticed under John-Pierre Laconte. I have cooked for princes and presidents. And I am at your service."

Alex turned to blink at Emma.

"I hired a caterer," she confessed into the silence.

He paused, his expression carefully neutral. "You hired a caterer?"

"Is that a bad thing?" Before the question was out, she knew it sounded ridiculous. Mrs. Nash was about to call up the Royal Navy. And Philippe's complexion was turning an unnatural shade of purple.

Alex didn't answer, but his eyes widened.

Mrs. Nash sniffed. "You *are* the bride, of course."

Emma might be the bride, but it was easy to see she'd stepped on some very important toes. She hadn't wanted to hire a caterer. It had been an act of self-preservation.

Though she had to admit, Philippe was wonderful. He'd cleared her lobby and emptied her mezzanine of unwanted wedding planners and reporters. Since then, he'd been nothing but professional and helpful. She didn't want to fire him.

But Mrs. Nash, who was obviously the uncontested mistress of her domain had very concrete plans for Alex's wedding. Emma sure didn't want to alienate her, either.

She glanced at Alex. No help there. He was obviously waiting for her next move.

She looked from Mrs. Nash to Philippe and back again. "Could we, um, compromise?" she asked.

Alex coughed. "You want the English and the French to compromise over food?"

"Is that a bad thing, too?"

No one seemed inclined to answer.

"I am willing," Philippe finally put in, with a long-suffering sigh, "to make a few—how do you say—concessions."

Emma glanced hopefully at Mrs. Nash.

Mrs. Nash's lips pursed.

"Mrs. Nash?" Alex prompted.

"It's tradition," she spouted.

Emma struggled to come up with something helpful. "Perhaps you could do the main course? And Philippe could do dessert?"

"Mon Dieu." Philippe crossed himself. "I will be ruined."

Mrs. Nash clacked her teeth together. "The admiral would turn over in his grave."

Emma looked to Alex once more. He should feel free to jump in anytime.

"Any more good ideas?" he asked her.

That did it. This whole mess was his fault anyway. "*You* were the one who proposed in public. You unleashed the dogs."

"What dogs?"

"Philippe is the one who saved me. He cleared out the reporters. He sent the other caterers packing—"

"Thirty-five years," Mrs. Nash put in. "Thirty-five years I've been with the Garrison family."

Philippe made a slashing motion with his hand. "Yorkshire pudding and boiled cabbage has *no place* on my table."

"*Your* table?" cried Mrs. Nash. "I think you mean Mr. Garrison's table."

"Can we get back to the dogs?" asked Alex.

"They were metaphorical," said Emma.

"I got that much," he drawled.

"The press," said Philippe, providing a few more dramatic hand gestures. "They were everywhere. Ms. McKinley was forced into hiding. I saved her."

"He saved me," Emma agreed. And she wasn't about to fire the man for his trouble. Surely to goodness four sane adults could come up with a compromise.

She turned to Mrs. Nash. "Why don't we pull out your recipes—"

"Water, salt and a big ol' slab of beef," said Philippe.

"At least it's not the legs of amphibians—"

"That's it." Alex took a decisive step forward. "Philippe, Mrs. Nash, you'll work together. I want three recommendations for a compromise by Wednesday."

The two immediately stopped talking.

"Morning," said Alex.

After a pause, Philippe and Mrs. Nash eyed each other suspiciously.

"Can I get a yes?" Alex prompted.

Philippe lifted his chin. "But of course. I will do everything in my power to assist."

"We can certainly discuss it," said Mrs. Nash, canting her chin at an equally challenging angle.

"Then, thank you," said Alex. "If you'll excuse us, Emma and I were picking out some jewelry."

Both Philippe and Mrs. Nash nodded stiffly and exited the room. Mrs. Nash closed the door behind them.

Alex gave Emma an exaggerated sigh of exhaustion. "A Frenchman?"

"How was I supposed to know you had a rabid housekeeper?"

Alex ambled back to the open safe. "You're right. Silly me.

Anything else I should know about? A Greek limousine driver? A Romanian florist?"

"What does Mrs. Nash have against the Romanians?"

His back was to her, but Emma could tell Alex smiled at that.

"Maybe you should run any future plans by me first."

"To pander to your control freakish nature?"

"To avoid murder or dismemberment during the ceremony. Ahhh. Here it is."

Emma's curiosity got the better of her, and she stepped closer to the safe. "What did you find in there?"

He popped open a purple velvet box. "The Tudor diamond."

Emma glanced down at the jewel in his hands and instantly stopped breathing.

It was gorgeous.

Old, unique, luxuriant and gorgeous.

The band was fashioned from strands of platinum, woven together to form an intricate Celtic pattern. Rubies tapered up the curve, highlighting the centerpiece—a glittering oval of a flawless gem.

The Tudor diamond.

"Try it on," said Alex.

She shook her head. Fake brides didn't touch a piece like that. At the very least, it had to be bad luck.

He moved the box toward her. "Mrs. Nash is right. The family jewels work in our favor."

Emma shook again, shifting from one foot to the other, her heart rate increasing. No way. No how. The ring he'd given her at casino night was perfectly fine.

"It is insured," he said.

"Against bad luck?"

He glanced at the ring in confusion. "What bad luck? It's nothing but metal and stone."

"It's a precious family heirloom."

"And it's my family heirloom. And I want you to wear it."

"That's not your choice to make."

Alex frowned. "It is my choice. I own the ring. I own the collection, the safe, the house. And I can give them to any damn person I please."

She couldn't do it. She just couldn't do it. "I'm talking morality, not legality."

The frustration in his voice was obvious. "How is it immoral for you to wear my ring?"

"Because I'd be disrespecting all the brides who came before me."

Alex blinked. Then he squinted, and a funny little smile flexed his face. "Emma. Do you honestly think you're the first Garrison bride to marry for money?"

Emma wasn't marrying for money. At least not the way he was insinuating she was marrying for money. She had her own money. He was simply… Well, he was helping her out, for a handsome return, that was all.

It was mutually beneficial, and she resented him making her feel otherwise.

"This has been going on since the early eighteen-hundreds," said Alex. "Even my father—" Then he clamped his jaw. "Hold out your hand, Emma."

She started to retreat, but he reached out and snagged her left wrist, coaxing it toward him.

"I don't—"

He slipped the band over her first knuckle.

She shut her mouth and stared at the endless circle of platinum, at Alex's dark hand against her own pale skin, at the antique rubies and diamond winking in the light.

"Believe me when I tell you," said Alex, pushing it a little farther. "You're carrying on a proud tradition."

The ring thudded reluctantly over her second knuckle, but then it settled at the base of her finger.

A perfect fit.

"There," Alex breathed, stroking his thumb over the surface of the diamond. "Now we're really engaged."

Where Alex had ended up with Hamilton's fortune and Hamilton's looks, his third cousin, Nathaniel, had ended up with Hamilton's life. The second son of the current earl of Kessex, Nathaniel had been forced to seek his own fortune, just as Hamilton had done so many decades before.

With little more than seed money from the family estate, Nathaniel had founded Kessex Cruise Lines. Then he'd added Kessex Shipping and quickly grew his fortune to the hundreds of millions.

He now had his finger on the pulse of the transportation industry from Paris to Auckland. And the transportation industry was the lynchpin of global commerce. Alex might know how to run a successful hotel chain. But Nathaniel could manipulate the world.

He'd provided Alex with a thick dossier on DreamLodge, then he'd hung around an extra couple of days. He should have been on his way back to London today. His continued presence made Alex nervous. Nathaniel didn't stick around unless something was interesting. And things that Nathaniel found interesting usually made Alex sweat.

The two men, along with Ryan, waited until Simone exited and closed the door to Alex's office.

"What's going on?" Alex asked his cousin without preamble.

Across the round meeting table, Nathaniel inched slightly forward in his chair. "You ever met David Cranston?"

That sure wasn't what Alex had expected to hear. "You mean Katie McKinley's boyfriend?"

Nathaniel nodded.

"Sure," said Alex.

Nathaniel strummed a single staccato beat with his fingertips. "He's on my radar."

Ryan jumped in. "Why?"

Nathaniel's mood became contemplative. "Don't know yet."

"Gut feeling?" asked Alex, knowing the answer already.

Nathaniel's gut feeling was legendary in the family. He made million-dollar deals based on nothing but a vague shimmer of a theory.

His uncanny luck used to freak Alex out. But then Nathaniel explained his luck was, in fact, the sum total of several hundred subconscious observations, from facial expressions and stock trends to weather patterns and newspaper articles. He wasn't sure himself how it worked. He only knew that it did.

The phenomenon didn't freak Alex out anymore, and he'd quit calling it luck years ago.

"Gut feeling," Nathaniel confirmed. "Did you know McKinley Inns just hired him?"

"Cranston?" asked Alex, more than slightly bothered that he had to hear news like that from his cousin. "Doing what?"

"Overseas marketing. VP Special Projects."

Ryan snorted. "*Special* projects?"

"Pathetic," Nathaniel agreed.

"What's his background?" asked Alex. And what was Emma thinking?

Nathaniel shrugged. "Some kind of mediocre project manager for Leon Gage Consulting."

"Did they can him?"

Nathaniel shook his head. "He quit."

"McKinley actually headhunted him?"

Nathaniel nodded. "Offered him a salary bump."

"The guy's a mooch," said Ryan. "Takes a cushy job with the girlfriend's firm…"

Alex hated the thought of McKinley Inns supporting a do-nothing executive, particularly where nepotism was involved.

Then again he wasn't stupid enough to get between his fian-cée's sister and her true love, either. Of all the battles he wanted to take on at McKinley, this sure wasn't on the top of his list.

Nathaniel stood up. "That's all I wanted to tell you."

Alex stood with his cousin. "You're offended on an ethical level, aren't you?"

"Nothing worse than a wussie who rides on his woman's coattails. You should have a talk with this Katie person. Tell her to dump the bastard."

Alex scoffed out a laugh. "Right. Like that's going to happen."

"She's got rotten taste in men."

"She's also got fifty acres of beachfront property on Kayven Island. She can marry her St. Bernard for all I care."

Nathaniel gave him a mock two-fingered salute. "Thanks for the visual there, Al."

"Not a problem, Nate. Everything still on track for the Kayven Island project?"

"Minor problem with the dockworkers' union, but I straight-ened it out. Everything still on track at your end?"

"Absolutely." Emma had a ring on her finger, and they'd had very positive coverage in three major newspapers.

Nathaniel slid his chair back under the meeting table. "In that case, gentlemen. I've got a girl and a plane both waiting on the tarmac at JFK."

Alex reached out and shook Nathaniel's hand. "Thanks for the intel. On both fronts."

"Anytime." Then Nathaniel nodded to Ryan. "Catch you later."

Ryan rose to his feet. "Have a good flight."

Nathaniel grinned and turned for the door, tossing his parting words over his shoulder. "Plane's my new Learjet Sixty. Girl's a licensed masseuse from Stockholm."

Alex crossed to his desk as the door clicked shut behind Nathaniel. "Guess he *will* be having a good flight."

"How do I get his life?" asked Ryan.

"Most people want his brother's."

Wednesday evening, Katie grasped at the unwieldy ring on Emma's left hand. *"No way,"* she exclaimed.

"Way," said Emma, still struggling to get used to the weight of the thing and still worrying about the insurance implications if she lost it.

Katie looked up, her eyes shining under the lights of Emma's penthouse. "A real earl?"

"About four generations ago."

"Alex *gave you* his family heirloom?"

"Don't go getting all excited." Emma liberated her hand and sat back down on the couch. "He's only lending it to me. And it has a dubious history."

Katie took the seat opposite, kicking off her sandals and curling her feet beneath her. "Oh, do tell."

"The brides all married for money."

Katie stared at her, waiting. "That's it?"

"That's it."

"I thought you were talking about sex and scandal and murder."

"Sorry. No murders." Emma thought back to her afternoon. "Well, except for Mrs. Nash. Alex's housekeeper. I have a feeling she's capable of it."

"And did you upset her?"

"Not so much me. But Philippe better watch his back."

Katie grinned. "I have a feeling Philippe can take care of himself."

Emma had to admit, she had that feeling, too. She stroked her thumb over the big diamond and was assailed by a vivid body memory of Alex. She determinedly shook it off. "So what did I miss at the office?"

Katie tossed her wavy blond hair back over one shoulder. "I got David to come and work for us."

Emma didn't understand. "Your David?"

"Yes, my David."

"But he has a job. With Leon Gage."

"I convinced him to quit."

An uneasy feeling trickled through Emma. "Why would you do that?" David was a great guy. And Katie obviously loved him. But working together? Day in and day out? Could that be good for any couple?

"Because we need him," said Katie, the tone of her voice subtly shifting to petulant.

Emma regrouped.

She wished Katie had discussed it with her. Not that Emma would have overruled her sister, but she might have been able to curb Katie's impulsive nature.

"Did you at least get help from Human Resources?" McKinley had a top notch HR department.

"What? I can marry him, but I can't hire him?"

"Katie—"

"Really, Emma."

Emma clenched her jaw. HR checked references and aligned suitable people with suitable jobs. What would they do if David didn't work out?

Now she struggled to keep the censure out of her voice. "What's he going to do?"

Katie pushed out her bottom lip.

"Katie?"

"Vice President of Special Projects Overseas."

Emma pressed her thumb against the jagged facets of the ring

This time when the memory of Alex popped up, it was strangely comforting. "I see."

"He's got contacts in Europe and all over the Caribbean."

Emma nodded. She wasn't aware they had problems in Europe or the Caribbean.

"He's going after convention business and tour clubs."

Emma couldn't hold her tongue completely. "Are you sure that's not too much togetherness?" She wanted Katie to be happy, truly she did. But there was something about this situation that made her uneasy. For Katie's sake. For the company's.

"You and Alex are going to work together," said Katie.

"But Alex and I aren't—"

"Getting married."

Emma jerked her thumb away from the ring. "Falling in love."

"So? Love makes it easier for me and David to work together."

Emma struggled to find fault with that logic. Technically, she supposed it should be true. Katie and David actually liked and respected each other. Where Alex and Emma couldn't come within ten feet without arguing or...worse.

Fingers spread, Katie raked her blond hair back over her forehead. "Quite frankly, Emma, if you're going to worry about anyone working together, I'd worry about you and Alex."

Emma was already worried about that.

She resisted the urge to touch the ring again.

Quite frankly, she was getting more worried by the hour.

Seven

Emma braced herself for Alex's entrance.

Her admin assistant, Jenny, had just spent three minutes warning of his arrival, an excited lilt to her voice as she watched him walk through the long office foyer and relayed his every move to Emma.

According to Jenny, Alex was wearing a charcoal suit, a black shirt and a silver-and-blue striped tie that picked up the sunshine through the skylights. He didn't look upset, but he didn't look particularly happy either. And, by the way, had Emma ever noticed the delicate cleft in his chin or the way his gray eyes sparkled silver in direct sunlight?

By the time Emma got off the intercom, she only had thirty seconds to smooth her blazer and brace herself for the onslaught of emotions that were sure to be brought on by his presence.

She'd stay on this side of the desk. He'd stay on that side. She wouldn't touch him, or smell him or look too closely into his eyes. And she would not touch that annoying diamond while he was in the room.

The oak door swung open, the air current swaying the leaves on her ponytail palm.

She came to her feet to face not happy, not angry Alex, with his sparkling silver eyes.

"Hello, darling," he greeted for Jenny's benefit before he clicked the door shut behind him.

She drew a bracing breath. "Can I help you with something?" They hadn't made another appointment to meet, although she knew they had an endless number of things to work out.

"Brought you a present."

Please, God. No more jewelry. Her right hand went to the ring before she remembered to jerk it back.

But he tossed an envelope on her desk. "Our prenup."

She glanced at the thick manila envelope. "You wrote it without me?"

He eased down into one of her guest chairs. "Trust me."

"Ha." She peeled back the flap and took her own seat.

It was a single page, duly signed and notarized. Alex got half of McKinley upon their marriage, and if either of them initiated divorce proceedings within two years of the marriage, the other got ten percent of their net worth.

She looked up to see him smile. There wasn't a single thing she could complain about. It meant she couldn't have a relationship for a couple of years. But she'd expected that. If anything, the agreement favored her.

Then she set the paper down on her desk. "What exactly is your net worth?"

"Less than Nathaniel's. More than yours."

"Who's Nathaniel?"

"My cousin. He'll be the best man."

She glanced back down at the agreement. "You've already signed."

"I have."

"You're obviously not planning to divorce me anytime soon."

"Not a chance."

Emma picked up her phone and dialed the two-digit extension for Jenny's desk. "Can you bring somebody over from Legal?"

"Right away," Jenny confirmed.

"Thanks." Emma hung up the phone. "Probably be about five minutes," she told Alex.

He nodded. "I hear you hired David Cranston."

"Where'd you hear that?"

Alex shrugged. "I told you the hotel business was a tight-knit community."

"Katie hired him," said Emma, then she immediately regretted the admission.

"Without talking to you?"

Emma hesitated. "We talked."

"You're lying."

"I am not. And how dare you—"

"And you agreed to this?"

Emma compressed her lips.

Alex stared hard into her eyes. Despite her resolve, and despite the knowledge that she'd ramp up her unruly hormones, she gazed right back into his.

"She told you after the fact," he guessed.

"But I wouldn't have stopped her."

"But you don't like it."

Emma stood up. "No," she admitted, pacing toward the picture window. "I don't like it. But it's her relationship, her decision. And it's certainly none of your business."

Alex stood. "Oh, yes it is."

She turned. "You going to micromanage Katie's staff?"

"He's working directly *for* her?"

"Alex."

Alex crossed the room to stand in front of Emma. "Between the two of us—"

"No," she barked.

"You don't even know what I was going to say."

Anger rising, she punctuated her words by poking him in the chest with her index finger. "Oh yes I do. And don't you ever *dare* suggest that we gang up on my sister. McKinley Inns doesn't work that way. I don't care who the hell you are."

He trapped her hand. "It's a bad decision."

"It's *her* decision."

"And you're just going to stand there and watch her make it."

"I am. And so are you."

He moved closer. "I wouldn't be too quick to tell me what I am and am not going to do."

Emma paused. She couldn't force him. But then he couldn't force her either. And a tie went to the status quo. Which meant the tie went to Katie in this case.

Emma didn't smile, but she came close.

But then she became aware of Alex's hand on hers. The warmth of his skin prickled its way into her bloodstream, and those appalling feelings of lust and longing surged to life inside her.

His voice dropped deep and throaty. "We're going to have to deal with it, you know."

"With Katie?" she asked in a small voice, clinging to the slim hope that that's what he meant.

"With the fact that we turn each other on like original sin."

"We do not," she lied.

"Want me to prove it?"

She tried to step back, but he kept hold of her hand.

He smiled. "You really need to stop lying to me, you know."

"You really need to develop some manners."

"Yeah? Okay, how's this? Would you care to accompany me to a luau?"

"A luau?" The sudden switch left Emma's head spinning.

"Kessex Cruise Lines is launching a new ship, the *Island Countess,* specializing in Polynesian trips. We're invited to the launch party, and I thought you could wear the ruby-and-diamond choker."

Emma had already resigned herself to being seen in public with Alex. She'd made a deal, and she was going to stick by it. Besides, being with him in public was quickly becoming a preferable choice to being with him in private.

In public she could pretend she was still pretending. She'd have an excuse to talk to Alex and laugh with Alex and touch Alex without examining the reasons why.

Doing those things in private forced her to admit she liked him. She even liked arguing with him. His self-confidence and strength of purpose made her feel…safe somehow.

And she trusted him. Probably not the smartest move in the world. But she had to trust somebody. And he was learning things about her that nobody else would ever see.

For now, for this moment in time, he was pivotal to her life. Not that she'd admit that to him. And not that she'd make things easy.

"You really think rubies and diamonds will go with orchid print cotton?" she asked.

"Hey, you want to look good or make your future husband happy?"

"Can't I do both?"

"Not in this case."

They stared each other down for a long minute.

"Well?" he demanded.

She tilted her head sideways. "Don't you sometimes wish you'd picked the pretty one?"

"Watch it."

"Watch what?" She was only joking. Besides, it was an acknowledged fact that Katie was the pretty one.

"Mess with me, and I'll make you admit I turn you on."

"How do you plan—"

His eyes darkened and his nostrils flared.

She quickly backtracked. "Never mind." Then she swallowed and squared her shoulders, voice going unnaturally sweet. "I *live* to make my future husband happy."

He smiled and brushed her hair back from her temple. "There. Was that so hard? Friday at seven. And I'll bring the necklace."

Climbing the short gangway to the *Island Countess,* Alex told himself everything was fine. He'd expected Emma to be a knockout in her deep-red, Hawaiian-print dress. And he'd expected the Garrison jewels to look stunning against the smooth honey tone of her throat. He'd even expected the sucker-punch sensation he was coming to associate with being in her presence.

What he hadn't expected was his burning desire to keep her all to himself.

Tonight was about parading her for the press, letting the other ladies ooh and ahh over the Tudor diamond on her finger, and solidifying their position as a couple with other players in the New York tourism industry, so that when Alex started representing McKinley, no eyebrows would be raised.

Trouble was, Alex couldn't bring himself to care about any of those things. There was a steel drum band playing by the pool on the aft sundeck, and all he wanted to do was hold Emma in his arms under the stars.

He knew she hated publicity, but she was doing it anyway. She hated deception, but she'd gone along with his scheme. And she probably hated him, but she was smiling up at him, holding his hand, and plastering her body against his for the benefit of photographer after photographer.

Until now, he hadn't given much thought to how much of a trooper she really was. There was an entire company being saved, her sister, the board, the executives and thousands of jobs. Yet, it was all on Emma's shoulders.

Had she complained?

Of course she had. But she'd made logical, reasonable arguments. She'd looked for options and solutions that would suit her better. But when she didn't find them, when Alex had prevented her from finding them, she'd bucked up and done what was needed.

He admired that.

He admired her.

He motioned to the glass elevator that ran up the five stories of the central atrium.

"Ready to go upstairs?" he whispered against her glistening chestnut hair. He inhaled the scent of her shampoo, his gaze darting to the ruby earrings dangling from her delicate lobes.

His earrings.

He closed his hand over hers, letting the diamond press into his palm.

She leaned up to laugh in his ear. "You think they got enough pictures?"

"Absolutely. Besides, there'll be more photographers on the deck."

She set her empty champagne glass on a waiter's tray. "Then, lead on."

"You're awfully agreeable tonight."

She smiled and waved to a cluster of brightly dressed women. "That's because I live to make you happy."

"Seriously," he said. "You're…" He wasn't quite sure how to put it into words. He finally came up with, "sparkling."

"It's the rubies."

He took the excuse to run his thumb over the bracelet on her wrist. "They suit you. But that wasn't what I meant."

The elevator door opened in front of them, and they moved inside alone.

"Then it's the champagne," she said, bracing her hands on the small railing and leaning back against the glass wall.

The posture brought the cotton fabric tight against her breasts, and Alex felt his body involuntarily take note. The dress was strapless and fitted, with a tie cinching up the waist and a narrow skirt delineating her hips before falling softly to just above her knees.

Most of the women had gone with island styles, the men sticking with casual slacks and open-collar shirts. Alex had gone with tan and buff, not being a fan of wearing palm fronds across his chest.

From the shine of her soft hair to the tips of her painted toenails, Emma looked like an island goddess.

"Are you drunk?" he asked. That might account for her relaxed mood.

She eased away from the wall, moving sinuously toward him, stopping to walk her fingertips up his chest and grasp the small lapels of his shirtfront. She shook her hair and gazed slumberously up into his eyes. "I'm acting, Alex. I thought that was what you were paying me for."

He leaned down ever so slightly. "Well, you're very, very good."

She smiled.

"Almost too good."

Her expression faltered. "What's that supposed to—"

The door glided open to some new passengers, and he slipped his arm around her narrow waist. "Let's dance."

Without waiting for a response, he drew her into his arms, and they joined dozens of other couples under the stars, swaying to the calypso beat.

Her movements matched his, stiff at first, but then she found his rhythm. He snuggled her closer, pressing her hips to his thighs. She was just the right size, just the right shape, just the right height to be a perfect partner.

His thoughts turned to movements of a sexual nature, speculating on how perfect things could be between them. Of course, he was only talking about sex, not about life. Life with Emma was going to be a challenge from the minute he got up in the morning to the minute he went to bed at night.

Alone.

Because their marriage wasn't about intimacy. It was about convenience. And for the first time, Alex wondered if Mrs. Nash might be right. He didn't really like the thought of a cold, lonely death.

Nor did he like the thought of a cold, lonely bed. In fact, he didn't like the thought of a bed with anyone in it but Emma at the moment.

Which was impossible, in so many ways.

But she was in his arms now.

He closed his eyes and gathered her to him, tipping his head to the crook of her neck, inhaling her scented skin and letting the smooth, warmed gems of her necklace rub against his cheek. A camera flash penetrated his lids. And even though it was what he wanted, he resented the intrusion.

He danced Emma to a quieter corner of the ship's deck, where the lights were dim and the music was muted by wind baffles.

She tilted back her head and stared at the panorama of stars above them. "A romantic tryst for the press?"

"Something like that." He focused on the smooth skin, delicate neck.

She thought they were playacting? What the hell?

He leaned down and feathered a kiss on her collarbone, just below his necklace.

He heard her quick intake of breath, so he tried another one, this time on her shoulders, working his way slowly backward, then up toward the lobe of her ear, which he drew gently into his mouth.

Her fingers dug into his, and he splayed his hand wide on the small of her back, bringing her tight against him as his mouth sought hers.

Their bodies knew each other's this time. There was no fumbling, not the slightest hesitation. Their lips met full on. Their mouths opened. And their tongues parried in a way that sent sparks shooting straight to Alex's groin.

This was a bad idea.

No. This was a great idea. What it was, was a bad location for a great idea.

They were screened from the crowd at the moment, but that could change. All it would take is one rogue reporter or one straying couple, and they'd be caught in a compromising position.

Not that he'd compromised her yet.

He was only kissing her.

But judging by her quiet moans, and the way his hand was inching down her bottom, it was only a matter of minutes.

He dragged himself back.

She blinked in confusion, her lips red and swollen, her eyes clouded with passion.

"I want to show you something," he whispered.

He led her past the deck chairs, through an air-lock door, up a small staircase to the Empress Deck and the door to a vista suite. There he inserted the card key.

"What's this?" she asked.

He opened the narrow door. "The captain thought we might like to freshen up."

Emma walked inside, glancing around at the dining table, the sofa cluster and wet bar. "But there are no reporters in here." She looked back at Alex in confusion.

Had she really been acting the whole time?

He couldn't believe it.

"The veranda," he quickly improvised. "It overlooks the party."

He crossed the spacious room and pressed a button to pull back the drapes. He'd back off from the seduction plan. Really, nothing ventured nothing gained.

The drapes slid out of the way to reveal a huge, wraparound veranda with views of the portside pool, the ocean and the New York skyline.

He opened the two French doors, letting in the night air and calypso music and party laughter. "Nothing like a clandestine telephoto lens shot to convince people we're in love."

Emma peered through the doorway at the crowds dancing one deck below. "You're frighteningly conniving, you know that?"

He reached for her hand, muttering under his breath. "You don't know the half of it." Then louder. "Shall we get cozy on the double lounger?"

She stepped outside on her strappy sandals, her dress billowing gently around shapely legs. "Why not. You think they'd bring us up one of those pineapple drinks?"

"You got it," said Alex, picking up the phone to push the button for the butler.

Emma felt much safer out on the veranda than inside the suite with Alex. She'd thought, planned, *hoped* to spend the entire evening in a crowd of people. And she sure hadn't counted on Alex going for quite so much realism. Those kisses had all but sizzled her toes.

When she thought about it though, it made perfect sense. A newly engaged couple wouldn't stay in the thick of the party all night long. They'd steal away for a kiss or two in private. Letting the press spot them on the suite's veranda was inspired.

She sat down on the thick padding of the double lounger and

kicked off the tight high heels she'd borrowed from Katie. The dress was Katie's, too. While Emma was well outfitted for business events, she'd never built up her party and vacation wardrobe. Luckily, she and Katie were the same size.

Alex set a tall, frosted glass on the mini table beside her. "One frozen Wiki Waki."

"You made that up."

He held up a hand. "Swear it's true. That's what they're serving at the party."

The frost slipped against Emma's fingers as she lifted the glass and stirred the mixture with the straw. It was crisp and tangy on her tongue, and the blend of liquors definitely left an afterglow.

The cushion shifted as Alex sat down.

"What have you got?" she asked.

"Glenroddich on the rocks."

"Wrong hemisphere."

He leaned back and closed his eyes. "That's as exotic as I get."

She smirked, wiggling her bare toes in the cool ocean breeze. "I knew you'd be a dud as soon as I saw the outfit."

He opened one eye. "You messing with me again?"

She took another sip of the tropical drink. "I'm merely entertaining myself while we pose for the photographers."

"By playing mind games with me?"

"Afraid I'll win?"

He snorted and closed his eyes again. "Afraid you might sprain something trying."

Emma glanced at his slacks, then she glanced at her slushy drink.

He made a show of settling back to a more comfortable position. "But, go ahead and give it your best shot."

"Really?" she simpered. "Can I?"

He grinned, and she upended her drink in his lap.

He shot up straight, his roar loud enough to attract attention from the dancers directly below them. Then he turned to stare at her in horror.

"That was my best shot," she explained, scrambling for the courage to hold her ground. Dousing him had seemed like a good idea about ten seconds ago. Now…

"I can't believe you did that." He gritted his teeth as the sticky peach-colored mixture trickled between his thighs.

"You might want to make it look like we're having fun," she suggested with a quick glance at the crowd below.

Alex curved his mouth into a pained grin. "You asked for this."

Without further warning, he scooped her up, and sat her square in the middle of the mess on his lap.

"It's Katie's dress," she shrieked. Then she cringed as the ice seeped through her panties.

His fingertips went to her ribs, and she shrieked a second time when he started tickling. "Don't," she gasped. "Stop."

"Don't stop?"

"No. Stop!"

"Try to sound like you're having fun," he advised.

"No." But she kept laughing. She couldn't help it. She wasn't sure where he'd learned to tickle, but he was definitely a master.

"Help," she called weakly to the crowd below.

But they couldn't hear her over the music.

Alex's hands suddenly stilled, but it was only to lift her from the lounger and carry her unceremoniously back through the French doors.

He set her down and closed it to the whoops and hollers of those below.

"What did I tell you?" he asked, eyes flashing dark and purposeful in the dusky suite.

"About what?" She took an involuntary step backward.

He matched her pace, keeping the distance constant between them. "About messing with me, that's about what."

His meaning hit, and she scooted up against the wall. "Oh, no." She shook her head.

He moved forward, trapping her between the sofa and the wet bar. "Oh, yes," he said menacingly. "It's a matter of pride now."

Her glance darted to his ruined trousers. "You already got me back." Her dress was just as wet as his pants.

He shook his head. "Not good enough. Admit I turn you on, Emma."

She knew she should say it. She should say it and get it over with. He'd make good on his threat, that was for sure. And ten kisses from now, she'd be admitting the earth was flat and that she was a witch, never mind that he turned her on.

But she shook her head anyway. She couldn't bring herself to go down without a fight. He might get her admission, but he was going to have to work for it.

He moved even closer, his voice instantly seductive. "You know I'll do it."

She nodded.

"You *want* me to do it?"

She shook.

He raised his hand and tenderly stroked his palm over her cheek, tangling his fingers into the hair behind her temple. "You think you have a hope in hell?"

She stared defiantly up at him. "I know I have a hope in hell."

He cracked a half smile. "Just one?"

"Maybe two."

"I do like those odds."

She almost smiled in return and wondered why she wasn't more wary of the situation. Maybe it was his soothing tone, or his reassuring strength or his comforting scent. Or maybe it was because she was looking forward to his kiss.

His kiss? Who was she kidding?

She was looking forward to anything and everything he'd do before she said uncle. Confidence mounting, she stared directly into his slate dark eyes. "Go ahead, Alex. Give it your best shot."

Eight

Alex went still, his eyes narrowing as he stared down at Emma. "Are we playing chicken?" he asked her. "Because it feels like we're playing chicken."

She forced herself to hold her ground. "Are you all talk and no action? Because it feels like you're—"

He swooped down and enveloped her mouth in a hot, passionate kiss. His strong arms held her protectively, lovingly. Sensations racked her body as the damp of his slacks seeped through to her dress. His tongue flicked out, and his fingers anchored firmly at the base of her neck.

The room spun, even as her world came to a full stop.

Okay. Now *that* was action.

"Say it," he rumbled.

She shook her head, no.

His hand moved to her rib cage, stroking upward to engulf her breast. Through the thin cotton fabric, his thumb unerringly zeroed in on her nipple, circling it once then abrading the tip.

Her body was instantly flooded with desire.

"Say you want me," he tried again.

She locked her knees to keep them from buckling but refused to concede the test of wills.

"Have it your way," he muttered, kissing her once more.

She tasted the mellow, nutty flavor of his scotch, inhaled the heady scent of his musk then felt his warm fingertips creep beneath her neckline. He inched his way closer, closer, closer still. Until she arched her back, pushing her aching breast into his hot hand.

He groaned in response, assuaging her nipple with an expert motion. Goose bumps rose on her skin. Her body clamored for more.

What was he doing?

He did it again, and she cried out loud.

"Say it," he hissed, his mouth brushing against hers.

She whimpered a no.

He swore under his breath.

Then he scooped her up into his arms and carried her through the narrow doorway, depositing her on the thick comforter of the king-sized bed.

Before she had time to breathe, he bent over her, staring into her eyes as he released the tie of her wraparound dress. Silver flecks smoldered in the depths of black slate as he eased the dress open, revealing her cleavage, her navel, the lace front of her panties.

His breathing grew ragged. "Just say it, Emma."

She reached beneath his shirt, running her fingers up his chest, through the sparse hair and over the flat of his nipples, giving back at least some of what she was getting.

He trapped her wrist. "Me wanting you was never the question."

Right. Damn.

He slowly released her, sending his own fingertips on a sensual journey between her breasts, over her stomach, dipping ever lower. He touched the detailed top of her panties. Then he traced a line over the translucent fabric, zigzagging across her sensitive flesh, before stopping and cupping her, rubbing the heel of his hand on the center of her passion.

With his free hand, he separated her dress, exposing her naked breasts. His eyes feasted on her pale skin and her pink, tightly contracted nipples as her chest rose and fell with labored breathing.

He kissed one nipple, laving it with his tongue, pulling it into a tighter and tighter bud. Then he blew against the damp spot, and she went hot, then cold, then hot all over again.

"All you have to do is say it," he repeated.

In answer, she flexed her hips. His hand was doing such delicious things down there that she didn't think she could speak if she wanted to. And she didn't want to. She didn't want him to win, and she sure didn't want him to stop.

He eased down beside her, burying his face in her neck, planting sharp kisses beside the necklace while he pushed down her panties and sought her warm wet flesh.

She grasped his shoulders, pinching tight as his fingertip found her center. He lingered and circled while her thigh muscles tightened, her toes curled and a small pulse came to life beneath his hand.

"Emma," he gasped, fixing his mouth on hers, plunging his tongue in deep, dragging the dress from her.

He closed a hand over her breast, held it there, then seemed to hold himself back. His eyes were dark as midnight as he gazed down at her. His mouth glistened with moisture, and the dim light from the living room highlighted the planes and angles of his face.

Emma dragged in a lungful of oxygen.

"Either you tell me you want me," he growled, "or I stop right now."

He wouldn't.

He couldn't.

Her inner muscles convulsed with need.

"I want you," she said hoarsely.

"Thank you." His mouth came down on top of hers, and his finger sank inside.

She scrambled with the buttons of his shirt, tearing it apart, holding him tight and pressing her breasts against the roughness of his skin. The heat of his chest seared her even as his mouth found hers, and their tongues began an intimate dance.

Somehow, he kicked off his slacks and located a condom. She raked her fingers through his hair, stroked his stubbled chin, rubbed a finger over his lips and tucked it inside.

He kissed her palm, the inside of her wrist, the crook of her elbow. Then he rose above her and she brought up her knees.

"Emma," he breathed. Trapping her hands, their fingers entwined, he kissed her hard as he plunged to the hilt.

She moaned his name, rising to meet him. The music, the party, the *world* disappeared in a haze of passion as his strokes grew harder and faster and her nerve endings converged on the place where their bodies met.

She closed her eyes as the fireworks pulsed. Small explosions at first. Then they grew higher and brighter and faster until the entire sky erupted in light and color and sound.

"Alex," she cried, and his guttural moan told her he'd followed her off the edge of the earth.

The fireworks slowly ebbed to a glow. The music returned, and the sound of laughter filtered up from the party on the lower deck.

She willed the sounds away. Alex's body was a delicious weight holding her down on the softness of the bed, and she didn't want to surface just yet.

"You okay?" he asked, easing up.

She nodded. "But don't move. For now." She didn't want to break the spell.

"Okay." Then he sighed against her hair. "So nice to know I won."

She tried to work up an appropriate level of indignation, but she was too satiated. "You couldn't give me five minutes, could you?"

"You're a hard nut to crack, Emma McKinley."

"Funny. Here I was thinking I was easy."

His fingers flexed between hers. "Easy? I've never worked so hard for sex in my life."

Okay. The afterglow was officially ebbing. "You can get off now."

He rolled his weight to one side, giving a deep sigh of satisfaction. "You want me."

She bopped him on the shoulder. "Oh, get over yourself."

He held up his hands in mock defense. "I distinctly heard you say it."

"Well, you want me, too."

"Of course I do."

"So, we're even."

He grinned. "Not quite. You don't want to want me. That's not the same thing."

"It was the night," she waxed sarcastically. "The champagne. The cruise ship."

"You telling me this was a shipboard romance?"

"Correct." It had to be. She couldn't go around wanting Alex for the duration of the marriage. The mere thought was…well… unthinkable.

"And it's a very short cruise," she said tartly, sitting up and drawing her dress firmly around her, already regretting having let herself go—with Alex of all people. Talk about taking a complicated situation and blowing it right off the charts.

She glanced around the room. What had she done with her shoes?

Alex sat in silence for a moment, then muttered to himself. "I'll say it was short. We never even left the dock."

"We should go back out to the party," she said.

"Our clothes are covered in Wiki Waki."

Emma made a face.

"I'll call the concierge. I'm sure they can bring us up something we can change into."

And walk back into the party wearing a different dress? "I think I'll hide out here," she stated.

Alex picked up the telephone from the table next to the bed. "Are you kidding? This is perfect."

She turned her head to glare at him. Why were things that were so perfect for him always so embarrassing for her?

I slept with Alex.

Or, maybe: *The funniest thing happened last night... Alex and I accidentally...*

No, that wasn't the right way to start a conversation either.

"Emma?"

Startled, Emma glanced at Katie across the office desk. Her sister had wandered in about five minutes ago, wanting to talk about Knaresborough in central England.

"You okay?" asked Katie.

"Fine." Emma should spit it out, get it over with so she wouldn't feel as if there was this huge secret between them.

"Did you hear what I said?"

"Sure," Emma replied. "The bed-and-breakfast in Knaresborough."

"Right," said Katie. "It's over two hundred years old now, and David was saying..."

Emma had never kept a secret from Katie before. Not that this was a secret, exactly. But she'd sure never slept with a man and not told her sister about it the next morning.

"...because with the new competition," Katie continued. "The probable payback on the redecorating costs would be fifty years."

Emma blinked.

"Does fifty years make sense to you?"

"Uh, not really. Katie, there's something—"

Katie stood up, a beaming smile on her face. "I totally agree. I'll tell David."

David? Wait. No. Emma wanted to talk about Alex.

"He can leave in the morning."

"Alex?"

Katie stared at her for a second. "David."

"For where?"

"Knaresborough, of course. What can he do from here?"

Right. The redecorating. "Okay. But, before you—"

Katie started for the door. "I'll get Legal to draft up an authorization for us to sign."

"Sure. But—"

"Can we talk later? He's going to be so excited."

"Katie—"

"Lunch?"

Emma sighed. "I can't. I promised Alex I'd stop by his place."

Katie waited, her hand on the doorknob.

"You know," said Emma, her stomach buzzing at the very thought of formal wedding plans. "Invitations, flowers, catering."

Katie's eyebrows waggled. "You have fun now, you hear?"

"Yeah. Right."

Have fun facing Alex after he'd seen her naked?

Have fun watching Philippe and Mrs. Nash reenact the Battle of Hastings?

Or have fun trying on a wedding gown while Amelia Garrison turned over in her grave?

None of it sounded particularly promising.

Amelia, it seemed, was a flapper, and maybe a bit of a rebel. Emma decided she liked that.

Her nineteen-twenties dress was made of gorgeous cream satin with a long, overlay bodice of ecru lace. Sleeveless, it had a cluster of ribbons at the shoulder and hip, and a flared skirt that shimmered to her ankles.

"You were right," she said to Mrs. Nash, turning in the wood-framed, oblong mirror in the Wiltshire bedroom, enjoying the whisper of satin against her skin.

"A perfect fit," Mrs. Nash agreed, brushing the skirt and arranging the scooped neckline. "And exactly right for a garden party wedding."

Emma paused. "Thank you for understanding about the church." Instead of an altar, she and Alex had decided on a rose arbor in the garden, overlooking the ocean.

"No point in lying to God along with everyone else."

It was a small consolation, but Emma was taking whatever she could get. "I said no to the proposal at first."

Mrs. Nash fussed with the ribbons at her shoulder. "But you said yes eventually."

"I did."

"And Alex got his own way again."

"Does he get his own way often?"

"He's a billionaire. He gets his own way pretty much whenever he wants to."

"But not with you?" Emma guessed.

Mrs. Nash gave her a sharp-eyed look. "Never with me."

"I bet he appreciates that. Somebody keeping him grounded, I mean."

"He hates it. So did his father. But his mother wouldn't let the man fire me."

Emma attempted to shift the conversation to the positive. "She obviously valued your help."

Mrs. Nash straightened. "No. She did it to spite him."

Emma honestly didn't know what to say to that.

"She was a misguided young woman, and he was a bitter old man."

"But, why—" Emma quickly cut off her inappropriate question.

"The money," said Mrs. Nash. "She wanted it. He had it." Then Mrs. Nash shook her head. "She just didn't count on...the rest."

Emma tried to swallow the lump in her throat. She reminded herself that she had her own life, her own money, her own business. Alex wouldn't have any real power over her.

Mrs. Nash's voice turned brisk again. "I suspect she thought she'd outlive him."

Even though part of her dreaded the answer, Emma had to ask. "How did she die?"

"Horseback riding accident. Poor thing. Alex was only ten and a regular protégé for that cynical old bastard."

Emma shivered, struggling to find her voice. "Am I getting into bed with the devil?"

Mrs. Nash cocked her head, silent for a moment as she assessed Emma. "I'd say you'd already been to bed with the devil."

Emma was speechless. Did Mrs. Nash mean it literally? How could she possibly know?

Mrs. Nash gave an out-of-character chuckle as she went to work on the back buttons of the dress. "That's the trouble with the devil, young lady. He's irresistibly charming. Even to an old woman like me."

But Alex couldn't hurt Mrs. Nash. Where he could definitely hurt Emma. If she wasn't careful. If she didn't resist his charms on every possible level.

There was a sharp rap on the bedroom door.

"The invitations have arrived, ma'am."

"Thank you, Sarah," Mrs. Nash called. Then to Emma, "Philippe and Alex will be waiting downstairs."

* * *

Alex knew he had a problem as soon as he saw the expression on Emma's face.

"Six hundred and twenty-two?"

"You can add some more names if you'd like," said Mrs. Nash, her attention on one of the invitation samples. "We are *not* sending out scrollwork, script and purple fleur-de-lis under the Garrison family name." She gave Philippe a sharp look over the top of her glasses.

Emma waved the list at Alex. "Who are they? Your ex-lovers?"

The remark was uncalled for, and Alex clenched his jaw. "Hardly any of them."

Emma sniffed.

"The fleur-de-lis is a beautiful and honorable symbol," said Philippe. "It's an iris. For the goddess."

"I don't know six hundred people," said Emma. "I sure don't know three hundred."

Mrs. Nash squinted at the sample. "Good Lord, that butterfly hurts my eyes."

"You were thinking black and white?" asked Philippe.

"Silver," said Mrs. Nash.

"Blah," Philippe retorted.

"Maybe a little royal blue. Something dignified. Not this tacky, froufrou Technicolor explosion."

Alex couldn't care less what his invitations looked like. "Why are you making this into a thing?" he asked Emma.

She dropped her hand and the list into her lap. "I'm making six hundred and twenty-two things out of this."

"The garden is huge."

"That's not the point."

"What is the point?" He honestly wanted to know. What difference did it make if they got married in front of fifty guests or six hundred?

"Beef Wellington," Philippe suddenly sang out.

Emma turned to stare, while Mrs. Nash stilled.

"A compromise," said Philippe. "I will give up the fleur-de-lis if you agree to the *boeuf en croûte,* instead of your Yorkshire puddings."

"The Duke of Wellington's dish?" asked Mrs. Nash.

"Which he stole from Napoleon."

"After defeating him in the war."

Alex jumped in before the two could get going again. "Let's just say yes."

"And *I* have a compromise for you," said Emma.

Alex raised his brow.

"Your six hundred and twenty-two guests for a drive-through wedding in Vegas."

"Three hundred of them are yours," said Mrs. Nash, flipping her way through the invitation samples.

"What?" Emma's astonishment was clear.

"I spoke with your sister, and with your secretary."

Alex didn't even try to disguise his smug expression. "Three hundred of them are yours."

"Shoot me now," said Emma.

"Ahhh, mademoiselle," said Philippe, rising to put an arm around Emma. "It is no matter. You will be beautiful. The dinner will be magnificent. And people will forgive us for the insipid invitations."

"The flowers?" Alex quickly put in, before Mrs. Nash could make a remark that did justice to her expression.

Standing on the wide, concrete veranda, Emma watched a team of gardeners working on the expanse of lawn that stretched out to the cliffs at the edge of the Garrisons' property.

The tent would be set up on the north lawn. The arbor and

guest chairs for the ceremony were slated for the rose garden. And a band would play in the gazebo. If the weather looked promising, a lighted dance floor would be constructed near the bottom of the veranda stairs.

The print shop would work overtime on the invitations tonight, and come next Saturday, she'd marry Alex. The guests likely had plans for that day. Heck, Emma already had plans for Saturday. But she'd cancel them and so would they. A garden wedding at the Garrison estate was too hot a ticket to miss.

Alex was counting on that.

And, as Mrs. Nash had said, being a billionaire, he usually got his way.

"Everything okay?" his voice rumbled behind her.

She coughed out a laugh. "What could possibly be wrong?"

He came up beside her. "Thought you might like to know they've agreed on the centerpieces."

"Yeah?"

"White roses and purple heather. Okay by you?"

The timbre of the lawn-mower motor changed, and she shrugged in response to Alex's question. "I really don't have an opinion on the centerpieces."

"You should."

"Why?"

"It's your party."

She pulled her gaze away from the two men in the rose garden to look up at him. "You feel at all funny about this?"

"Funny how?"

"Like a fraud?"

His eyes squinted down for a moment. "A little. I didn't expect to…."

"It's not like we're breaking the law," she said, more to herself than to him.

"We're throwing a great party, solidifying a business relationship, and giving the tabloids something good to write about for the next two weeks. I don't see the harm."

Emma didn't either, at least not from the logical perspective he'd outlined. But there was a problem at a visceral level.

"I guess I should ask you who pays for it," she said.

"Pays for what?"

"The party. The wedding. The six hundred guests. Are we splitting it down the middle?"

"I'll get this one," he said, crossing his arms to lean them on the rail, shifting his attention to the distant horizon. The ocean was growing restless, frothing up green and white as the tide rolled in. "You can catch the next one."

"The next wedding?"

"The next dinner."

"I doubt it'll be for six hundred."

Alex just shrugged.

"We need to talk about that," she said, matching his posture, leaning on the top rail and gazing out at the rhythmic waves.

"About dinner?"

"About how we're going to work this. Where are we going to live."

"Here. I thought we'd decided."

"*You* decided."

There was a smirk in his voice. "And your point?"

She elbowed him. "My point is, I get a vote, too."

"I'll pull a Philippe."

"How so?"

"A compromise. We stay here on weekends. Weekdays, we hang out in the city at one of the penthouses."

Emma had to admit that sounded reasonable.

"You do know we have to stay together?" he asked. "At least at first."

"I know. That solution sounds fine."

"Given any thought to the honeymoon?"

"Not even a moment." In fact, she'd been avoiding thinking about the honeymoon. This wasn't exactly any girl's dream scenario.

"What about Kayven Island?"

She twisted her head to look at him. "A McKinley resort?"

"Sure."

"I thought you'd fight tooth and nail for the *home court advantage*."

"Will we be making any business deals on our honeymoon?"

"Wasn't on my agenda."

"Then you can have the home court advantage."

"It's not our best resort." Paris was bigger, and Whistler was most recently renovated.

Alex shrugged again. "I'd like to check out the island."

"A couple of days only—I'll book it. And I'm taking my laptop and PalmPilot."

"You afraid we'll get bored if we're alone together?"

A salt breeze gusted in off the ocean, and an image of Friday night when they were alone together bloomed in her mind. "Alex."

His expression said he was reading her mind.

"About Friday night…"

He waited.

"We can't do that again."

"Wanna bet?"

"Alex."

"I'm just saying we could if we wanted to."

"Well, we don't want to."

"You sure?"

"Yes! I'm sure. It was crazy and stupid."

"I thought it was exciting and satisfying."

She knew it was those things, too. But that didn't change the fact that it couldn't happen again.

"Just out of curiosity," said Alex. "What is your objection to it happening again?"

"This is a business deal."

"It's also a marriage."

She shook her head. What they were doing bore no resemblance whatsoever to a marriage. He was looking out for his interests, and she was looking out for hers. It was as simple as that.

"If we mix things up," she said. "If we get confused. One of us—and by one of us, I mean me—is going to get hurt."

Her hair lifted in the breeze, and he reached out to brush it back from her cheek. "I won't hurt you, Emma."

Despite the lightness of his touch, she knew it was a lie.

"Yes you will," she said. "Let's face it. You're not marrying me because, of all the women in New York, I'm the one you want to spend time with." She gave a harsh laugh. "Heck, even when you narrowed the pool down to *McKinley* women in *New York City,* I came last."

"You did not."

"Alex. Don't rewrite history."

"I'm not—"

"At least do me the courtesy of being honest. You want my hotels. Well, you've got them. And that means you've got me for a while, too." She was falling for Alex. There was no point in denying it any longer. But the idea that Alex might also be falling for her was laughable. He could have any woman in New York City, probably any woman in the country. And he liked them glamorous, sophisticated and fashionable.

He was being kind right now, because deep down inside he really was a decent guy. And he seemed to like her. Sometimes, he seemed to like her a whole lot.

But she wouldn't delude herself. She wouldn't set herself up for heartache. They both knew he wasn't about to fall for plain old Emma McKinley just because he happened to be marrying her. Her chest burned as she forced herself to voice the bald truth. "But don't pretend it's anything other than a business deal."

He was silent for a full minute, his eyes dark as a storm-tossed sea, and just as unreadable.

"Fine," he finally said, a sharp edge to his voice. "I'll pay for the party. You live at my house. And we'll both bring our laptops on the honeymoon."

Then he turned from the rail and marched down the stairs.

Emma was glad. She'd said what needed to be said, and cleared the air between them. It was the only way to move forward.

Really.

Alex knew he had to back off. He was pushing Emma too hard and too fast. But he had a burning need to figure out what was going on between them. Truth was, at this moment, he had a feeling he'd pick Emma over anybody anytime anywhere. And that scared him.

From the moment they'd made love, he knew things had gone way past a business deal. They had something going on, and he needed to figure out what it was. To do that, he needed to talk to Emma. But she didn't want to talk to him. She especially didn't want to talk to him about them.

Them.

What a concept.

Alex stopped at the edge of the rose garden and gave his head a quick shake. His brain couldn't wrap itself around the idea of a them. He liked her. Sure. And he respected her, and she definitely turned him on. But what did that mean?

Did it mean he should give their marriage a chance? Or did it mean he was getting too caught up in the whole wedding charade?

He turned toward the balcony where she gazed out at the ocean, her hair lifting in the breeze. His heart gave a little hitch at the sight of her, and he knew one thing for sure. He wouldn't be getting any perspective at all while Emma was around.

Backing off was probably a good idea, for his sanity if nothing else. Besides, they'd ridden the publicity wave about as far as they could. From a business perspective, there was nothing left to do but get married.

And then they'd be together on the honeymoon, and maybe things would start to make sense. And, if it didn't, they'd have plenty of time to talk things out. After all, Emma had made it pretty plain they wouldn't be doing anything else.

Once Philippe and Mrs. Nash joined forces, the wedding plans shifted to high gear, barely leaving Emma time to take a breath. She stopped asking questions along about Wednesday, seeking sanctuary in her business problems instead. It was less stressful to worry about the proposed tourist tax regime in France than the music to which she'd say "I do."

Yesterday, Mrs. Nash had couriered a set of cardboard index cards, telling her where to go and what to do over the two days of festivities. Tonight the rehearsal dinner kicked things off. She and Katie were to dress at Alex's mansion in Oyster Bay. Then a limo would pick up the wedding party at seven. Alex's cousin Nathaniel would host a dinner for fifty at the Cavendish Club.

Afterward, the women would stay over at the mansion. Where, tomorrow morning, a veritable army of hairdressers, manicurists and makeup artists were due to arrive.

For the moment, Emma's stomach did a little flip-flop as her car rounded a curve and the mansion came into view. What the neatly typed index cards didn't cover was her reaction to Alex.

Katie popped forward in the passenger seat. "*This* is where you're going to live?"

"Only on weekends," said Emma, her voice firm with conviction. "And only for a few months."

Over the past week, she'd refocused her priorities. Her mind was on business now. Alex was simply a means to an end.

She wouldn't picture them together—not in his breakfast nook over a cup of coffee, not on his deck sharing a bottle of wine, and definitely not in his bedroom, in a tangle of sheets, his hot, naked body pressed up against hers.

"Can I come visit?" Katie asked, twisting her head as they passed the front rose garden.

Emma sucked in a bracing breath. "Sure," she said with determined cheer. Then Katie's phraseology penetrated. She'd said *I* not *we*. "What about David?"

Beneath her gauzy, mauve blouse, Katie shrugged her shoulders. Her lips pursed every so slightly. "He's been working a lot of hours lately."

David's job interfering with his personal life?

"He works for you," Emma pointed out.

Katie tossed her head and let out a chopped laugh. "Never mind. It's nothing. Sometimes he hangs out with the guys at the club."

Emma pulled to a stop in the round driveway, turning to peer at her sister. "Is everything okay?"

Katie stared straight back. "Everything is great." She gestured to the wide staircase and the towering stone pillars. "Everything is fantastic! The Cavendish Club tonight, and the wedding of the year tomorrow. Now get your luggage and let's move in."

Emma nodded sharply in agreement. She could do this. She was ready for this.

Her cell phone buzzed, as two of Alex's staff members trotted down the stairs. She flipped it open and saw the Paris area code. Business before marriage. As it should be.

Nine

Alex stood at the bottom of the mansion's main staircase and listened to the hustle and bustle of the preparations. Mrs. Nash was taking a strip off a delivery man. Philippe was fussing over the temperature of the butter cream icing. And Katie was running around in a robe, worried about rose petals in the bathwater.

Only Emma seemed calm, serene really as she went along the hallway past Hamilton's portrait.

They were getting married tomorrow—in less than twenty-four hours—and she was talking to somebody in Paris, making sure the McKinley Inns convention display had arrived on time. She laughed at something the caller said, and her smile lit up the room.

He tried to remember the last time his house had felt like this. Maybe when he was a boy. Maybe when his mother was still alive.

His father had hated parties, but his mother had planned them anyway, sometimes for upward of a hundred. Alex could remember their arguments, and the way his father's jaw had tensed when the first guests arrived.

His gaze strayed to the landing at the top of the main staircase. As a young boy, he'd crept out of his room and peeked through the railing, watching finely coiffed women and snappily dressed men stroll through the foyer, drinks in hand, voices animated.

His mother had been happy on those nights. And the house had felt warm and alive. Like it felt now—with a woman present.

A certain glow worked its way up from the pit of his belly when he thought about Emma staying for a while. She looked up from her call and smiled at him before saying something in French into the phone.

Emma spoke French. And she seemed pretty much unflappable in the face of chaos.

Maybe they'd entertain some more. No harm in making the most of their time together. And fine parties with key contacts would do nothing but help their businesses thrive.

His own cell phone buzzed in his breast pocket, and he retrieved it, flipping it open.

"Garrison here," he said.

"It's your best man."

"Hey, Nathaniel. Where are you?"

"Just touching down in your backyard."

"You better not be blowing my tent over."

Nathaniel chuckled. "Relax. We're on the other side of the garage. You know you've got news crews circling, right?"

"They can circle all they want. We're going to the Cavendish Club tonight."

"Exactly. Still, I'm glad I'm not trying to get in your driveway."

"Did you happen to see a white cube van back there?"

"It's stuck behind a couple of semis and about a dozen limos."

"Good God. That's Philippe's tenderloin. I gotta get somebody out there to direct traffic."

"See you in a minute," said Nathaniel, signing off.

"Mrs. Nash," Alex called.

Emma plugged one ear and moved into an alcove.

Alex strode down the hallway and nearly ran into Katie.

"Can you please help me get her into the bath?" Katie pleaded.

"She's on the phone. Have you seen Mrs. Nash?" He continued toward the kitchen.

Katie scurried behind him. "I know she's on the phone. That's the problem."

"Well, I can't get her off. I have to rescue—"

The kitchen was a maelstrom of activity. That was the only way to describe it. A dozen cooks vied for space on the countertops. Two more were working over the stove. A cleanup crew was elbows deep in the sinks. And Mrs. Nash's voice rose clearly above the din as she spoke to a young man with a perpetually bobbing head.

"One *hundred* tables," she said. "The order was for white cloths with the royal blue skirting. And I don't want a single wrinkle. If you can't guarantee—"

"Never mind," Alex muttered to himself, doing an about-face.

"Alex," said Katie. "The hairdresser will be here in less than an hour."

Alex shook his head as he paced back down the hallway.

In the foyer, he picked the phone out of Emma's hand.

"Hey!"

"You, in the tub, now," he ordered, snapping it shut.

"Alex," she protested, grabbing for the phone.

"Save it. I've got four hundred pounds of tenderloin to rescue." He swung open the big oak door.

"Hey, cousin," sang Nathaniel.

"Point me to the cube van."

Nathaniel ignored him and elbowed his way in. "This must be Emma," he cooed, taking Katie by both hands.

"I'm Katie," she corrected, tugging her hands away and closing the neckline of her robe.

"Ahhh," said Nathaniel, hitting Alex with a sidelong look.

"What ahhh?" asked Katie, eyes narrowing.

"I'm Emma," said Emma, stepping forward to hold out her hand. "Alex has told me nothing but good things about you."

Nathaniel took Emma's hand with great fanfare and bestowed a kiss on her knuckles. "You're more beautiful than I imagined. And a most charming liar."

"What ahhh?" Katie repeated.

Nathaniel gave her a sharp look. "Wait your turn."

"Excuse me?" she said.

Nathaniel ignored her, clinging to Emma's hand.

"Would you do something for me?" Emma asked him sweetly.

"For you, anything."

"Make Alex give me back my phone."

Alex grasped her shoulders, turning her toward the staircase. "Bath."

Then he turned to his cousin. "And *you,* keep your hands off my bride."

"She's stunning," said Nathaniel with an exaggerated sigh, then he deigned to gaze down at Katie.

Katie stared back with a clenched jaw.

"Ahhh means I've heard about you, too," he said.

She was about to ask what he'd heard. Alex could see it in her eyes. But, to her credit, and to what had to be Nathaniel's disappointment, she didn't take the bait. She kept completely silent.

Head held high, she turned to link arms with Emma, and the women headed up the stairs.

"You're losing your touch, cousin," said Alex.

Nathaniel straightened his tie. "We already know she has terrible taste in men."

Alex slapped him on the back. "You cling to that thought. And help me get the damn tenderloin into the house."

After the wedding rehearsal and the dinner at Cavendish, Alex leaned on the railing of his veranda. It was after midnight, and the mansion was mostly dark. But the yard lights were on, and a few clouds teased a faraway moon.

"Not too late to back out," said Nathaniel, approaching with a crystal tumbler of single malt in each hand.

"I'm not backing out," said Alex. Worst case scenario, he'd make millions of dollars. Best case... He accepted the drink from Nathaniel and took a long swallow.

Best case, Emma decided to give them a real chance.

He'd given it a lot of thought over the past week, and there was something going on between them. It went past business, even past friendship, and he intended to use the honeymoon to figure out exactly what it was.

"The sister's prettier," said Nathaniel.

Alex straightened and shot his cousin a warning glare. "Excuse me?"

Nathaniel chuckled low.

"Emma happens to be gorgeous."

"Do you happen to be falling for your bride?"

"I'm simply pointing out the obvious."

"That she's gorgeous?"

"She is." Anyone could see that.

"And Katie's a pale second?"

Alex took another swig.

Had he once called Katie the pretty one? Because Katie couldn't hold a candle to Emma. Emma was one of those rare women who got prettier as you got to know her. She had a stunning smile, eyes that glowed when she was happy and sparkled when she laughed. She had an inner radiance that nobody could fake.

"Katie's a pale second," he agreed.

Nathaniel sobered, and his jaw went tight. "You do remember she has an ulterior motive, right?"

"Katie?"

"Emma."

"I'm fully aware of all Emma's motives." She was doing exactly what she'd promised. The woman didn't have a scheming bone in her body.

"Al—"

"Back off, Nate."

"I'm just saying."

"Well stop saying it. My wife is not plotting against us."

"Everybody's plotting against us."

"You're paranoid."

"She's marrying you for your money."

"Because I forced her to."

"Just keep your guard up."

"Just mind your own damn business."

Nathaniel shook his head. Then his mouth curved into a knowing smile.

"What?" Alex asked.

"It's ironic," said Nathaniel.

Alex waited.

"That you fell for her."

"I did not." Alex snapped his jaw shut.

Okay. No point in disagreeing. He had fallen for Emma. But it hadn't clouded his judgment. For the first time in his life, his judgment was clear.

He was marrying Emma in the morning, and it was absolutely the right thing to do.

* * *

Emma told herself over and over that this wasn't a real wedding. But somehow it didn't ease the pain of her father's absence. Marriage of convenience or not, he should have been here to hold her hand, to escort her down the aisle, to tell her everything was going to be all right when, deep down in her soul, Emma feared it would never be all right again.

The weather had cooperated. So, under the glare of a brilliant blue sky, the gazebo band struck up the traditional version of the "Wedding March." Mrs. Nash's choice, no doubt.

That was Katie's cue to start down the long strip of royal blue carpet that bisected seven hundred white folding chairs filled with smiling friends, relatives and business associates. Lilac ribbons streamed from the floral pew ends, fluttering in the breeze while Emma kept her attention fixed on Katie's purple dress.

Proving Alex lived in a whole other world, Mrs. Nash had hired a team of seamstresses to design and sew Katie's dress in less than a week. The same nineteen-twenties style as Emma's, it was shorter and simpler, and perfectly suited to Katie's slender shape.

They'd both opted for upswept hairstyles. To match the color of her dress, Katie's had a light sprinkling of irises at the back, while Emma had had a pinned French twist and the antique diamond tiara to match her cream-colored vintage gown. A veil seemed excessive, so she'd left her head bare.

Katie passed the midpoint of the long aisle, Emma's cue to start walking. She took a deep breath and pasted a smile on her face. She couldn't bring herself to meet anyone's eyes, and she sure didn't want to look at Alex, so she fixed her gaze on the rose-covered arbor.

Everything else faded to her soft vision, and she told herself her father would be proud. At least, she hoped he would be proud. She'd give anything to have him here to tell her one way or the other.

By the time she made it to the front, her eyes were misty with memories and regrets. Striking in his tux, Alex took her hands in his and stared at her quizzically while the preacher welcomed the congregation.

His eyes narrowed in a question, and she shook her head and forced a smile. She was fine. She would get this over with, and her life would get back to normal. Well, almost normal.

He gave her a smile in return and a reassuring little squeeze. Then the preacher addressed the two of them, talking at length on the solemnity of marriage and their obligations to each other as lifelong partners.

Emma grew more uncomfortable by the second. Was Alex listening to this? Had he known it was coming? Could they not cut to the "I dos" and get out?

Finally, the preacher started on the vows. Emma almost breathed a sigh of relief. But then her gaze caught Alex's, and his deep voice seemed to penetrate her very skin. She felt a tingle envelope her as he promised to love her and honor her.

It wasn't real. She'd repeated that to herself over and over again. But when she whispered her own vows, something shifted inside her. And when he slipped the antique wedding band on her finger, she felt the weight of a dozen generations on her shoulders. For better or worse, she was now a Garrison bride.

The preacher pronounced them husband and wife, the crowd erupted in a spontaneous cheer, and Alex leaned down to kiss her.

"For the record," he whispered as his palms cupped her face and lips grew close. "I *did* marry the pretty one."

Then his tender kiss exploded between them. He pulled back, far too soon. For a moment, and only for a moment, with her head tucked into the crook of his neck, inhaling his scent, feeling the strength of his arms and the power of his heartbeat, she let herself believe. But then she heard the helicopters in the distance and realized it was all for the benefit of the telephoto lenses.

Alex was grinning happily at her. He planted one more kiss on her forehead before taking her hand for the recessional. The band struck up, and the standing crowd congratulated them all the way down the aisle.

Back on the veranda, Katie gave her a quick hug and kiss, then they assembled into a receiving line to greet ambassadors, celebrities and captains of industry.

"You did great," said Alex nearly two hours later as they made their way across the lawn. The sky had turned a glorious pink. The champagne was flowing, and succulent smells were beginning to waft from the tent.

"I want to jump up on the nearest table and confess to them all," said Emma. The deeper they went into their deception, the guiltier she felt.

"I wouldn't recommend that," said Alex.

"Afraid I'd tarnish the Garrison name?"

He smirked. "Afraid you'd convince six hundred people you were a lunatic. I'd be forced to tell them you were merely drunk. It could get ugly."

"I didn't drink a thing."

"You mean I'd be, gasp, *lying?*"

"Don't you feel the least bit guilty?"

"At the moment, I feel…as if it's none of their damn business."

"You invited them to our wedding."

"To eat Beef Wellington, not to pass judgment on my life."

"They're your friends and family."

"You're my family now."

His words made her chest ache. "Don't say that."

In response, he took her hand and kissed each of the knuckles.

"Alex, don't." His playacting made her want things she couldn't have, things they could never have together.

"Emma. It's you and me now. And we'll make whatever damn decisions we want."

If only. But they weren't living in a vacuum. "What about Katie? And Ryan? And Nathaniel."

He sighed. "Are you always going to be this contrary?"

"My contrariness is a surprise to you?"

Before he could answer, Mrs. Nash bustled from the crowd, and he muttered in Emma's ear. "Knew I should have put obey in the vows."

"*There* you are." Mrs. Nash swiftly plucked some imaginary lint from the bodice of Emma's dress. Then she straightened Alex's tie. "They need you two at the head table."

"Nathaniel's written a great toast," said Alex.

Emma's stomach sank. She didn't think she could take any more benevolent smiles and heartfelt well wishes. "Surely you told him the truth."

"I haven't told him a thing."

"So his toast will be sincere?"

"He's going to call me lucky, and you gracious and beautiful."

The words, "I *did* marry the pretty one," suddenly rushed back into Emma's brain. What could Alex have meant by that?

Katie was stunningly gorgeous tonight. Even though she was on David's arm, half the men in the yard were staring openly at her, including Nathaniel, who looked annoyed about something.

"You *are* beautiful," Alex continued in a gentle voice. "And I *am* lucky. Focus on the truth, Emma."

It wasn't as simple as that. "Yet all those so-called truths are couched in one very big lie."

Had Nathaniel guessed what they'd done? Was that the reason for the scowl on his face?

"The head table," prompted Mrs. Nash.

"You have a half-empty attitude," Alex said to Emma.

"And you have flexible ethics."

"Emma, Emma." He put his hands on her shoulders, slowly guiding her toward the giant open-air tent. "Don't fail me now."

The speeches were over. The cake was cut. The Beef Wellington had been magnificent. And Emma was still holding up.

As the conductor cued up the first waltz, Alex counted his blessings and pulled her into his arms.

"Home stretch," he whispered, as much to have an excuse to lean in close as to reassure her. She knew her only remaining duty was to throw the bouquet.

To his delight, she almost immediately softened against him, matching his step to "Color My World." He'd chosen it because it was short. But it also seemed appropriate. He might not be in love with Emma, but she'd brought more life to his cavernous old house than he'd seen in years. He couldn't help but think his father would gripe about the noise. He also knew his mother would be pleased.

Vaguely aware of the oohs and ahhs of the crowd around them, he was infinitely more aware of the soft, sensual woman, pliant in his arms. Her guard was down, he imagined from exhaustion, but he wasn't going to dwell on the reason.

He planted a gentle kiss on the top of her head. Yeah, it would look good in the pictures. But, honestly, he felt like doing it. She'd been terrific today. In the receiving line, he'd been impressed with her graciousness all over again.

Maybe they could host some kind of Garrison-McKinley companies social function. Ryan would certainly be thrilled with the personal touch.

"We staying here tonight?" Emma asked, fatigue evident in her voice.

He shook his head. "Chuck will fly us to the airport."

A genuine laugh left her lips. "A helicopter ride from your backyard to the roof to the airport?"

"That's right."

"Okay. I'm not going to complain about that."

"You're *not?*"

She shook her head against his chest. "Not tonight. You can go ahead and spoil me to death."

He couldn't help but smile. "You got it."

The song ended, and a new one started up immediately. Emma would be relieved to have Nathaniel and Katie join them on the dance floor.

Alex caught sight of David scowling in the crowd. It was mean-spirited, but he was glad Nathaniel was making the man think. Taking a cushy job at his girlfriend's company? That was just tacky.

Nathaniel danced up beside them. "May I?" He nodded to Emma.

Alex's arms automatically tightened around her. *No.* He didn't want to stop dancing with Emma. And he didn't want lady-killer Nathaniel holding her close.

He felt a sudden pang of empathy for David.

"Certainly," he said smoothly, smiling at his cousin and forcing his arms to release her.

Then he turned to Katie to complete the switch.

"Great party," she told him, doing a hop step to catch up to his rhythm.

"Thanks."

"Think you'd be willing to host your sister-in-law's wedding?"

"My who?"

She tipped her chin to look up at him. "Me, of course."

"Oh."

"Think about it?"

"Sure."

They danced a few more steps. "So what's the story with your British cousin?"

"What do you mean?"

"He's very nosy."

"Is he asking about Emma?"

Was Nathaniel yanking his chain? Or did he still think Emma was a threat? And why was her smile so bright?

"Is that jealousy?" teased Katie.

"Don't be ridiculous." Alex dragged his attention away from Emma.

Nathaniel wouldn't flirt with his bride. Or would he? Had he come up with some bizarre plan to prove she was opportunistic?

He glanced at them again.

"You're as bad as she is," said Katie, digging her elbow into his ribs.

"Huh?"

"You can't keep your hands off each other."

Alex's jaw dropped. "Excuse me?"

"You heard me."

Had Emma actually told her they'd made love?

Katie waved a hand. "Give it up, Alex. You're not fooling anybody."

His heart thudded heavily in his chest. Katie knew they'd made love. Had she guessed how he felt?

He didn't even know how he felt.

He had to throw her off track. He carefully arranged his features and shrugged, feigning unconcern. "You know the score." He waited. "That thing on the cruise ship was…you know, just a thing."

Katie drew back, confusion on her face. "What thing on the cruise ship?"

Alex cursed himself and scrambled for a recovery. "We… had a fight."

"You two have fights all the time. One more would definitely not be memorable." Katie peered suspiciously into his eyes. "What happened on the cruise ship?"

"Nothing."

He knew the exact second comprehension hit her. "Oh my God."

"It's not—"

"And she didn't *tell* me? I'm going to kill her."

"No!" His arms reflexively tightened around Katie. "Don't you say a word."

"Why didn't she tell me? Why wouldn't she tell me?"

Alex could have kicked himself. "Back off, Katie. She's had a tough day."

"There's only one reason she wouldn't tell me," Katie muttered to herself, her feet tangling over the dance steps so that Alex had to recover for both of them.

"Because she regrets it," he said. She was afraid he would hurt her. And he might still. But then she might hurt him right back.

It was a chance they'd both have to take. They needed to work it out together. And alone.

Katie was shaking her head. "No, that can't be the reason."

He steered Katie toward Emma and Nathaniel.

She resisted his pressure. "Oh no you don't. You're not dumping me with him again."

Alex sure as hell was. "He's your official escort."

"He's my inquisitor."

"Katie?"

"Yeah?"

"Don't say anything to Emma about the cruise. It was a mistake. We both made a mistake."

Katie opened her mouth. But then she closed it again and nodded.

"Nate," said Alex.

Nathaniel glanced up and gave him a cocky, knowing grin. "Need your girl back?"

"I'm sure she's had enough of you."

"Why don't we ask her?"

But Alex latched on to Emma's arm, forcing Nathaniel to let go of her.

"Ahhh," said Nathaniel, staring down at his returning partner. "The charming Katie. Where were we?"

"Let me save you some time," she said, adjusting her arm to keep a careful distance from him. "No. None of your business. And when hell freezes over."

Despite her efforts, Nathaniel dragged her closer, his voice fading as they spun away. "You know, you really shouldn't make promises you can't keep."

Emma blinked up at Alex. "What was that all about?"

"I don't think Nathaniel likes David."

She moved into step with him. "Well, neither do you."

Alex grunted. "That's because he's hiding behind Katie's skirts."

Emma punctuated her opinion with an exasperated sigh. "He's got an MBA. And he's a respected project manager."

"Then why's he hiding behind Katie's skirts? Why not make something of himself?"

"I'm way too tired to have this fight."

Alex felt like a heel. "Sorry."

"Hey, will you look at that."

"At what?"

Emma nodded across the floor. "Philippe is dancing with Mrs. Nash."

Alex followed the direction of her nod. Sure enough. And they were laughing about something.

"I guess they finally found some common ground," he said.

"That's good to see." Emma settled back in. "So what time is our flight to Kayven?"

"Whenever we want to go."

"You haven't booked the tickets yet?"

Alex smiled as he shook his head. "We don't need tickets. I have a plane."

Her shoulders relaxed, and she closed her eyes. "Naturally you have a plane." Then she rested her cheek against his chest, just the way he liked it. "And I'm not going to complain about that one either."

He rubbed his hand up and down her back. "I have to say, I really like your attitude."

"Don't get too used to it. All I need is a good night's sleep."

Ten

Alex was a perfect gentleman all the way to Kayven Island.

They'd stopped in L.A. for a late dinner. After which, Emma had had a surprisingly restful sleep across the Pacific, arriving at the local Kayven airstrip in the early morning hours.

Partway between Hawaii and Fiji, the island boasted white sand beaches, world-class reefs and turquoise seas dotted with brightly colored sailboats. The McKinley Resort consisted of a main building with traditional hotel rooms, an open-air lounge and a restaurant, along with several dozen bungalows scattered between towering palm trees.

Emma and Alex's bungalow opened onto a wide, covered patio with three steps down to the beach.

They quickly discovered their PalmPilots didn't work. Neither did their cell phones. Internet service was only available in the main building, and it was intermittent at best.

So, after an open-air breakfast of pastries and tropical fruit,

Alex declared they should chuck their business obligations and rent a catamaran for the day. Inspired by the salt breeze and laid-back atmosphere of the island, Emma wasn't inclined to argue.

So, at 10:00 a.m., along about the time she usually attended her senior staff meeting, she was dressed in a lilac bikini, skimming over the waves of the South Pacific, the breeze in her hair and the salt spray dampening her skin.

"Dolphins," Alex called from the stern, and she twisted on the pontoon seat to see a dozen dorsal fins cutting through the green water.

"How do you know they're not sharks?" For the first time since leaving the dock, Emma cast a suspicious glance at the clear water below her.

Alex pulled the tiller. "Let's take a closer look."

"No!" she squealed. What did Alex know about sharks and dolphins? He'd spent his entire life in a city center just like her.

He laughed. "Chicken."

"I like my legs, thank you very much."

"They're dolphins."

"No offense, but you're hardly an expert."

He corrected their course to follow the towering cliffs of the shoreline. After a set of rudimentary instructions on sailing the two person catamaran, the man at the rental shop had provided a map to a snorkeling beach and one of the islands scenic coral reefs.

"I've watched the Discovery Channel," said Alex, his tone tinged with mock offense.

"I rest my case."

"You've got to learn to trust me on something."

"I'm letting you drive, aren't I?"

"*Letting* me?"

She whooped as they crested a particularly big wave, then sang out, "My turn on the way back."

"I don't think so."

"Hey, Alex. You've got to learn to trust me on something."

"You can decorate the main floor."

"The main floor of what?"

"Of my house."

She turned to stare at him. "We're decorating your house."

He stared out over the waves, and she had to fight to keep from ogling his wet, tanned body. His calves were sculpted with muscle, and his pecs were something out of a beach-boy magazine. His face was handsome as ever, but the rakish swirl of his windblown hair left him looking softer, less intimidating than he had in New York.

She was suddenly aware that they'd be spending the day on a deserted beach, far away from the problems and constraints of their real lives. She'd sworn up and down, to herself and to Alex, that they were never, ever making love again. Now she found herself questioning that promise, exploring the rationale and trying to remember exactly why it was so important that she keep her hands off him.

"I thought we'd decorate before the party," he said.

She shook herself out of the fantasy. "Huh?" *What party?*

"I thought a Garrison-McKinley company party might be a nice idea. Ryan is always after me to soften my image."

She gave her head a shake. "You want another party? After yesterday? Or was it the day before?"

"Actually, I think this might be our wedding day."

"Don't mess with me."

"I'm not messing with you. The International Date Line takes a funny jog around Kiribati."

She refused to be impressed by his knowledge. "Well, it's only noon," she retorted. "That means we're not married yet."

He squinted. "Hmmm. That means there's time for one last fling."

Emma made a show of glancing around the empty ocean. "With who?"

Alex waggled his eyebrows.

"In your dreams." Or in her dreams, depending on how you looked at it.

"Look," he said. "There's the point and the bent palm tree." He abruptly turned the tiller, sending the blue-and-red sail swinging crossways over the catamaran.

Emma shaded her eyes as a sparkling white, crescent-shaped beach came into view. Cliffs towered over it on both sides, and a white, frothy waterfall spilled into the little cove.

"Wow." She let out a long breath of appreciation. "I don't think we're in Manhattan anymore."

"Screw the cell phones," said Alex. "The world can live without us for a day."

Emma laughed and shook off the remaining vestiges of her guilt, while the sail caught a gust of wind, pushing the front of the floats onto the soft sand.

She quickly hopped off the net platform, sinking calf-deep in the warm water, and grabbing the rope as the floats bobbed free again.

Alex joined her and tugged the boat onto the sand and removed their supply sack.

She pulled her messy hair free of the elastic and raked it into a new ponytail. Without the breeze from the moving sailboat, the sun was burning hot. And the water was more than inviting.

"Swim first or snorkel?" asked Alex, reading her thoughts.

"Anything that gets me wet."

They swam in the cove and snorkeled around the reef for hours. With the swim fins for propulsion, Emma easily maneuvered through the salt water, seeing thousands of fish in every color imaginable, crabs, sea urchins and sea stars, plants and shells, and what seemed like mile upon mile of vibrant coral.

Thirst and hunger finally brought them to the surface. The sun had moved far enough in the sky that they could find shade from one of the cliffs. They spread their blanket out near the waterfall, where the fine spray brought the air temperature down a few degrees.

Emma leaned back and inhaled the scent of the tropical flowers, then she closed her eyes to concentrate on the calls of birds and the low hum of the insects. A sigh slipped out. "Do we really have to go back?"

Alex's sexy voice was full of promise. "No, we don't."

She opened one eye, squinting at him through her sunglasses as he lay down on the blanket, propping himself up on one elbow.

She matched his pose so that she was facing him. "Eventually, we'd starve."

He pushed his sunglasses up on his forehead, shifting almost imperceptibly forward. "We'd survive on fish and coconuts."

"You're going to fish."

"I'm a versatile guy."

"How are you going to cook them?"

He moved her sunglasses up on her forehead. "I'll gather firewood from the forest."

The mere whisper of his touch spiked her pulse. "And rub two sticks together?"

"If I have to. I didn't become a billionaire by giving up."

"I thought you became a billionaire by inheriting lots of money."

He moved closer. "Yeah. There was that. But it doesn't mean I'm not a resourceful guy." His gaze dipped to her cleavage, and a buzz of sexual awareness ran through her.

"Alex."

"It's okay." He reached for the spaghetti strap on her bikini top, running his index finger beneath it, then trailing it down her arm. The fabric peeled away, exposing the barest millimeter of her nipple.

His eyes darkened, and she could feel the sensuality radiating from his very pores. Next, he leaned forward and kissed the tip of her shoulder, his cool lips gentle on her sun-warmed skin.

She knew she should fight it, but the last thing in the world she wanted to do was interrupt a sexy man on a tropical beach, making her feel like she was the most desirable woman in the world.

He left her shoulder to kiss the mound of her breast, trailing his fingertips along the curve of her waist.

She gasped in a breath, and his arm went solidly around her, turning her onto her back, his dark head blocking out the bright sunshine.

"I want you," he said.

And she wanted him, too. So much that it hurt to breathe. Her chest was tight. Her skin was tingling. And her thigh muscles pulsated with the need for his touch.

"Oh, Alex."

He bent his head close to hers, kissing the corner of her mouth.

"It's okay," he muttered. "It's after three. We're married now."

Before she could smile, he kissed her full on the lips, his broad hand swooping beneath her bottom to pull her against him.

She opened her mouth, tangling with his tongue. And her hands framed his face, pulling herself closer and deeper, trying desperately to fuse her body to his.

The waterfall roared in her ears, and the breeze off the ocean sensitized her skin. She kissed his cheek, his shoulder, the bulge of his bicep, tasting the sea salt, reveling in the flavor of his arousal.

He flicked the clasp of her bikini top, and the purple fabric fell away, exposing her breasts to the heat of the sun and Alex's avid gaze.

"The pretty one," he muttered. "The beautiful, sexy, charming sister. I am so glad you stormed into my office that day."

Emma tried to comprehend his meaning, but the words didn't make sense. And then he drew her nipple into his mouth, and the entire world stopped making sense. It was Alex. And they were married. And she was falling fast and hard and unconditionally for him.

The rake of his teeth and the swirl of his tongue sent pulses of delight streaking down her body. She arched her spine, tipping her head back, closing her eyes against the rainbow of light taking over her brain.

She had to feel him. She had to touch him. She had to make sure he was experiencing *half* the intensity she was.

She ran her hands up his arms, resisting the urge to linger, exploring his biceps and strong shoulders. Then she tangled her fingers in his hair, pulling him tight against her breast, releasing a pent-up moan of desire.

He moved to the other breast, and she trailed her fingertips down his back, shifting her knees and pressing his arousal into the cradle of her thighs.

He drew back. "Whoa. You sure?"

"Yes," she blurted. "I'm sure. I *want you.* Whatever. Just tell me what to say."

He chuckled as he kissed her mouth. "I meant are you sure you want it this fast."

"Yes. Now. Right now." She didn't think she could wait another second.

He sobered, his thumb hooking her bikini bottom and sliding it off over her sweat-slicked skin. Then he made short work of his own trunks, positioning himself over her, staring down at her with tousled hair and dark eyes, like some kind of sea god bent on conquest.

His fingertips trailed down the slight indentation of her belly, and she squirmed beneath him, holding her breath, waiting, anticipating. He stared deep into her eyes and smoothed over her curls, parting her thighs and easing his finger into her body.

She sucked in a breath with the exquisite pulse that came to life deep inside her. She slid her own hand down his body, cupping him, controlling him, pulling him toward her to satisfy her growing impatience.

He swore under his breath.

Then he pushed her hand away and flexed his hips, pressing himself at her entrance, widening her, stretching her, sliding slick and thick and hot inside her, inch after delicious inch as his hands tangled with hers and their mouths fused once more.

Primal passion took over.

The birds called in the treetops, the waterfall cooled the raging fever of their skin, and Alex's rhythm matched the pulsating waves taking over their gleaming stretch of beach.

He sped up, then slowed down, and she bit her lip, pushing back against his hands, arching her spine and tipping her hips to bring his thrusts faster and harder against her.

Then the world seemed to freeze. Her breathing stopped, and the sun disappeared, the trees went silent and she cried his name as the rainbow sensations washed over her again and again and again.

His own cry was guttural, and the parrots took flight above them, a cacophony of surprise and confusion. Then his weight finally settled, pressing her into the warm sand, his arms, his breath, his heartbeat surrounding her.

By the time they made it back to their bungalow, dusky pink clouds were gathering above the island.

Then, while the maître d' sat them in the resort's open-air restaurant, the first fat raindrops plunked on the palm leaves and turned the wooden deck a dark mottled brown. Lightning flashed in the distance, and the growing rainstorm clattered against the restaurant's thatched roof.

Grateful for the cool air, Emma settled back in the cushioned teak chair, dangling her sandal from her toes while the cool breeze swirled around her cotton print dress. The hurricane lamps on the tables seemed to brighten as the orange ball of the sun disappeared below the horizon.

Emma gazed at the flickering light on Alex's handsome face, hardly believing they'd so thoroughly consummated their marriage.

"What are you thinking?" he asked.

She grinned. "That I'm married to the best-looking man in the room."

He glanced around. "Okay," he said slowly. "But the other guys are mostly over sixty."

A waiter in a pristine white jacket approached. "Mr. and Mrs. Garrison. I am Peter, the restaurant manager. The chef was delighted to hear you would be dining with us tonight. He has asked if he might present some additional entrée suggestions?"

Alex stood up and shook the waiter's hand. "Good to meet you, Peter. Please, tell the chef we would be delighted to hear his suggestions."

"Very good." With a smile and a nod, Peter retreated, only to be replaced by their cocktail waiter.

"Champagne?" Alex raised his eyebrows in Emma's direction.

"For our wedding night?" she asked with a stupid, sappy grin. But she couldn't help it. It was still Saturday and, if the expression in Alex's dark eyes was anything to go by, they were about to spend a glorious night together.

He nodded to Emma, then turned to the waiter. "Cristal Rose? The ninety-six?"

The waiter nodded sharply. "Excellent." Then he swiftly removed their red and white wineglasses and left the table.

Alex reached for her hands and took a deep breath. "So, you want to talk about this? Or do we just let it happen?"

She let the warmth of his touch penetrate her skin. "The champagne?"

He shook his head, stroking his thumb over her rings. "No. Not the champagne."

"Let me see." She tilted her head. "The chef?"

"No. Not the chef."

"Your inability to steer a catamaran?"

"Hey."

"You nearly took out those two tourists."

"Their dive to the left was incredibly sudden."

"They were scattering in terror."

Alex paused, then he sobered. "May I assume your redirecting the conversation means you just want to let it happen?"

His words sent a shiver through her, and she leaned forward, lowering her voice. "I'm not even sure what 'it' is yet."

He gave her fingers a gentle squeeze. "I am," he said softly.

An unaccountable panic burst through her belly. "Don't—"

"I won't. Not tonight."

"Mr. and Mrs. Garrison," Peter interrupted. "May I present Chef Olivier."

Alex released Emma's hands, and she tucked her hair behind her ears as the wind picked up another notch.

Alex got to his feet. "A pleasure," he said to Chef Olivier, shaking the man's hand.

"The pleasure is mine," the chef replied.

"Are you cold?" Peter inquired of Emma. "Shall we close the shutters?"

"Please, don't," said Emma. There was something wildly beautiful about the pounding rain, the distant lightning, and the crazily undulating palm fronds. There was a potent storm brewing out on the Pacific, and a potent storm brewing inside her. Both were frightening, unpredictable and exhilarating all at the same time.

Eleven

"I want to say it," said Alex, propping himself up on one elbow in their huge four-poster bed.

"You can't say it," Emma responded, her sun kissed breasts glowing a golden honey against the stark white sheets.

"But I mean it," he insisted. He'd realized hours ago that he was madly, passionately, incredibly in love with his wife.

She reached up to place her index finger across his lips. "You promised."

He drew her fingertip into his mouth, turning the suction into a kiss. "Bet I can make you say it."

She shook her head in denial, but he knew that he could. The right kiss, the right caress, the right whisper in her ear, and her secrets were his for the taking.

It wasn't ego. It simply was.

He feathered his fingers up the length of her thigh.

"Don't," she gasped.

He smiled. "Say it."

"Play fair."

"All's fair in—"

"Alex."

He moved his hand and kissed the tip of her nose. "I'm just messin' with you."

"Well, I don't like it," she said tartly.

"Sure you do. At least give me that."

Her mouth twitched in a reluctant half smile.

The telephone next to the bed jangled in his ear.

He swore out loud.

"What time is it?" she groaned, covering her ears in time for the second ring.

"Around one," he said, picking up the receiver before it could vibrate his eardrums a third time. "Yeah?"

"Where the *hell* were you?" barked Nathaniel.

"Dinner. The beach. Why?"

"Because you're about to lose half a billion dollars, that's why."

Alex sat up straight, his brain shifting gears faster than a Formula One driver. "What happened? Where are you?"

"David happened. And I'm still in New York."

"David?" asked Alex.

Emma sat bolt upright. "What about David? Is Katie all right?"

Alex held up a finger. He wasn't trying to be dismissive, but he needed to hear what Nathaniel had to say.

"David, that slimy, underhanded son-of-a-bitch, is attempting to *sell* the Kayven Island Resort."

Alex reflexively glanced around. "Huh?"

"Please, cousin, tell me you're a director of McKinley Inns. Tell me the paperwork is done. Tell me Emma and Katie don't still have control of that company."

Alex's gaze shifted to Emma.

"What?" she asked.

"Alex?" Nathaniel prompted.

"The lawyers are drafting right now."

"Are you telling me *nothing's* been signed?"

"Only the loan to McKinley."

"Shit."

Alex's tone was harsh. "What the hell is going on, Nate?"

"Cranston's flashing a power of attorney signed by those two women."

That didn't make any sense. None at all. "Hang on." Alex covered the receiver.

Emma was watching him with an impatient look of confusion.

He kept his voice even. It had to be a mistake, or maybe a forgery. "Nathaniel says David Cranston has a power of attorney."

She drew back on the bed, shifting the covers away. "For what?"

"Did you sign anything for him?"

She shook her head. "No." Then she stopped shaking and her eyes narrowed. "Wait. There was one thing. An authorization to redecorate a bed-and-breakfast in Knaresborough. It's a tiny little place. Nothing important."

Alex returned to the phone. "She says all he can do is redecorate some bed-and-breakfast."

"It's not redecorating. And it's not a bed-and-breakfast. The man is authorized to sell any and all McKinley properties. He's cutting a deal with Murdoch and DreamLodge. For an obscene commission."

"How do you know—don't answer that." Alex went back to Emma. "Did you read it carefully?"

Her eyes went wide, and her face paled.

"Did you read it at all?"

"We'd already talked about it…" Her features pinched, and her hands fisted around the blanket. "With the wedding and all… I signed so many stacks of paper."

He let out a pithy swearword.

"Yeah," said Nathaniel. "Now you're catching on. You get your ass on a plane."

Alex glanced to the rain battered window and the pitch black beyond. "Can you stall?"

"I've already put his entire legal team on retainer, had them declare a conflict of interest, and forced him to find new attorneys. You don't want to know what that cost me."

"Did you talk to Katie."

"Hell, yes."

"Can she stop it?"

"Not without Emma."

Alex closed his eyes and willed the wind and rain to *stop*. "We'll be there as soon as humanly possible."

"Get here now." The line went dead.

Alex set down the phone.

"Alex?" Emma whispered hoarsely.

He stared at her. There was no easy way to say this. "David is trying to sell the Kayven Island Resort."

She blinked back in silence. "Why?"

Alex's stomach clenched to walnut size.

Why?

Because its value is about to rise to half a billion dollars. Sorry I forgot to mention that before you married me.

Emma understood the words "trying to sell Kayven Island." It was the meaning that eluded her.

David was redecorating in Knaresborough. And, as far as she knew, hadn't had anything to do with the Kayven Island property.

"Why would he do that?" she repeated into the rain-dotted silence. She got that something was wrong. But she couldn't get the puzzle pieces to connect inside her head.

"For a big, fat commission from Murdoch." Alex raked a hand through his hair. "Why didn't Katie see—"

"Back up," said Emma, clambering off the bed and shrugging into one of the hotel robes. "Murdoch?"

Alex's eyes went hard as granite. "Murdoch bribed David to find a way to sell him Kayven Island."

"He wanted it that bad?" Sure it was a nice resort, but it served a small niche market. It commanded steep rates, so it was often half empty. Nobody was getting rich off Kayven Island anytime soon.

A muscle clenched near Alex's right eye. He grabbed his boxers and retrieved a pair of slacks from the closet. "We have to get to the airport."

"In *this?*"

"It'll let up eventually. As soon as there's a break in the ceiling, we're taking off."

"But what did Nathaniel say?"

Alex seemed completely serious about heading for the airport, so Emma discarded the robe and pulled on a cotton dress.

"Just what I told you," said Alex.

"You haven't told me anything."

Keeping his back to her, he moved around the room as he spoke. "David duped you and Katie into signing a power of attorney that somehow allowed him to make a deal on Kayven Island. Nathaniel is trying to hold him off, but we need to get back to New York."

Emma watched his furtive packing. "What aren't you telling me?" Was it a done deal? Had they already lost the resort?

"Nothing."

"Has the sale gone through?"

"No."

"Because if it has, it wouldn't be the end of the world."

Alex froze.

"It wouldn't," she repeated. "As long as David got a decent price."

Alex pivoted to face her. "Your employee, your sister's *boy-*

friend, is trying to defraud your company and you're saying it'll be okay *as long as he got a decent price?*"

"If you're afraid to tell me it already happened, you—"

"I'm not afraid to tell you it already happened. It *didn't* already happen."

"Then why are you acting so weird?"

"I'm not acting weird. I'm acting normal. Acting weird was earlier."

His words hit Emma like a sledgehammer, and she staggered back. Was that it? Had the kinder, gentler Alex been an illusion? Was he mad now because he thought she'd made a mistake?

She supposed she had made a mistake. But Katie had—

Katie.

Katie would be devastated.

Emma went for the phone.

But as she reached for the receiver, Alex latched on to her wrist.

"What are you doing?"

"Calling Katie."

"You can't do that."

Emma glared up at him. "Yes, I can." This wasn't some random whim, this was her sister's life.

"Emma…"

"Let go of me, Alex."

"We have to talk."

She tried to shake him off. "We can talk on the plane."

"We have to talk *before* you talk to Katie."

The look in his eyes sent a shiver of fear through her body. She almost couldn't bring herself to say the words. "Is she hurt?"

"*No.* No. She's not hurt."

Emma shook her arm, and Alex let her go.

"Then what the hell is going on?" she asked.

Alex squeezed his eyes shut for a second. "There's something about Kayven Island you don't know."

"But Katie's not hurt?"

"Katie's fine. I think she's with Nathaniel. No, I know she's with Nathaniel. He won't let her out of his sight until we get back."

Emma's fear cranked back up. "Is she in some kind of danger?"

"Emma, listen to me."

She closed her mouth.

Alex took both her hands in his. "The local government is putting a cruise ship dock on the island."

"What island?"

"This island."

"So?"

"So, that's why Murdoch wants the resort. That's why he's willing to bribe David."

"Because the value will—" Emma stopped.

She got it. In a blinding flash she understood exactly what had happened to her.

"Alex!"

"I wanted it, too," he confessed.

No kidding. She yanked her hands from his, stumbling back against the bed.

"You kept this from me?"

"Yes."

"You… You… *I* could have sold it to Murdoch."

Alex nodded.

"And then I wouldn't have had to marry you."

He nodded again.

She raised her fist, battling a split second temptation to pummel his chest. "And you didn't *tell* me?"

"It was business."

"Business?"

"I knew what I knew, and I did what was best for my company."

The fight suddenly left her.

Of course he'd done what was best for his company. He'd never pretended to do anything different. He'd even warned her. He'd suggested she do the same.

And she thought she had, she thought she was. But Alex had been working against her all along.

"And you have the nerve to criticize *David?*" she challenged.

Alex gritted his teeth. "I am *nothing* like David. David's a con artist and a criminal."

"Yeah," Emma agreed. "Just look what he did? He romanced Kayven Island out from under Katie."

Emma had never felt like a bigger fool in her life. She might be stuck with Alex for better or worse, but that didn't mean she ever had to speak with the man again.

"And wasn't that reprehensible of *him?*" she ground out in a parting shot, then turned away and cut him out of her life forever.

Emma forcibly tamped down her troubles with Alex as soon as she saw Katie's stricken face.

They were in the McKinley offices. It was six in the evening. She wasn't even sure what day.

"Oh, honey," she crooned, drawing Katie into an embrace.

Alex and Nathaniel immediately put their heads together and began talking in low tones.

Katie hiccoughed out a sob. "I've made such a mess."

"It's not your fault." Emma shook her head, then shot Alex and Nathaniel a look to ensure they kept any stray opinions to themselves. "The only thing you're guilty of doing is trusting too much. We were coerced and lied to by criminals."

Katie swallowed. "I should have guessed—"

"Guessed what?" asked Emma, her gaze still boring in on Alex's profile. "That a man could make love to you one minute then stab you in the back the next?" Emma hadn't guessed that, either. But she'd know better next time.

Alex spared her a fleeting glance, his expression neutral. She wasn't even sure her words had registered. Not that her condemnation would mean a thing to him anyway.

"The important thing is to fix it," she said, switching her attention to Katie, pulling back and striving for a look of reassurance.

Katie gave a shaky nod, her gaze darting nervously to Nathaniel, and Emma worried what the man might have said before they arrived.

"We have to both sign a revocation," said Katie. "The lawyers…"

Alex stepped forward. "The lawyers have it drafted, and they're waiting across the hall."

Emma refused to look at him. "And then what?" she asked Nathaniel.

Alex gave a frustrated sigh.

"Then we make certified copies and have a sheriff waiting to serve it to both Murdoch and Cranston first thing in the morning."

"And that's it?" asked Emma.

Nathaniel shrugged. "That's it."

She turned to Katie. "See? It's going to be fine."

Katie shook her head, mutely blinking back tears, and Emma felt like a heel.

"Hey, I know you'll miss him."

Katie's face crumpled, and Emma pulled her back into her arms. Then she motioned for Alex and Nathaniel to leave. The papers were ready. All it took was their signatures before the start of business tomorrow. She could afford to comfort Katie for a few minutes.

The door snapped shut behind the men.

"I'm such a fool," said Katie.

"You're not a fool."

Emma had made a much bigger mistake. And, while they could recover from Katie's, Emma's was permanent. Alex would soon own half of their business, and there wasn't a single thing they could do about it.

Katie pulled back, a funny expression coming over her face. "If it wasn't for Nathaniel, we'd have lost millions."

"If it wasn't for me, we'd have made millions."

Katie shook her head. "That was just business."

"You're *defending* Alex?"

"He could have had our loan called and cut us out completely."

"Or he could have been *honest*."

"He was honest. He gave us the choice between a hostile takeover or a merger. We took the merger."

A merger? That's all it was to Katie?

Then Emma forced herself to regroup.

Yes, that's all it was to Katie.

Katie didn't know about Kayven Island. She didn't know that Alex had tried to seal the deal by pretending to fall for her. She didn't know that he'd been willing to coerce some friendly sex out of his bride of convenience before they got down to the business of flipping her resort for half a billion bucks.

Alex Garrison in love with Emma McKinley.

If anyone had told her two months ago she'd have dared to even think that phrase, she'd have laughed them out of the room. But she'd not only thought it. For a moment in time, she'd believed it. On that faraway beach, she'd believed it with all her heart. And he heart was what she'd given to Alex. And her heart is what he'd crushed with his bare hands.

He'd wanted her hotel, and she'd been stupid enough to hand him that and more on a silver platter.

Katie looked aghast. "How will I ever trust my own judgment again?"

It was Emma's judgment that needed remedial attention.

"I asked…" Katie tapped her fingertips against her mouth. "I asked Alex if he'd host our wedding someday." Then she have a helpless laugh. "What a fool I was."

"Katie, please—"

The office door opened. "Emma," said Alex. "We have to do this."

Emma looked at Katie. "You ready?"

She gave a shaky nod. "Yeah."

By 8:30 a.m., ten cups of coffee to the good, Alex was ready to jump out of his skin waiting for the sheriff to show.

"Screw it," he growled to Ryan who was sitting across the boardroom table, tapping a pen against the polished, inlay pattern.

Ryan's brow jerked into a furrow. "Screw what?"

Alex slid the manila envelope into his palm. "I'm delivering them myself."

Ryan stood up, pushing the chair back behind him. "Whoa there, Alex. I don't think that's such a good idea."

"Why not?" He couldn't stand sitting there another second. And at least he'd know it was done right.

"Because we don't want to have to waste our lawyer's time clearing you of assault charges."

"David won't even be there."

"Murdoch will."

"Murdoch's too old to defend himself."

"My point, exactly."

Alex snorted as he stood. "Right. Like I'm going to assault an old man." But he did want to see Murdoch's face when they presented the documents that would undo what he'd done.

The negotiations had moved far enough, with David legally entitled to conduct them, that backing out now could get dicey.

Their lawyers had advised the most expedient way out was for Alex's company to present an outrageous counteroffer so that Murdoch would be forced to withdraw. Quick and neat, and Alex was at the helm. First things first though, they had to deal with that proxy.

"It's not like there's anything to negotiate with him," said Ryan. "You don't even have to have a conversation."

"I just want to see his face." Alex was still doing a slow burn. "I told him *I* was the contact. He ignored me. That makes it personal."

"You sure it's not Emma that makes it personal?"

Alex slid a glance Ryan's way.

"How was the honeymoon?" Ryan asked mildly.

"Short," said Alex.

"You didn't call in yesterday. Not once. Not to anyone."

Alex retrieved his briefcase and placed the envelope inside. "No cell service."

"No phones in the hotel."

"We were busy."

Ryan grinned. "It went well?"

Alex snapped the case shut. "I guess that's irrelevant now that she knows about Kayven."

Ryan sobered. "Yeah. I guess it is."

"Yeah," Alex agreed, trying very hard not to care.

Sure, Emma was upset. But she'd get over it. And he had what he wanted. He had what they'd all wanted: a ring on her finger and a fifty-percent share in McKinley Inns.

And… He scooped the briefcase from the table and headed for the door. He was about to rescue the jewel in the McKinley crown and visit revenge on an annoying rival.

"You okay?" Emma whispered, walking up behind Katie and stroking the back of her soft blond hair.

Her sister was sitting on the bench seat in the bay window of the penthouse dining room, staring at the wispy clouds on the eastern horizon. The coffeemaker dripped and hissed on the countertop.

Katie nodded. "What about you?" They'd sat up most of the night talking, so Katie knew all about Alex and the honeymoon.

Emma took the other end of the bench seat, curling her legs under her robe. "My stomach aches, but I think it's embarrassment more than anything else."

At least that's what she was telling herself.

She closed her eyes and sighed. Alex and Ryan and Nathaniel must all be having a good laugh at her expense. She'd fallen for his act hook, line and sinker.

"They must have been afraid I'd back out," she whispered, leaning one elbow on the white windowsill, supported the weight of her achy, sleep-deprived head.

Thinking about it, she realized her decreasing objections to the marriage correlated to when Alex started acting as though he liked her. He'd obviously figured out really quick that she was a desperate, lonely, plain-Jane woman, ripe to fall for pretty much anybody.

And he'd used that as a way to control her. Who knew if he even wanted sex with her. Maybe he just thought she wanted sex with him. And he was willing to play the gigolo, if it meant sealing the deal.

The pretty one. He'd actually hinted she was prettier than Katie. What's more, she'd actually started to believe him.

Alex had earned his millions through acting alone.

Katie squeezed her shoulder. "It's going to be okay." But her voice was too hollow to be convincing.

"I can't divorce him," said Emma. "I'd lose a fortune."

"Then we'll go away. We'll go on a very long vacation."

Emma nodded. She'd promised to live with Alex and hang on his arm like some kind of accessory. But that part wasn't in writing. So he'd just have to learn to live with the disappointment.

She only hoped she could learn to live with it. Despite her resistance, she'd started to like the life he'd made up. She'd even started looking forward to that goofy McKinley-Garrison office party. And redecorating his main floor. It would have been fun to redecorate his main floor. Even if it was only temporary.

A tear slipped out of the corner of her eye.

Who was she kidding?

She'd stopped thinking about it as temporary somewhere on the hot beach at Kayven Island, along about the time Alex pretended he loved her, and she realized she loved him right back.

She inhaled a shuddering sob.

Katie wrapped her in a tight embrace. "Oh, Emma. It's going to be okay."

But it wasn't going to be okay. It might never be okay again.

Twelve

Alex was going to make things right. And he was going to make Clive Murdoch regret the day he even considered crossing Alex Garrison.

He slapped the envelope down on Murdoch's desk.

"What's this?" the old man asked, glancing from the envelope to Alex.

"Our counteroffer."

Murdoch's eyes narrowed.

Alex plopped down in one of the guest chairs. "To bring you up to speed. David Cranston's authority to negotiate for McKinley's has been revoked."

Murdoch's face went from pasty to ruddy. "That's—"

"He's lucky he's not in jail. You're lucky—"

"He has a duly executed power of attorney."

"*Had.* I'm the man you have to deal with now."

Murdoch snatched up the envelope. "We'd already agreed on a price."

Alex nodded. "That you had. And I'm willing to stick to that price, provided you agree to the in-kind contribution McKinley's requesting."

Murdoch peeled away the envelope and stared at the first page of the contract. Then he stared bug-eyed over the page at Alex, and his ruddy complexion turned near purple.

For a second, Alex worried the man was going to have a heart attack.

"*Free* staffing?"

"For all McKinley properties, around the globe, into perpetuity."

"That's—"

"Perfectly legal, according to my, and your former, legal team. You are, of course, free to turn it down."

Murdoch opened his mouth, but nothing emerged except a damp squeaking sound. It took him a few seconds to recover the power of speech. "This is outrageous."

"This is business," said Alex, clamping his jaw. "I told you to deal with me and me alone. What's more, I told you *nothing* of McKinley's was for sale."

"Because you wanted it for yourself."

"That's true," said Alex. "And I got it." But things had changed.

Murdoch's mouth twisted in an ugly sneer. "I sure hope it was worth the mercy screw."

Alex was out of his chair in a flash, reaching across the desk and grabbing Murdoch by the collar, Ryan's warning obliterated from his mind. "Don't you ever *dare*—"

"You trying to tell me this is something other than a media-palatable land grab? Don't waste your breath, Garrison. You know as well as I do that this deal suits *nobody* but you. You screwed her in more ways than one."

Alex's fist clenched. He wanted nothing more than to smash the self-satisfied smirk from Murdoch's face.

Trouble was, Murdoch was right.

Alex had screwed Emma. He'd used her, and he'd lied to her. And what he'd won was a half-billion-dollar property, a ridiculous prenup that forced her to stay with a man she probably hated, and half of her business, when she could have bailed herself out financially if he'd only been honest with her.

He got what he'd set out to win. But he'd lost so much more in the process.

He slowly let Murdoch go, then sank back into his chair.

How exactly was he different than Murdoch, or even David for that matter? If Alex could go back in time, he'd tell Emma all about Kayven Island, wait for her to sell it, then romance her, no strings attached.

He almost laughed at the absurdity.

He wanted Emma more than he wanted the island, more than he wanted the money, more than he wanted anything, really. All he wanted was for Emma to redecorate his house so they could throw party after party and fill that mausoleum with life and laughter.

Well, he couldn't have that. Not anymore. But he didn't have to take Emma down with him.

He took a deep breath. "I'll sell it to you," he said to Murdoch.

"Not with free staffing, you won't."

"I'll sell it to you for double the agreed-upon price, no staffing, no other conditions."

Murdoch's eyes narrowed.

"That's the only offer I'm making," said Alex. "Take it or leave it."

He could give Emma the money, and give her back McKinley. She could bail the company out of debt, and his partners... Well, his partners would just have to learn to live with it. Worst they could do is gang up and fire him as CEO.

If they did, he'd live with it. Just as long as he'd done right by Emma.

* * *

After two days and four pints of caramel pecan dream, Emma swore to herself that she was through with grieving. She had lost, and Alex had won. And that's the way it happened in the big bad world.

At least she still had half her company. And she and Katie could still work toward buying him out. Someday, anyway. For now, he was her partner. She wouldn't allow herself to think of him as anything more.

She wouldn't divorce him, but she wouldn't live with him either. If he wanted to talk to her, he could do it at the office. Her door was always open to all of her business associates.

An associate.

Yes. She liked that term.

In fact, she almost looked forward to seeing him again. She wanted him to know she was over him, that she'd picked herself up, learned from the experience and carried on.

Katie appeared in the bedroom doorway.

"This just came for you," she said, entering the room, holding out a cardboard envelope.

"From downstairs?" asked Emma, coming briskly to her feet. It was time to get back down to the office anyway.

"Crosstown courier," said Katie.

Emma took the envelope and tugged on the tab. The Garrison offices return address jumped out, but she refused to let it rattle her. There'd be plenty of correspondence between her and Alex from here on in. She could handle it.

"What is it?" asked Katie as Emma's gaze focused on the letter.

Emma read the brief paragraphs then shook her head and started over again.

"What?" Katie repeated.

The message finally sorted itself into some kind of order inside Emma's brain. "He sold Kayven Island."

"What?"

Emma squeezed her eyes shut, then refocused on the bank draft clipped to the top of the letter. "Alex sold Kayven Island to Murdoch."

Katie moved closer. "I thought the whole point was to *not* sell Kayven Island to Murdoch. How much…" She peered over Emma's shoulder. "Holy *crap!*"

Katie tried to read the letter, but Emma's hand was shaking too hard. So Katie had to still it.

"He's giving it back?" asked Katie.

Emma reread the words. "He says we should use Murdoch's money—" Her gaze went involuntarily to the amount on the bank draft. Holy crap indeed. "—to pay off McKinley's debts. And then it's ours. A hundred percent. Free and clear."

"He's tearing up the prenup," said Katie as she continued reading. "What's this about redecorating his house?"

"It's a joke." Emma laughed weakly. "When we were goofing around on Kayven…" When they were goofing around on Kayven, all her dreams were coming true. She'd dared to hope. Now, her eyes stung with the need to give him another chance. Was Alex truly that sweet, funny, sexy man? Or was that man a fraud, contrived to distract her? And which one of them had written the letter.

How would she ever know for sure?

Katie stared at her. "You do know what this means?"

Emma nodded. It definitely meant one thing. "We own our company again."

Katie elbowed her in the arm. "It means he wants you to *redecorate his house.*"

Emma scrambled to keep her emotions out of it. She had to thank logically. "That was just a joke."

"A joke? A guy who's giving up this many million dollars doesn't make jokes for the sake of a joke. He wants you. He probably loves you."

"Then why is he tearing up the prenup? Without the prenup, I can divorce him." Her voice caught. "He wants me to divorce him."

Katie squealed in frustration. "He wants you to come to him. Because you *want* to. Without coercion. He gave you back your money." She stared at the draft. "And *then* some. He gave you your freedom. But at the same time he mentions redecorating? Earth to Emma."

Emma's mouth went dry, and her heart thudded in her chest. Could Katie be right? Did she have the guts to find out?

"Go to him," said Katie. "Thank him. *Redecorate* him for God's sake. And do it now."

Emma bit her bottom lip. She wanted this, desperately wanted this. But if Katie was wrong... "You really think—"

"Go! I'm going to the bank." Katie glanced down again. "Holy crap."

Emma swung the mansion's big oak door wide open and strode into the foyer.

"Mrs. Garrison. So good to see you."

"Good to see you, too, Mrs. Nash. Is Alex in?"

If she was wrong, Emma had already decided to pretend it was all a joke. She'd pretend she'd only stopped by to thank him for his gentlemanly, yet fair, behavior. And the rest was just a big joke.

No hard feelings. No harm done.

Mrs. Nash stepped back, a wry smile on her lips. "He's out back. Oh, have you had lunch? I can bring out some tea or sandwiches? Philippe has this great—"

"Philippe is here?"

Mrs. Nash laughed, and her cheeks turned slightly pink. "Oh, no. Of course not. Not at the moment."

Despite herself, Emma grinned. "Is it fair to say he'd be willing to help with future parties?"

Mrs. Nash nodded. "I think that would be fair to say."

Okay. That was a happy outcome.

Emma would cling to that.

She made her way past Hamilton and the other Garrison portraits, her chest tightening and her pulse increasing.

Oh, please let Katie be right.

Emma cut through the breakfast room, onto the deck, then down the stairs to the pool.

Alex was at an umbrella table, reading the *Times*. He glanced up at the sound of her footsteps.

"Emma." He was on his feet in an instant.

She slowed to a stop in front of him, not sure any more what she should say. The moment took on a surrealistic quality and her bravado evaporated. "Hello, Alex."

The sea breeze whispered through the aspen trees while they stared at each other.

"You got my letter?" he finally asked, his expression giving nothing away.

Emma nodded stiffly. "Thank you."

He moved forward. "It was just business, you know."

Her heart sank slowly in her chest, her palm going slick against the briefcase. He wasn't going to buy that it was a joke. This was definitely going to be embarrassing. "I know."

"It was nothing personal."

She flinched. "Of course not."

"I knew what I knew, and you knew what you knew, and I made the best deal possible for my company."

She'd been a fool to come here. A fool to think… "So you said."

"There was no reason to tell you up front." He gave a harsh laugh. "A guy wouldn't get very far telling his competition his secrets, would he?"

"Right." She'd only hoped she could get out of here in time. "Well, I just—"

"But then…" Alex's tone softened, and the harsh slate look went out of his eyes. "Then I proposed to you. And maybe, maybe that was when the rules changed."

Emma stood frozen to the ground.

"And then I married you. And that definitely meant the rules had changed. And then…" He took her left hand, rubbing his thumb over the Tudor diamond. "Then I fell in love with you, and any right I'd ever had to treat you as a business adversary was gone."

The aspen trees rustled into the silence.

"Emma?"

She couldn't help smiling. It was going to be okay. It was really going to be okay. "You fell in love with me?"

"Yeah, I fell in love with you. What did you think I meant by 'saying it'?"

"That you were in love with me." At least that was how it had seemed in the moment.

"Damn straight."

"Or that it might only be part of the game." She had to admit, the thought had crossed her mind.

"You thought our time on the beach was a game?"

She shook her head, her chest tightening with joy. "No. Not the beach."

On the beach, she'd believed him. On the beach, she'd dared to hope they were starting a glorious life together. Kind of like she did now.

"The beach was real," he rumbled. "That beach was the most real moment of my life."

Emma's, too. Oh, Emma's, too. She felt moisture heat the insides of her eyelids.

"I love you, Emma," Alex whispered, lifting her hand to place a gentle kiss on her knuckles.

Her mouth curved into a relieved smile.

Alex loved her.

He *loved* her.

"Well?" he asked.

"What?"

"Do I have to make you say it?"

She gazed into his dark eyes, her smile turning impish. "Yeah."

"Later," he whispered with a nod to where Mrs. Nash emerged onto the deck. A stream of people trailed out behind her.

"Hello?" Alex's brow shot up.

"I hope Mrs. Nash doesn't have anything against Italian decorators," said Emma, as the troop rounded the sun umbrella.

There was an unmistakable grin in Alex's voice. "We're redecorating?"

"I took a chance," she admitted. "And I mentioned your name. They have swatches and flooring samples."

He chuckled and he shook his head. "In that case, you don't have to say it."

"Why not?"

He took the case from her hand. "Because you just proved it."

She playfully elbowed him in the ribs. "Oh, make me say it anyway."

Alex leaned down and kissed her mouth. It was a warm, tender kiss, full of love, full of hope, full of the promise of a lifetime.

"I love you," she whispered on a sigh.

He drew back only slightly. "See, that was way too easy."

She leaned her cheek against his chest, enjoying the feel of his strong arms around her. "When it comes to you," she crooned, "I'm always easy."

He snorted his disbelief. But his fingertips sent a different message, trailing lightly along her spine. "You know, we have a honeymoon to finish."

"I guess we do."

"The *Island Countess* leaves for Fiji tonight." He paused. "And I know a guy who can get us a suite."

She pulled back. "I've seen those suites. They're fabulous."

"I have fond memories of them myself."

By the time the *Island Countess* blew her horn and pulled away from the dock, Emma was naked and wrapped tight in Alex's arms. The sounds of the late-night launch party tinkled up from the aft sundeck pool.

She buried her face in the crook of Alex's neck and inhaled his masculine scent. "I love you," she sighed.

He kissed the top of her head. "Wonder what else I can make you do."

"Pretty much anything at the moment. As long as it doesn't require movement. Or thinking. Or staying awake, actually." She stifled a yawn.

"You hungry?"

She shook her head. "Not hungry."

"Thirsty?"

"I'm fully satisfied, thank you."

He chuckled against her hair. "That's what I like to hear from my wife."

She smiled.

The phone on the bedside rang.

"Uh-oh," she said.

"Nothing else can go wrong," he assured her.

Then he picked it up. "Garrison here."

He listened for a moment. "So it's done?"

Another pause.

"It'll be public?"

Emma came up on her elbow to watch his expression.

He smiled. "Yeah. Thanks. I owe you one."

Then he hung up the phone.

She waited.

"So, who was it?" she asked.

Alex closed his eyes. "Nathaniel."

"Oh." She waited again. "Well?"

He opened one eye. "What?"

"Is it a secret?"

"No." He opened the other eye and a smug grin took over his face. "Turns out, when the local government heard Kessex Cruise Lines had some concerns with the Kayven Island dock, they decided to move it."

Emma sat up. "What?"

"To another island, about five hundred miles east."

"You didn't."

"I didn't do a thing."

Emma leaned in closer, pasting Alex with an openly skeptical look. "You just told Nathaniel you owed him."

"Oh, that." Alex wave a hand. "That was—" He grinned. "Yeah. I did it. Murdoch needed to learn not to mess with us."

Emma tried hard not to be happy about getting revenge. "Remind *me* not to mess with you."

Alex pulled her into a hug. "You, woman, can mess with me any old time you like."

She pulled back and batted her eyelashes. "Like now?"

"I thought you were tired."

"I changed my mind. Apparently you vengeful types turn me on."

He slipped his hand across her hip and snuggled her up tight against his body. "Better not be any other vengeful types onboard."

"Better keep a close eye on me. Just in case."

He kissed her then. "You bet I will." Then he drew back. "By the way. I made an investment on behalf of McKinley."

She studied his eyes. "What did you do?"

"Bought a piece of property. Little bed-and-breakfast on Tannis Island. That's about five hundred miles east of Kayven.

Not much to look at really. But I think it's going to be extremely valuable by the end of the week."

Emma fought a smile of astonishment. "You didn't."

His eyes softened, and he gazed at her with a love that sizzled through every fiber of her being. "You can bet I did."

* * * * *

TALL, DARK & CRANKY

KATE LITTLE

Kate Little claims to have lots of experience with romance—'the *fictional* kind that is,' she is quick to clarify. She has been both an author and an editor of romance fiction for over fifteen years. She believes that good romance will make the reader experience all the tension, thrills and the agony of falling madly, deeply and wildly in love. She enjoys watching the characters in her books go crazy for each other, but hates to see the blissful couple disappear when it's time for them to live happily ever after. In addition to writing romance novels, Kate also writes fiction and non-fiction for young adults. She lives on Long Island, New York with her husband and daughter.

One

"**Y**our recommendations are impressive, Ms. Calloway. In fact, they were positively glowing. One of your former employers even called you a miracle worker," Matthew Berringer said.

"I love my work and I'm good at it," Rebecca said in her usual straightforward fashion. "But I'd hardly call myself a miracle worker."

"You wouldn't, eh? That's too bad, because I'm not sure that anything short of a miracle will restore my brother Grant, to his former life. To any sort of productive life at all."

She saw instantly that her reply had dampened Matthew Berringer's enthusiasm, and Rebecca wondered if she should have been more...diplomatic. She could have soft-soaped her answer a bit. She'd been warned that her pungent honesty was sometimes a shortcoming. Rebecca bit her lower lip. She needed this job. But she wouldn't be hired on false impressions and she would never make any false promises.

She knew how demanding, physically and emotionally, a home assignment like this one might be. From what she'd heard about the patient, she wasn't sure she'd succeed in rehabilitating him, much less getting him up and about his business by the summer's end, which was Matthew Berringer's explicit request. She wasn't sure anyone could. From what she'd seen in the medical records, the problem wasn't so much Grant Berringer's physical condition as his attitude.

Miracle worker, indeed. All the Berringers' money and then some couldn't buy a miracle. And Rebecca knew she couldn't live up to such high-flown accolades...and didn't want to break her heart trying.

"Mr. Berringer, your concern for your brother is very touching. He's fortunate to have someone so involved in his recovery—"

"Your kind words seem to be leading up to something, Ms. Calloway." Matthew Berringer interrupted her. "Perhaps you should just say it?"

Rebecca was taken aback, then found his frankness refreshing. There *was* something more she wanted to say.

"You can't will your brother to get well again, to resume a productive life, if he doesn't want to. You can hire a hundred therapists. Even some that *will* promise you miracles. But no one can snap their fingers and give your brother the will to fight his way back. He has to want it. He has to want it very badly.''

He stared at her, looking angry at her words, she thought. Or at least greatly irritated. Then, without replying, he looked at her résumé and letters of reference again, as if reviewing the pages for final questions.

She'd blown it totally, Rebecca realized. She wasn't going to get this job. She could always tell when the interviewer started studying her résumé in the middle of everything. She predicted he would soon lift his head, bestow a dismissing smile and send her off with some polite comment that would let her know she was low on the list.

Rebecca glanced at her surroundings. She'd been so intent on answering Matthew Berringer's questions, she hadn't taken much notice of the room. Sunny and spacious, it appeared to be a library or study. The walls were lined with floor-to-ceiling bookcases, and the furnishings were large, comfortably worn pieces upholstered in leather and tapestry fabrics. There were many framed photos. Some looked quite old. Most looked like family groups.

Area rugs in traditional designs covered the polished wooden floor, and an impressive carved oak desk stood in front of glass doors that led to a covered terrace. The doors stood ajar, allowing the spring air to fill the room.

When the interview began, she'd expected Matthew Berringer to take a seat behind the big desk. Instead, he'd sat on a couch across from her and offered her coffee from a silver service. The gesture, though small, had helped put her at ease.

She took a moment to raise her china cup and take a sip. The coffee was cold, but at least it gave her something to do.

In the tense silence, Rebecca could hear the ocean, just steps away from the terrace of the beachfront property. The steady rhythm of the waves was soothing and helped her relax.

It was a pity she wasn't going to work here. The Berringer mansion—merely Grant Berringer's summer home—was so beautiful, the kind of grand old place she'd so far only admired from a wistful distance. Earlier Matthew Berringer had told her a little about the estate, which was set on ten acres of oceanfront property. The twelve-bedroom mansion, designed in the style of a French Norman manor house, was built in the 1920s for a wealthy oil magnate, part of New York's aristocracy. The stones had been shipped from Europe, as well as the craftsmen who had put the place together. The carved stone architectural details included gargoyles with all too human faces. With its wide, rambling structure, courtyards, slate roof and turrets, the place looked more like a miniature castle, Rebecca thought, nestled in a grove of woods near the sea. The decor within was fit for royalty, as well.

Not only did she need a new job, but she and Nora, her six-year-old daughter, needed a new place to live by the end of the month and an apartment in one wing of the huge house was part of the deal, in addition to a generous salary. Matthew Berringer had already shown her the rooms, which were lovely. Certainly enough space for her and Nora for the summer. If Grant Berringer required her services for longer than the summer and Nora had to return to school, Rebecca had told Matthew Berringer some other arrangements would be necessary. But he hadn't seemed put off by that potential complication. He'd stated that he'd be happy to hire a tutor for Nora or enroll her in one of the fancy private schools nearby. Rebecca felt satisfied by his reply. Although she had read Grant Berringer's medical records and discussed his condition with Matthew, she still needed to see him with her own eyes to gauge how long he would need her help.

Living on the beach for the summer, in such luxurious surroundings, no less, would have been heavenly. But...she'd blown it all with her irrepressible need to be honest.

Well, she wasn't really sorry. She'd only told Matthew Berringer the truth. People always say they admire honesty. In theory, perhaps, but not in actuality, she'd noticed. Not in her case, anyway. Perhaps she'd helped him, in a way. He'd be wary of the next applicant, who might claim to be able to have Grant Berringer behind his desk in no time flat.

Finally, Matthew Berringer looked at her. The irritation in his expression had disappeared.

"I know what you've told me is true, Ms. Calloway. I know the real motivation has to come from within Grant. I just don't want to believe it, I guess. I keep wishing I might find someone who could snap their fingers and make my brother well again," he admitted.

"I understand. I really do," she sympathized. "Just about everyone I meet who is caring for a loved one feels the same."

"But my brother's case is different from most you've had in the past," Matthew Berringer said. "He has had an extraordinary loss. Many people use the word tragedy when they're describing a sad but not necessarily unusual event. My brother, however, has lived through a tragedy, a devastating event that cost him…everything. And left him with an impossibly heavy burden of guilt, in the bargain."

So far, Rebecca had only learned that Grant Berringer had been in a car accident. She'd heard that he'd been the driver and there was one passenger involved who had died instantly. Grant had escaped with multiple injuries the most severe to his right hip and leg. Those were the basic facts, but obviously there was more to the story.

"Why don't you tell me everything about your brother's accident? Everything you think is relevant to his recovery, I mean. I do need to know the complete details in order to evaluate the case."

Loss was something she knew about. She could empathize with Grant Berringer. But at the same time, she had been through so much in her life, Rebecca wasn't sure she had the resources to handle an unusually demanding assignment.

Matthew Berringer's cool blue-eyed gaze met hers, then he looked away. It seemed he was gathering his thoughts. "I'll try to keep this brief and to the point," he said. "My brother was engaged to be married. He and his fiancée, Courtney Benton, were returning to the city after spending the weekend at the country home of one of my brother's clients. It was bad weather, a sudden heavy rainstorm, and my brother apparently lost control of the wheel. The car skidded off the road and crashed into a cement wall. Courtney was killed instantly. My brother was in a coma for two weeks. When he woke up and learned what had happened, he barely had the will to go on living."

"Oh, dear…that is heartbreaking," Rebecca said softly. She had heard many sad stories during her career, but this was one of the saddest. That poor man. She couldn't imagine his grief…or his guilt.

"And to complicate matters even further, my brother has some memory loss. He can recall events leading up to the accident. Leaving the home they were visiting and such. But he can't remember anything that happened right before the crash occurred. He can't even remember if he and Courtney were trying to pull over and wait out the rain."

Matthew Berringer sounded amazed but somewhat frustrated. "The doctors say he may never remember."

"They may be right," Rebecca agreed. "I have heard of such situations before. It's a reaction to extreme trauma or stress. It's the mind's way of protecting itself from memories that are too painful to relive."

"Yes, I understand all that." As Matthew Berringer nodded, a lock of his smooth brown hair dropped across his brow, and he impatiently brushed it back. "But I often suspect that if Grant could remember all that happened that night—no matter how distressing those memories might be—perhaps he'd be able to move forward, to work through his grief and rebuild his life.''

''Yes, it might help him a great deal. But it's a catch-22 of sorts, isn't it?'' she added. ''He *will* get stronger if he remembers. But he'll only be ready to remember when he gets stronger.''

''It's a riddle inside a riddle.'' Matthew shook his head, and Rebecca could sense his frustration and sadness. Matthew had also experienced a loss, she realized. The loss of a brother who was once vital and strong, an equal in friendship and camaraderie, for it was clear that the two were quite close.

Rebecca did not know how to reply and thought it best to say nothing. Sometimes it helped people to talk, even if she couldn't supply an easy answer. She sensed that Matthew Berringer needed to talk right now to someone he thought could understand not only his brother's dilemma, but his own, as well. ''So you see, if he's fallen into some dark pit of despair and is reluctant to return to the land of living, I believe, that after all he's been through, it's an understandable reaction.''

''Completely understandable.'' Rebecca nodded and looked at her hands, which were folded in her lap.

Now that she knew the tragic story, she could see why Matthew was looking for a therapist who might be part superhero, part saint. The question loomed even larger—was she the right person for this job?

''I know the will to return must come from him,'' he added, echoing her earlier words, ''but I was hop-

ing—praying, if you must know—that I could find
the right...messenger. Someone who understands
such matters and is willing to go down into that dark
place and convince him to come back to us.''

His voice, which had been calm, increased in emotion, so that finally, Rebecca was quite moved by
Matthew Berringer's caring speech.

He was an uncommonly good man, she thought. A
kind man. The type who would never give up on
someone he loved. Rebecca admired that. Yet, despite
his striking good looks and admirable qualities, she
did not feel the least bit attracted to him.

It was funny how that worked, Rebecca reflected.
The chemistry was either there...or it wasn't. In this
case, it clearly wasn't. Not for him, either, she suspected. She could tell these things by now. Though
he seemed to respect her professionally and to like
her well enough in a friendly way. Which was all for
the better, she thought, if he was possibly to be her
employer.

''I'd like you to meet my brother. Will you come
with me now and talk to him?''

''Yes, of course.'' Rebecca was surprised at the
invitation. Then pleased. She usually wasn't asked to
meet the patient if the interview was a total loss. Perhaps there was more hope of being hired here than
she thought.

Besides, she was curious to meet Grant Berringer.
It would help them both to decide if she was right for
the job.

Matthew led her through the elegantly decorated
mansion, and Rebecca quickly peeked through door-

ways and admired her surroundings. The house was furnished with a mixture of antiques and traditionally designed pieces, with sumptuous drapery, original artwork and interesting porcelain and statuary. Yet the decor didn't look at all stuffy or museumlike. The rooms retained a fresh, light-filled look Rebecca found inviting.

"Grant has a few rooms upstairs, but when he was released from the hospital, the doctors advised me to set him up on the ground floor. I fixed a suite of rooms for him in the west wing of the house, including an exercise room with all types of equipment for his therapy. I'm in the city during the week, but I've hired a private nurse to take care of him during the day. A young man named Joe Newton. He's been great with Grant, very patient."

While most health-care professionals needed to extend patience to their charges, Rebecca sensed Grant Berringer required an extraordinary effort in that respect. *Not* a good sign.

"Our housekeeper, Miriam Walker, lives in," Matthew continued. "There's an intercom system throughout the house, so Grant can call her if there's any need."

Rebecca listened and nodded. It sounded as if Matthew had thought of everything. They had passed several large main rooms—a banquet-size dining room, an impressive parlor and a huge kitchen stocked with professional-looking cooking equipment. Lured by the view, Rebecca couldn't help but slow her step to glance inside the doorway.

"Great kitchen," she remarked when Matthew turned to glance at her.

He smiled. "You must like to cook if the sight of all those pots and pans and gadgetry turns you on."

"I do. When I have the time." She thought of the tiny, ill-equipped kitchen in her apartment in the city. It was a challenge, but she still managed to turn out some great meals for dinner guests or for herself and Nora when she had the time and inspiration to experiment. What a treat it would be to cook in a kitchen like this one.

"It's a very relaxing hobby, I hear," Matthew said. "Never caught my interest, though. I much prefer to work out my frustrations on a golf course...then visit a good restaurant for dinner," he joked. "But my brother loves to cook. He had just had the kitchen redone before the accident. He was quite a chef. He had so many interests—tennis, sailing, skiing, traveling to the most exotic places. He played hard and worked hard. He's known on Wall Street, too. Notorious, in fact, for being tough, even ruthless, some say. Grant is a successful, self-made man who knows how to live life to the fullest. Or did, before the accident," Matthew added. "You couldn't guess it, though, to see him now."

"He could be that way again," she said optimistically. "In time."

"Yes, I suppose," he agreed with a heavy sigh. "But it's hard to believe when you see him now."

They had arrived at double doors at the end of a long hall. Matthew knocked once, and a male voice answered. "Just a moment."

A young man with short dark hair answered the door. Joe Newton, the private nurse, Rebecca assumed. He smiled at Rebecca in greeting. He had a kind, gentle manner, she thought, if first impressions were any clue. He looked quite strong, as well. Was Grant Berringer so incapacitated that he required a weight lifter's aid? From what she'd read of his injuries, it shouldn't be as dire as all that.

Matthew led her into the room and made some quick introductions.

"How's Grant doing this afternoon?" Beneath Matthew's casual tone, Rebecca could sense his concern.

Joe shrugged a hefty shoulder. "About the same, I'd say. I persuaded him to go out on the beach after breakfast, then he wanted a nap. He refused to do any exercise today. Said his hip hurt too much," Joe reported with a frown. "He's been resting for some time now. I was just about to try to get him up."

A nap, in the middle of a day like this one? His depression was deep. While she had a degree in psychology as well as one in physiotherapy, she wondered if she was professionally equipped to treat this man.

"Let me go into him alone first," Matthew said.

Matthew disappeared into the adjoining room and Rebecca was left alone with Joe. "Are you interviewing as a physical therapist?" he asked her.

Rebecca nodded. "Have there been many others here so far?"

"Matthew has hired plenty. But they don't last

very long. Grant scares them away,'' Joe replied with a laugh.

Matthew Berringer had neglected to add that tidbit of information during their talk, Rebecca realized. Perhaps her chances of getting this job weren't as bad as she thought.

"I don't scare easily," Rebecca told Joe with a smile.

"He's tough," the nurse assured her. "I try to help him as much as I can. To get his strength back and such. But he prefers me to be more of a glorified baby-sitter."

"Matthew said you were patient with him. He appreciates that," Rebecca confided.

"I try to be." She could see that the compliment had touched him. "Grant's a good guy underneath it all. I'd like to see him get back to his old self."

It seems everyone who knew Grant shared the same hope, Rebecca reflected. Then she heard Matthew's voice. "Ms. Calloway, could you come in here, please?"

"Be right there," she replied. She turned away from Joe and began walking to the open doorway.

"Good luck," he whispered as she passed. She simply smiled in reply. She didn't know why she felt such a fluttering in her stomach. She was never nervous about meeting prospective patients.

She entered the room slowly. It seemed very dark and stuffy, considering the weather outside. Her eyes took a moment to adjust to the dim light, then she could still see that the place was a mess, with books and newspapers scattered about, a tray of food that looked barely picked over and an unmade bed in the midst of everything. Considering the appearance of the rest of the house, she could only assume that Grant Berringer preferred his personal area to be left in such a state.

Some distance from the doorway, she could make out Matthew's tall form, and beside him a man in a wheelchair who she assumed was Grant. His back was turned to her. Not a good sign, she thought.

As she walked toward them, Rebecca's first instinct was to pull open the long curtains that covered one wall. From the layout of the adjoining room, she guessed the drapery covered glass doors that led to the long deck and framed an ocean view. Some sunlight and fresh air would do a world of good in here, she thought.

But she didn't touch the curtains. Instead, she continued to approach the two men. Matthew's voice cut through the tense silence.

"Ms. Calloway, I'd like you to meet my brother Grant." His tone was so smooth and sociable, Rebecca thought she might have stumbled into a garden party instead of this dark, stuffy lair.

"I would like to meet him," Rebecca replied, standing just a few feet from them. "If he'd be so kind as to turn around."

Matthew looked at Grant, a tense expression on his face. But he didn't say anything. They waited what seemed a long time, though it was perhaps only a moment or two.

Then finally Grant Berringer spun his wheelchair around and Rebecca had her first look at him. His hair was dark and thick. Appealingly so, she thought. She couldn't tell if he was growing a beard or had just neglected to shave for a day or two. His cheeks had a scruffy appearance that could not detract from his strong good looks. With his hair combed straight back from his forehead and his broad, high cheek-bones and angular jaw, his face had a distinctly regal, lionlike appearance.

He was extremely attractive, she thought, though not in a smooth, typical way, the way his brother, Matthew, was handsome.

She'd learned the basic facts of his physical appearance from his medical records—six feet in height, one hundred and seventy-five pounds. At thirty-eight years old, he was almost ten years her senior. Yet the basic facts had not prepared her for some undefinable quality he possessed—his sheer intensity, which was as much a characteristic of the man as the dark eyes that took her in from head to toe.

"You'll forgive me for not getting up." He greeted her in a gruff, sarcastic voice.

His eyes, framed by thick brows, looked large and luminous in the dimly lit room. The rugged lines of his face held a serious, almost angry expression.

"No apology necessary," Rebecca replied lightly. "Of course, considering your condition, Mr. Berringer, you could be out of that chair by now, you know."

"You think so, do you?" he challenged her. He gave a bitter laugh, then turned to his brother. "Did you find yet *another* Mary Poppins for the job, Matthew?" His voice sounded weary and vaguely amused. "One would think the supply would be exhausted by now."

"One would think your brother would be exhausted by now, trying to help you, Mr. Berringer," Rebecca replied quietly.

She saw Matthew Berringer's eyebrows pop up at her tart response. But he said nothing. Grant finally lifted his head and stared into her eyes. He seemed impressed. Almost animated. She gave herself two points for that achievement, anyway.

"Well, well...this one's got some spunk, I'll give her that much," he said to Matthew. Rebecca thought she'd noticed a spark of appreciation in his eyes as he gazed at her, then thought she must have been mistaken. His gaze remained flat and dispassionate. "I've always preferred a tart, cool taste myself, as opposed to something sticky and overly sweet."

"None of my patients ever accused me of being too sweet," Rebecca replied. "More like the opposite."

"I'm not your *patient* yet, Ms. Calloway," he reminded her harshly. "Not by a long shot."

Rebecca was taken aback, but only for a moment. The wounded lion, cornered in his den, she thought. All he could do was give a loud roar and hope to scare the intruder away.

There was a small chair near his wheelchair, and she walked over and sat in it. She knew that being on the same eye level as the patient—not staring down at them—should help ease a tense moment like this one.

"You're right. My mistake," she said simply.

He stared directly at her, and she had her first good look at him, up close and personal. Intimidating was the word that first came to mind. But as she gazed unflinchingly into his dark eyes, she saw his vulnerability, as well, and the wellspring of pain and fear that had driven him to this dark place.

A thin white scar extended from the corner of his eye to his jawline, marring one cheek. Rebecca had read in the medical report that Grant could have easily had the scar erased with plastic surgery, but for some reason preferred not to. Did he keep it to help him mourn his loss? Or as a penance he felt bound to pay?

Her heart was touched by him, moved by him. Not by pity or compassion, exactly, but by some inexplicable urge to restore him, physically and spiritually, to siphon into him some of her abundant strength and will.

She had never felt quite this reaction to a prospective patient before, Rebecca thought with a mental jolt. Why this one?

Then suddenly, Grant's voice broke into her thoughts.

"I like a person who can admit when they're wrong," he said in a low, deep voice.

"I do a lot of that," she admitted. "Maybe you'll end up liking me, after all."

He suddenly laughed, and the deep, warm sound skimmed along her nerve endings, lighting a path in its wake—a reaction that alarmed Rebecca and one she forced herself to ignore. Still, she couldn't ignore the sudden change in Grant Berringer's appearance. His smile was like a sudden burst of light exploding

in the shadowy room. His face was transformed, softened, making his dark good looks even more appealing, Rebecca thought, as her gaze lingered on the
small, attractive lines fanning from the corners of his
eyes and deep dimples beside a full, sensual mouth.

Rebecca quickly pulled her gaze away. What was
going on here? Was she attracted to him?

No, it couldn't be. *Mustn't* be. She'd been warned
about this but it had never happened to her. She tried
to find some rational reason it would happen now. It
was his sad story, she told herself. Matthew had
drawn Grant as a tragic—even romantic—figure. The
story had gotten to her. It had to be. She couldn't
compromise her professional standards by taking on
a case when she had a romantic interest in the patient.

As if reading her mind, Grant said, "You know,
Ms. Calloway, there are women, like yourself, who
have come here hoping to bag a rich husband. If that's
your intention, I may as well warn you now, you'd
be wasting your time."

Rebecca knew his insult was merely a tactic, a ploy
to drive her away, but it stung nonetheless to hear her
ethics—and those of her colleagues—disparaged.

"Grant, please," Matthew urged his brother.
"Why do you have to do this?"

Matthew had been quiet until now. He seemed to
think Rebecca and his brother should sort things out,
and she was grateful for that. She could hear his frustration and embarrassment for Grant's rudeness.

"No, it's okay," she assured Matthew. She turned
to Grant again. "Mr. Berringer, I can promise you,

the last thing in the world I'm looking for is a husband, rich or otherwise.''

She watched him blink in surprise, but he showed no other reaction to her words.

''All right, point taken,'' he replied. He paused, then looked at her. ''My brother says you're highly qualified. The best he's found so far. But I want you to give me one good reason I should hire you for this job. Especially when so many others before have clearly failed at it. One good reason, Ms. Calloway,'' he added, the note of challenge in his voice growing sharper. ''That's all I'm asking for.''

Rebecca sat straight in her chair. She was being tested, like some character in a myth, required to answer the riddle before a magic portal to another realm would open or some treasure would be handed over.

She wasn't sure what she should say or do, and on a sudden impulse, she stood and pulled open the heavy curtains. Sunlight flooded the room. God, she'd been itching to do that since she'd come in.

From the corner of her eye, she could see Grant Berringer reel back in his chair, one arm raised to shield his eyes from the sudden flash of light. Rebecca ignored his reaction.

''Here, come with me a minute, I want to show you something.'' Without waiting for Grant's reply, she flipped off the brakes of his chair and quickly wheeled him toward the open glass door.

''What are you doing?'' he demanded. ''Have you lost your mind?''

''Maybe. But that doesn't mean I'm not a nice person,' Rebecca answered lightly as she pushed his chair onto the deck. Inside the room, she could hear Matthew softly chuckling. She pushed Grant's chair to the middle of the balcony, near the railing.

"That was quite a ride," Grant said. "You're stronger than you look."

"Strong enough to handle you," she promised.

He grunted something in reply, but Rebecca couldn't make out any distinct words. The sound of his dismay made her smile.

"So why have you brought me out here, Ms. Calloway? To catch pneumonia, maybe?"

"It's not that cold," she countered with a laugh. "It's not cold at all."

"Or maybe you plan to push me off the balcony? Put me out of my misery?"

His words were spoken in a jesting tone, but they touched an alarm in Rebecca. She knew his cynical joke came from a deep, frightening place, and she knew with almost utter certainty that Grant Berringer had considered ending his life, perhaps in that very manner. Still, she managed to answer him in a joking tone.

"I've rarely been known to push a patient off a balcony. On purpose, I mean," she said casually. "And I certainly wouldn't choose such a low one," she added, peering over the edge to the beach below. "I'd definitely take you up to the second or third floor for something like that."

"Thanks, I feel much better now," he said. Rebecca restrained herself from laughing. "That still doesn't answer my question, though. Why are we out here, Ms. Calloway?"

"For the view, of course," she replied, as if he should have guessed. "It's breathtaking, isn't it?"

Rebecca stood straight and took a deep breath. The ocean air was wonderful. And the view of the water and the blue sky above... Well, they reminded her of how great it was just to be alive. Couldn't he feel that, too?

"Oh, that." He dismissed her enthusiasm with a sarcastic laugh. "You get used to it. Believe me."

"I never would," she countered. She moved around his chair and stood beside him.

He glanced at her, then at the horizon. "Yes, you're the type who probably wouldn't," he said quietly. "But most people do. Besides, you still haven't given me a reason to give you the job."

Rebecca felt suddenly nervous, anxious. This wasn't working out as she had expected. He was tough. Maybe too tough for her?

She stood behind him again, and on impulse covered his eyes with her hands. His skin felt warm to her touch, and she could feel his entire body grow tense and alert. Yet he didn't roar a protest, as she expected. Or try to pull away. She felt his brow furrow in a puzzled frown. Then his large hands came up to cover hers.

"What are you doing now, playing peekaboo? The woman is mad, definitely," he murmured to himself.

Rebecca ignored his complaint. "I know you're used to the view, take it for granted, in fact. But what if you couldn't see the ocean ever again. How would you feel about that?"

"It wouldn't matter to me one bit. I don't really

see it now," he confessed in a flat voice. "I don't deserve to see it at any rate."

Her heart clenched at his words. Yes, it all came down to his guilt. He wouldn't allow himself to reach out for life again. He believed he didn't deserve it. He was trying to punish himself—and scare off anyone who tried to stop him from punishing himself.

She took her hands off his eyes, yet for some inexplicable reason, her hands floated down to trace the line of his lightly bearded cheeks. With the fingertips of her right hand, she felt the thin ridge of his scar, and a wave of emotion for him washed through her as she lifted her hands.

His hands did not prevent her from moving, but they held her, transmitting a sense that he was reluctant to feel her break contact.

But she did break contact and stood behind his chair with her arms dangling at her sides, her body feeling subtly charged from the brief touch.

"I'd like to say I understand," she said quietly. "But I'm sure you believe that nobody really can."

"Very wise. I don't see how anyone could."

Standing behind Grant Berringer, she couldn't see his face. But his voice was filled with emotion, the most she'd heard from him so far.

She paused and took a deep breath. She was losing him. Not just losing her chance at getting the job. But losing her chance to help this man who had mysteriously touched something within her. She suddenly wanted to be the one to help him. She suddenly believed she could succeed where all the others had failed.

She moved to face him. "I took you out here because I thought that the sight of this beautiful day would remind you it's simply great to be alive. And that's the best reason to want to recover."

"Spare me, Ms. Calloway. I've heard all these little sermons before."

"Yes, I'm sure you have. But maybe we're both right. It doesn't have to be one way or the other, you know."

"I don't quite get your meaning."

"Well, if what I'm saying is true, maybe you think that means your loss is without value. That what you've been through isn't truly important. But that's not what I mean at all," she assured him. "If you allow yourself to look at the ocean, Mr. Berringer, and truly see it again and wonder at the sheer power and beauty of it…well, that's okay," she said quietly. "It doesn't diminish your loss or make your pain meaningless. If you choose to go on with your life and build yourself up again, physically and emotionally, it doesn't erase the past or make you disloyal to the memory of your fiancée."

He held her gaze for a moment, then looked away, smoothing his hair with his hand. He seemed disturbed by her speech, and Rebecca braced herself for a tirade. Then he appeared to settle into his own thoughts as he stared at the sea. She wondered what those thoughts were. She couldn't begin to guess.

He had a strong profile, she noticed, one that spoke of determination, even a stubborn streak. If looks were any indication, maybe he'd make it, after all.

"I'll take you back in now," she offered after a

few moments. "Unless of course you'd like to stay out here alone for a while?"

"I can get myself back in, when I'm damned good and ready," he replied curtly. "But is the interview over, Ms. Calloway?" he asked, his tone mockingly polite. "I thought that small formality was the employer's prerogative."

Rebecca suppressed a laugh. "My mistake...once again."

"Yes, that's two. But who's counting? Frankly, I'm amazed that I'm still interested in hiring you at all."

"Yes, so am I," she replied honestly, feeling her heartbeat quicken at his words.

"So...do you want the job or not?" he asked impatiently.

Her immediate impulse was to answer "Yes." But she restrained herself.

"I'm glad you want to hire me, Mr. Berringer. But I do need to think it over for a day or so. I hope that's acceptable to you."

"As you wish. You can call Matthew with your decision," he instructed.

"All right, I'll do that," she replied. Had she hurt his feelings when she didn't accept right away? He was pouting like a small boy. Well, she couldn't help that.

"Did I scare you?" he asked suddenly. His black eyes were narrowed in a brooding look that had already become familiar to her. "You hardly seem the timid type."

"No, not at all," she called over her shoulder. "You'll have to try much harder if I come back."

"Yes, I will try harder. I'll be absolutely impossible," he promised. "See, you've motivated me already."

Rebecca met his glance quickly then continued on her way. His brief smile was heart-stopping. Both a good sign...and bad, she thought with dismay. She kept going, through the glass door, through Grant's messy bedroom to the outer room, where she found Matthew waiting for her.

"How did it go?" Matthew asked eagerly, rising from his chair.

"All right, I suppose. He offered me the job."

"That's great!" Matthew smiled, and his blue eyes lit with pleasure. "When can you start?" he asked eagerly.

"Well, I haven't accepted yet. I need some time to think it over. A day or two, at the most. Your brother told me I should call you with my answer."

"Yes, call me with your answer as soon as you decide, Ms. Calloway. And if there are any questions, any questions at all—about the salary or living arrangements—please know I'll do all I can to make the situation comfortable for you."

Rebecca promised she would call as soon as she came to a decision, and Matthew showed her to the front door, where they said goodbye.

As Rebecca started up her car and drove down the long driveway toward the main road, she wondered why she hadn't accepted on the spot. While she dithered, the Berringers might interview someone else and offer them the position. The salary they'd spoken of was very generous. As were the extras. It was a plum assignment, really. Except for one thing. The patient.

Grant Berringer hadn't scared her. But her feelings and reactions to him certainly had.

Two

Although Rebecca had expected to deliberate over the job offer for at least a day or more, she could think of nothing else during the long drive back to the city. By the time she arrived at the front door to her apartment in a brownstone building on Manhattan's Upper West Side, she had more or less decided that she had no real choice at all. She felt compelled to accept, despite a niggling, intuitive warning that the job would be a hard one, perhaps the hardest she'd ever faced.

Yet each time she'd pondered turning it down, the vision of Grant Berringer's dark, luminous eyes and bleak, haunted expression would rise before her, and she'd feel herself swaying again toward a positive answer.

Rebecca had faced some hard cases but prided herself on the fact that she had never failed to inspire her patients to work hard and heal. She had a solid reputation in her field—which was why Matthew Berringer had gotten in touch with her in the first place. Did she dare put that professional reputation on the line for a man she barely knew—and didn't even necessarily like? If she failed with a well-known man like Grant Berringer—and joined the ranks of his rejected therapists—the word would soon get around. It might make it difficult to find another assignment.

Well then, she couldn't fail, could she? Somehow, she had to break through the fortress he'd built around his wounded heart and soul. The injuries to his body were serious but irrelevant, Rebecca believed. It was the inner man who needed to recover. And once that began to happen, the rest would follow easily, as night follows day.

Rebecca quickly changed from her interview suit into comfortable, worn jeans and a striped T-shirt. With a tall cold drink in hand, she dialed Matthew Berringer. He sounded surprised to hear from her. But when she accepted the offer, he seemed so pleased and grateful, Rebecca felt she'd made the right choice, after all. She arranged to move into the Berringer mansion the following weekend, which was right after Nora's last day of school.

Since her stay would be temporary, Matthew insisted on paying her moving expenses and any unexpected costs, such as rent on her apartment or storage for furniture. While Rebecca appreciated his consideration and concern, she had been asked to move out of her apartment at the end of the month to give way to the landlord's brother. And as for items to put in storage, since her divorce, she and Nora had been traveling light, and Rebecca thought she could fit most of their belongings in the back of her Jeep Cherokee.

"Grant will be very pleased to hear the news," Matthew said. "He was impressed by your meeting."

"Yes, I'm sure," Rebecca replied, smiling. "The same way a bored cat is impressed with a particularly feisty mouse."

"Well...that, too," Matthew conceded with a laugh. "But I think he's finally met a worthy adversary. My money is riding on you, Rebecca."

Rebecca thanked him for the vote of confidence. They discussed the terms of her contract and ended the conversation on a cheerful note. The moment she hung up the phone, however, she felt a knot of dread in the pit of her stomach. Well, she'd accepted. The contract would arrive in a few days, and once she signed it, she was committed to the assignment.

Rebecca shoved worrisome thoughts aside and began making a list of all she had to do in the next week to prepare for the move. She looked up to see that it was time to pick up Nora at school, a task that was performed by a sitter while Rebecca was working. But Rebecca liked to meet her daughter whenever she was able.

Nora greeted her with a giant hug. They walked down the tree-lined street toward home hand in hand while Nora chatted happily about her adventures of the day. With the school year coming to a close, the teachers were clearly growing weary, and the children were getting wilder every day. Rebecca was barely able to interrupt Nora's conversation long enough to offer her some ice cream at a favorite shop. They sat at the counter and each ordered their usual flavor, strawberry for Rebecca and Rocky Road for Nora. Once Nora had settled down, Rebecca told her about her new job and explained that they'd be moving to the patient's house for the summer.

"You mean, like when we stay at Grammy's, in the guest room?" Nora asked, sounding puzzled.

Rebecca had to smile at the comparison. Her mother lived in a lovely old Victorian house on the Connecticut shore, the house where Rebecca had been raised along with two sisters. But the entire home would fit quite neatly into the space of the Berringers' east wing, she thought.

"Not quite like Grammy's guest room. We'll have our own private apartment, about the size of the apartment we have now. But it will be part of the Berringers' house," Rebecca explained. "Their house is very large. The kind you call a mansion."

Nora's lovely little face was still puckered in a frown. "Oh, you mean sort of like a castle?"

"Well...not exactly. But a little like a castle, I guess," Rebecca conceded, taking a spoonful of ice cream. There *was* a genuine, fire-breathing dragon on the premises, she reflected.

Nora seemed satisfied by that answer and excited to be living at the beach. Rebecca realized she would have to enroll Nora in a day camp or some type of summer program so her daughter would be occupied during working hours, but Rebecca was sure she would easily find something suitable.

"I think Eloise will love living in a castle," Nora said. "Maybe she'll learn how to swim."

Oh, dear, the cat, Rebecca thought. She'd almost forgotten about Eloise. But the cat, who had been with Nora since she was only two, couldn't be left behind. She'd have to tell Matthew Berringer about Eloise, of course, and hope he didn't mind.

"Cats don't like water much, Nora," Rebecca reminded her. "But I'm sure she won't complain about seafood dinners."

Nora laughed. As they walked home, Rebecca felt relieved that her daughter had taken the news of their sudden move so easily. Some other children would have been upset about the unexpected change. But Nora had always had an easy temperament, even as a baby. She'd always taken changes in stride, too. Even the breakup of their little family. Nora had only been four years old when Rebecca's husband had asked for a divorce, claiming he'd fallen madly in love with a co-worker.

Rebecca had been crushed by the betrayal, but not truly surprised. In the years since Nora's arrival, it seemed that she and her husband, Jack, had been growing increasingly distant and they spent little time together as a couple—except to argue about money, or Jack's late nights out with his pals, or all the day-to-day problems in every married life. But while Rebecca had noticed the change in their relationship and wondered how to rekindle their romantic spark, she'd never imagined that Jack had found someone else.

She'd never once considered being unfaithful to him. No matter what.

They had been sweethearts since high school, and his disloyalty was a great blow to her. Still, for Nora's sake, Rebecca had offered to forgive and forget, if Jack was willing to end his affair and try to work on their marriage. She was even willing to recognize that she had played some part in his seeking passion elsewhere.

But Jack had claimed it was too late and any efforts in that direction would be useless. He also claimed that he loved her…but not the way a man should love his wife. Maybe they'd married too young, or simply knew each other too long and too well. While it all sounded like the typical excuses of an unfaithful spouse, Rebecca knew there was some truth to his words. Maybe she *had* always been too devoted to Jack, her love and loyalty too easily won. His great romance hadn't held together very long, but that, too, was predictable, Rebecca realized.

The blow was awesome, but it was a clean break and irrevocable. As painful as it had been to face the truth, her loving feelings for Jack had withered and grown cold soon after she'd learned about his deception. In fact, in the passing years, she'd come to see him differently. It wasn't just bitterness, either, she knew. While they were married, she'd accepted and overlooked his immaturity and self-centered tendencies. But now she saw him objectively and often felt relieved that she didn't have to put up with his inconsiderate behavior anymore.

Except that Nora often did, which inevitably made

Rebecca livid. Jack had never been a very consistent father, sometimes showering Nora with the attention and affection she deserved and sometimes ignoring her existence completely. His sales job kept him on the road a lot, and even when he was in town, he often forgot plans and special dates he'd made with Nora. Rebecca was left to make excuses and soothe Nora's hurt feelings…and to give their daughter a double share of love and attention. It was at those times especially that Rebecca wondered why she'd ever put up with him all those years.

Rebecca had swiftly regained her pride in the years since her divorce, yet she'd never found the courage to have a real relationship again. She'd dated a bit, even met a few men she genuinely liked. But nothing ever went too far, and Rebecca knew that the fault was hers alone. She never let her fledgling relationships progress very far and always found some reason to bail out before things grew serious.

It was fear, plain and simple. She didn't need a therapist or self-help guru to diagnose her problem. Logically she knew all men weren't faithless, but emotionally, she just didn't trust the opposite sex any longer. Besides, she'd found that earning a living and taking care of Nora required her full attention and effort. Though she was occasionally lonely and from time to time imagined a perfect romance that could magically sweep away her fears, Rebecca was largely content with her life and always put off the idea of dating for some future time in her life.

When Nora was older, she told herself, or when her professional life was less demanding of her time

and energy. She knew these reasons were all thin excuses, convenient shields. But she allowed herself the
pretense and fended off friends and relations—mostly
her two sisters—who never grew tired of trying to fix
her up with dates.

At least by living at the Berringers' for the summer
she'd be out of that loop, Rebecca reflected, and the
relative isolation would give her the perfect excuse to
neglect her love life, or lack thereof.

The week passed quickly and the morning soon
arrived for Rebecca and Nora to drive to Bridge-
hampton in Rebecca's aged and overloaded car. She'd
hired two college students with a van to move her
furniture and many of the boxes.

All in all, she didn't have much to show in the way
of worldly goods, which was more or less the way
she preferred it. Rebecca had never been impressed
by wealth or the privilege and power it commanded.
Her ex-husband had often accused her of what he
called reverse snobbery, and though she was sure she
wasn't usually judgmental, she sometimes thought
she did have an automatic bias against rich people.
Matthew Berringer, however, had impressed her fa-
vorably, and for all his money, she had found him
quite down-to-earth. As for her new patient, Rebecca
thought as she turned down the long drive that led to
the mansion, well…any snobbery Grant Berringer
possessed was the least of her problems right now.

"Wow…we're going to live in *there?*" Nora asked
with a gasp.

Rebecca had to laugh at her reaction. "That's
right."

"It does look like a castle...practically," Nora conceded.

"It's as close as we'll ever get, honey," Rebecca replied. As if to underscore her advice, Eloise, in her cat carrier, released a long, plaintive yowl.

As soon as Rebecca and Nora arrived, Matthew sent down some of the house staff to help, and the car and van were unpacked in no time flat. Rebecca felt a bit disoriented by the moving-day confusion, especially since Nora insisted on opening various boxes, looking for favorite toys and other belongings she feared Rebecca had left behind. Rebecca had hoped to put their things away in an orderly fashion, but soon the place was topsy-turvy.

In the midst of the confusion, the phone rang, and Rebecca was greeted by Grant's deep, commanding voice.

"So, you've finally arrived. When did you plan on seeing your patient...next week, perhaps?" he asked in a cranky tone.

For a man who had to be persuaded to hire her, he was certainly taking a different tack today, she reflected. Different, but no less imperious.

"I was just doing a bit of unpacking. Do you feel neglected already?" she countered.

She was probably starting off on the entirely wrong foot—and would be fired by dinnertime, hence wasting energy with all the effort of moving in—but he sounded so much like a spoiled little boy, she couldn't resist answering him tartly.

"That's not the point." He bristled. "I believe that you're to be paid very well for your time here, Ms.

Calloway, and I expect your complete attention. Is that clear?''

"Quite clear. Though, in fact, you don't start paying me for my time until Monday morning, and today is Saturday," she reminded him politely. "Also, please feel free to call me Rebecca."

She heard him grumble but couldn't make out the words. She didn't expect an apology, and there was none.

She did expect him to hang up, but instead he said, "It's almost twelve o'clock. If you haven't had any lunch yet, please join me. On the terrace off the library, in about half an hour or so."

It was more of a command than an invitation, Rebecca noticed, but it seemed to indicate that he was eager to see her again, which was a hopeful sign.

"Thank you, I'll see you then." She hung up the phone, checked her watch and quickly glanced at herself and then Nora. They both looked as if they'd been dragged through a trashbin by the hair. They'd never be ready on time, but Rebecca knew she had better try.

Miraculously, a half hour later, she had bathed Nora, dressed her in a yellow gingham sundress and sandals and put her long hair in a ponytail. No time for a braid. Nora didn't understand why she had to suddenly dress up but submitted to the treatment with little complaint. Rebecca had quickly showered, pulled on a long floral skirt and silk tank top she'd found at the top of the clothes pile and then whisked on some lipstick. She grabbed Nora's hand, and they scurried down numerous hallways until they finally found the library. Nora thought it was a game and raced ahead, despite Rebecca's hushed warnings to slow down.

A bit out of breath but right on time, Rebecca composed herself at the door to the library. She took a deep breath and smoothed her hair before entering. The room was empty, but she heard voices outside the glass doors that opened to the terrace. As she stepped onto the terrace, she saw Matthew and Grant sitting at a table set for lunch. Rebecca stopped a few feet away from the table and smiled at them both.

"Well, here we are," she said brightly.

"And right on time," Matthew replied with a smile. He rose to greet them. "How nice to be joined for lunch by two lovely ladies."

Rebecca smiled in reply as he held out her chair. But when she turned to greet Grant, his dark gaze was narrowed, his brow knitted in a frown. He stared at her, looking positively shocked. She couldn't quite figure it out. Then she realized he was staring at Nora.

"Who's that?" he demanded, indicating Nora.

Rebecca felt her daughter clutch her hand and looked to see the child's expression grow wary and tense. She pulled her protectively to her side. "My daughter. Her name is Nora."

"You never said you were bringing a child," he bellowed.

Rebecca glanced nervously from Grant to Matthew, who seemed to shrink into his seat. "But...I told Matthew. I assumed he told you," she explained.

Grant's dark eyes widened, and his mouth tightened into a hard, grim line. He stared across the table at his brother. "You knew she was bringing a child here?" he demanded.

"Rebecca told me about her daughter during her interview," Matthew admitted smoothly. "We'll discuss this later, Grant. No reason to frighten the little girl."

"No reason, eh? No reason to tell me about the child, either, I suppose...until it's too late. Because you knew I wouldn't permit it!" he roared. His fiery gaze swept from Matthew to Rebecca. "And I won't," he insisted.

Rebecca took a deep breath and stood tall against his outburst. She didn't know what to say. If Matthew knew his brother had such strong objections to having a child in the house and had hidden Nora's arrival from Grant, then she could understand Grant's anger. Not that it excused his manner of expressing it.

"Grant, please." Matthew approached his brother. "Calm down. Try to be more reasonable—"

"Why in heaven's name should I be reasonable? You've purposely tricked me. The both of you. Just because I'm in a wheelchair, does that mean you have a right to control and manipulate me? To completely ignore my opinion?" He backed his wheelchair away from the table, then came directly toward Rebecca and Nora.

His dark hair looked longer and shaggier than at their first meeting, Rebecca thought. And his glowing lion's eyes burned bright and wild. Even in his anger, Rebecca still felt that irksome tug of attraction she tried so hard to deny.

He was acting like a child, she told herself. Still,

she understood his side of the situation. He was a proud man, now forced to rely on others for every need. It was a question of self-respect. She was sorry she had not been aware of his objection. She would have confronted him directly about it, as an equal. Now he seemed to believe she was in on the deception.

"I wasn't aware that you didn't want to hire someone with a child," she said honestly. "It's a big house. Nora will do her best to stay out of your way. If that's not a satisfactory solution, we can go."

He rolled the chair closer, glaring at her. "I would like you to go," he announced in a low, harsh tone. "Today, if at all possible."

"Grant—come on now," Matthew urged. "Rebecca has a contract."

"What's the difference? Pay her out. Pay her for the whole damn summer. What do I care?"

"But why must she go?" Matthew persisted. "It was all my fault. You can't just—"

"Don't tell me what I can and cannot do!" Grant turned toward his brother and pounded his fist on the tabletop. The plates and silverware clattered. "I'll do as I damn please! Do you understand that?"

Clinging to Rebecca's side, Nora suddenly burst into tears and buried her face in her mother's skirt. Rebecca was overwhelmed by a wave of protective instinct.

"Nora, sweetheart," she crooned. "It's okay." She crouched and wrapped her arms around the little girl in a sheltering embrace.

"Can't we go, Mommy? He's...scaring me," Nora whispered between sniffles.

"Don't be afraid, sweetie. We're going right away," she promised.

She scooped Nora up in her arms, though the child was well past the age of easy lifting. Nora clung to her and buried her face in her mother's shoulder. If this was the atmosphere Grant would create, then perhaps it was best if she took Nora away. As she turned to leave the terrace, Rebecca glanced at Grant with a searing look.

"Proud of yourself?" she asked, though she didn't know how she dared to be so insolent to him.

The look he gave her in answer stopped her cold in her tracks. His eyes flashed, and he looked away, quickly turning his chair so he didn't have to face her.

"You don't have a clue about me, Rebecca Calloway," he said in a hushed, almost apologetic tone. "It's best you get away now, while the going is good. Best for your little girl, too."

Rebecca stood stone still for a moment, feeling dazed and confused. But before she could think of anything to say in reply, Grant turned his chair, and she was suddenly facing his back. Matthew glanced at her and made a small motion with his head, indicating that she should leave them.

Hugging Nora close, she made her way through the study and down the labyrinth of hallways to their rooms. Nora had calmed down considerably and didn't need to be carried all the way—which Rebecca considered a small blessing, since her back was already sore from moving, and she faced repacking many boxes and loading her car again.

Once in their rooms, Rebecca explained that Grant was not a bad person and that his outburst didn't have anything to do with Nora personally. She told her daughter he was terribly unhappy because of his accident and slow recovery. Nora seemed to understand.

A few minutes later, Matthew brought them some lunch on a tray. Nora immediately ran over and chose a sandwich. Rebecca had lost her appetite and picked up a cold drink. Matthew moved a few boxes to the floor, then sat on the small sofa and sighed.

"I need to apologize," he began. "This whole mess is all my fault. I knew Grant would object to having your daughter here, but I'd hoped that once you arrived, he'd get used to the idea," he explained.

"What does he have against children?" she asked. "Does he think having Nora with me will distract me from my work?"

"No, it's not that." Matthew met her gaze then looked away. "I'm not free to say. But maybe you can talk to him about it. He might explain it to you."

"Why bother?" Rebecca asked honestly. "I doubt he'll change his mind."

"Won't you stay? At least until Monday. Maybe by then I can persuade him to reconsider."

Rebecca's first impulse was to say no. She found the start an ill omen and had the instinct to bail out. Something told her this job would be jinxed. Perhaps it was best to get out now, before she'd begun. As for her contract, she'd never accept the full summer's salary for work she did not perform, as Grant had suggested. But she did feel that the Berringers owed her expenses for her trouble in getting here and moving out.

Still, Rebecca knew she couldn't answer abruptly. Her professionalism demanded a rational pace. And though she hardly knew Matthew Berringer, she was beginning to feel as if they were friends. She couldn't just run out on him. Again, she wondered why she felt no attraction to Matthew, with his calm, considerate manner and even temperament. The two brothers were opposite in every way. It was just her luck that only the brooding, titanic Grant drew her.

"I don't know," she said finally. She crossed her arms over her chest. "Grant feels very strongly about the issue. And I do understand why he's angry."

Matthew dragged his hand through his hair. "Yes, yes. I know you're right. I made a big blunder there. It was wrong of me to hide the truth from him. I can see that now," he admitted. "But you only just got here. You can't turn around and go. Won't you stay the night? You and Nora must be exhausted. Grant isn't such a monster that he won't understand."

Rebecca shrugged. She glanced at the boxes. She had to laugh or she would cry.

The truth was, she had no place to go with Nora. They'd probably end up at a motel somewhere for the night, and maybe even until she could rent a new apartment. She might make the long drive to Connecticut and stay with her mother. But that wouldn't solve everything. Her head spun.

"Mommy!" Nora raced in from the other room, wild-eyed. She ran straight to Rebecca and clutched her arm. "Mommy, something horrible has happened," she gasped, on the verge of tears.

Rebecca gripped her shoulders and remained calm. Sometimes Nora's emergencies were nothing more than a lost button or a bit of chocolate candy melted in a coat pocket.

"What is it, Nora? What's happened?"

"Eloise," she gasped. "She's gone. I wanted to feed her some of my sandwich and I looked everywhere. She must have run away."

Rebecca felt her stomach clench but tried to be reasonable. "She must be around here somewhere, sweetheart. She's probably scared from the move and hiding in one of the boxes."

Nora shook her head. Tears welled in her eyes. "We only opened a few boxes and I checked them all. I've looked in the closets and under the bed. Everywhere," she insisted. "She's gone."

Rebecca hoped that was not the case. But a cold chill in her gut told her it was so. Nora was a smart girl, and if she said she had looked thoroughly, she had.

"What's happened?" Matthew asked quietly. "Did she lose something?"

Rebecca nodded. "Our cat. Seems she's disappeared."

"What a day." Matthew sighed and shook his head. "Well, I'm sure we'll find her. Though the cat could be anywhere in the house by now if she's wandered outside these rooms."

And it was a large house, Rebecca reflected grimly. A very large house.

"We've kept the door closed since we got here. But I guess she could have slipped out when we weren't looking."

"No," Nora insisted. "She was sleeping under the bed when we left. But look." She pointed to a sliding glass door that opened to a deck. "That door was open. She could have gone out onto the beach and run away."

Rebecca looked at the door then at her daughter. It seemed to be the only explanation. She rested her hand on Nora's soft hair. "We'll go out and look right now. She's such a lazy old thing," Rebecca added. "She probably didn't get very far at all."

"Okay." Nora nodded. "Let's go." Rebecca could tell she was trying to be brave but was imagining the worst.

As Rebecca and Nora started toward the door to the deck, Matthew picked up the phone. "We'll get some help from the household staff. We'll make a complete search of the house and grounds. Don't worry, Nora. We'll find your cat," he promised.

Nora thanked him, and her eyes brightened. Rebecca was grateful for the help.

Three

With the help of several members of the Berringer household staff, including the housekeeper, Mrs. Walker and Matthew, they searched for hours—the house, the grounds and the beach. They searched the large garage, the pool side cabana, the guest cottage and gardener's shed without a sign or fleeting sighting of Eloise.

It was dark by the time Rebecca convinced Nora to give up and return to their apartment. The little girl was too exhausted to argue and too tired to eat any supper. Rebecca washed her quickly and pulled on her nightgown.

"Don't worry, we'll look again tomorrow morning," Rebecca promised her as she tucked Nora in. "She couldn't have simply disappeared."

"Oh, yes, she could," Nora murmured sadly.

"Don't you remember the cat in Alice in Wonderland? The Cheddar cat?"

"The Cheddar cat?" Then Rebecca realized she meant the Cheshire cat. But before she could reply, Nora had turned her tearstained face into her pillow and fallen asleep.

Rebecca felt bone tired, and after a quick shower, she climbed into her bed and shut off the light. Losing a job, a cat and the roof over their heads all in one day had been draining, to say the least.

She wondered if Grant Berringer knew they had not yet left. Well, there was no hope for that. But tomorrow morning, with or without Eloise, they had to be on their way. Tomorrow had to be a better day, she reflected as she drifted off to sleep. What else could possibly go wrong?

Rebecca was awakened by the shrill sound of the telephone. Early morning light filtered through the drawn curtains. She glanced at the clock on the nightstand. It was barely seven, and she wondered who could be calling so early.

It was Grant. He greeted her in his deep, sonorous tone, which danced along her nerve endings like an electric charge. Rebecca was annoyed at herself for feeling the least bit affected by him.

"If you're checking to see if we've left yet, don't worry," she said curtly. "We'll be gone in an hour or so."

"Well, don't forget your cat," he replied in a voice that could almost be called cheerful. "A large calico, on the plump side? The tag says her name is Eloise."

Rebecca quickly sat up. "How did you find Eloise?"

"She found me. When I woke this morning, she was sleeping at the foot of my bed. She's now helping herself to my breakfast. She's enjoying the cream cheese and lox but doesn't have much interest in the bagel."

As if Grant wasn't mad enough at them already, now the cat was prancing through his breakfast. She decided she ought to get over there in a hurry, before he lost his temper and frightened Eloise back into oblivion.

"I'll be there right away. Try to hold on to her."

"I don't think she's going anywhere," he replied, clearly amused at her urgency. "Not as long as the smoked salmon holds out."

Rebecca ended the conversation abruptly and jumped out of bed. As she frantically searched through a box of clothes for her bathrobe, Nora woke up and came into her room.

"What's the matter? Who was that on the phone, Mommy?"

"Mr. Berringer found Eloise. I'm going to get her."

Nora beamed and jumped with excitement. "I want to come get her...please?"

Rebecca pulled on her robe and tied the sash. "You wait here, honey. It's better if I go alone. I'll be right back."

"Please? Why can't I come, too?" Nora pleaded. "Matthew won't mind if I come with you."

"It wasn't Matthew who called. It was Grant," Rebecca explained. Suddenly, Nora did not seem as eager to come.

"Oh. Was he angry?" she asked.

"He didn't sound angry," Rebecca answered honestly. "Not at all. He's feeding Eloise breakfast. I'm sure she's safe and sound."

"All right. But come right back." Nora made her promise. Then she ran into her room and returned with the cat carrier. "And be sure to put her in here right away, so she doesn't run away again."

"Good thinking." Rebecca took the carrier and left on her mission.

It wasn't until she knocked on Grant's door that she suddenly gave a thought to her appearance. She hadn't bothered to comb her hair, which hung in loose, long reddish brown waves past her shoulders. She'd pulled on the first nightgown she'd found last night, a short slip style in shell pink, and a handy robe—a peach-colored floral print that ended midthigh. She suddenly felt exposed and vulnerable, and at a distinct disadvantage, facing him again wearing such flimsy attire. But there was no help for it now.

"Come in," he replied from the other side of the door.

Rebecca opened the door slowly and spotted Grant, sitting near the doors that led to the deck. The curtains had been pulled back and the room was filled with soft morning light. As she entered, she held the cat carrier in front of her, hoping it would distract him from her scanty attire and long, bare legs.

She didn't see the cat anywhere and wondered if she had gotten away again. Then she realized Eloise was sitting in Grant's lap, curled in a comfortable ball and cleaning her face with one paw.

"Oh, dear. I'm sorry," Rebecca apologized, quickly walking toward him. "Let me get her off you."

"It's all right." Grant held up his hand. "She's not bothering me...and I did want to speak to you."

"Oh. About what?" Rebecca took a step closer and held the cat carrier at her side. She felt self-conscious as Grant paused, seeming to forget what he wanted to talk about.

His dark, assessing gaze moved over her from the top of her head to her bare feet. When their gazes met again, the smoldering light in his eyes was one of pure male appreciation—and more than that, desire.

"You came straight from your bed, I see," he commented finally. His voice was low and husky, and she was sure that wasn't at all what he'd meant to say.

She swallowed hard, feeling a hot blush sweep up her neck to color her cheeks as her body responded to his lustful look. She struggled to ignore the frisson of heat arcing between them and forced herself to sound businesslike and impersonal.

"You wanted to speak to me about something?" she reminded him.

He looked away and shifted in his chair. "I wanted to apologize for my outburst yesterday. I'm ashamed of myself. Totally. And very sorry for frightening your daughter. Will you tell her that I'm sorry and didn't mean to scare her?"

She was surprised, not just by his words, but his sincere, heartfelt tone. "Thank you for saying that.

Yes, I'll give Nora your apology,'' she promised. ''I'm sure she's already forgiven you since you found the cat.''

''And what about you, Rebecca? Do you forgive me?''

Rebecca took a breath. ''I do...though I can't see why it should matter,'' she answered honestly. ''After today, we'll probably never see each other again.''

She knew the words were true, yet somehow the thought of never seeing him again seemed impossible. Unthinkable, actually. She felt a powerful, uncanny connection to him. The intimacy caused by the fact that they were both in their pajamas, just out of bed, somehow didn't seem strange at all.

''Would you consider staying? I know it's a lot to ask after the way I acted.'' He shook his head. ''There is a reason for my reaction. Though it's still no excuse.''

''Oh? And what's that?''

He seemed to be collecting his thoughts. A lock of his dark hair fell across his forehead, and he brushed it back. He hadn't shaved yet, and a day's growth of beard shadowed his lean cheeks. He wore long striped pajama bottoms. Either he'd been in excellent shape before the accident, or using the wheelchair for weeks had built up his shoulders, chest and arms. His dark blue silk robe hung open, exposing his muscular, hair-covered chest, completing an image that was thoroughly masculine and totally appealing. Rebecca realized she was staring and forced herself to look away.

''My fiancée, Courtney...she was expecting our

baby when she died. Now I find it hard to be around children.'' Rebecca felt her breath catch in her throat at his admission. Poor man. If there was an acceptable excuse for his outburst, this had to be it.

''I'm so sorry...I had no idea,'' Rebecca replied. She didn't know what more to say. She watched as he took a deep breath, struggling to maintain control.

''Of course you didn't,'' he replied. ''But the world is full of children, and I can't hide from that fact forever.'' He paused again. ''Yesterday, after you ran off with Nora, I had to face myself—my own selfishness and insensitivity. The sight was repellent to me. I have to do better.''

He met her gaze for an instant, then looked away. His face was as devoid of emotion as his calm, even voice. But in his eyes Rebecca discovered a world of anguish and remorse.

She didn't know what to say, how to answer him. She sat on the edge of his bed next to the wheelchair. Her bare leg brushed the cool, smooth fabric of his robe. She had the urge to take his hand, to offer some gesture of physical comfort, but didn't quite dare.

''If you'll stay, I'll treat your daughter with kindness and respect,'' he promised. ''And the cat, too, of course,'' he added, stroking the contented feline who sat with eyes half-closed, like a furred Buddha in his lap.

''Yes, we'll stay,'' she replied in a quiet but firm tone. She had no need to think the matter over. But she knew she had to change the mood, to snap him out of this reverie and get him looking to the future.

''The clock starts running officially tomorrow.

We'll start very early in the morning, too. I'm going to put you to work,'' she warned him. ''Hard work.''

''Oh, hard work, eh? You sound as if you think I've had it easy so far, Rebecca. Lolling about, reading girlie magazines or something?'' The grief that had shadowed his handsome features had faded. A sexy, winsome smile played at the corners of his full lips and set her pulse on an erratic pace.

''I won't comment on your taste in literature. But you asked me to get you out of that wheelchair by the end of summer, and I mean to do it.''

''Yes, sir!'' He teased her with a curt salute. Alarmed at the gesture, Eloise jumped off Grant's lap and strolled to an armchair, where she jumped up and settled.

''Okay, laugh if you like.'' Her take-charge tone had amused him. That was fine for now. He wouldn't be quite so amused come tomorrow, she reflected with a secret smile.

''I'm not laughing at you…but you do make me smile a lot,'' he admitted. He regarded her with a thoughtful expression. ''Maybe that's the reason I hired you, after all.''

''Maybe,'' she replied, her gaze still locked on his.

His dark gaze made her feel warm. She wanted to look away but couldn't and watched, mesmerized, as his gaze wandered over her face, studying her—liking what he saw, it seemed—finally dropping to her lips.

''You know, you're very lovely. Beautiful, really,'' he said. ''Not many women could sit in the full morning light without a drop of makeup on looking as lovely as you do.''

Compliments about her physical appearance always made Rebecca uncomfortable, mostly because she could never quite believe them. She felt herself flush with embarrassment. He sounded as if he knew what he was talking about when it came to women, and she imagined he'd seen more than his fair share of females first thing in the morning. The thought was a sobering one.

"Did you hire me for my good looks?" she asked curtly. "I thought it was for my brains."

"To be honest, I hardly noticed what you looked like when you came for the interview." The statement stung, but Rebecca knew he was being truthful. "Now that I have, let's just say that if I'm going to be saddled with a tyrant all summer, she may as well be easy on the eyes." He gave her a tigerlike grin. "And blush so prettily when I tease her."

She opened her mouth to protest, but before she could utter a sound, he reached out and cupped her cheek with his hand. He was about to kiss her, and her breath caught in her throat. He couldn't kiss her, her mind protested. This moment between them had gone way out of control.

But somehow, she couldn't move away. As his large hand stroked her cheek and the pad of his thumb swept over her full bottom lip, instead of moving away, she leaned closer, so close she felt the heat of his breath on her skin. When his long fingers sifted her hair, urging her closer, she rested her hand on his forearm and felt his formidable strength.

"Grant...this is not a good way to start things off," she finally whispered.

"We don't start officially until tomorrow morning. You just said so yourself," he reminded her, his lips barely a breath away from hers.

"But I didn't mean..." Her halfhearted protest was abruptly interrupted as his mouth covered hers. His lips were warm, his touch coaxing and persuasive.

Though she wanted to pull away for a moment, struggling to resist, the sensation of his mouth on hers quickly melted her defenses. There was nothing tentative in his kiss. Not in the least. His lips moved over hers masterfully, savoring her response and persuading her to give him more and more. His strong arms wrapped around her, and his tongue slipped into her mouth, and she heard herself give a small moan of pleasure, a sound that encouraged him even more.

She knew she had to stop him...but she couldn't stop herself. All her hesitation and doubts about taking this job boiled down to one thing—her compelling attraction to him. A powerful pull that was all the more dangerous because he seemed to share the feeling.

Their attraction had simmered below the surface since they'd met—and now, sitting here in such an intimate atmosphere, it had exploded.

Rebecca couldn't reason, couldn't protest. She couldn't stop kissing him or resist the mounting pleasure of him kissing her. Their intense attraction had somehow moved them to another place, and the moment seemed separate from the real world. Pure and elemental. She wasn't his therapist, only a woman expressing her longing, and he was not her patient, but a passionate man who desired her totally.

She leaned her head back and felt him clutch her shoulders. Her mouth opened under his, and the kiss deepened, rising in intensity and hunger. She pressed her hand to his chest. At the opening of his robe, she felt the whorls of dark hair and warm skin. Instinctively, her fingers glided across his chest in a smooth caress.

She heard him moan deep in his throat, and the sound excited her. His strong hands pushed her robe down her arms, then slid down her bare arms, leaving a fiery path in their wake. Then she felt his caressing touch on her breasts, the heat of his hands penetrating the thin silky fabric of her nightgown. Her nipples grew instantly tight and tingled as he stroked them with his fingertips. She pulled her mouth from his, and her head dropped to his shoulder. She covered his hands with hers and stilled them. She felt too weak to pull away from him, but knew it could go no further. She was shocked and amazed it had gone this far.

"We have to stop. Please," she whispered.

He pressed his cheek to her hair and didn't say anything at first. She wondered if he had heard her. Finally, she lifted her head and stared into his eyes.

"Yes, you're right." He nodded.

He looked at her body and then gently pulled up her robe. The lightest touch of his fingertips on her skin set her nerves jumping with excitement. She pulled away from him and struggled to ignore the sensation.

"We're attracted to each other. It happens," she said, trying to regain some control.

"Oh…does this happen *often* to you? With your patients, I mean?" he asked, eyes wide, dark brows raised.

"Of course not!" she exclaimed. "It's never happened…I've never so much as… Well, I've certainly never kissed a patient before," she insisted.

"I've never kissed a therapist, so I suppose we're even."

He didn't sound as if he believed her, and though the thought made her angry, she couldn't entirely blame him. She'd behaved like a love-starved loon. What did he think she was, a paid companion? How was she ever going to set things right here?

"Look, what I meant to say was, it shouldn't have happened. But it did. We're attracted to each other… and curious, I suppose," she reasoned. "Maybe it's a good thing it happened now, and we've gotten it out and over with."

"You sound as if kissing me was some distasteful but necessary task, Rebecca." He sounded stung. Rebecca nearly laughed.

"I didn't say I didn't enjoy it," she argued. "But it was totally…inappropriate."

"Inappropriate, yes. The best ones usually are."

His smug, sexy grin was infuriating. She had enjoyed it. More than he could know or she'd ever be willing to admit. But it wouldn't happen again.

She stood up and pushed her hair from her face. He'd gotten her so confused, her head was spinning.

"Look, let's get the ground rules straight right now." She commanded his attention with her best professional manner. "As the weeks pass, we will have a close relationship. Even a physical relationship. But *not* a romantic one. This cannot happen again. Or I'm out of here. Contract or not. Understand?''

''Yes.'' He nodded. ''I understand completely.''

She thought for a moment he might apologize. But he didn't. Although his face held a completely serious expression, in his eyes she could still detect a gleam of male satisfaction. As if they'd been playing some game and he'd won the first round, hands down.

Of course, it had all been a game to him.

An amusement for a man who was by now probably bored with his own company. He couldn't really be attracted to her, she reasoned. Not seriously, anyway. She suspected that he was still too much in love with his fiancée, for one thing.

He was testing her. And testing his ability to attract and relate to women again. It was important to remember that, she realized.

From that perspective, it was probably a good sign that he'd made some move toward her. It was all part of his recovery process, and she felt a great deal better about the encounter thinking of it in those terms.

The awkward moment was cut short by a sharp knock on the door. Rebecca quickly put some distance between herself and Grant. She checked her robe to make sure it was securely fastened. Even if it was one of the housekeeping staff, coming to clear away his breakfast tray, she thought it looked awfully questionable to be found in her nightgown and robe in Grant's room so early in the morning.

''Come in,'' Grant called.

The door opened slowly, and Nora peeked from behind it.

Rebecca could see in a glance that her yearning to see Eloise had overruled her fear of disobeying her mother and facing Grant, the monster.

"Nora. Did you follow me? I asked you to wait in our rooms," Rebecca reminded her calmly. Secretly, she was most grateful that Nora had not interrupted them a few moments earlier.

"But I waited and waited and you never came back. Did Eloise get lost again?"

"Don't worry. She's safe and sound," Grant assured her. He wheeled his chair toward Nora.

"Where is she?" Nora asked, glancing around the room. "I don't see her."

"Right there, on the chair." Grant pointed to Eloise. "She ate a hearty breakfast and needed a nap."

Nora leaned around the door and saw the cat. But Rebecca could tell she was still afraid of getting too close to Grant.

"Come in, come in," he urged her. "I won't bite you."

"You won't?" Nora asked doubtfully. Her abrupt reply made the adults laugh.

"I deserve that," Grant said, shaking his head. Rebecca could see genuine regret in his dark eyes, and his caring spirit touched her. "I'm sorry I scared you, Nora. Very sorry. I'm not usually like that. It was wrong of me. I won't do it again," he promised. "I've just got a bad temper, being in this chair," he explained, slapping the side of the chair with his hand.

"Mommy said you got hurt in a car accident and sometimes when people take a long time to get better, they feel angry. She said it didn't have anything to do with me," Nora explained.

Grant glanced from Nora to Rebecca. Their gazes met for an instant, and his look was a mixture of embarrassment at being read so clearly and respect for Rebecca's insight.

"Your mother is a very smart woman."

"Yes, I know," Nora replied in a matter-of-fact tone.

"I've asked her to stay here and help me get better. Is that okay with you?"

Nora took a moment to appraise him with intelligent eyes. Rebecca felt quite proud of her. "It's okay. She has to do her work." She finally stepped into the room. "Thank you for finding Eloise, Mr. Berringer."

She walked to the armchair to get her cat and Grant's gaze followed her. "You call me Grant," he told her. "And actually, your cat, found me. By the way, I was wondering, how did she get that name, Eloise?" he asked with genuine curiosity.

"I named her after the character in the books. You know, the little girl who lives in the Plaza Hotel in New York City." Nora sat next to her cat and began to pet her. The cat lifted her head and pressed against Nora's hand, then rose and jumped into Nora's arms. "She's very rich and spoiled and orders anything she wants from room service, and does whatever she likes and never has to pay attention to grown-ups."

"She sounds...charming," Grant remarked with a sly smile, and Rebecca found herself smiling, too.

"I'd like to read about her sometime. Maybe you could loan that book to me."

"Maybe. Or I could read it to you," Nora suggested. "I can read, you know."

"Can you really?" he replied, sounding suitably impressed. "Well, I'd like that very much."

His warm, delighted laugh transformed his features completely. His dark eyes flashed, and Rebecca felt her heartbeat quicken. She forced herself to look away.

"Have you ever been to the Plaza Hotel, Nora?" he asked.

Nora shook her head. "Mommy says she'll take me there when I'm a little older. Maybe for my next birthday. There's a portrait of Eloise there, you know. Right in the lobby."

"Is there? I've never noticed. You must see it then. I'll take you there myself. To make up for yesterday. How does that sound?"

Nora's eyes widened. "Would you really? That sounds great."

Rebecca could tell from Nora's expression that all was forgiven. She felt pleased and proud of both of them. Nora had been brave to face Grant and work out her problem with him without her mother's help, Rebecca thought. And as for Grant, Rebecca felt heartened to see she had not been so far off in her impression of him as a kind, sensitive man—despite the way he'd behaved yesterday. It was obvious he wasn't around children much, but still, he had a nice way of relating to Nora, she thought.

Promising to take Nora to the Plaza was a grand

gesture, but would he really carry through on it? Rebecca wondered. Perhaps he didn't realize Nora would not easily forget the idea. Oh, well, she'd manage to make it up to Nora once they got back to the city. She was happy to see that Grant could treat Nora kindly and that Nora had gotten over her initial fear of him. This newly forged truce between the two would certainly make her work easier.

Now if only she could negotiate a truce in her own heart with her seesawing feelings of attraction for him.

Four

"**S**eventeen, eighteen...come on, lazy bones," Rebecca chided him. "You're not getting off this bench until you give me thirty good ones."

"Twenty-five...and I'll raise your salary." He huffed as he completed two more lifts.

"You can't buy yourself out of this torture," she teased. "Besides, I thought you knew by now I can't be bribed. Twenty-one... That's good, nine more."

"Nine more! Ugh," he groaned, completing another lift. "You're a slave driver...a cruel, heartless wench. It's hard to believe it, looking at you..." He huffed.

"No pain, no gain, pal."

"You sadists all love that line, don't you?" Grant grunted.

"Do save your breath for the exercises, Grant,"

she counseled him. "You still haven't hit the bench press today."

She watched the muscles in his thighs bunch and his jaw clench as he pushed himself to reach number thirty. He was making an effort, a painful one. Pleased with his physical progress and spirit, she didn't care a whit what he called her.

"The bench press!" He railed between breaths. "What are you trying to turn me into, woman? I work on Wall Street, remember? Not as a bouncer in a nightclub."

Rebecca had to laugh. "True, but a little bulk under your Armani suits couldn't hurt. You still need to intimidate the other guy when you swing those big deals, don't you?"

"I intimidate them with my intelligence, daring and reputation as a financial piranha, not with my neck size." He gasped.

"Breathe," she reminded. "In through the mouth, leg up, out through the nose, leg down. Slowly now. I want concentration and control."

His nostrils flared as he exhaled a long breath. "Yes, master," he replied.

"That's the idea." She praised him with a laugh.

In a month's time, they had made impressive progress. As she had feared, Grant was resistant and hard to motivate at first. Yet during those early days, he never challenged her so seriously that she gave up on him and quit. Little by little, day by day, she watched his resistance slowly wear away and saw him become increasingly committed to his recuperation.

When she came to him in the mornings, he looked

pleased to see her and begin their workout—though he greeted her with every disparaging name in the book. But Rebecca knew he didn't really mean it. It was just his way of dealing with the fear of trying hard and maybe failing.

But he wasn't failing. Not in the least. He was succeeding by leaps and bounds. In a day or so, he'd be ready to leave his wheelchair and graduate to crutches. When Rebecca had reported the news to Matthew, she saw tears in his eyes. But he briskly brushed the emotional moment aside.

Although Matthew insisted she was indeed a miracle worker to get Grant interested in a therapy program, Rebecca knew it was not merely her coaching and praise that motivated him. She knew Grant was far more motivated and inspired each time he could see that he'd gained strength and some use of his injured body. Getting out of the wheelchair was a particularly enticing carrot to dangle in front of him. She knew the move would be a great boost to his spirits and his self-image. Once on his feet, even supported by crutches, he would start to see himself again as the vital, energetic and confident man he once had been.

Rebecca looked forward to the change with a mixture of pleasure and fear. It had been hard enough to handle her feelings of attraction toward him and keep their relationship within professional limits while he was wheelchair-bound. But as he grew stronger, her willpower seemed to grow weaker. She didn't know how she'd manage to hold up her defenses against him once he got his full strength back.

Though he'd never tried to kiss her or encourage a romantic embrace after that first time weeks ago, Rebecca could always feel the powerful chemistry simmering between them, like some highly potent, combustible element that needed merely a spark to explode. No matter what she did, no matter how ultraprofessional she tried to act, how poker-faced and detached, it was always just there. The way he held her gaze when she smiled. The way he looked at her when he thought she didn't notice. The way his breathing changed and his body grew taut, affected by her slightest touch.

It had been so very long since Rebecca felt this way about a man. It was all so confusing, so disturbing to her peace of mind, and yet at the same so amazing. So downright...wonderful.

But she knew she could never let herself get carried away by high-school-girl feelings. To encourage any type of romantic relationship with a patient was totally unethical, even predatory in a way. In relationships between patients and medical professionals of any kind, so many patients mistook gratitude for feelings of love when they were recovering. Grant had experienced a serious blow to his ego and needed reassurance that he was still attractive to the opposite sex—thus the reason for that mind-blowing kiss and all the lingering looks that had come after. Since she was the only woman in his life right now—with the exception of Mrs. Walker, who had to be in her mid-sixties—Grant's need to build up his macho confidence would have to be worked out with her.

It all sounded so simplistic, so obvious. She knew

if she ever tried to explain it to him, he'd laugh in her face and act as if he was above such predictable, textbook responses. But while Grant was a highly sophisticated man, he was no less vulnerable to his reactions and needs. Whatever he felt for her right now was a side effect of his recovery, Rebecca assured herself, and she would be foolish to take his admiration to heart.

Rebecca knew she, too, was especially vulnerable right now. Since Jack's betrayal, she hadn't been able to trust men. She certainly had let Grant closer emotionally than any man she'd met since her divorce. But was she attracted to him because his admiration was a great ego boost? Rebecca knew that was highly possible.

And what about Courtney? Was she his past love, or were Grant's feelings for her still very much in the present? Although he never spoke about his loss, he kept Courtney's photo at his bedside. She had been quite beautiful, with thick blond hair and a model's perfect features and figure. Rebecca had heard that Courtney had been a successful lawyer, as well.

Grant slept with Courtney's image just inches from his pillow. Rebecca could only imagine the tortured thoughts that ran through his head each night. Clearly he had never resolved his feelings of love for Courtney, and due to his memory loss, perhaps he never would.

Rebecca knew any woman with half a brain and an ounce of experience would be wary of losing her heart to a man who carried such a burden. Rebecca's heart went out to him, but the shadow of his past was certainly one more good reason to avoid any real involvement with Grant Berringer.

Turning her attention to the red-faced Grant, Rebecca realized he'd finally reached his goal.

"Thirty!" she announced brightly. He finished his last leg lift and immediately collapsed onto the cushion of the machinery with his eyes closed. "I knew you could do it," she praised him. "Here, have some water."

She handed him a water bottle and watched as he tipped his head back and with eyes shut drank thirstily. His thick hair was damp, and sweat ran freely down his face and chest, causing his thin tank top and shorts to cling to his body. He paused once, to take a deep breath and stretch, his hard chest expanding and his arm muscles pumping up.

Rebecca felt a knot of attraction and longing for him tighten in the pit of her stomach. She took in a sharp breath and turned to grab a towel from a nearby chair.

"Here you go," she said lightly, while inside, she felt anything but light. "How do you feel? How is your leg?"

He had most severely injured his right leg, and the last group of exercises was designed to strengthen those muscles.

He shrugged and slung the towel around his neck. "Okay, I guess. It feels a little tight today," he admitted.

He looked at his leg and flexed his foot. She saw the corner of his mouth twitch and guessed he felt some pain but wouldn't admit it.

"Get up on the table and let me have a look," she said with concern.

She thought he was going to argue with her, but he submitted with a frown and a peeved look. With a little help from Rebecca, he maneuvered himself off the seat of the weight machine, moved to the padded massage table on crutches and hoisted himself to a sitting position, his long, muscular legs dangling over the edge of the table.

She ran her hand over the back of his bare leg. His skin felt damp, and the dark hair on his legs tickled her palm. She gently tested the tension in his calf muscles with her fingertips. They were knotted, and she wondered if she'd pushed him too hard. If he strained a muscle, they'd have a setback, which would affect not only his healing process but his spirits, as well. And his spirits had improved so much since she'd arrived.

"Does this hurt?" she asked, gently massaging the muscle.

"No...it feels good, actually," he replied in a husky tone.

She massaged the muscle until she felt the knot dissolve. She moved her hand to the front of his leg, stroking from his ankle to his kneecap. Her hand finally came to rest at the hard quadriceps at the top of his thigh. She felt the muscle with her fingertips, tenderly testing for any knots or signs of overwork.

"How about this leg?" she asked in a concerned, professional manner. With one hand still resting on his right thigh, she used her other hand to examine his left leg.

When her tenderly probing fingertips slipped beneath the edge of his workout shorts, she heard his quickly indrawn breath and saw him grip the arms of the chair. She looked at his face. From the tight expression, she couldn't tell if he was in pain or if her ministrations had elicited another, quite different response.

When her gaze met his, she realized in a flash what was happening. She felt a hot blush race up her neck and drew her hands off his legs as if she'd been touching stove burners.

But before she could move away, he reached out and grabbed her shoulders.

"You don't have to stop, Rebecca. I like the way you touch me," he murmured. His husky, seductive tone seemed to set every nerve ending in her body on fire. "I like it very much."

"Grant, please..." She tried to pull away, but he wouldn't let her. His arms and shoulders had become more powerful in the past weeks, and she knew she was no match against him. She felt trapped between his open legs. She tried to pull her gaze from his, but his shining black eyes commanded her full and complete attention.

"You know very well I wasn't touching you that way." She finally managed to speak. "I only needed to see if you have a cramped muscle."

He laughed low in his chest. "Well, I have one now, ma'am," he reported blithely. "But definitely not in my leg."

Rebecca didn't dare let her gaze drop below his waist. She already knew his claim to be true. He still held her arms, but his hold had loosened. He gently stroked her upper arms and shoulders.

She stared at him, her lips pursed in dismay, not realizing for one moment the tempting and provocative picture she presented to him. Wisps of reddish brown hair had come loose from her ponytail and curled around her face in long tendrils. Her fair skin—which never quite tanned—looked smooth and sun-kissed from her hours on the beach. Her white tank top and navy blue shorts showed off her figure to advantage, and she knew his steamy gaze roamed appreciatively over her full breasts and tight waist.

The way he looked her over made Rebecca's heartbeat race. It had been a long time since any man had showered her with such blatant appreciation. And Grant wasn't just any man. He was an extraordinary person, she'd come to see that. Not only because he was rich, a self-made millionaire and a brilliant success at his work. But for so many reasons…just because he was Grant.

As he stared at her hungrily, she felt herself softening under his touch, like a chocolate bar left in the sun. She felt herself leaning toward him, staring at his mouth, imagining what it would be like to kiss him again.…

But some rational part of her mind valiantly fought, and would not allow her to move one breath closer. Still, neither could she find the will to move away.

"Let go of me, Grant, please…" Her plea was a hushed whisper.

Grant shook his head. A small smile played at the edges of his mouth.

"No, I don't think so. I want you right where you are, Rebecca. In fact, I want you even closer," he decided, his voice low and compelling.

His large hand moved to cup her head, and an instant later, his mouth merged with hers in a kiss that was wild and hungry and almost violent in its intensity.

Rebecca struggled against him, then finally gave herself over to the moment. She moaned under the hard pressure of his lips. Not in protest, but in answer to his passionate assault. She felt an explosion of sheer desire and longing for him. Grant groaned, too, and his kiss deepened, his tongue swirling and melding with hers, his large hands sliding seductively down her back to stroke and cup her bottom and pull her even closer against the warmth at the juncture of his thighs.

Rebecca sighed, kissing him with her whole heart, her whole being. Her senses were suddenly filled with him—the taste of him, the scent of his warm body, the feeling of his hard muscles and smooth skin. Her head spun, and her knees turned to water. She clung to his shoulders for support. She felt intoxicated and in over her head.

But more than that, as the embrace continued, she felt an amazing sense of completeness and utter calm, as if she were suddenly sitting in the eye of a storm. She felt a total and utter connection to this man— heart, mind and soul—that she'd never experienced before. Could this really happen to a person outside of a book or a movie? Her rational mind demanded to know. Could this be happening to her?

A sharp knock on the door brought them both to their senses. Rebecca pulled away, and Grant finally released her. He rubbed his face with both hands as Rebecca moved a safe, discreet distance away. With her back turned toward the door, she struggled to get her breathing under control.

The knock sounded again, more insistent this time. "Come in," Grant shouted.

"Hi, guys, I'm back. Need a hand with anything in here?" Joe greeted them.

If she hadn't felt so muddled and light-headed, Rebecca knew she would have laughed at Joe's innocent question. Instead, she stared at the male nurse as if he'd just dropped down from the moon. Joe sometimes helped with Grant's morning workout, but since Rebecca's arrival, his work hours had been reduced, and he usually arrived at the house around noon. She was half grateful for his early appearance, and half annoyed at it.

"We've just finished the exercises," Rebecca replied in as natural a voice as she could manage. "Grant has some muscle soreness, but the whirlpool should help. Why don't you help him change into his swimsuit and bring him to the pool?"

"But we never did our cooldown, Rebecca," Grant reminded her. "I hardly think it's fair that you work a guy into a lather and totally skip the cooldown." His reminder sounded innocent enough, but Rebecca knew when she was being baited.

She glanced at him just long enough to catch his taunting grin, then forced herself to look quickly away. She felt an annoying blush color her cheeks and sensed Joe regarding them with a curious stare. Somehow she maintained a placid expression.

"Just dump him in the pool, Joe. The deep end," she instructed calmly. "That ought to cool him off fairly quickly."

And before either man could reply, she gathered her belongings and left the room.

That night, Rebecca took Nora out to dinner in town and then to a movie, a G-rated family comedy. She was glad they had planned the evening out and relieved that she was able to avoid Grant at dinner. But while the movie flashed before her eyes, she could barely concentrate. All she thought about was Grant, picturing him eating his dinner alone in his room, most likely wearing that brooding expression. *He can survive very well without us,* Rebecca assured herself, *with a house full of servants to do his bidding besides.* Still, she felt she'd somehow snuck out and left him flat.

Not that they ate with him every night. Some nights, she fixed an easy supper for herself and Nora in the bachelor kitchen in their suite. But most often, they took dinner with Matthew and Grant in the large dining room or on the terrace off the library.

Sometimes it was only the three of them, Rebecca, Nora and Grant. Since Rebecca had arrived, Matthew had returned to his responsibilities in the city and stayed there during the week, returning to the seaside mansion on the weekends. Rebecca missed his company. He was not only a friendly face and ally when Grant grew surly, but he provided the perfect buffer—

and even convenient chaperon—for herself and her too-attractive patient.

Even with Nora at the table, Rebecca often felt a pull between herself and Grant that was almost too intense to be ignored—or resisted. Especially when dinner was over, after Nora had run off to get ready for bed and Rebecca remained, sipping coffee and chatting with Grant about nothing in particular. Considering how much time they spent together every day, it was amazing to her that they had so much to talk about. Sometimes they talked little, preferring to sit together and listen to the night sounds and admire the sight of the rising moon over the water.

The air was so clear compared to the city, Rebecca and Nora were amazed at the display of stars in the night sky. Grant seemed amused at first by their reaction, and Rebecca felt a bit self-conscious. Then one night, he surprised them with a huge, high-quality telescope, which one of the maids brought out with their dessert. Rebecca had little interest in learning the names of constellations. But she greatly enjoyed viewing the heavens, and she appreciated Grant's thoughtful gesture. She knew he didn't have to go out of his way to please her, and the fact that he had secretly thrilled and worried her.

After the movie, she and Nora stopped for ice cream, and Nora was eager to bring some back for Grant. She already knew his favorite flavor—Rocky Road—since they'd had a long, careful discussion on the topic. At first, Rebecca thought, why not? Then she discouraged the idea. She didn't need to be knocking on his door late at night, bearing gifts. He might misinterpret the gesture and assume she'd found an excuse to see him and continue the amorous episode from early in the day.

That was just the problem. She had to be very careful to avoid provocative situations. Or very soon she'd be in real trouble. Rebecca shook her head dolefully as she started the car and headed to the Berringer mansion.

The house was quiet and dark when they returned, and Nora went to sleep quickly. Rebecca, however, tossed and turned as sensual memories of Grant's embrace made it impossible for her to sleep. She finally got up to make herself a cup of herbal tea. But when she searched her cupboard, she realized she was out of tea. She slipped on her robe and headed to the kitchen, which seemed miles away through the dark house. She was about halfway there when she heard a low but distinct moaning sound. She realized she was near Grant's rooms and the sound was coming from within. She drew closer and kept very still, listening. The sound came again, louder. It sounded as if he was in real pain, and without giving propriety a thought, she opened his unlocked door and entered his bedroom.

The room was dimly lit with a night-light near the bed, and she could see the outline of his body laying flat, under the covers.

"Grant, it's me, Rebecca. What's wrong?" she called softly. Her first guess was that she had overworked his injured leg and that, as a result, he was experiencing severe leg cramps. But if so, he hadn't sat up to rub his legs, she noticed.

He moaned again, then screamed and moved his hands to his head. "No, no…let go. Damn it, let go," he called in an anguished tone.

Then she realized he was asleep. Asleep and having a nightmare. She knelt next to his bed and gently shook his shoulder. "Grant, wake up. You're dreaming. You're having a bad dream. Wake up now," she said.

He took her hand in a viselike grip, still asleep, she realized. "Oh, sweetheart…how could you?" His tone was bleak, tortured. Rebecca felt stunned.

"Grant." She spoke louder. She shook his hand. "It's me, Rebecca."

Suddenly he opened his eyes, shook his head as if to clear away the remnants of his nightmare, then lifted himself to a sitting position in the bed.

He stared at her, looking shocked. "Rebecca…I thought you were…" He paused and looked away. "Never mind," he mumbled.

She watched him rub his face with his hands. *You thought I was Courtney. Of course. Who else?* Rebecca knew she had no right to feel hurt, yet her heart stung at the realization.

"I was on the way to the kitchen for some tea and heard you moaning. I thought maybe you'd fallen down, or had a leg cramp."

"Yes, yes, of course." He nodded, though she wasn't sure her words had fully registered. His eyes still looked shadowed, dazed, as if he was somewhere between his frightening other realm and the real world.

She reached for the light on the bedside table, but

he stilled her hand. "No, don't put the light on," he said.

"All right." Rebecca complied. He did not let go of her hand. He held it securely in his, which rested on the sheet.

She heard him breathing hard, as if he'd just run a five-minute mile, and guessed that his heart was pounding, as well. Whatever he'd been dreaming of, it had been terrifying. She wasn't sure if she should ask him about it.

"Can I get you anything? A glass of water?" she offered. "A cup of tea?"

"No, thanks." He paused and took a deep breath. "Just stay a minute more, will you?" he asked quietly.

"If you like," she replied.

"Don't kneel on the floor like that. Sit up on the bed," he commanded her. He sat with his back resting against the wooden headboard and shifted to make room for her.

Rebecca hesitated. Being on a bed with Grant—no matter how stressed he seemed—was not a good idea. Now that her eyes had gotten used to the dark, she could see him clearly. Too clearly, she thought. He was wearing a form-fitting T-shirt with a deep V-shaped neckline that emphasized his broad shoulders and muscular, hair-covered chest. He smelled of bath soap and a spicy cologne, all mingled with another scent that was distinctly his alone. Distinctly male.

Then she chided herself for being silly. The man was practically traumatized from a nightmare. He was hardly in the mental state to be planning a seduction.

She sat on the edge of the bed with Grant still holding her hand. He was quiet for a long time. Rebecca heard his breathing return to normal and wondered if he'd fallen asleep.

"Where were you tonight?" he asked suddenly.

"I took Nora out for a bite in town and to the movies."

"You didn't tell me you were going out." He was trying hard not to sound as if he'd been pouting, but she could tell otherwise.

"Sorry." She laughed. "I didn't know I needed to."

"I didn't say you needed to," he echoed, mimicking her slightly defensive tone. "It's just common courtesy, Rebecca. I missed you tonight at dinner...and Nora, of course."

Rebecca felt suddenly guilty for hurting his feelings, though she wasn't sure why.

"Nora wanted to bring you back some ice cream. Rocky Road," she admitted. "But I thought it would be too late to bother you."

"Are you always so sensible, Rebecca? Don't you know that it's never too late to wake somebody up for Rocky Road?" he asked, sounding amazed at her lack of life experience.

"Yes, I'm always sensible. It's one of my more annoying qualities," she informed him. "Would you like some ice cream? I could find some in the kitchen and get it for you."

"Don't bother. I was only teasing you." She couldn't quite make out his expression but sensed that she had cheered him up a bit and helped him get past the dark images.

He took her hand and held it between his two larger hands. "Do you know what I would really like right now?"

Something in his quiet, thoughtful tone set off alarm bells within her. "What's that?" she asked, feeling a giant lump form in her throat.

"I'd like to hold you... *Just* hold you," he said sincerely.

Rebecca's first thought was to bolt. Here it was, happening all over again, despite her best intentions for it not to. How did she get herself into these situations?

But something—some undefinable but totally potent force that had been working on her ever since she'd set eyes on this man—made her stay. And the longer she stayed, the more she imagined how wonderful it would feel to be held in Grant's arms, to be embraced by him and embrace him in return. And suddenly, all the loneliness and longing of so many empty years, feelings she had denied and kept carefully locked away in a secret place, came rushing in on her. She couldn't refuse Grant's simple request or deny herself a few moments of such simple satisfaction and contentment.

"Just holding. You promise?" she asked him.

"Absolutely," he replied. "I'm under the covers, you're on top. Completely and *totally* sensible. Wouldn't you agree?"

She nodded and sighed, a deep sigh of surrender and affection. "Very sensible," she replied.

Five

He opened his arms to her, and she moved into the circle of his strong, warm embrace. As she settled beside him, he turned toward her and physically coaxed her to curl against him. She dropped her head, then rested her cheek on his chest. She felt his chin graze the top of her head and his hand came up to stroke her hair. She vaguely recalled that she had gone to bed that night with her hair pulled back loosely in a ribbon. It seemed the ribbon was gone. Either it had fallen out or Grant had removed it.

It hardly mattered. She closed her eyes and savored the moment. She felt utterly at peace and totally complete. Here in the dark, in the middle of the night, listening to Grant's steady heartbeat and slow, deep breaths, she felt transported to a special place, as if together they'd created a private world.

"You have such wonderful hair," he murmured. "You look like a girl with it long and loose down your back like this. How old are you, anyway?" he asked suddenly.

Rebecca laughed. "Why do you want to know?"

"Why don't you want to tell me?" he replied, sounding vaguely amused. "I'm thirty-eight," he offered quite matter-of-factly.

"I know," she said simply. She knew his age from his medical records, though he looked much younger.

She was usually not shy at all about telling her age. But for some reason she felt reticent tonight.

"I don't think a woman should be asked to tell her age...or her weight," she said finally with an imperious air.

"I'd bet you're not even thirty yet," he guessed. "You're still a baby, Rebecca," he teased her. "A baby with a sassy tongue."

"I think that part of a compliment was mixed up in there someplace," she teased him in return. "So thanks...I guess."

"You're very welcome, I'm sure," he replied. His touch on her hair was so tender and loving, Rebecca realized it hardly mattered what he had said to her.

"Why don't you wear your hair like this more often?"

"Gets in my way when I work," she said simply.

"How about when you're not working? When you're going out on a date, for instance?"

Rebecca felt her body tense slightly at this line of inquiry. She wondered if she should lie and lead him to believe she had a boyfriend…or several. It might scare him off. But deception was not her. Besides, some part of her didn't want to scare him off.

''I don't date much,'' she admitted. ''I usually work long hours and then need to take care of Nora.''

''Of course you do.'' She felt him shrug. ''But everyone has a social life.''

She laughed. ''I don't.''

''I find that hard to believe,'' he persisted. ''Men must ask you out all the time.''

''I do get invitations,'' she admitted.

''But you're not involved with anyone right now?'' he asked.

''There's been no one, really, since my divorce.''

He was quiet for a moment. She felt his hand in her hair again and wondered what he was thinking. She itched to ask him about his romantic past, but didn't dare broach the subject—and doubtless ruin the mood.

''Your ex-husband must be a complete fool to have let you go.''

''Yes, he is,'' she replied succinctly. Her blunt reply made Grant laugh.

''What happened? Another woman?'' he asked quietly.

She nodded against his chest.

''The stupid jerk.'' The note of anger in his voice surprised her.

''It took some time, but I got over it.''

''But not enough to try again,'' he reminded her.

She didn't reply. She knew why she felt so emotional all of a sudden. She hadn't talked so openly with a man in a long time. Longer than she could remember.

It was frightening to reveal herself to someone else. Terrifying, actually. Like jumping from a great height and trusting someone to catch her. But just as it would feel taking that leap, it was exciting as well to share secrets in the dark and to be entrusted with Grant's intimate truths. Maybe she had recovered from Jack's betrayal more than she'd guessed. Maybe getting to know Grant had helped her do that.

"It's all very much in the past for me," she said, and meant it. "My only concern now is that Jack, my ex-husband, is good to Nora."

"Is he?" Grant asked, sounding concerned.

"Jack isn't a bad guy. But he's a very self-centered person. He's always been that way. He's an attentive father when it's convenient for him. Otherwise..." Her voice trailed off. She didn't want to sound bitter. "Well, he tries, but he could do a lot better."

"Nora's a great kid. I don't know how any father could ever ask for more," Grant said sincerely. "You've done a great job with her, Rebecca. You should be very proud."

"Thank you. I am," Rebecca replied quietly. "It's one reason I can never really regret my marriage to Jack. If we hadn't married, I'd never have had Nora. No matter what, she's always the bright spot in my day."

"She's gotten to be the bright spot in my day, too," he said with a warm, low laugh. "Except for you, Rebecca…when you're not being a slave driver, I mean.''

"Thanks, I think." She laughed.

"Nora is the spitting image of you, you know. Even her personality is a lot like yours. I bet you were just like her growing up. I bet you grew up in a happy family, too.''

His personal question about her background took her by surprise. Mostly because she could tell from his tone he'd been thinking about her, wondering about her past. As she had been thinking about him.

"I was a lot like Nora, I guess. But I grew up with two older sisters who spoiled me and bossed me around a lot. We had a happy family, though. My mother was a nurse, retired now. She worked part-time until we were in high school. My father owned a hardware store in our town.''

"Which was?"

"Guilford, Connecticut. It's a very small town on the sound. It still hasn't changed much, though the real estate values have gone through the roof since the yuppies discovered it. But when I was growing up there, it was really very quiet and off the beaten track. And we were a very typical, average family, I suppose,'' she added.

"Nothing about you is typical or average," he corrected her, his fingertip trailing against the line of her cheek. "Your parents must be very special people, to have raised you.''

"I think they're good people," she said quietly.

"But you'll have to meet them sometime and decide for yourself."

"I'd love to," he replied.

She wasn't sure why she'd added that last part. It had slipped out. It sounded silly to her once she'd said it. Of course Grant would never meet her family. How would that happen? It would have to be quite by accident, after she'd finished her work for him and their lives had gone on in two very separate paths.

"How about you?" she asked suddenly, wanting to shift attention from herself. "Did you and Matthew have a happy family life growing up?"

"We had everything kids could ask for, if that's what you mean. We went to private schools and spent summers out here, in this house. That was probably the best part of growing up for us," he replied quietly. "But our family wasn't really happy. My parents were both very successful and focused on their work. They never seemed to have much time for me and Matt...or make much time for us. But we got by. We had each other," he added on a brighter note.

Rebecca could tell he was trying to present an unhappy picture in the best light. Perhaps it was wrong of her, but she wanted to know more. She wanted him to feel open enough with her to show her the worst.

"That must have been hard for you," she said simply. "Children need to feel appreciated and loved. No matter how much they're given materially, it can't make up for a parent's time and love."

"Yes, that's very true," he agreed. "I'm not sure

why our parents ever married, actually, or bothered having children. They didn't get along and only stayed together for our sake.''

"Oh…that's too bad,'' Rebecca said. She understood so much more about him. "Are they still together?'' she asked.

"My mother died when I was fourteen and Matt was nine. My father must have loved her, despite their problems, because he really grieved. He worked constantly once she was gone. Matt and I hardly saw him. But we grew even closer. So that was a plus.''

"I'm sorry to hear about your loss.''

"It was a shock when it happened. But that was a long time ago. In some ways, I suppose it made me stronger.''

Stronger? Or just more guarded and distant? For once, she managed to hold her tongue. No wonder he was having such a difficult time recovering from losing his fiancée, she realized. The recent tragedy had only reinforced the fears incurred by his earlier loss.

"I spent a lot of time looking after Matt. In some ways, I feel I raised him myself. More than my dad ever did. But now, the roles are completely reversed,'' he observed with a harsh laugh. "The kid's doing a pretty damn good job, though, I think.''

"Yes, he is,'' Rebecca agreed. She was glad Grant had shared his unhappy memories with her but sad to learn he'd suffered so much emotional damage growing up. She had an urge to soothe him and comfort him for those long past hurts. But she chided herself for the impulse. She'd asked him personal questions, and he'd answered her. He wasn't asking for her comfort or sympathy. He'd probably be appalled by such a reaction.

They lay together silently for what seemed to Rebecca a long time. She wondered if Grant was falling asleep. Yet his hand still moved restlessly through her hair and up and down her back.

The warm, steady pressure of his touch was tender and soothing, lulling her into a sleepy state. But she knew she couldn't fall asleep in his bed. Good heavens! That wouldn't do. She knew she had to go, the sooner the better. But her body felt so warm and relaxed, tucked against Grant's hard, muscular form, it was hard to budge.

"I guess, because of the way I grew up, for a long time I just didn't get it about marriage and kids," he said finally. "Especially about the children. Oh, I thought it was nice enough for other guys I knew to settle down and start a family. But secretly, I always thought, 'Gee, another poor sap got himself caught. I'm too smart for that.' I know it sounds cynical, but I just couldn't understand why any guy in his right mind would tie himself down that way."

"Well, at least you're honest," Rebecca replied. It was shocking but certainly refreshing to hear a man make such blatant admissions. Most men she met were willing to say anything to get a woman into bed. But when it was time to make a commitment, their story changed quite a bit.

"Back then, I suppose I kept telling myself I was just waiting for the right woman to come along."

Rebecca lifted her head and pulled away from him enough to see his face.

"Then the right woman did come along." She forced herself to speak. She was referring to Courtney.

He was silent. She felt her throat go suddenly tight. He was about to start talking about Courtney. She had encouraged him. Yet she wasn't sure she could handle it.

Still, there was no earthly reason she should feel so upset and unsettled to hear him reminisce about the woman he had loved. Still loved, probably. Maybe Rebecca was lying in his arms right now, but this stolen hour together was nothing more than a bit of friendly comfort for him, wasn't it? A chance to clear his head from his terrifying dreams. Dreams about losing Courtney.

"No," he said finally. "It wasn't quite like that. I realized what I was missing out on well before I met Courtney. I'm not sure how it happened, really. One day I just knew I had enough—enough money, enough success, enough exotic trips, enough dinners at fancy restaurants and late nights out at exclusive clubs."

Wow, what a lifestyle he'd enjoyed. Rebecca's mind reeled. A far cry from her leisure hours, which usually contained a pizza and a rented video.

"It all came to a head one year during the holidays. You're supposed to be so happy and cheerful. But I felt awfully down that year. Matthew was in California on business, and I didn't have any plans or anyone to spend Christmas day with. I was dating a model at the time—''

A model. Rebecca silently moaned. *Please, spare me the details.*

''She was off on a shoot somewhere hot and tropical. She asked me to join her, but I didn't want to, so I guess that says it all about that affair.''

Rebecca suddenly felt much better. At least he found the model boring. It was some consolation.

''Anyway,'' he continued, ''here I was, feeling pretty sorry for myself, when I ran into an old college buddy—you know, one of those poor saps I was telling you about. I don't know how it happened, but I ended up going to his house for Christmas Eve. It was a big party, with a lot of family and friends, so I didn't stick out quite as much as I had feared. He had a great wife and two adorable kids. It was fun watching them tear open their presents,'' he added.

Rebecca could tell from his voice how much the experience had affected him. Even now, the memories of that visit were still very vivid for him, she could tell.

''I remember the ride back to the city. I couldn't believe it. This college chum, who I'd never thought was very sharp or had amounted to much, suddenly looked like the smartest, richest, most successful guy in the world. I would have changed places with him in a second. It was like a lightbulb going off inside my head. A big lightbulb. Then I realized how for so long I'd felt empty and bored. Yet I didn't understand what was missing in my life. Making a real commitment, having a true partner to share the ups and downs. Raising a family. That was it. The answer I'd been looking for.'' He was quiet. ''Then Courtney came along, and it all fell into place for us, more or less. And I had a chance to have what I really wanted out of life. But now I guess I'll never have that chance again.''

The light, conversational tone of his voice could not completely mask his sadness and pain. Rebecca wasn't sure what to say. There seemed no answer to his dilemma, and yet she knew in her heart that the only thing keeping Grant from having the life he'd once dreamed of was his will, his thwarted perspective.

''I'm sorry...I must be boring you,'' he apologized.

''No, not at all,'' she assured him. ''I was just thinking about what you said at the end, how it's all lost for you. It's not, you know. Only if you want it to be.''

''Please, Rebecca. It's been so good to talk with you like this tonight. I don't want to end up in an argument. This is the way I feel, and by God, I can't help it.''

His voice held a harsh note, and she braced herself. She feared she'd made him angry.

''I'm sorry. I didn't mean to upset you.'' She was sorry, but she wouldn't contradict herself and agree with him to soothe his feelings. She'd only told him the simple truth.

''Listen, I know you're only trying to make me feel better. But unfortunately, it doesn't work that way.

Even if I could some day get over my feelings about Courtney and the accident—which I don't believe will ever happen—I don't know if I could ever take that…that leap again. I'd be too afraid of losing someone I loved. Too afraid of some awful unforseen event taking everything away from me.''

His voice was so quiet and bleak, Rebecca instinctively moved closer. Maybe it was best not to argue with him. But she couldn't keep from saying what was on her mind.

''I know what you're saying. It's understandable that you'd feel this way. But I want to ask you one thing. You don't have to answer me. I think you should ask yourself, if the situation had been reversed, if you had died in the accident and Courtney had survived, would you want her to live the rest of her life alone? Without a husband or children?''

''No, of course not,'' he said adamantly. ''I'd never wish that for her…for anyone.''

''Then why are you wishing it on yourself?'' she asked bluntly.

He stared at her as if the truth of her words was sinking in. Then he shook his head. ''You don't understand, Rebecca. It's just not the same. I was driving the car. I caused the accident that took her life…and our child's. It was all my fault.''

''Was it? There was a terrible storm that night. The road was treacherous. Maybe you skidded to avoid another car, or maybe you hit a bad stretch of pavement. You don't know for a fact that it was your fault, Grant,'' she reminded him.

"That's the problem...I can't remember. Not about the actual accident or much of the time right before it." He rubbed his forehead. "Except when I have one of these horrible nightmares, and then everything is so dark and distorted it's impossible to tell what's a real memory and what's just part of the dream. If only I could remember."

"Well, even if you do, what then? Would you be blaming yourself for not avoiding someone who stopped short in front of you or a cat who ran into the road? You're not superhuman you know Grant. An accident like that could happen to anyone."

"Yes, I know that rationally, Rebecca...but it's not the way I feel deep inside. In here," he added, touching the middle of his chest. "I blame myself for what happened. And because I do, I don't believe I'll ever be free to truly love again. Maybe I'm just afraid. Afraid of what might happen now that I've lived through the worst. Isn't that what you're trying to tell me?"

"Grant, no, that's not what I mean. It's not what I mean at all."

"Or maybe I believe I don't deserve a second chance after what I did. I know that's not rational, either, Rebecca. But maybe that's just the way I really feel."

Her mouth opened to reply. Then she could see it was useless to argue with him.

"If you say so, then I guess that it must be so," she finally agreed. "But whether it's fair or true is another story, I suppose."

"Another story for another day," he replied in a tone that warned her to let the topic go. "Some day, a long time from now, maybe I'll feel differently... And my future—what's possible for me—will look a great deal different, too."

"Maybe," Rebecca said wistfully. "I truly hope so."

"So do I," he replied. "So do I."

He swallowed hard and lifted his hand to cup her cheek. He met her gaze and stared deeply into her eyes. She thought he wanted to say something more. Something important.

But Rebecca abruptly broke the silence. "I need to go now. I've stayed way too long."

He looked sorry to hear she wanted to leave, but his expression quickly turned to one of resignation.

"Yes, of course. You'd better return to your own bed. If anyone finds you here, they might get the right idea about us."

"The *wrong* idea, you mean," she corrected him.

"Oh, right. The *wrong* idea. That's what I meant to say," he assured her with a teasing grin.

Before releasing her, he leaned over and kissed her softly. His warm mouth lingered tenderly. She knew he was savoring the taste and feel of her lips against his, hinting at unimaginable pleasures.

But the kiss ended as quickly as it had begun. Much too quickly, Rebecca thought.

He pulled away with a soft, reluctant sigh, and she stood up and looked at him. Sitting back against the pillows, his arms folded behind his head, his chest bare and the sheet draped around his waist, he was so impossibly handsome and appealing to her, she didn't know if she had the willpower to go.

"Well…good night," she said in a tender whisper. "I hope you won't have any more bad dreams."

He smiled softly. "No chance of it now. I'll only have sweet dreams of you…but not as frustrating as our real-life encounters, I hope," he added with a sexy grin.

Rebecca felt herself blush, and with another quick good-night she left the room.

In the hall, she wasn't sure which way to turn—toward her bedroom or the kitchen. After nearly an hour in Grant's bed, she did really need something to calm her down so she headed for the kitchen.

She sipped her tea, but it didn't soothe her ragged nerves very much. Her mind was filled with Grant and his intimate confessions. Despite his argument to the contrary, she did believe that someday, his feelings about the accident and losing Courtney would change. If he wanted them to.

But would it be too late? Too late for Grant to rejoice in love, marriage and children—those deeply satisfying experiences he valued far above success and material possessions.

And more important, would it be too late for anything serious to develop between them, as well?

Yes, it probably would be too late. It hurt to admit the truth, even to herself.

The conversation had ended painfully for both of them. But it had been an eye opener. She understood him far better now, and it was all for the best that she knew any secret hopes of romance between herself and Grant were vain and foolish fantasies.

Maybe that was why he'd confided in her so openly. Consciously or unconsciously, he'd wanted her to know he wasn't able to become emotionally involved with her. Not in a real relationship, one that would stretch beyond their time together as therapist and patient.

He was healing on the outside. But inside, Rebecca realized sadly, he still had a long way to go.

Six

Grant woke at dawn without the aid of his alarm clock. Soft sunlight filtered into his room, and before he opened his eyes, he heard the raucous sea gulls cruising the beach for their breakfast.

He liked to wake up early these days, and he never slept with the curtains pulled closed anymore. As he opened his eyes and slowly stretched, he smiled, anticipating the day. He had promised to meet Nora on the beach this morning and teach her how to surf cast. He had spent hours after dinner last night preparing their equipment, testing the reels on old fishing rods and rethreading the lines. He hoped the fish were jumping this morning. By heavens, if he could bribe somebody to stock the shoreline behind his house, he would, just for the pleasure of seeing Nora's adorable little face light up when she felt that first real tug.

He leaned over and checked the clock. It was only half past five. He didn't need to rush. He took a deep breath and realized he felt happy this morning. Happy to be alive. Happy to wake and stretch his arms and legs without feeling pain. Well, a cramp or two perhaps, but nothing like before. He was inordinately pleased to know he could sit up, swing his legs off the side of the bed and stand on his own two feet. With the aid of a cane, he could get just about wherever he wished to go.

He was starting to feel his old self again. And, in some mysterious, unfathomable way, not just his old self, but a new self. A better self. He had always imagined that once he'd reached this point in his recovery, he'd be rushing to the city, diving headlong into the mayhem of Wall Street.

But he felt no pressure to return to the madness and competition. From a distance, it looked so senseless to him, like so many eager rats, futilely running on their little wheels. Getting no place fast. All in the pursuit of money and more money. He once felt that being rich was the only true measure of success. But he felt differently now. Very differently. Not to mention that he had enough money to last several lifetimes.

And if he sometimes missed the mental challenge and stimulation of his work, he could keep up with everything he needed to know from here. The high-flying world of finance was no farther away than his computer.

The nightmares still returned from time to time. And bad headaches, as well. But each time he was plunged into that dark world he emerged with some precious fragments of his lost memories. He was keeping a journal, a private notebook where he tried to record the images before they faded. From time to time, when he felt strong enough, he looked through the scribbled notes and tried to piece the bits together. Sometimes he felt on the verge of remembering. Then something held him back, some force so strong he'd feel physically ill, dizzy and shaken and short of breath, trying to remember.

The doctors had told him he shouldn't try to force it. His memory would return in its own time, in its own way, they said. Yet Grant felt an irresistible compulsion, a driving need to remember that night, to remember everything that had happened to him in that car until the moment of impact.

He wasn't sure why he felt so compelled to remember. Many people would prefer to forget, he guessed. Sometimes he wondered if he was trying to torture himself. To punish himself for recovering, for feeling better and starting to take some simple pleasure in life again.

But other times, he had a more positive view. He saw it as a search for a key that would unlock both his missing past and his future. For without those lost hours and true understanding of the tragedy that had befallen him, he believed he could never be totally free of the grief and the guilt he carried.

His hand slipped under his pillow, and he felt the satin ribbon he had hidden there. He took it out and looked at it, curled it in the palm of his hand. It was apricot in color and frayed a bit on one end. He'd die before he'd ever let anyone know he kept it there. It was Rebecca's ribbon. It had fallen out of her hair the night she'd come to his bed and lain in his arms. He'd discovered it the next morning, a wonderful surprise. He'd thought of returning it to her, then knew he never would. He had to have it, a precious souvenir of their hours together.

That night had been so special to him. A turning point in his recovery, he believed, though he'd never told her so. Although they had not shared physical intimacy, he'd felt closer to her that night than to almost anyone he'd ever known. Grant knew very well that he could share his body with a woman without the experience being the least bit intimate or personal. Rebecca was different. With just a smile or a glance, she never failed to touch his soul.

It had been at least three weeks ago, and he'd struggled like hell to keep his hands off her. He knew she was wondering why, after sharing such tender intimacy, he suddenly chose to keep a cool, polite distance between them. But the reason was simple. He didn't dare let himself fall in love with her. He knew he was already falling. He knew his feelings for her ran very strong and deep. But somehow he hoped he could manage to keep them under wraps until her work here was done. He hoped he could keep her from growing more attached than she might feel already. And though he fantasized endlessly about truly loving her and knowing that she returned his love, it was a dream from which he was always harshly awakened.

He rolled the ribbon in his hand and crushed it into

a small ball. How could their relationship ever work out? It couldn't.

He had the world to offer her and Nora in a material sense, but nothing to offer Rebecca emotionally. Though he was almost healed physically, he knew he remained broken and damaged. He was hideously scarred inside, a monster no woman could ever really love.

Rebecca deserved so much more. She deserved the very best of men, not the worst. She deserved someone free to love her completely, without shadows of the past hovering over her happiness. No, he was damaged goods. Damaged beyond repair, perhaps. Still, Rebecca gave him hope. Hope of recovering physically, and in more optimistic moments, hope of somehow working through the demons that plagued his soul.

The summer was passing day by day. Minute by minute, hour by hour, his precious time with Rebecca was coming to an end. Every day he grew stronger, every step he took on his own was another step he took away from her. He knew it. And she knew it, too.

At times, he regretted the fact that he hadn't made love with her that night. How easy it would have been to pull her close and kiss her. How easily their kisses would have turned to something more. God, he would have adored every inch of her. He would have made love to her as she'd never been loved before.

But then what? Once she'd returned to her ever-sensible self, there would have been hell to pay. She probably would have quit on him. Left him flat. And he would have felt horrible for taking advantage of her attraction to and affection for him. Now there was something new about him. In the past, he could rarely recall feeling guilty for making a move on a willing woman. Had he developed a conscience with all these extra muscles Rebecca had put on him?

He could never use Rebecca for the purposes of a one-night stand, a casual, convenient affair that would end once she left the house. He knew women very well. Too well, he thought at times. Rebecca was definitely not the type for a quick fling. She was the type a man cherished for a lifetime. Anything less would hurt her deeply. And he would never hurt her, not for the world. Not even in exchange for the pleasure of making love to her, which he was sure would be heavenly. He gazed at the ribbon and touched it to his lips. She would never be in his bed again. Of that, he was sure. The hours they'd shared together were a special gift, a stolen, guilty pleasure. And that was all there would be, no matter how it tortured him to hold her at arm's length. Maybe that was why the ribbon seemed so precious. He knew he'd never get physically close to her again, though in his heart, he'd treasure her for a lifetime.

Sometimes, when Grant found himself lost in thoughts of Rebecca, he felt a sudden pang, thinking he was being unfaithful to Courtney. He stared at her picture on his night table. If he was totally and coldly honest with himself, he knew he could barely recall any deep, soul-stirring feelings for Courtney. He remembered their mutual strong attraction and common interests, common friends. He remembered an affectionate, warm feeling toward her. Even a possessive feeling. But it was nothing like the feelings he held for Rebecca. Had he ever really loved Courtney? he wondered. Maybe his feelings for her were one more item lost to his memory. Yet, if all he had felt was what he could remember…well, it seemed disrespectful to Courtney's memory, Grant had to recognize that his feelings for his past love seemed pale and superficial compared to his feelings for Rebecca. Feelings that grew stronger each moment he spent with her. Emotions that seemed to penetrate to the marrow of his bones, to his very soul.

Courtney, did I ever know that kind of love for you? he silently asked the picture. Of course, the blond, blue-eyed image posed no answer. She stared at him, frozen in time. Lost to him forever. On impulse, he picked up the photo and slipped it into a drawer.

The sunlight was stronger. It streamed into the room and warmed his bare skin as he sat at the edge of his bed. Time to get moving. It wasn't polite to keep ladies waiting. Nora and Rebecca, no less. Rebecca would give him the sharp side of her tongue if she'd got up at dawn for this outing and he dawdled. He smiled, anticipating her sassy remarks.

Yes, it could be a wonderful day, he told himself, *if you let it.*

The surf-casting lesson was a great success. Grant hardly minded having to sit in a wheelchair to be stable enough to fish. He knew he'd progressed far beyond the chair, and it was only a precaution. Besides, sitting in the chair, he was able to hold Nora on his lap and help her with her fishing line. When they felt a mighty tug, he savored the expression on her face—so much so that he lost focus on the line, and the reel spun like crazy.

When they finally got the pole under control, he and Nora battled their prize catch together. At one point, the fish pulled so hard, they felt the wheelchair rolling toward the shoreline. Luckily, Rebecca caught them before they were pulled in. Nora thought a ride into the pounding surf on a runaway wheelchair was terrific fun, and after their initial shock, Rebecca and Grant had a good laugh.

Finally, the fishing lesson ended and they made their way to the house, feeling tired, hungry and happy. Nora insisted on carrying the fish they'd caught in a pail of ice and water, though the load was heavy for her. She and Grant had reeled in a huge bluefish, a real beauty, he thought. He couldn't wait to get to the house and take a picture of Nora holding up her catch.

Rebecca had caught some small fish and tossed them back. Grant could see that fishing would never be her favorite pastime, but she was a good sport and got just as excited as Nora when the bluefish was landed.

Once they'd all cleaned up, they gathered for breakfast in the kitchen. Grant had rarely eaten a meal in the kitchen in all the years he'd spent in this house. But lately, since he'd been able to amble around on a cane, he'd started cooking again, and it seemed convenient and cozy to have Rebecca and Nora with him in the kitchen while he played master chef and they followed his orders or simply sat chatting, waiting to be fed.

This morning, he made waffles with fresh fruit. As Nora carried the platter to the table, Rebecca rubbed her hands together in hungry anticipation.

"Yum, my favorite," she said, hungrily eyeing the platter. "Pass that platter right here to Mom, darling," she teasingly coaxed Nora. She helped herself to a waffle and all the trimmings. He liked to see her enjoying the food he cooked. That was half the fun. "With all the fuss you made over that fish, Grant, I was half-afraid I was going to experience my first blue fish omelette."

"I'm saving that beauty for dinner. I was thinking of a mustard sauce." He was about to describe some recipes he had in mind when Nora interrupted him.

"You're going to cook it?" she squeaked. "You're going to cook my fish?"

Grant and Rebecca stared at her. Grant glanced at Rebecca, not knowing how to handle this delicate situation.

"Well, what do you think we should do with it, Nora?" he asked her very seriously.

"I don't know." Nora shrugged. He could see the tears in her eyes, but she valiantly held them back. She stared down at her waffle. "But I didn't think we were going to eat it."

"But honey, I thought you knew that's what people did with the fish they catch," Rebecca said.

Nora shrugged again. Grant caught Rebecca's eye.

"Listen, Nora, would you feel better if we put the fish back in the ocean?"

She lifted her head, and he knew from her expression that he'd hit pay dirt. "Can we? I thought it was dead. I thought we killed it once we took it out of the ocean."

"Well, we left it in a pail of cold water outside. Maybe it's still breathing. Let's go check."

Walking at a slow pace behind Nora, Grant sent up a silent prayer that the glorious bluefish was still breathing and would be strong enough to live if they tossed it back in the waves.

With his fingers crossed, Grant peered into the pail over Nora's slim shoulder. By golly, it looked good. Very good. The fish was flipping and flapping about with loads of life left in it.

Without more conversation, they returned to the beach and Grant had the honor of flinging the fish far out over the breakers. They stood silently watching. Rebecca shielded her eyes against the sun with her hands.

"I think you threw it far enough," she said finally.

"I hope so." Grant watched the shoreline to see if the fish had been caught in a wave and dashed toward the beach. He didn't see it pulled back in.

"I think he's swimming home as fast as he can," Nora said. "He wants to tell his family how he got caught by some big ugly humans and they nearly ate him for dinner. With mustard sauce. But somehow, he escaped."

Rebecca and Grant laughed at her story. Grant reached out and playfully tugged Nora's braid. "I'm sure that fish is bragging all over the Atlantic about his clever escape,'' Grant agreed. "Feel better?" he asked kindly.

She nodded, then impulsively flung her arms around Grant's waist and hugged him tight. Grant hugged her as best as he could, balanced precariously on his cane. "There now...what's this all about?"

"Thank you," she said, lifting her head.

"You're welcome," he replied. "Hey, but I never got a picture of you with that fish," he said regretfully. "I was looking forward to saving it in my album."

"I'll draw you one at camp today," she promised.

"Deal," he replied with a wide smile.

They shook hands in a very official manner, and when Grant caught Rebecca's warm, admiring grin, his heart swelled with warmth and affection for both of them.

After Nora left for camp, Grant and Rebecca met in the exercise room for Grant's daily workout. Grant arrived a bit early and began his requisite stretches. Rebecca entered and spared him a quick, approving smile. While she moved around the room, checking the equipment, Grant took the opportunity to check her out.

The day had warmed up considerably since the early morning fishing adventure, and Rebecca was dressed in white cotton shorts, a ribbed black tank top and white running shoes. Her hair, which she usually wore in a ponytail or long braid, was loose today, pulled back from her face with a wide black hair band that emphasized her high cheekbones, large, hazel eyes and thick dark lashes.

She looked wonderful, he thought. Absolutely. But seemingly not conscious of it at all. He'd never met a woman who was so naturally beautiful yet so unaware of her good looks. Or the effect she had on a man.

Seated on the floor, Grant took a deep breath, leaned forward and reached for his toes. Her shorts were very short, he thought, greedily taking in an eyeful of her gorgeous long legs. As his gaze surreptitiously traveled upward, he couldn't help but notice that the tank top she wore was a bit skimpy. He didn't remember seeing it on her before. Perhaps it was new. Was he imagining it, or was it tighter and cut a bit lower than the tops she usually wore?

With her back toward him, she leaned over and picked up some hand weights. He swallowed hard. She was gorgeous. Sometimes he wanted her so badly it hurt. This was going to be an extra difficult session to get through, he realized, gritting his teeth.

His consternation and distress must have shown on his face, he realized, for when she turned to him she met his gaze with a curious stare. "Are you all right?" she asked with innocent concern.

"I'm fine," he insisted. Holding the exercise table for support, he pulled himself to a standing position.

"You looked like something hurt while you were doing the stretches," she replied, walking toward him. "Any pain or soreness?"

"No, not at all." He crossed his arms. "Let's get on it with it, shall we? I have work to do today. I can't spend the day in here like some mindless bodybuilder."

"My, my, aren't we cranky today," Rebecca replied lightly as she scanned the notations on her clipboard. "Anything you'd like to talk about?"

"I just have things on my mind, that's all," he explained abruptly. "Work...other things."

He certainly couldn't confess to her that his foul mood was largely due to his effort to keep her at a safe distance. If he didn't keep up a solid defense of grouchiness and sarcasm, he might give way to the temptation to pull her into his arms and make passionate love to her right on the exercise table.

She watched as he got on the treadmill and gripped the hand supports. "You must be eager to get back to work now that you're doing so much better," she said.

"Sometimes I am," he admitted. *But not for the reasons you might think, Rebecca. Sometimes I wish I was back at my desk because the bedlam of my demanding job would provide some distraction from my longing for you.*

"Well, it won't be too much longer. You're improving every day," she replied.

He glanced at her. She was fiddling with some settings on the machine, and he couldn't see her expression.

Her voice had sounded so cool and impersonal, he would have thought the idea of their time together ending meant little to her. Yet he didn't believe that. Maybe she felt as badly as he did about their relationship. Sometimes he thought she was angry at him for drawing her so close that night she came to his bedroom, then pushing her away. For showing her a glimpse of how wonderful it could be between them, then taking that treasure from her. Maybe she felt rejected by him and didn't realize that keeping his distance was the only way he knew how to protect her, to save her from some far greater pain that following through on their feelings for each other would surely cause down the road.

"That reminds me. I'm going to test you today to gauge your progress. Then maybe I can give you some approximate date in regard to returning to your office."

He met her gaze. Her expression was calm and poised, but in her eyes, he saw a flash of sadness and regret. He longed to reach out to her, to frame her lovely face in his hands and kiss her tempting lips. To promise her he'd never leave her, if that's what she wished.

But of course, he couldn't do that. He couldn't act on any part of his fantasy. He turned and faced forward, gripping the support railing. "Sounds good to me," he replied.

She checked to see that he was ready to begin, then turned on the machine and carefully noted his distance and speed. They went through the rest of the exercise circuit with little conversation.

After they completed the cooldowns and more stretching, Rebecca carefully measured flexibility and range of motion on Grant's injured leg. It was absolute torture for him to sit still and remain relaxed as she handled his body with her soft, tender touch. When she saw his grim expression, he thought she mistook his effort at self-control as an effort to hide physical pain.

But soon enough, the sweet torture was over and Grant sat sipping a large bottle of water while he watched Rebecca review the notations on her chart. She was concentrating, jotting notes here and there, flipping through pages to check records. He could watch her for hours, he thought. He just loved looking at her.

Finally, she looked up to find him grinning at her. He could tell she was trying hard not to smile, and finally she couldn't help herself.

"What's so funny?" she asked him.

"Nothing." He shrugged and took a long cooling sip of water. "I just like watching you try to tally me up and figure me out."

"I could never figure you out," she assured him. "I won't even waste my time trying."

He laughed. "Oh, I think you do a lot better than you give yourself credit for, Rebecca," he answered with a grin. "A lot better than most women I've known," he added.

"Well, thanks. But that's not saying much," she muttered, looking at his chart.

"So, how did I do? Am I ready for the Olympics?"

"Definitely. The wise guy competition. I'm sure you'll stun the judges," she replied dryly.

He laughed heartily and again fought the urge to pull her into his arms. "No, seriously, Rebecca. What's the bottom line here?"

"I need to look at these records closer, of course, but it all looks very good to me. I think that if there are no unforseen setbacks for the next few weeks, you should be able to return to work after Labor Day.''

A slight smile played at the corners of her mouth, but it didn't reach her eyes. Her pleasure at delivering this piece of good news was bittersweet, he could see. He knew how she felt, for he felt exactly the same. He sat quietly, taking it all in, then he saw that she was puzzled by his lack of obvious reaction.

''Aren't you happy?'' she asked him quietly. ''You did say back in May that your goal was to return to work by the end of the summer.''

''Yes, I remember,'' he answered. ''I guess it's sort of a shock to hear that it will finally happen. Maybe I've gotten lazy and grown too comfortable living the easy life out here,'' he added, trying to strike a lighter note.

''Maybe,'' she agreed, yet her tone sounded doubtful. ''You've made remarkable progress. You've worked very, very hard and have a lot to be proud of,'' she said sincerely.

The look in her eyes was almost his undoing. He swallowed hard and looked away. ''Thanks, Rebecca,'' he said simply. ''That means a great deal to me, coming from you. I couldn't have done it without you. I remember how you marched in here that first day, yanked open those curtains and told me I was wallowing in self-pity.''

''I opened the curtains, but I never said such a thing to you,'' she denied.

''You didn't have to say it. I could see it in your eyes, as plain as day. It made me feel ashamed of myself, thank God. I sometimes wonder what would have happened to me if you had never come along. I'd probably still be sitting in that chair, in that dark room, feeling miserable and sorry for myself. And making everyone around me miserable, too.''

''You were ready to help yourself,'' she insisted. ''I just gave you the means and a jump start.''

More than that, Rebecca, he longed to say. *So much more. Your smile gave me a reason to get out of bed every morning.*

But he restrained himself from confessing his feelings. Instead, he glanced away from her and tugged on the towel that was slung around his neck.

''And don't forget a good tongue-lashing when I didn't push myself to meet your standards...Your Highness.''

''That, too,'' she replied, smiling at him warmly. She crossed her arms and regarded him in a way that made his heart race. He was glad she was done checking his pulse and blood pressure for the day. He imagined his readings would jump off the chart.

''Listen, before I go I want to thank you for what you did for Nora this morning, Grant,'' she said finally.

''Taking her fishing? That was no trouble. I loved every minute, even when the wheelchair nearly rolled into the ocean.''

Rebecca laughed. ''That was a close call, wasn't it? I think you need a life preserver tied on the back of that thing.''

''Maybe, or an outboard motor,'' he joked.

''Actually, I didn't mean the fishing, though it was fun. I meant later, when she got upset. Even I didn't understand what was going on with her. It was very sweet of you to talk to her the way you did and figure out what was bothering her. She's waiting to hear if her father will be visiting for her birthday this week, and I guess she's a little sensitive right now."

"I hope he comes," he replied.

"Yes, so do I. We should hear from him tonight. But it was nice of you, all the same."

She gazed at him with gratitude for the consideration he'd shown her child, and Grant felt overwhelmed. He felt so proud that he had won the respect of this very special woman. It had seemed such a small gesture on his part, but she obviously thought otherwise. If only she knew how much he would do for her and Nora if he were able. He'd give them both the world.

Finally, he couldn't resist touching her. He reached out and took her hand, holding it in both of his.

"It was nothing. You don't need to thank me. I'm crazy about Nora. You must know that by now."

"Yes, I know. And she's crazy about you, too," she confessed. He felt the answering grip of her hand, and the sensation raced along his limbs like a brush fire. "But I worry about it sometimes, to be honest. I mean, we won't be here forever."

"She's getting too attached to me...is that the problem?" he asked quietly.

"Something like that."

"Don't worry," he assured her. "I'm not your ex-husband. I won't disappoint her if I can ever help it."

He rested his hands on her shoulders, and when she

wouldn't look at him, he gently lifted her chin with his fingertips.

"Didn't you hear what I said, Rebecca?" he asked quietly.

She looked upset, her eyes shining with unshed tears. She nodded, seeming too moved to speak.

"Yes, I heard you," she answered finally. "It's just that maybe you won't be able to help it. Maybe we don't mean to hurt someone we care about, but sometimes we just can't help it."

Her words struck a deep note in his heart. She seemed to be talking more about herself than about her daughter. He knew she had struggled to understand why he had set up an invisible barrier between them since their night together. She had struggled to understand and had tried her best not to blame him. Still, it had hurt.

He had no choice. He couldn't stop himself from kissing her and holding her tight, from stealing a few precious minutes of paradise in her arms. His head dropped, and their lips met. He felt her resistance for an instant, then he felt her relax and melt into his arms. Her mouth opened under the pressure of his, and he heard a small sigh of satisfaction deep in her throat that thrilled him down to the marrow of his bones.

Their kiss went on and on, his tongue plundered the honey sweetness of her soft, warm mouth in a mindless foray of tasting and savoring. His hands roamed up and down her sleek body, stroking her breasts through the thin fabric of her tank top and then moving, to the silky bare skin at the hem of her shorts. His hands moved around her hips and gently cupped her bottom, pulling her against his building heat.

He heard her groan with desire as their bodies pressed tightly together, heat seeking heat. He was ready to make love to her. He kissed her deeply, bending her head back as he nearly robbed her of her breath. Leaning against the wall for support, he held her tightly and turned her slightly to the side, slipping his hand between her smooth, lean thighs, then stroking her most sensitive and intimate place. She sighed, her hips rising to meet his rhythmic touch, then she shuddered with pleasure in his arms. She seemed half inclined to break away and half inclined to ask for even more.

He gazed at her beautiful face. While one hand continued to caress her lower body, his mouth covered the peak of one breast, his tongue swirling in lazy circles around her hardened nipple. He heard her moan and sigh, felt her move restlessly against him and finally felt her fingertips dig into his shoulder as he absorbed the tremors of excitement that rocked her slender body.

He longed to be inside her, to love her completely and bring her to the very height of pleasure, to give her everything he had to give and more. To make love to her like no man had ever loved her before.

''Rebecca, Rebecca,'' he sighed, raining soft kisses on her cheeks, her closed eyelids and her soft lips. ''God, I want you. I want you so much,'' he confessed.

She turned in his arms and buried her face in his

shoulder. Then she lifted her head and stared deeply into his eyes. "I want you, too," she admitted in a silken whisper. "But it's not right. It's not enough."

Her words were quietly spoken. But their impact was deep. Grant felt as if a door within him had opened for a moment, letting in fresh air and sunlight—and then, just as quickly, slammed shut.

He didn't know what to say. He let his hands linger on her waist and felt her slowly pulling away.

"I need to go now," she insisted.

"Okay." He nodded, his expression grim. "I'm sorry, Rebecca. Maybe I shouldn't have…"

She raised her hand and pressed her fingertips to his lips. "No, don't say that, please," she insisted. "It only makes it worse."

Ducking her head, she pulled away and swiftly left the room.

Grant sat alone at the long dining table, drumming his fingertips on the linen cloth. He'd spent the last half hour reading the newspaper but had grown bored with it and laid it aside.

He glanced around, suddenly conscious of the vast, banquet-size room. It seemed like an empty cavern stretching out around him, echoing his slightest movement or sound. Classical music floated through speakers hidden in the wall, and he rose stiffly, walked to the control and turned up the sound. Bach usually had a soothing effect on his nerves, but tonight not even Bach and a tumbler of premium Scotch whiskey calmed him while he waited for Rebecca and Nora to appear.

Mrs. Walker poked her head into the room. "Shall I have the maid serve, sir?" she asked quietly.

"Not yet." He glanced at his watch. "Let's give them another few minutes."

"Do you want me to call Ms. Calloway for you, sir?"

"No," he said abruptly. "That won't be necessary, Mrs. Walker, but thank you," he added more politely. "She did say she was coming down to dinner tonight, though, didn't she?" he asked, checking for perhaps the third time.

"Yes, she did, sir. I asked her myself this afternoon, when the cook needed to know how much food to prepare for the meal. She said she was planning on dining with you tonight."

"All right." He nodded, then carefully lowered himself into his chair. "I'll just wait then. Perhaps they were held up for some reason."

"Perhaps," Mrs. Walker agreed. Grant caught a flash of sympathy in her eyes. Feeling embarrassed, he looked away. "Can I bring you anything, sir?"

"No, thank you. I'll ring when I'm ready."

With a nod, Mrs. Walker retreated to the kitchen, and Grant was left alone again with his wandering thoughts. He had made a special effort with his appearance tonight, though he wasn't quite sure why.

After his shower, he had given himself an extra close shave and combed his hair carefully. Rebecca always teased him about needing a haircut, and for once, he was starting to believe her. He was wearing a collarless white linen shirt, khaki trousers and a navy blue blazer. When he glanced at his reflection in the mirror, he looked like his old self again. His before-the-accident self. Except for the thin scar that ran across his right cheek.

He touched it with his hand. He might have that removed someday. Someday soon. The doctor said it wouldn't take much. Though he'd never been one to fuss much with his looks, the scar was jarring whenever he caught sight of it. An unnecessary reminder of the accident.

As if he could ever forget that fateful night. He didn't need a scar on his face to remind himself, as he had once thought. The true scars were within, marks that no surgeon, however skillful, could ever erase.

He sighed and picked up the newspaper. He worried that he had scared Rebecca away with his ardent embrace this morning. He must have terrified her. He knew he'd terrified himself. If he could express that much explosive passion holding her for five minutes, fully clothed, what would happen if they ever made love? The question was nearly too much to contemplate.

Was she avoiding him on purpose, as she'd done in the past? Or was there some other reason for the delay? He checked his watch again. It was nearly half past seven, and she knew that dinner was served at seven sharp. He suddenly felt foolish. Surely she had a right to eat her dinner wherever she pleased. She didn't have to join him if it made her feel uncomfortable. She knew better than he did that whatever they felt for each other, however strong and real their feelings seemed to be, this was a temporary situation.

He would soon return to his office, to his life in the city and all the complications and distraction there that usually kept the loneliness and emptiness at bay. Rebecca would go on to another job in another house and work her special magic on some other needy soul.

He hoped to God her next patient wasn't a man. The thought of her tender, loving hands on some other man made his blood boil. But of course, that was inevitable, wasn't it? Once they went their separate ways, sooner or later she'd find someone to love. Some lucky man would find her. It was a miracle she was still unattached this long after her marriage. The men in New York City had to be either blind or just plain stupid, he thought bitterly.

Though it brought a sharp stab of pain to his injured leg, Grant stood abruptly and rang the dinner bell.

Mrs. Walker came running. "Yes, sir?" she inquired breathlessly.

"Have the maid serve, please. I don't think they're coming," he said simply.

"Yes, of course, sir. She'll be right in," Mrs. Walker replied. She paused in the doorway and turned to him. "Shall I have her clear the extra place settings?"

He glanced at the table. The empty chairs and place settings where Rebecca and Nora usually sat seemed to mock him. He felt sad and angry—mostly angry at himself for encouraging his vain hopes.

"Yes, clear them away," he said sharply. "Clear them right now."

"Yes, sir." Mrs. Walker hurried over carrying a silver tray and cleared the places herself.

Grant turned his back to her and sipped his whiskey and soda as he stared out the window. When he was finally alone again, he let out a deep sigh.

He tried to enjoy his food, a shrimp dish that was one of his favorites. But at every bite, he thought only of the bluefish they had returned to the sea. He skipped dessert and instead of returning to his rooms, he decided to walk on the beach.

The sun was setting and the horizon was tinged with color, deep lavender and amazing hues of gold and pink. As the sky in the east darkened, brilliant stars appeared.

He didn't see Rebecca and Nora sitting on a long driftwood log near the shoreline until he was only a few yards away. His first impulse was to turn and walk in the other direction. Then he realized that Nora wasn't leaning on her mother in a casual embrace, she was crying hard, and Rebecca was trying to soothe her.

He stopped and wondered what he should do. He didn't want to intrude on them, especially since their absence at dinner seemed to signify Rebecca didn't want his company tonight. Yet he felt concerned. Very concerned. Maybe there was something he could do to help, some problem he could solve. He thought he should at least offer his assistance.

Rebecca didn't notice him until he was standing right next to her. She looked up, clearly surprised. "Oh, Grant. It's you," she managed to say.

Nora didn't lift her head, but her crying did slow down a bit, Grant noticed.

"Is something wrong with Nora?" he asked quietly.

Rebecca stared at him, then looked away. The light wind blew wisps of hair across her cheek and mouth. He had the urge to brush them away but carefully restrained himself.

"Nora feels upset tonight. Very upset. That's why we didn't come to dinner," she added hurriedly. "Her father called and said he won't be able to make it back to New York this week for her birthday."

"Oh... That's too bad," Grant said sincerely.

He crouched in the sand next to them, not knowing what to say. Nora was sniffling, too embarrassed to look at him. He felt a pang in his heart, empathizing with her. His own father had disappointed him so many times in the same way—missing an important birthday, a big game, even his college graduation. Grant knew how it felt, how much it hurt. He had once promised himself that if he ever had children, he'd walk through fire to be there for them. He suddenly hated Rebecca's ex-husband for the heartless way he'd treated Nora...and for hurting Rebecca, as well.

"I've got an idea," he said on impulse. "Why don't we make that visit to New York City we were talking about. You know, when I promised to take you to the Plaza to see the portrait of Eloise?" he reminded her. "Do you remember?"

Nora slowly lifted her head. "Of course I remember," she replied.

She didn't smile, but she did look interested in the proposition, he noticed. He could feel Rebecca staring at him intently. He should have checked with her before blurting out the invitation, he realized. She probably would have opposed it.

"Can we really go there? For my birthday, I mean?" Nora said.

"Yes, definitely... If your mother says it's all right, of course," he added. He glanced at Rebecca and caught her eye. She looked furious but was holding back a smile, he could tell by the way the corner of her mouth twitched.

"Can I, Mommy? Please?" Nora begged.

"I guess you have to now," Rebecca replied, sounding cornered.

"Can my mom come, too?" Nora asked Grant.

"Of course. If she wants to. I for one would love to have her along. I could take you shopping to F.A.O. Schwartz...and take your mom down the street to Tiffany's," he teased.

"Come on, Grant. I won't go at all if you're going to joke like that," Rebecca replied.

"Who's joking?" he asked innocently.

"Cool!" Nora exclaimed as her bright blue eyes lit up. "My birthday is Friday. Can we go on the exact day?"

"Sure, why not? I'll make all the arrangements," Grant promised. "We'll stay in for the weekend at my place. There's plenty of room there for everyone."

"The weekend? I thought we'd just go in for the day," Rebecca said warily. Grant guessed that Rebecca knew very well about his place, a huge, duplex penthouse on the Upper East Side, with a view of

Central Park from one side and river views from the other. He would bet good money that Mrs. Walker, who sometimes worked there, had given Rebecca an earful about the city home. In her expression he could see her curiosity warring with something that looked like sheer terror at the mere mention of staying there. He wasn't at all surprised when she came up with a handy excuse.

"I'm sorry. It's a lovely invitation, really, and very generous of you, Grant, but we really can't stay over," she replied, not surprising him in the least.

"Oh, really? Why is that?" he asked calmly.

"Why can't we, Mommy? I really want to," Nora said.

"But you have to leave for your camping trip very early on Saturday morning," Rebecca reminded her. "The bus leaves at half past seven. We'll never make it back in time."

"Oh, that's right. I nearly forgot," Nora said to Grant. "I'm going on a real overnight in the woods, with my camp," she explained to him. "We're going to sleep outside in tents and everything."

"Sounds great," he said with a smile. He knew it would be a terrific experience for Nora, but he was sorry to learn that the trip put a damper on his plans. "Well, you'll have to visit my house in the city another time then, okay?"

"Of course we will," Nora promised brightly. "When we go back at the end of the summer. We'll all be back in New York then...right, Mommy?"

The mention of the end of their time together put a bittersweet twist on the conversation for Grant. He glanced at Rebecca and could tell she shared his feelings.

"Of course, we'll visit Grant sometime when we get back...if he wants us to," she added in a more tentative tone.

"Of course I do. But let's talk about Nora's birthday. We'll make a real day of it," he promised. "There's the Plaza and then maybe the Central Park Zoo." He began planning out loud. "Have you ever ridden in a helicopter, Nora? That would be something fun to do, don't you think?"

"A helicopter ride?" Rebecca exclaimed. He could see that the mere mention of it made her stomach lurch. "How about a plain old horse-drawn carriage?"

"I want to go in a helicopter, Mom," Nora insisted. "Wow, this is going to be great!" Nora jumped up and did a little jig in the sand. "This is going to be the greatest birthday I ever had."

"Guess I need to bring along some earplugs," Rebecca said as she shook her head and smiled.

"I believe they supply the earplugs," Grant offered. Nora held out her hands to him and pulled him. He smiled at her, holding her small hands in his as she danced around in the fading light. He felt like a hero, the ten-foot-tall variety, his injuries and shortcomings magically forgotten. It felt amazingly good to do something like this for Nora—and Rebecca, too, of course. He felt protective toward them...and needed.

Rebecca hugged her knees to her chest, and the long, loose sweater she was wearing slipped off one shoulder. Silhouetted against the sunset, he found her more beautiful and appealing than ever.

She tipped her head back and smiled at him, a secret smile that warmed his heart. She silently mouthed the words "Thank you."

"My pleasure," he silently answered.

It *would* be his pleasure, too. His utmost pleasure to show them the time of their lives. He knew only too well that they'd be parting soon enough…and forever. For despite what Rebecca had told Nora, he truly doubted they'd see each other in the city. He knew too well she'd only said so to appease Nora.

At least they'd have one special day together, something to look back on and treasure. The idea had been a gift from above, he suddenly realized.

One day would never be enough, of course. A thousand wouldn't satisfy him. But given the chance to spend this time with Rebecca and her daughter, he was determined to make it wonderful.

Seven

For the remainder of the week, Rebecca's head spun with doubts about spending a day in the city with Grant. It was a grand gesture on his part and a generous one. But carrying through on it made her feel obligated to him somehow.

Nora was so thrilled with the idea she talked of little else, and Rebecca didn't have the heart to call a halt to the outing. Especially since her ex-husband had almost ruined Nora's birthday entirely with his typical last-minute excuses.

It had been very kind of Grant to rush in and rescue the situation. More than kind, she knew. Even if he had wanted to cheer Nora up, she knew he hardly had to go so far out of his way to do so. He could have bought Nora a present or taken her into town for a movie or some special treat. When Rebecca considered the time, trouble and expense involved in the schedule he'd put together, she had to wonder why he was going to such lengths.

Well, he was a man with an active mind, and he was stirring with energy these days. Maybe planning this trip gave him something to do. A project for a man who had been burdened with responsibility not so long ago but lately had had none. Or maybe it was an easy way for him to get on his feet again, get reoriented to the city. He hadn't been to Manhattan, except to visit doctors, for months. Maybe he was wary about going back, and showing Nora around the town made it more palatable to him.

In more optimistic moments, she imagined his impulse sprang from deeper feelings—specifically, feelings for her. Maybe he felt more than mere attraction. Perhaps he had begun to see a future for them.

Then reality would sweep in like a giant wave, washing away all traces of her heart's lovely sand castles of hope. Yes, the attraction was real, mutual and as powerful as ever. But it still led nowhere, she reminded herself. Maybe to Grant's bed. But certainly not to a real relationship. Not as long as memories of the accident hung over him like a cloud. Or, to be more precise, his inability to remember the accident.

Even though they knew each other far better now, Rebecca feared that his attraction to her was still inspired by the reasons she'd suspected from the start— his need to regain his male confidence and his feelings of gratitude toward her for his recovery. Hadn't he admitted as much to her? He had told her he'd never have made it without her help. Hadn't that con-

fession been voiced right before their last smoldering
encounter, when his passionate kisses and persuasive
touch had her ready and willing to make love with
him atop the nearest horizontal surface?

Rebecca felt her cheeks grow warm just thinking
about it. She'd behaved so wantonly, with such utter
abandon, in his arms. She'd never responded quite
that way to any man before Grant, and wondered if
she ever would again. What would it be like to surrender finally to all the heat and hungry desire that
simmered between them, to love him completely and
feel his love in return? How many long hours she'd
tossed in her bed this summer, fantasizing about that
very question. Obsessing, she had to admit. He had
become an obsession for her. She was stuck on him
totally. He lived in her mind, in her heart, in her soul.
She only hoped to heaven that once they were apart,
her need for him would gradually fade, though she
was sure the process would be a painful one. In light
of her intense feelings, she often thought it had been
a blessing they'd never made love. Wouldn't it be far
worse for her later if they had? Or would it give her
something of him to have and cherish in the lonely
future? Rebecca was never sure of the answer.

Perhaps he'd try to persuade her to make love this
weekend, while they were alone in the house with
Nora and Matthew gone. For once, despite her lev-
elheaded, ever-sensible side, Rebecca didn't know
what she would do if that happened. Surely she could
avoid him and hold the line for just a few more
weeks. Surely, she could keep herself from having a
real affair with him. He'd progressed so much this

summer. He was gaining strength every day. He wouldn't need her much longer. They both realized that.

She knew she ought to see September as a light at the end of the tunnel. Yet having the end in sight made their remaining time together feel all the more precious, all the more intense and emotionally charged. For that reason and so many more, she felt wary of the upcoming weekend, when they would be alone together.

Her will to avoid an empty affair with Grant was strong. But she was only human. And probably—no, make that *definitely,* she mentally amended—totally in love with him. Did all her ethical, logical reasons to resist him stand a chance against those odds?

Rebecca couldn't help but feel nervous on Friday morning as she and Nora got ready to meet Grant. She fussed more than usual over Nora's outfit and her hair until even her typically even-tempered daughter had to complain.

Grant had the car waiting for them at the front of the house, and they were already five minutes late. But Rebecca couldn't get her hair right. For some reason, it wouldn't stay where she pinned it in a neat French roll. As she pulled the pins out and attempted to fix it, Nora tugged at her sleeve. ''Mommy, we're late. Grant is waiting for us. Can't you do that in the car?''

Rebecca considered the suggestion. But she didn't want to be fixing her hair in the car in front of Grant. It made her feel too self-conscious. She glanced at her watch. They *were* late. ''I'll just wear it down,'' she said finally. She tossed the pins on her dresser and whisked a brush through her hair.

"That looks good," Nora said, standing behind her. "You don't have to wear it pinned up like Mary Poppins all the time."

"Nora...since when do you think I look like Mary Poppins?" Rebecca replied, feeling genuinely shocked at the comparison.

Nora shrugged. "Not in a bad way...I'm just saying your hair looks nice loose, too."

Mary Poppins, indeed. Rebecca silently bristled. Did she really look like the stuffy British nanny? She hurriedly closed their door, grabbed Nora's hand and walked as briskly as she dared through the big house, to the front door.

Finally, she opened the door and stepped onto the covered portico, feeling breathless and unaccountably nervous. It was silly really. She knew Grant so well, yet she felt as jumpy as if she were in high school, going on her first date. At least she had on a new outfit, a form-fitting wheat-colored linen sheath and matching three-quarter-length jacket, worn with a pearl necklace and small gold earrings. Nothing Mary Poppins about it, either, she assured herself.

The first thing she saw was the long, white limousine. She knew Grant owned several cars, one to suit each mood, it seemed, including a sleek black Jaguar and a sturdy metallic gray Land Rover. But she'd never seen the limo.

"Wow, we're going to ride in *that?* Awesome!" Nora exclaimed. She raced toward the car, and the uniformed driver opened the door for her. Then Rebecca caught sight of Grant, who had been standing on the other side of the car.

"There you are. I was starting to get worried that you'd stood me up."

He greeted her with a smile, his white teeth flashing against his richly tanned skin. He was dressed in a charcoal gray suit with a pale pinstripe, along with a white shirt and patterned burgundy silk tie. He looked so handsome, her breath caught in her throat.

"We had a little...delay," Rebecca explained, not wishing to admit she'd been fussing with her hair. "Nothing important," she added.

He'd come around the car and stood facing her. He seemed very tall today, tall and imposing, towering over her. Maybe it was the suit, she told herself. Or his confident attitude. Or the way his dark gaze moved over her, appraising her appearance.

"Let's get going then, shall we? We have an early reservation for lunch, and we'll be cutting it quite close as it is."

"Yes, of course," she agreed. Yet she still didn't move.

"Why are you staring at me?"

"Was I?" She felt herself flush. "Sorry...I didn't mean to. You just look different today," she admitted.

"It must be the suit," he said.

"No, I don't think so," she replied, still staring but unable to help herself. "It's something else." She met his puzzled gaze, then realized what it was. "Your hair. You had it cut."

"Yes, I had a haircut. Don't I always?" he asked defensively.

His surly tone made Rebecca smile. It brought back memories of their early days together. As far as she could see, it was only Joe who chopped into his hair every few weeks, when it got so shaggy not even Grant could stand it anymore. But she held her tongue, knowing he already felt self-conscious under her scrutiny.

"Well, maybe you've found a new barber then. It looks very nice like that," she added gently. "Shows off your handsome face."

She saw a smile tugging at the corner of his mouth. He was pleased with her compliment. Very pleased.

"Thank you, Rebecca," he said smoothly. His dark gaze swept her body, taking in every inch of her. "You look pretty wonderful yourself, if you don't mind me saying so."

She smiled, feeling warmed from head to toe. "I don't mind at all," she admitted. Hoping the shadows in the car would hide her blush, she ducked her head and got in.

The drive to the city passed very quickly. Nora had seen plenty of limousines before but had never been inside one, and she occupied most of Grant's time asking for demonstrations of all the gadgetry. To his credit, Rebecca noticed, he had unlimited patience with her curiosity and seemed to enjoy letting her use the phone, the notebook computer, stereo system and TV—complete with a VCR, of course. Not to mention the minibar, where Nora found many drinks and snacks suited perfectly to her taste.

"Do you always stock your car with Yoohoo?" Rebecca asked him in an amused tone.

"Always," he answered with a shrug. "I keep it right next to the Dom Perignon." His quick comeback made her laugh.

At the Plaza Hotel, they were showered with star treatment from the moment they arrived. Although a line of guests waited for tables in the Palm Court, they were ushered through the crowd and seated in a choice location. It was a beautiful setting, with the fabulous palms and sumptuous decor. Two musicians in formal attire played classical pieces on a violin and cello. Rebecca felt as if she'd been transported to another world. The look on Nora's face expressed the same feeling, only more so.

Grant had thought of everything—he'd even brought along a slim automatic camera to take pictures. Rebecca thought it looked awfully expensive and delicate, and she shuddered when Grant offered Nora a chance to take a few shots. But it was obviously simple to use and a perfect amusement for Nora while they waited for their lunch. She was thrilled to take photos of everything she saw, including Grant and Rebecca.

"You're sitting too far apart," her little voice insisted as she gazed at them through the shutter.

"How's this?" Grant asked. He leaned over and swiftly drew Rebecca to him in a close embrace. For the blink of an eye, Rebecca savored the heat of his nearness.

"Perfect," Nora said, snapping the photo. Rebecca turned to see Grant wearing a wide grin. She was sure her expression in the photo would be one of pure shock.

"That could be a good one, Nora. I can't wait to see it," he joked as he took the camera.

Before Rebecca could comment, the waiter arrived with their lunch. The food was as splendid as the setting, and just when Rebecca thought she couldn't eat another bite, the waiter appeared with a birthday cake decorated with a sparkler and real miniature orchids and satin ribbons. The other waiters gathered around and sang a rousing round of "Happy Birthday."

Nora squeezed her eyes shut and blew out the candles in one breath as Grant captured the moment on film. Everyone in the restaurant applauded, and Nora looked totally pleased. Rebecca could only imagine what she had wished for.

Rebecca had given Nora her presents that morning, a new watch, some clothes she'd asked for and a book by her favorite author. Nora had seemed very pleased by the gifts, and Rebecca knew she didn't expect more. Now Rebecca wondered if she should have saved at least one box to open after the cake. She was sorry she hadn't thought of it.

"Chocolate, my favorite," Nora said as she took a huge bite of cake. "How did you know?"

"Lucky guess," Grant teased with a grin. "I almost forgot." He leaned over and pulled a slim box from his pocket. "Here's a little present for you. Happy birthday, Nora."

A present? And it looked like jewelry, no less. Rebecca couldn't quite believe he'd gone and got Nora an expensive present on top of everything else. It was just too much.

"Thank you, Grant," Nora said sweetly, as she eagerly undid the wrapping. She opened the box and peered inside. "Wow...a real gold locket. Look, Mommy," she exclaimed, holding her gift for Rebecca to see.

"It's beautiful, Nora," Rebecca said honestly. She glanced at Grant. "It is lovely, Grant. You shouldn't have gone to such trouble, though."

"It was no trouble." He sat beaming at Nora, clearly pleased his choice had been a hit. "Here, let me help you put it on," he offered.

Nora came around to his side of the table, and Grant fastened it for her. "It opens up, you know, to put pictures inside."

"Does it really?" She quickly figured out how to open it, and did so. Rebecca watched her look inside the locket, then saw her sudden wide grin. "Grant, you're so silly," Nora said to him.

They were both laughing, and Rebecca felt left out of the joke. "What's so funny?" she asked.

"Look, Mommy." Nora turned the locket so Rebecca could see. "Grant put a picture of Eloise in here for me. Isn't that silly?"

Rebecca didn't know why, but the simple gesture was very touching. Jack had never given—or even mailed—Nora such a lovely, thoughtful gift. She felt her eyes glaze over then forced herself to be bright.

"Yes, very silly," she agreed. She turned to Grant and smiled at him, then reached across the table and took his hand in hers. "You really can be awfully silly sometimes," she told him.

"Yes, I know...in addition to all my other shortcomings, of course," he admitted with a sly, sexy grin as he returned the pressure of her touch. "How long can you put up with me, Rebecca?" he asked cryptically.

"As long as you need me, I guess," she answered quietly, unable to break her gaze from his.

It was Nora's excited voice that broke the spell, drawing them back to reality. "We didn't see the portrait of Eloise yet," she said. "Can we go look for it now?"

"Of course," Grant said. "That's a great idea."

Rebecca was about to help him from his chair, but in the blink of an eye, he was standing up, discreetly aided by the use of his cane, and helping her out of her seat in a very gentlemanly fashion.

It took Rebecca a moment to orient herself to the role reversal. She felt him pull back her chair, and she rose smoothly and smiled. "Thank you," she said, meeting his eye.

"Not at all," he replied with a small smile. "Shall we?" he asked, gesturing for her to go before him.

After lunch, they visited the zoo in Central Park and took a carriage ride. There was shopping on Fifth Avenue, where Grant insisted on buying Nora the largest stuffed dog Rebecca had ever seen. When they found it was too large to fit in the trunk of the limousine, Grant had it sent to Bridgehampton that very day so Nora would have it when she got home.

As they strolled down the avenue past Tiffany's, Grant pointed out a pair of breathtaking emerald earrings displayed in the window.

"Emeralds would be perfect for you," he remarked, as if suddenly inspired. "When is your birth-day, anyway, Rebecca?"

Rebecca turned to him, not knowing what to say. Did he really think he would buy her emerald earrings for a birthday gift? No, he had to be teasing, she reasoned.

"Oh, too bad," she said lightly. "My birthday's in June. You missed it."

"That was a well-kept secret, wasn't it?" he asked, meeting her gaze. "There's always Christmas. I'll make it up to you then," he added, his tone halfway between a threat and a promise.

She knew he had to be teasing her. By Christmas he'd be so immersed in his real life, she was sure he'd barely recall her name.

They reached the car, and she was saved from continuing the silly conversation. The rest of the day was a blur of activity, with Nora and Grant calling all the shots. Although she'd raised Nora in Manhattan, Rebecca rarely had the time or money to take Nora around the city in such a fashion. Of course, on rainy days she'd drag Nora through a museum or two, and once she took her to the top of the Empire State Building. But their outings had been nothing like this one.

Rebecca enjoyed seeing the city as a tourist would, and she was happy to sit back and take orders for once—though she did grit her teeth and squeeze Grant's fingers until he yelped with pain during the helicopter ride.

After an early dinner at a beautiful restaurant on the East River, Rebecca expected they'd return home.

But Grant had one more surprise up his sleeve—orchestra seats to a Broadway show Nora had been longing to see.

Nora jumped out of her seat with excitement when Grant made the announcement.

"How did you know she wanted to see that show?" Rebecca asked, totally surprised by his choice.

"I make it my business to know these things, Rebecca," he replied, sounding serious, but pleased that she was impressed.

Yes, he had made it his business to please Nora today, Rebecca had to admit. To please both of them, she added silently. His efforts made her love him even more. Which was a good thing and a bad thing. She silently pondered as she gazed out the restaurant window at the river view and the twinkling lights on the opposite shore.

Nora sat attentive and alert through the entire show, and Rebecca enjoyed watching her take it all in. After the show, they had barely driven a block in the car when Rebecca felt her daughter cuddle against her and rest her head in Rebecca's lap. Within seconds, Nora was deeply asleep.

"She's out like a light," she whispered to Grant. "I don't know how I'll ever get her up tomorrow for the camping trip."

Grant glanced at Nora, who sat between them, with a soft smile. "Don't worry. She'll get up. She'll be excited all over again about the camping."

Rebecca had to agree. She could see that he was able to predict Nora's moods and reactions almost as well as she did. With Nora asleep, the ride to Bridge-hampton was very quiet. Grant barely spoke, and Rebecca wondered if all the activity had been taxing for him, too. Perhaps he was in some pain but too macho to admit it. Despite all the time they'd spent together in the past weeks, for some reason Rebecca felt very tense in his presence tonight. Maybe it was the darkness, and the enclosed atmosphere of the car. She glanced at him. He was staring straight ahead. She wondered if he'd fallen asleep, as well.

"Grant?" she whispered quietly. He quickly turned to look at her, and she knew he hadn't been sleeping. "I just want to thank you for today. Nora was thrilled. It was wonderful. You went to far too much trouble, though. It was too generous of you."

"Nonsense," he replied curtly, looking straight ahead again. "It was a selfish gesture on my part, actually. I don't have anyone special in my life to please, Rebecca. I don't have anyone to surprise with a birthday cake or a helicopter ride. Watching the look on her face all day, and yours," he added, "was a rare pleasure for me. So maybe I should be the one thanking you."

"You're welcome," she replied. "Very welcome. You would always be," she added quietly. He met her gaze, and even in the car's dark shadows, she could see the intense emotion in his expression.

He reached over the back of the seat and slipped his arm around her shoulder with Nora cuddled between them. She welcomed his touch and dropped her head to his shoulder.

As they drove in silence, Rebecca felt his quiet

words deep in her heart. Underneath it all, he was a lonely man, trapped in a prison of his own making. He could reach out to her this way. With his tender insights, he could almost tempt her into believing there was a real future for them. But finally, what would it all add up to? A broken heart for her, she knew for sure. And maybe even for him, as well.

When they arrived at the house, Rebecca was surprised to realize she'd fallen asleep on Grant's shoulder. "We're home," he whispered in her ear without stirring a muscle.

She turned her head to find his face just inches away. "Oh, dear. I fell asleep on you, Sorry."

He smiled. "Don't be." He cupped her cheek in his hand and dropped a sweet, lingering kiss on her mouth. Rebecca sleepily kissed him back, feeling so warm and relaxed, the kiss could have lasted forever.

Finally, with a reluctant sigh, he withdrew from her and whispered, "Better wake up Nora."

"Yes," she agreed as they slowly broke apart. She had to wake up and stop dreaming, as well.

Eight

$\textbf{A}$s Rebecca had predicted, it was tough going the next morning, getting Nora out of the house and to her camp bus by seven-thirty. She felt a bit teary, waving to Nora as the bus pulled away. It was only a weekend, she reminded herself. But Rebecca knew she'd miss Nora's bright, sprightly company.

Rebecca had coffee and a roll at a café in town, then did some errands. She returned to the Berringer estate just before noon feeling tired and tempted to take a nap, an indulgence she rarely allowed herself.

The note taped to her door had the effect of a double espresso, jolting her out of her lethargy. She could see right away it was written in Grant's handwriting, and the simple message inside made her heart race. ''Had a great catch this morning. And won't have to throw it back this time. Have dinner with me? Grant.''

Rebecca leaned against her closed door. The silence of her rooms, a subtle reminder of Nora's absence, and the note in her hand caused reality to sink in. She was alone in the house with Grant. Utterly alone until Sunday night when Nora returned. Even Mrs. Walker had been given the weekend off to visit her grandchildren in Massachusetts.

Whenever Rebecca had considered this situation, she'd assured herself it was a very large house and that she could easily avoid Grant for two days, even more if she needed to.

But did she want to? That was the real question. She dropped onto the sofa and looked at the note again. She recalled the way he'd kissed her last night when they'd arrived home. He was the one who had pulled away. She had not wanted the kiss to end.

Yesterday, he'd given Nora a day to remember for all time. But while the memories were sweet, Rebecca knew what she and Grant could share together, intimately, as a man and a woman, would be a thrill far beyond that of a helicopter ride. A ride in the space shuttle might not even compare. She quietly smiled.

To accept his invitation to dinner would be, in her mind, a tacit agreement to spend the night with him. For she knew very well that's what this invitation was all about. If she refused, he'd be a gentleman, she was sure, and would leave her alone for the rest of the weekend.

She strolled to the glass doors that led to the deck. What did she want, she asked herself. The answer was simple. As simple as the sight of the brilliantly shining sun and rolling blue sea. She wanted him. She wanted to know what it was like to love him and feel his love in return. To join with him, be part of him. Maybe it tarnished her professional standards. Maybe it was a hopeless gesture, a tantalizing taste of a future that could never be.

But that's what she wanted. And by heaven, Rebecca knew, down deep in the pit of her soul, she would not—and could not—deny herself this experience. It would hurt later. Hurt plenty, she had no doubt. But when she looked back on the choice, years and years from now, it would be one she knew she'd never regret.

Before reason and secret fears could change her mind, Rebecca picked up the phone and dialed Grant's extension. He picked up on one ring, and before he had time to say hello, she accepted his dinner invitation in an embarrassed rush of words.

"Great," he replied, sounding genuinely pleased. He accepted Rebecca's offer to help fix the meal. "I warn you, I'm a tyrant in the kitchen. Worse than you are in the workout room."

"We'll see who's worse," she replied, smiling.

Rebecca found she was smiling after she hung up the phone, and still smiling when she strolled to the beach, took a swim and then napped in the sun. She was smiling the entire day, in fact, in anticipation of the night ahead.

Rebecca dressed casually, in a short, slip-style sundress with a peach background and a print of scattered flowers. An armful of silver bracelets and small silver earrings gave the dress a more high-fashion touch, as did her sleek long ponytail. She felt relaxed from her leisurely afternoon on the beach, and her fair complexion looked golden and glowing. For makeup, she needed only a dash of mascara, lip gloss and a brief touch of her favorite perfume at her wrists and nape.

She entered the kitchen and found Grant standing at the counter, chopping something on a wooden block. He turned and took her in with a long, sweeping stare, then let out a long, low whistle.

"If I knew you were going to look that gorgeous, Rebecca, I would have taken you out, just to show you off," he admitted.

Rebecca pursed her lips but couldn't hide her blush. "Thanks for the compliment," she replied. "Even though that's a perfectly chauvinistic thing to say," she added with a laugh.

"Now, now," he reprimanded her. "Would a true chauvinist be standing here up to his elbows in chopped parsley...wearing an apron, no less?"

With her hands on her hips and her head cocked, she looked him over. He looked pretty darned cute in his apron, she had to admit.

"No, I guess not," she agreed. She walked to him. "What can I do to help, boss?" she asked with a twinkle in her eye.

"First, pour yourself a glass of wine," he instructed, pointing out the wine bottle and glass. "Then you can help me chop up these herbs."

They worked together companionably, preparing the fish and other dishes. Grant was terribly bossy, scolding her about the way she chopped or carried out some other task. But Rebecca managed to laugh at him and patiently followed his exacting instructions.

They ate on the terrace, an array of glimmering candles on the table and glittering stars above. The fresh-grilled fish had a subtle but superb flavor, and Rebecca was lavish with her compliments to the chef.

"It was nothing," he said modestly. "Just some herbs and lemon butter. It's hard to ruin a nice fresh fish like this one. Although I do have to take some credit for catching it."

"Yes, you do," Rebecca agreed. "And I won't mention a word to Nora, if you don't," she added.

"Heaven forbid," he replied. He took a sip of his wine. "She might decide that it was the same fish she'd set free."

Rebecca paused, a forkful of food midway between the plate and her mouth. "It wasn't, of course...was it?" she asked quietly.

Grant met her gaze and laughed. "Of course not. That fish was too smart to come back in this direction."

They talked easily through the meal about varied and wide-ranging topics. Rebecca loved to talk with Grant. He knew so much about so many things. He had traveled all over the world and had packed so much experience into his life so far. Yet he listened quietly and seriously when she offered her opinions. His mind was quick, his wit sharp and irreverent. Although she often disagreed with him, their conversation was never boring.

Grant served coffee, and they both decided they were too full for dessert—a fabulous chocolate mousse that had been delivered from a gourmet shop in town. Rebecca sipped her coffee and felt a tense silence fall between them. She found herself toying with her napkin, then felt Grant's touch on her hand, stilling her fingertips.

"You know, I've really come a long way in my therapy these past few weeks, Rebecca. I can walk on my own, swim, fish, even cook dinner."

"Yes, you're doing very well," Rebecca agreed, wondering where the conversation was leading. "Exceptionally well," she added. Was he about to say, in a polite way, that he no longer needed her services?

"There is one thing I really wanted to try tonight," he said in a quiet, seductive tone. "Something I haven't been able to do for a long, long time," he added, with longing underscoring every word.

"Oh...and what's that?" she asked breathlessly. She felt his hand on her shoulder, adjusting the thin strap on her dress. She swallowed hard but didn't dare look at him.

"I'd like to dance with you," he said simply. "Will you dance with me, Rebecca?"

She met his gaze and caught the teasing light in his dark eyes. He knew he had scared her. On purpose, too. She felt a smile tugging at the corners of her lips, but held it back.

"Yes, Grant. I'd love to dance with you," she said. She waited until he rose and helped her from her chair. Then she turned and moved smoothly into his open arms. The first contact of his hard, warm body on hers was heavenly, and Rebecca realized she'd been secretly waiting for this moment the entire evening.

His arms circled her waist, and he pulled her close. She needed little coaxing to tuck her head against his shoulder. Grant had chosen some jazz CDs for their dinner music, and the song that played was a sultry jazz ballad. Their bodies swayed together in time to the beat. Grant's step was slow but steady. Her arms circled his muscular shoulders, her fingers moving into his dark hair as she breathed in the familiar scent of him, his warm skin and spicy cologne. She felt totally intoxicated. Her head spun from his nearness, his firm, muscular body moving against her own, the magic of the sultry music and her powerful longing.

When she felt his mouth moving against the skin of her bare shoulder, her head dropped to the side, giving him freer access to the smooth column of her neck.

"Hmm, you taste delicious. I wish I could have you for dessert," he murmured playfully as his hands moved firmly over her back and hips, molding her slim form. "May I?" he asked, in a husky, sexy whisper.

Rebecca turned her head, seeking and finding his mouth with hers. She tilted her head to kiss him fully, conveying the desire she felt more clearly than words could.

Finally, she pulled away, meeting his startled gaze with hers. "Yes," she said simply.

It took an instant for her meaning to register. Rebecca watched as his expression quickly turned from surprise to happiness to intense, ignited desire.

She felt his grip on her body tighten as he pressed her closer. His arousal at her nearness was plainly evident. It excited her.

"I could make love to you right here, on that lounge chair," he admitted in a low growl close to her ear, "but I won't. This is going to be perfect for you."

She pulled back and stared into his eyes as she lovingly touched his face with her hand. Her fingertips traced the hard line of his cheek to his jaw, grazing the slight ridge of his scar. "If I'm in your arms," she answered finally, "I can't imagine how it could be anything less."

He gazed at her. About to say something, she thought. And yet, no words came. Finally, his head dipped to the lure of her moist, red lips. Their mouths met and merged, his kiss questioning at first. Then, as he felt her eager response, the kiss quickly deepened to a passionate expression of Grant's deep need for her. And her need for him.

Finally, he drew away from her, his hands sliding up to cup her bare shoulders. He pressed his cheek against her hair, catching his breath and inhaling her flowery scent. "Come with me to my room," he whispered. Rebecca nodded in answer, too overwhelmed to speak.

Grant wrapped his arm around her waist and dropped a kiss on her hair as she fell into step with him. Rebecca was thankful his rooms were only a short walk from the terrace. Her legs felt so weak and rubbery, she wasn't sure she could make it very far. Within moments they arrived and went inside. Re-

becca heard Grant close the door behind them and
was glad to find there were no lights. The curtains
were open, and light from the full moon that had risen
over the sea bathed the room in a silvery glow.

When Rebecca turned toward him, she could discern only his tall outline. But then he came closer,
and her heart pounded wildly. He stepped toward her
and cupped her bare shoulders in his hands. He
pressed his cheek against her hair, breathing in the
rich scent of her hair and skin.

Rebecca moved smoothly into his embrace, her
arms looping around his waist, her soft, full breasts
pressed to his chest. She stirred against him, murmured his name, and his arms moved to encircle her,
gripping her tightly to him. His hands immediately
moved to her hair and unfastened the clip that held it
back.

"You make me feel so alive, Rebecca. You
brought me back to life, you know. But even better
this time than before," he murmured as he dug his
fingers into her hair and spread it across her shoulders. "Before I met you, even before the accident, I
never felt quite this way. So awake, so aware. So
eager for every sensation. You've done that to me,"
he confessed as he dropped soft kisses on her shoulders, then followed the soft curve of her neck. She
sighed, unable to answer him, unable to think.

He lifted her face to his. His eyes looked huge and
bright, dark as the sea and churning with a passion
that both thrilled and terrified her. She ran her hands
along the hard planes of his back and tipped her head,
unable to pull her gaze from his. He made her feel

alive, too. Full of life and eager to love him completely. She didn't have to say it. She was sure he could see it in her eyes, feel it in her touch, taste it in her kiss.

Finally, their mouths met and merged. Her hands glided over his muscular chest and shoulders, then to his back again, boldly caressing him. Grant answered her touch with a sweep of his large warm hands down the curves of her lithe form, from her shoulders to her hips, then up again, to gently cup her full breasts. Rebecca didn't realize when he slipped down the thin straps of her dress, but soon she was bare to the waist except for her lacy, strapless bra. Grant's warm mouth pressed against the soft curves of her breasts, his fingertips circling the hardened tips. The material of her dress felt like airy thin gauze that floated down her hips and pooled at her feet as he touched and caressed her. Her kiss was wild against his mouth for a moment before she softly moaned with pleasure, her body sagging helplessly against him. She felt his hand press against her flat stomach, his fingertips grazing the edge of her bikini underwear.

"You're so beautiful," he whispered in a husky voice. "You take my breath away."

Moments later, they dropped onto his bed. As their kisses grew wilder and more intense, Grant cushioned Rebecca's head with one strong arm, the other stroking her from hip to thigh. His mouth moved from her lips, down the smooth column of her throat and across the silky skin at the edge of her bra. With his fingertips and tongue he teased and tasted the soft, sensitive flesh at the top of her cleavage and removed the scrap of lace entirely, exposing her breasts to his passionate touch.

Rebecca's fingers moved restlessly through his thick hair as his mouth covered one rosy, sensitive nipple. She moaned and stirred under him, pressing her hips provocatively against his. She felt his readiness for her, his throbbing need to make them one. She heard him take a deep, ragged breath as he lifted his head and looked at her.

Her eyes were half-closed, dazed with passion, her face flushed, her glorious red hair splayed around her head.

"Rebecca," he whispered. He kissed her lightly and then swallowed hard. "If you want me to stop, I will," he whispered hoarsely. "I just want you to be sure."

She framed his face with her cool, soft hands and looked deeply into his eyes. "I've never been surer of anything in my life," she promised him.

He didn't answer, but in the tense set of his jaw she saw a small pulse beating madly out of control. She ran her hands along the sculpted planes of his back again, then slipped her hands under his shirt and pulled open the buttons. Her touch clearly thrilled him, and Rebecca felt her confidence to satisfy him grow. She pressed her mouth to his chest, kissing him, tasting him, her warm, wet tongue swirling around his sensitive flat nipples. She felt his body shudder and heard him moan with pleasure as her caresses moved lower, her mouth tenderly exploring his flat abdomen, her hands caressing his chest and then his thighs. She unfastened his belt and the top of his pants, then slipped her hand inside his pants to cup and caress his male hardness, stroking him until he groaned and grasped her hard, responding to the intense pleasure of her touch.

Finally, pulling back from her seductive caresses, Grant raised himself above her, his hand sliding up her smooth, strong leg. His fingertips found the lacy edge of her panties and his fingers slipped inside, seeking and finding her slick velvety warmth. Her hips arched into his touch, and she knew he could feel that she was ready for him, more than ready.

As she shifted restlessly against him, Grant stilled her with a long, lingering kiss. "Not so fast, sweetheart. I told you before, I want to make this perfect for you."

Rebecca clung to him and felt herself drowning in wave after wave of pleasure while his fingers expertly stroked the peak of her pulsing womanhood. He was the most sensitive and masterful lover she'd ever known, alert to the slightest shift of her body, the slightest change in her breath, eager to please her, to touch her exactly as she wanted. His mouth moved again to her breasts, sucking and soothing her nipples. Rebecca sighed and writhed with pleasure as his expert loving pushed her higher and higher. She gripped his powerful shoulders, her hips thrusting to meet the lovingly slow strokes of his hand.

Finally, she couldn't bear it anymore. She trembled and moaned and pressed her face into the hollow between his neck and shoulder. She took a deep, shuddering breath and pressed herself close to him.

"Was that good?" he asked quietly, kissing her hair.

"Unbearably good...and it can only get better," she added in a sultry whisper. "Come to me," she urged him. With her hands on his hips, she gently guided his body to cover hers. "I want you so badly," she confessed.

"I want you more," he whispered. "I never wanted a woman more than I want you...or waited longer to have her."

Then his mouth pressed passionately to hers, and he shifted his body and settled between her thighs. Moments later, he made their bodies one.

Rebecca drew in a sharp and ragged breath. Her body tensed, then trembled in his arms. He held very still, kissing her hair until he felt her relax beneath him. Then he began to move slowly inside her, and she moaned deep and low at the back of her throat. The sound of pure, uninhibited pleasure seemed to thrill him, inspiring him to move deeper, to give her even more.

Their bodies moved as one in an ageless rhythm, an echo of the steady pounding of the waves against the shoreline just beyond their door. Grant thrust faster and deeper as Rebecca met him sigh for sigh, rising to meet him, driving him wild with passion.

He was indescribably beautiful, powerful, unique and precious to her. Rebecca knew suddenly that she had never loved anyone more, and never would again, no matter how long she lived. As he brought her to a climax of pleasure and she felt him reaching his own, in some dim, distant part of her heart, she knew that this session of lovemaking had not served to satisfy one single drop of her longing for him. To the contrary, to hold him and love him this way had given her a taste of what could be and an everlasting longing that would never be satisfied.

Just as she felt herself reaching the peak, she heard Grant's cries of ecstasy and felt him shudder in her arms. Their mouths merged in a deep, devouring kiss as Grant moved within her with one last, powerful thrust. She shivered and gripped him close, calling his name as her body clenched around him, and they cleaved together as one, as close as two beings could ever be.

Rebecca lay with her eyes closed, unwilling to come down off her lovely cloud of bliss. She felt limp and spent, her body still tingling with tiny lights, like the last embers of fireworks left sparkling in the sky.

Grant remained on top of her. When he made a move to shift away, she held him fast. "No...not yet. I like the way you feel on top of me," she whispered.

He lifted his head, and she saw the flash of his smile in the darkness. "You're an angel, Rebecca," he whispered. He dropped soft kisses on her forehead, cheek and chin. "An angel to make love with, that's for sure," he added. He pressed his cheek to hers and sighed. "Will you stay here with me tonight, the whole night, I mean? I want to wake up next to you."

What a lovely idea, she thought. She smiled at him. "Well, you've already seen me first thing in the morning, so that part won't be any surprise."

"You look beautiful no matter when I see you," he replied. "You always take my breath away."

She blushed, unable to believe his compliment. "You don't have to tell me things like that, Grant. I don't need...outrageous compliments."

He shifted to his side and rested his head on his hand. "It's only the simple truth, Rebecca. Even looking at you right now, I want you all over again." He reached out and gently brushed a strand of hair off her bare breast, his fingertips lingering on her silky skin, teasing her until she felt her nipple harden, though he never touched her there. "Even more than before, if that's possible."

Staring deeply into her eyes, he pulled her long leg up to cover his hip, and she felt the hard evidence of his renewed desire. His hand covered her breast and his mouth sought hers again, his slow, deep kisses kindling her deepest fires.

Rebecca would have never guessed that she could be ready to make love again so quickly. But she was. And with tender touches and even more imaginative ways of pleasuring him, she showed Grant how much she wanted him, too.

Rebecca woke up the next morning in Grant's arms. At first she felt confused and disoriented. Then memories of their night together flooded back with amazing clarity. She realized she was naked under the sheet, and so was Grant. His warm, hair-covered body was curled next to hers, as intimately as two could be. She liked the feeling of his heavy arm draped across her waist. She held perfectly still, trying not to wake him. She wanted to enjoy the moment before he woke and pulled away.

She glanced at the clock on the night table and noticed that they had slept late. It was nearly nine. She also noticed that the large framed photo of Courtney was gone. Grant had put it someplace else or put it away altogether. She hadn't given the photo—or his lost fiancée—a thought last night. Everything had been so perfect between them, so passionate and loving. She didn't allow her mind to entertain a single thought or insecurity that would have spoiled it.

But now she wondered if Grant's feelings about the past had changed since they'd last spoken about his accident and unhappy memories. Clearly, he seemed happier, eager to embrace life and move forward with his recovery. Did that mean he saw a future for them? They'd made love endlessly, and he'd praised her and complimented her to the stars. Yet he'd never once mentioned the word love or anything close to it. Well, it was far too soon for that, Rebecca thought. She felt grateful for the precious hours she'd spent in his arms. Maybe that was all she would ever have with him, she realized, the sum total of their entire affair. But she knew that going in, she reminded herself. If that's all he could give her, she'd have no regrets. Certainly, compared to the alternative—having no chance to share her love with him—she'd take it. She turned her face on the pillow and watched him sleep. He was so handsome, so utterly masculine looking with his tanned skin, dark bearded cheeks and sleep-tousled hair. He'd been hers alone, at least for one night. In her heart, she knew she'd always belong to him.

She had no idea what the future would hold for them, and Rebecca was determined not to break the

fragile spell they'd woven last night with her inse-
curities.

Grant slowly opened his eyes to find her staring at
him. She smiled, and he smiled back. "I got my
wish," he said quietly. "There you are, the first thing
I see."

"Here I am," Rebecca greeted him. She touched
his cheek with her hand. "It's late, after nine."

His smile grew wider. "We were tired...under-
standably so." His hand skimmed the bare skin of her
hip, moving down to her slim thigh. "I'll make us
some breakfast," he offered. "How about pancakes?"

"Good, I'm hungry."

"I'm hungry, too," he replied, his gaze fixed on
hers. "Hungry for you again," he added before moving closer for a kiss.

Rebecca opened her arms to him and held him
close as he kissed her and kissed her again. As she
felt her body awaken to his touch, she realized she
could happily wait for her pancakes. If necessary, she
could wait all day.

After breakfast, which qualified more as brunch,
Rebecca and Grant decided to go out for the day.
Since Grant was still unable to drive, he persuaded
Rebecca to get behind the wheel of his Saab con-
vertible. Rebecca felt very nervous at first, thinking
she was going to dent the expensive car at every turn.
But she soon grew used to it and began to enjoy the
way the automobile handled so easily.

They drove around the countryside, stopping to
browse antique sheds and the beautiful shops that

lined the streets of the nearby towns, which catered to the wealthy summer visitors.

Grant wanted to drive to North Fork, which was considerably quieter, not quite as fashionable and still full of farms and vineyards. Late in the day, they stopped at a vineyard for lunch and sampled the featured wine, an icy cold Pinot Grigio, while a violinist played a beautiful classical piece, her backdrop the rolling acres of the vineyard.

Later, as they strolled the streets of the harbor village hand in hand, Rebecca felt truly hopeful, as if all the loose ends had finally come together for them. Could Grant have overcome the barriers of his past? She wanted so much to speak to him about it, but knew it was best to wait for him to say something. It was a struggle, but somehow Rebecca managed to hold her tongue, to relax and enjoy the day.

All too soon, it seemed, the sun began to set, and it was time to pick up Nora. As they drove to the pickup location in town, Rebecca was suddenly eager to see her daughter.

"I wonder if she had a good time," Rebecca said, thinking out loud. "I remember my first sleep away. I felt a spider crawling over my hand right after lights-out, and I didn't sleep a wink all night."

Grant laughed. "You poor kid. I'm sure Nora loved it. Even if she met a spider or two."

"She'll have a lot of stories," Rebecca agreed, knowing how her daughter loved to report every detail of her outings.

"Yes, she will," Grant said. "I can't wait to hear

them,'' he added, his hand gently stroking her shoulders as she drove.

Nora was elated but exhausted. As Rebecca had guessed, she talked nonstop all the way home. Grant encouraged her to tell all with his questions. After they returned and had all climbed out of the car, Nora turned to Rebecca and Grant and flung her arms around both adults. ''I missed you guys,'' she said, her face muffled in Rebecca's skirt.

Grant rested his hand on Nora's head. ''We missed you, too, Nora,'' he said. ''It was very quiet around here. Too quiet.''

She looked up and grinned at him. ''What did you guys do all weekend? I'll bet it got boring without me.''

Rebecca saw a grin on Grant's face, and he briefly met her gaze before looking at Nora. ''Not boring. No, I wouldn't say that at all,'' he replied slowly, choosing his words with care. ''Your mom and I managed to…keep busy,'' he said simply.

Rebecca smiled. That was one way of describing the weekend. She silently laughed.

The following days seemed to mark a new start for them, and Rebecca felt closer than ever to Grant. She didn't fear the end of the summer anymore, but looked ahead with hopeful anticipation. Grant's healing no longer seemed to signify the end of their time together. It seemed to be a step toward a new level in their relationship. It was hard to keep their intimate bond a secret from the household. Grant wanted to shout the news from the rooftops, but Rebecca didn't feel ready to share their secret with the world. The charade made Rebecca feel silly and childish sometimes. Especially at night, when Grant would visit her bed for a few precious hours of passionate lovemaking.

Secrecy was not natural to Rebecca's open nature. But she felt that in this case, it was for the best. She worried about Nora. She knew her daughter would be thrilled to learn that Grant was her mother's official "boyfriend"—but what if it didn't work out? Rebecca knew Nora had suffered enough disappointment over the divorce. She worried that Nora's hopes would be raised by the prospect of having Grant as a stepfather, but she might end up hurt and disappointed again. In the interest of protecting her, Rebecca persuaded Grant to keep their relationship under wraps, at least until they were in the city, living separately and feeling sure about where they were headed.

Sometimes Grant acted very confidently about their future. His casual comments about things they would do and places they'd go, would make her head spin in a happy daze. If it was up to him, it sounded as if they'd never be apart again, as he often hinted about her and Nora moving into his large city apartment at the summer's end. Rebecca had subtly let him know she thought it was too soon for her to think about living together. Especially with Nora involved. She'd been flattered, however, that he wanted such a domestic, permanent arrangement.

Still, she knew it was too early to count on things working out. Grant had never discussed his feelings about the accident. Was he over them? He had never told her point-blank that he loved her, either—though she believed he did, and felt it in his every look, his every kiss, his every loving caress.

They needed time, Rebecca kept telling herself. In time, it might all work out as she dreamed. About two weeks after Nora's camping trip, Grant finished his workout, then surprised Rebecca with a sudden announcement.

"I'm seeing my doctor in the city this week, on Wednesday. I think it's about time I went back to work. What do you say? He'll want your opinion, I'm sure."

Rebecca was startled. She felt blindsided. What did this mean? Was Grant suddenly looking for an easy escape hatch? Was he running to the city to get away from her? She turned, trying to hide her expression, which she was sure would show her distress. She hadn't been the one to pursue him, he'd pursued her. Persuaded her, despite her better judgment, to get involved with him. Was he running from her now? Avoiding a serious commitment?

"Well, what do you think, Rebecca?" he asked curiously. He hopped off the exercise table and followed her. "You seemed concerned. Is there something wrong I should know about?"

"No, not at all," she replied with a brief shake of her head. "You're probably ready to return to work, if you wish. Though you will need to keep up your exercise routine. I just didn't know you were so eager to go back to the city."

"Restless, I guess. I feel so much better lately, I need to do something more productive with my time.'' He lifted her chin with his fingertips and stared at her face. ''I'm not eager to leave you, if that's what you're worried about. Just the opposite, I'd say.''

''I never said I thought that.''

''No...but you didn't have to say it. I know you too well by now, sweetheart,'' he replied. He took her shoulders in his hands, then leaned over and kissed her hard on the mouth. ''I'm better now, finally. I can feel it,'' he told her. ''But it's not the end for us, Rebecca. It's only the beginning,'' he promised.

''Is it?'' she asked him, unable to hide her fears any longer.

He stared at her, then pulled her close in a sheltering embrace. ''Rebecca, please,'' he said, sounding shocked that she even dared to ask such a question. ''I didn't have a future until I met you. And now I couldn't imagine the future without you. You and Nora. I thought you knew that by now.''

''No, I guess I didn't,'' she admitted. She shook her head against his shoulder and felt him softly touch her hair. She felt tears in her eyes. She didn't want him to see her cry.

''I know you have your work, but we'll be together, won't we?'' he asked quietly. ''I mean, you aren't planning to take some new assignment in California or something?''

He was worried about losing her, too. She could hear it in his voice. And all the while, she thought she was the only one who yearned for assurances. Though he still hadn't said he loved her, Rebecca felt she'd heard as much of a promise as she needed. More than she needed to pledge herself to him.

"Don't worry, I can find an assignment in the city," she said simply, winding her arms around his waist. "You won't be getting rid of me that easily."

"Good," he replied, sounding satisfied. He hugged her close. "I won't lose you, Rebecca. Not after we've come this far."

She didn't say a word in reply. She didn't need to. Her heart felt so full of love for him, she thought it might burst. Her answering embrace was more eloquent than words. They *had* come far, she realized. With any luck, one step at a time, they'd make it all the way.

Grant returned from his visit to the city looking haggard and drawn. She worried that the doctor had given him distressing news, or not the news he'd hoped to hear.

But when she tried to draw him out over dinner, his answers were brusque, and even rude. His gruffness hurt her feelings, but Rebecca tried to act as if nothing was the matter. He was retreating into his old, dark mood, she realized, as if he was being pulled away from her by some unseen force. And there was nothing she could do about it.

That night, after Nora had fallen asleep, she went to his room. She knocked quietly, and he came to the door, seeming pleased to see her at first. But after she walked in and closed the door, he turned his back to her, and she heard him sigh.

"Grant, what's the matter? I know something is bothering you." She walked up behind him and rested her hands on his shoulders. "Please talk to me."

"There is something on my mind," he admitted. He glanced at her over his shoulder, then looked away again. "Something troubling. But it's none of your concern, Rebecca," he assured her.

She moved away from him and sat on the edge of his bed. "Please don't say it doesn't concern me. Don't you see? If it troubles you, it troubles me. If you can't be open with me about your problems, Grant, we don't really stand much of a chance."

He turned and gazed at her. She could see his expression softening a bit, though he still looked distant and grim.

"I want a chance with you, Rebecca. I want to have a life with you. I want to watch Nora grow up and have more children with you, too. I want us to grow old together, and stay together forever. I want that more than anything I ever wanted in this world. You believe me when I say that, don't you?" he asked solemnly.

"Yes. Yes, I do." That was exactly what she wanted, too. But his serious expression and tone scared her. She wished he would tell her what was happening. It had to be something bad. Something that threatened their future. She felt it in her bones.

He took a manila folder off his desk and handed it to her. "Here, look at this. These documents were received this morning by special messenger."

She opened the folder and saw some legal documents. She didn't quite know what she was reading but could discern that the form had to do with a lawsuit. It appeared that someone was suing Grant. As far as she could see, it was Courtney's family.

"You're being sued by Courtney's family," she said slowly looking at him.

"That's right. Wrongful death, they're calling it." He took the folder and took a deep anguished breath.

"But whatever for?" she asked, feeling a hollow place open in the pit of her stomach.

"They say it was all my fault, as the driver of the car," he said bitterly, staring at her. "The nightmare just never ends for me, Rebecca. I think it's going to end. I believe I deserve for it to be over. But it doesn't end. I can't get out from under. I can't escape this dark place. It will just keep pulling me back in, again and again."

Rebecca rose and put her arms around him. He dropped his head to her shoulder. She felt his body shake. He was distraught, and like most men, trying to hold it all inside.

She gently pulled him down so they lay on the bed together, then she turned out the light. She held him close and felt him answer her embrace. He soon grew calmer, his breathing even and slow.

"You'll get through this," she promised him, daring finally to speak. "We'll get through it together. It will be okay. You'll see."

He sighed deeply and kissed her hair. But when he finally spoke, Rebecca noticed he'd didn't say that he agreed with her. Instead, he changed the subject completely.

"Stay with me tonight, for a little while," he entreated her. "I want to make love with you. That's all I care about right now. The future will just have to take care of itself somehow."

Without waiting for her reply, he rose over her and pressed his lips to hers. Rebecca wrapped her arms around his strong body and answered his embrace. She was suddenly afraid of the future. Pushing fearful thoughts aside, she willed herself to follow Grant's lead and concentrate on the moment, on the pure and ultimate pleasure of holding the man she loved.

Nine

Several months later, long after Rebecca had left Grant's house in Bridgehampton for a new assignment in Madison, Connecticut, the last words he'd said to her that fateful night continued to prey on her mind. As well as the memories of the last time they made love.

Just as she feared, after he learned of the lawsuit, Grant slipped back to a shadowy place, where memories of the accident and his guilt ruled him. Rebecca's heart broke as she saw him withdraw from her little by little, day by day. She learned that the lawsuit would never go to court. Grant's lawyers were working on a quick settlement. Still, the situation had done its damage, and Rebecca felt her hopes sinking a little more each day, like a ship with a damaged hull.

They began to argue, not the bantering, playful arguments that had always sparked their relationship, but painful, bitter bouts. Rebecca knew that Grant was pushing her away. Time and time again, she wanted to run from him. But she hung on, because she loved him and hoped some miracle would save them.

Finally, one day, he angrily asked her to leave, telling her that her services were no longer required. Rebecca had heard it all before, but this time, the words hit home. Her heart couldn't bear any more pain. And her hope for a miracle had finally run out. She suddenly didn't know how she'd managed to stand it so long. She curtly agreed to his order and went straight to her room and packed.

Nora had been confused about the change in Grant's behavior, but she'd been satisfied by Rebecca's explanation that Grant had a business problem he was trying to work out. To Grant's credit, he was always kind and sweet to Nora, which somehow puzzled the little girl even more.

With tears in her eyes, Rebecca announced that they were leaving the next day. Thankfully, her daughter didn't question her. Rebecca knew she'd never forget the look on Grant's face as he hugged Nora goodbye. She had to look away, there was so much raw emotion there. Their parting was awkward. They stood staring at each other, Rebecca wishing to get through it before she burst into tears.

Grant looked uncomfortable and unhappy, yet relieved, as well, she had thought then. Relieved to be rid of her, relieved to be left alone with his sad, dark memories. She didn't wish to think badly of him—

she never really could. But he had disappointed her. He'd broken her heart as no one ever had before, or ever would again. She would never love any man again as she loved Grant.

She had thought that once they were separated she would gradually forget him, that her feelings would fade, even if she didn't wish it to be so. But she knew that wasn't true. It made no difference if they were together or apart. If she saw him tomorrow or never again. He lived inside her, and her love was an indelible mark on her heart and soul, marking her for him and him alone. She would live the rest of her life missing him as deeply as she missed him that very first day apart.

Her new patient was a ten-year-old boy, Jake Nelson. Jake had fallen out of a tree and broken several bones in his arms and legs. He was determined to play baseball again in the spring, and Rebecca was determined to see him do it.

Rebecca had purposely looked for an assignment near her mother's home, where she and Nora were staying temporarily. She decided not to return to the city for a while. She was not afraid of running into Grant, since New York was such a vast place and they moved in such different circles. But she was afraid of thinking too much of him if they were living in such proximity and thought a change would do her good. Since she'd given up her apartment when she'd started working for Grant, she had no reason to return to the city.

Her mother had guessed that Rebecca was suffering from some romantic disappointment. But she was not the type to pry, for which Rebecca was endlessly grateful. Rebecca did not think she would stay long in her mother's house and was starting to look for a place of her own. But it was the house she'd grown up in and a convenient and comforting resting place for the time being.

Rebecca tried not to think of Grant. But it was an endless battle that didn't get much easier as the weeks passed. As the holidays approached, her thoughts of him grew more intense. She found herself wondering where he'd be and what he'd be doing, remembering that he had so little family.

About a week before Thanksgiving, Rebecca sat with her mother in the kitchen, sipping tea and making a menu for the upcoming family dinner. Both Rebecca's sisters and their families would be arriving next week and staying for the weekend. Rebecca's mother, Alice, was in her usual tizzy, worrying about how she would find everyone a bed and get all the cooking and cleaning done. As Rebecca assured her they'd all pitch in, someone knocked insistently on the front door, and Nora ran to answer it.

"How about the cranberries?" Rebecca asked, trying to get her mother to focus on the menu. "I can make a cranberry relish, with orange and walnuts. It's really good," she promised.

"Sounds perfect," a deep, familiar voice replied.

Rebecca turned, her mouth dropping open. It was Grant. Standing in the doorway of her mother's kitchen, holding Nora's hand. For a moment, she thought she was having a hallucination.

"Look, Mom. Look who came to visit us," Nora

exclaimed happily. Rebecca could see that they had already exchanged greetings.

"My, isn't this a surprise," Rebecca said dryly. He was smiling at her, smiling with his whole heart showing in his eyes, the way he used to do. But it made her sad to look at him, sad and angry. She looked away, into her mug of tea.

"Rebecca?" her mother asked nervously. "Aren't you going to introduce me to your visitor?" she prodded.

Rebecca looked up again, remembering her manners. "Grant, this is my mother, Alice Calloway. Alice, this is Grant Berringer, a former patient."

Did Grant wince at her introduction? If so, he deserved it, she thought.

"It's good to meet you, Mrs. Calloway," Grant said smoothly. He smiled and took her mother's hand.

"Why don't you call me Alice?" Rebecca's mother replied.

Rebecca shook her head. Her mother looked a bit flustered receiving Grant's full attention. She always got that way around a good-looking man.

"And have a seat," Alice urged him, pulling out a chair for Grant to sit in. She glanced from Rebecca to the mysterious stranger. "I have some chores to do upstairs," she added hurriedly. "Nora, you come help me."

"But, Nana…" Nora began.

Alice looked at her over her glasses. "I really need your help, Nora," she insisted. "Upstairs."

Before Rebecca could prevent it, she was left alone

with Grant. He sat close to her, close enough to touch. Though she didn't dare.

"How did you find us?" she asked him.

"It wasn't too hard. I made a few calls. The specialist who first recommended you to my brother knew where you were."

"Oh, of course," Rebecca replied. She could hardly take her eyes off him, but she forced herself to. He was wearing a thick cream-colored sweater, worn, slim-fitting jeans and a leather jacket. He looked so good, so healthy and strong. So handsome and vital. His thick dark hair was cut short, the way she liked it, and combed back from his rugged face. He wasn't using the cane any longer, and his limp was imperceptible. When he turned his face toward her, she noticed that the long white scar on his cheek was gone, as well. She didn't know why, but it seemed like a good sign.

"It's good to see you, Rebecca," he said quietly. "I've missed you. Very much."

She forced herself to ignore his words, to ignore the way his soft tone melted her heart. "Why did you come?" she asked bluntly. "I don't understand what you're doing here."

"I have something important to talk to you about. It was too important to tell you by phone, I thought." She looked at him and saw the light in his dark eyes. Her heartbeat quickened, and despite herself, she felt a flicker of hope in her poor battered heart. "Besides, I thought if I called first, you would probably hang up on me. Or refuse to see me."

"Probably," she admitted. Still, she turned toward

him and felt her heart slowly opening to him again. "What happened? Did your memory about the accident return?"

His face grew serious, and he nodded. "Yes, it did. But it's more than that. Quite a strange series of events, actually. What I've learned has changed my entire life since I last saw you," he confessed. "It will change both our lives, I hope," he added.

Rebecca's heart skipped a beat at his words and at the hopeful look in his eyes. She could barely breathe as Grant explained what had happened to him in the weeks since her departure. The Bentons, Courtney's parents, were slow in negotiating a settlement, he told her. Oppressed by the cloud of the lawsuit, he returned to his office on Wall Street. He threw himself into his work, but he missed her constantly, he admitted to Rebecca. He wanted to call her every night but didn't dare.

"I knew I couldn't give you the love you deserved until I settled my past," he said. "And when I sent you away, I doubted that day would ever come."

Without a settlement in hand, Grant's lawyers continued to work on the case, he went on to explain. They took a deposition from Grant's former client, Mark Weyland. Grant and Courtney had been visiting Mark's country house the day of the accident, and Grant had not seen or heard from Mark since. Mark seemed reluctant to give testimony, Grant told her, and Grant didn't understand why. After the deposition was completed, it became clear. In his testimony Mark revealed that he and Courtney had been having an affair and that she had called him from her cell phone, from Grant's car, right before the accident.

The news had shocked Grant to the core. He had been sitting at his desk late at night, reading the document, and suddenly thought he was going to faint. Alone in his office, it all came back. The night of the accident, the drive in the rain from Mark Weyland's house. He and Courtney had been arguing. She confessed to Grant that she was in love with Mark Weyland and planned to leave Grant for the other man. They'd been having an affair for months, right under his nose. Grant had been stunned. He felt as if he had been stabbed in the back.

What about the baby? he remembered asking her. What will become of our child? Courtney had seemed sad, he recalled. She hadn't wanted to hurt him, but then confessed that she'd lost the baby weeks ago. Lost the baby, and you didn't even tell me? Grant remembered how he had roared at her.

She had grown angry with him. The real truth was that she'd never been pregnant at all. Knowing how much he'd wanted children, she'd lied to him about expecting a baby, just to get him to marry her. She didn't really want children. And neither did Mark, she had added. So they were very well suited for each other.

Grant remembered how the rain lashed at the windshield, blinding him as he drove. He was angry and upset at her betrayal. But Courtney grew tired of hearing his accusations and demanded that he stop the car and let her out. Mark would pick her up, she insisted as she started to call him on her cell phone. But Grant wouldn't stop the car. No matter how angry he was with her, he wasn't going to leave her on the highway in the rain, he argued. He'd find a gas station or a store. Courtney's temper flared. They argued, and she finally grabbed the wheel and pulled, trying to force him to pull over.

"That's when the car went out of control," he told Rebecca grimly. "I remember it all so clearly now." He shook his head as if to clear away the unwanted images. "At least I know the truth."

"It wasn't your fault at all," she said, in awe at the revelation. "And all this time, you were thinking about the child, but there was no child."

"No." He looked down and shook his head. "There was no child."

She reached out and touched his hands. Her hands were shaking. He quickly lifted his dark head and stared into her eyes. "So you see, it's finally over, Rebecca. The nightmares are over, too. And the Bentons have dropped the lawsuit." He took a deep breath, fixing her with his gaze. "I have my life back again."

"Yes, you do," she said, feeling her soul lift in happiness for him.

"But I don't have anything without you," he added, staring deeply into her eyes. "I know I was horrible to you at the end. But I couldn't bare to see everything I wanted so badly just ripped away again. I didn't want to push you away the way I did, but somehow, I had to. I love you so much, it hurt every time I looked at you and realized I couldn't have you, after all. Please." He lifted her hands to his lips and kissed her fingers. "Give me another chance. I'll spend the rest of my life making you happy, I swear it."

"I love you, Grant," she answered simply, as tears choked her words and blurred her vision. "I never stopped loving you...and I know I never will."

Grant stood and pulled her into his arms. His kisses were hard and demanding. Rebecca clung to him, answering his fierce emotion with deep longing.

He lifted his head and stared deeply into her eyes. "Will you marry me?" he asked.

She nodded. Then finally found her voice. "Absolutely," she replied. How had she ever managed to stay away from him this long, she wondered as his mouth found hers in a deep, hungry kiss.

Grant broke away. "I almost forgot," he murmured huskily. Without releasing his hold on her, he twisted and reached into his pocket, extracting a small velvet box. He flicked it open with his thumb. "I bought you this hoping you'd say yes."

Rebecca stared at a sparkling square-cut emerald ring in a simple gold setting enhanced by small diamonds. She felt her mouth drop open but she couldn't help herself. "Grant...my God. It's beautiful."

"I guess that means you like it." He laughed, sounding satisfied that he'd pleased her. "Here, put it on."

He took her hand and slipped on the ring. She gazed at it a moment, then wrapped her arms around him again. "Thank you. It's gorgeous. I'll never take it off."

"Just long enough to put on your wedding band,"

he amended. "I once told you I thought emeralds suited you. Do you remember?"

"Of course." She remembered exactly. "We were standing on Fifth Avenue, looking in the window at Tiffany's. You teased me about buying me emerald earrings for Christmas," she recalled. "And meanwhile, I was thinking I wouldn't even be part of your life by then," she admitted.

"Did you really think that?" he asked, sounding amazed. He hugged her closer. "Couldn't you tell, even back then, I couldn't live without you?" He sighed and kissed her hair. "Now, we'll be married by the New Year, Rebecca," he promised. "It's funny how things work out. In a way, that lawsuit was a blessing in disguise. At first it broke us apart. But if it hadn't been for Weyland's deposition, I'd never have regained my memory. And maybe I'd never have been able to come after you."

"I'm glad you feel free of those sad memories, Grant. But if you hadn't come here, sooner or later, I would have come to you," she admitted.

"Would you?" he asked her. "Even after the way I treated you?"

"I know in your heart you didn't really mean it. I don't think I could have lived with myself without trying, at least once to make you see that, no matter what, we belong together. Besides, in all the time we were together," she said, realizing that in fact, it was true, "I never told you how much I love you. Wouldn't that have made a difference?"

"Your love has made all the difference in the world to me, Rebecca," he confessed, as his mouth moved slowly along the line of her cheek. "It's changed my entire life."

His mouth came down on her parted lips and she softly moaned. Very soon they'd be alone together, in a world of their own, sharing their love completely and taking each other to the heights of passion. Rebecca could hardly wait.

As she held him close and thrilled to his passionate embrace, she felt joy in her heart that he'd sought her out this way. But she also knew that what she'd told Grant was true. Whether he'd regained his memory or not, nothing would have kept her from him for much longer. They belonged together, it was an irrefutable truth.

The sound of quick steps in the hallway brought Rebecca to her senses. She looked up to see Nora standing in the kitchen door, with her grandmother following close behind.

"Nora...come back upstairs. Your mother and her friend need some privacy," Alice scolded in a hushed tone.

"It's all right, Mom," Rebecca said, learning back in the circle of Grant's arms.

"We have some news for everyone," Grant said, glancing at Rebecca with a secret smile. He released her and she turned toward Nora.

"Grant and I are going to get married," she told her daughter. "What do you think?"

She carefully watched Nora's expression, having a brief anxious moment that perhaps she'd sprung the news too abruptly.

Nora looked shocked for a moment. Then jumped

up, clapping her hands. "Yippee!" She hugged Rebecca around her waist so hard it knocked the wind out of her, then immediately ran toward Grant and flung herself into his arms.

Laughing, Grant lifted her high and enclosed her in a huge hug. "I guess you approve," he said happily.

Nora hugged him around the neck. "Absolutely."

"Oh dear…I thought it was something like this… But I had no idea," Alice said. She dropped into a chair and began to fan herself with the Thanksgiving menu.

Rebecca touched her shoulder. "Mom, are you all right?"

Alice looked up at her, her expression tearful and happy at the same time. "I'm just so happy for you, dear. I knew when you came home that something was dreadfully wrong. But I didn't want to pry. I was hoping that…well," she quickly glanced at Grant. "I was hoping it would turn out all right for you, in time."

Still holding Nora's hand, Grant stood next to Rebecca and put his arm around her shoulder. "Now that I have her, I'll never let her go, Mrs. Calloway," he promised, tugging Rebecca close.

Alice beamed. "Will you have Thanksgiving with us, Grant? You'll get to meet the whole family."

"I'd love that," he replied. "And you will all be my guests at Christmas, I hope. For our wedding."

Rebecca met his dark gaze, about to protest that less than two months was far too little time to plan a wedding. But then she looked into his eyes and felt herself lost in his loving smile. She knew that Grant could do anything he set his mind to.

And tomorrow wouldn't be too soon to start a new life with the man she would love for all time.

* * * * *